Surf the
Milky Way

BOOKS BY E.R. HARRIS

SURF THE MILKY WAY
"I'm Never Going to Galaxy's End."
Award-Winning enovella - OUT SOON

CHRONICLES OF THE MERMAID
The Twelve Moons of the Dolphin Princess
The Eight Clans of the Merfolk
The Twins of Land and Sea
Fantasy Trilogy - BOOK ONE OUT 2022

Surf the Milky Way

Dear David

Thank so much for your support!

E. R. Har...

E. R. Harris

gatekeeper press™
Columbus, Ohio

Surf the Milky Way

Published by Gatekeeper Press
2167 Stringtown Rd, Suite 109
Columbus, OH 43123-2989
www.GatekeeperPress.com

Library of Congress Control Number: 2021947752

ISBN (paperback): 9781662920318
eISBN: 9781662920325

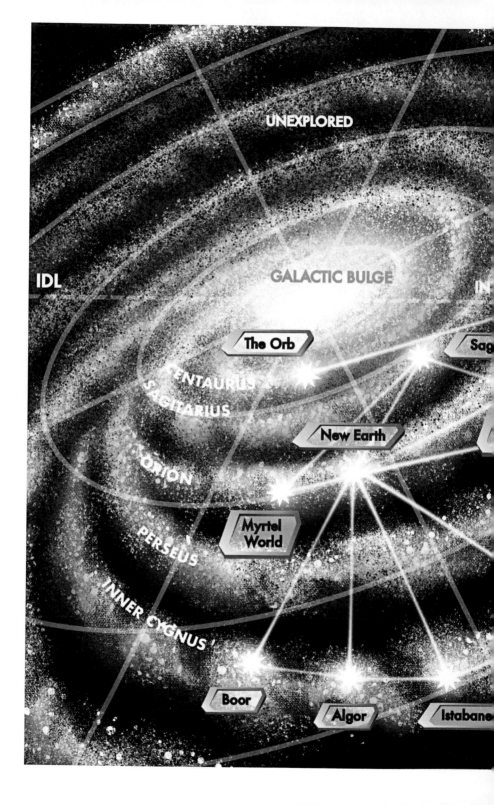

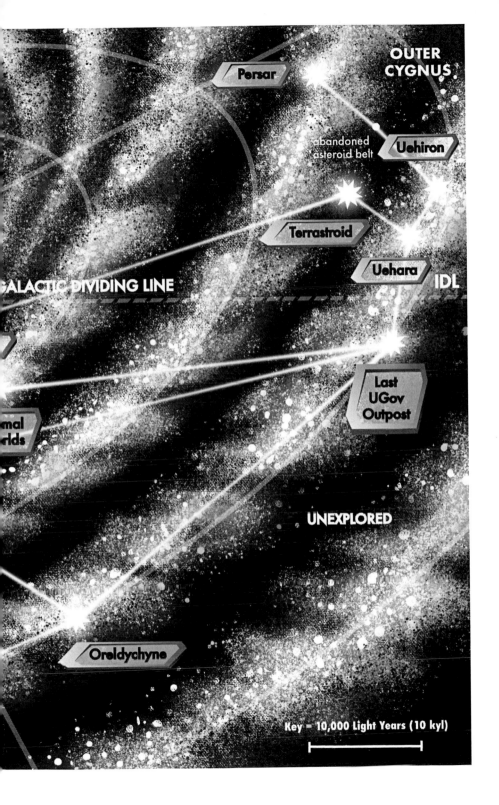

Acknowledgements

I must thank my loved ones. Without such creative parents, my mother Rohmana, a goddess arts painter and illustrator, and my deceased father Latif, a surrealist poet, there is no way I would have been prolifically writing stories as far back as elementary school. The genesis for my love of reading and writing starts with them.

Secondly, my stepparents Alpha and Jeff, all the love and support in my adolescent and adulthood helped me understand what it means to be a good man and a good human being.

I've got to shout out Martin Cruz Smith (of Gorky Park fame), my very first writing teacher—way back in fourth grade! Thank you for sharing your valuable time with me and giving me the impetus to be a writer. Ms. Chick—my fifth grade teacher—you were instrumental in my development as a writer. Mr. Nicholson my English teacher in high school, you showed me the importance of grammar and sentence structure. And Professor Eliot Butler-Evans, you opened my eyes to the marginalized writers and their stories. You brought empathy and understanding to my developing world of prose.

To my heroes of prose—Brandon Sanderson, Patrick Rothfus, Kim Stanley Robinson, J. R. R. Tolkein, George R. R. Martin, Thomas Pynchon, Don Delillo—to name just a few, thank you for inspiring me to world build and entertaining me everyday of my life with your amazing work.

Beta readers are essential, and Zane Summers is my top dog there. You have given me an incredible boost of confidence and your timely questions and comments make me want to improve.

This project would have gone absolutely nowhere without me investing in a shrewd, experienced, honest, and hardworking editor—Phil Athans. Thank you, Phil, for helping me recognize that "info dumping" is a sure way to kill interest in a good story.

Artwork is essential to my genre, and Gabriel Leonudikis you propelled my characters and settings to the visual realm. Thank you so much, Gabe!

But none of this happens without the beautiful love of my life, Carrie. You are my inspiration, my everything... you make all the hard work worthwhile Thank you for being in my corner, always!

Contents

CHAPTER ONE

Uehara Bay

Paddling at a smooth, steady pace, Max looked over his shoulder in time to see his crew mate Claude drive his surfboard into such a crisp, hard turn that a massive splash of water flew off the back of the wave and rained down upon him.

Max, grinning the whole time, gained speed as he stroked his muscular blue arms through the brackish mixture, the water heavy from all the chunks of soil, plant material, and a variety of other debris.

Next in line to catch a wave was Blob, the origin of his nickname easy to spot, as his stomach bulged way out—a perpetual integrity test of the synthetic carbon fibers of his protective suit. As Blob stroked his thick arms and kicked with his four-toed feet, his right hand slid down the rail of his board to press the paddle booster. In a flash, the oversized surfer was propelled to his feet and sliding down the steep face. He dropped all the way to the bottom of the trough and pressed back hard on the tail of his board, fins catching, to make a huge bottom turn. If successful, he would get ahead of the crumbling whitewater and be in a good position to attempt to navigate the first of its many dangers.

From Max's vantage point, Blob was up to the task, although his board did sag in the middle as he pumped down the line. He plowed right over a clump of plant matter without losing much speed, and zipped out of sight.

A voice shouted from behind. It was Mike, Claude's brother, who was paddling from calmer waters, careful to avoid the turbulent influence of the impact zone. Max smiled at Mike as the giant mutant rabbit twirled his elongated forepaws through the water as fast as he could.

"Did you see that one, Cap?" Mike was practically frothing at the mouth. "My bro was shredding! This is so epic, Max! Some of these waves—I swear—they're gargling up logs larger than the compression rods firing the *Planet Hopper!*" Mike loved to make the surf conditions seem more intense than they really were—but there was no need for embellishment with the Ueharan tidal bore wave. *Totally legit.*

"Yeah, I saw him all right!" Max called back. "That spray off the back of the wave was massive! He is absolutely ripping! Vern too! He got such a good one earlier!"

Wow, Max chuckled to himself at the impossibility of it all, *Uehara Bay! We finally made it! This is absolutely insane!* He sat on his board and slapped his hands down into the surging water as they waited for the next wave to form.

Pretty soon they were chatting about the infamous Ueharan tidal bore. It was the rarest of unicorns for galaxy-traveling surfers like themselves. Sure, there were plenty of *stories* of guys surfing it, but his crew had never met someone who actually had. The wave was merely a whisper among the ashes of alien surf culture, a forgotten rumor on the wrong side of the Intergalactic Dividing Line. Not only that, but it also happened to be located on a

Category C planet, as defined by the Ugovernment's classification system, and therefore it was strictly forbidden to land there. A beautiful little green oval, sitting out on the far edge of the explored portion of the galaxy—that just so happened to have the best wave they had ever ridden.

Max was more than ready for his turn, and a bulge loomed beyond the mud flats, stretching all the way to the horizon. It was a pulse produced by the largest of the planet's three moons, and a particularly nasty-looking wave formed. The tidal bore was about to oblige Max with all he could handle.

The Captain of the *Planet Hopper* locked in on the trajectory he wanted to take and used shoulder, back, and arm muscles to propel himself forward. Paddling straight at the triangular, bulging, frothing peak seemed… *suicidal.* An alien would have to be crazy to put himself in the way of something so devastatingly powerful… something so fixated on its mission to obliterate whatever strayed in its path. In actuality, the tidal bore was a series of mini-tidal waves, slicing their way along the same stretch of coastline each Uday.

In a laser-quick motion he spun his board around and pounced to his feet.

For a nanosecond all one hundred and fifty kilos of Algorean blue-skinned beef was airborne.

When his fins caught, and he was able to put his weight on the deck of his board, the sensation came—the satisfaction that accompanied a critical drop-in. With the most difficult part behind him, he glided into the crackling trough ahead of him, pumping to gain speed. When the wave face opened up he shifted his weight from back foot to front in order to stay ahead of the foam ball.

Uh oh. He had been too casual and his lapse in concentration might end up costing him some down time. Underwater time. And a *lot* of it, according to projections by the AI models they had run. If he fell he might suffer the same fate as one of the many unaware creatures that didn't make it out of range of the tidal bore, sucked under by brown, liquid tendrils, never to surface again. It was a daily carnage, occurring like clockwork, and Max would be a veritable feast for the bottom suckers. Even with a helmet on, the oxygen supply had a limit, and if he got pinned to the bottom by debris...

The oncoming section was about to throw. Max took a high line, slicing across the voluminous closing door, and made it around, *but...* a hazard waited on the other side.

A chunk of hardened mud, big enough to jar him from his board, was wedged right in his path!

At the last Usecond Max was able to avoid the trouncing of a lifetime by stepping back on the tail of his board and activating the riser function. He popped over the mud chunk, hardly losing any speed, riding on triumphantly. *Yesss!*

Blob and Claude hooted and hollered as they flew overhead in the botcopter on their way back to the top of the headlands to do it all over again.

Max was stoked and he returned a loud roar of approval. Being the best surfer among them, Max always got to be in the best position, closest to the take off spot.

About a half kilometer of huge roundhouses cutbacks later, it was time for the finish line. The river saved the fastest section for last, a part of the wave they aptly named "the racetrack," where the wave uncurled all its might into a wide emptying bay. It was as if the water of the bore sensed it was finally going to be allowed to rest, so it raced for the opening, eager to be free of the chaos. Max needed to pump with everything his Algorean thighs were worth, remaining ahead of the breaking lip by a fraction of a Usecond. Any slight displacement of his weight on either rail and the bore would guillotine him. *Not Captain Max of Algor, you know I'm not going down like that!*

Max made it to the edge of the terminus and now it was time for him to show off a little more. As the wave fizzled out, he carved a sharp-angled turn for the bank of the river, punched the tail thruster with his heel, and launched his board up and over the edge of the bank. While in midair, he jumped off his board and activated the anti-gravity feature on his suit, snatching his board as he floated down, landing comfortably on his feet. It *had* to be a perfect ten-out-of-ten on the rubric scale!

While riding the botcopter back up to the take-off zone, there was the *Planet Hopper,* perched up on the bluff, far away from the river's grasp, and Max couldn't help but smile at the glinting spacecraft. His pride and joy. The monitor display inside the botcopter retrieved Max's attention, as a live image showed Blob taking off on another monster wave. Even an alien of Blob's prodigious size was reduced to nothing more than a speck underneath the great Ueharan maw.

"Dudes!" Max yelled through the intercom, which broadcast audio throughout the ship and into the helmets of all the surfers. "Isn't this epic? The greatest tidal bore wave of them all… way out here? I can't believe this place is real!"

The botcopter holoscreen switched from Blob's ride to the twins sitting on their boards at the top of the river mouth. "Beyond epic, Captain!" Mike yelped. "But check this out… Hey Claude, catch this next one with me!"

"No way, bro," Claude, the cautious one, replied. "Too much debris in the water for a double drop!"

"Nah," Mike gave his typical nonchalant reply. "It's all good. Come on, here comes another pulse. Good galaxy—look at that thing spit! Follow me, bro!"

Mike lay flat, paddling straight for the hollow cylinder of fluid forming ahead of them. The breaking part of the wave's brownish color was a sharp contrast to the rest of the translucent blue waters stretching out to sea, a testament to how much debris was in there.

Max cheered in his deep baritone, manually forcing the botcopter into hover mode so he didn't have to use the holoscreen to check out the action below. From his bird's-eye perspective the nasty ten meter wall of crashing water forced him to think twice about egging on the twins.

Mike let go of all regards and stroked his forepaws to put himself in position, turbo-thrusting away from the apex of the breaking wave, but giving enough room for his brother to paddle in behind him. Sliding into his drop, Mike made a couple of subtle, yet perfectly-timed adjustments with the rail of his board, allowing him a nice easy line to make it around the first section of the wave, right as Claude crisscrossed in front of him. From there the twins zigzagged expertly back and forth across each other's lines. An occasional hazard—generated by an increasing mass of plant debris and tree limbs—threatened to force the brothers to have to kick out of the wave. But slipping off the back would mean missing out on the best parts of the wave… and that wasn't going to happen, not if Mike could help it.

Arc after arc the brothers progressed down the line in circular turns, unfazed by a jumble of animal carcasses forming a blockade of rotting flesh. The local fauna were always well-represented among the many items torn to shreds by this menacing, daily tidal bore phenomenon.

Max smiled, taking his eyes off the live feed on his holoscreen for a moment to take in the scenery around him. As he rode the botcopter back to the lineup, resting his sore muscles for a moment before his next ride, in the sky three moons hung there, their pale hues peeking through the atmosphere of Uehara. It was a special planet, still unblemished by the colonization of the Milky Way. *A portal back to another time,* thought Max. His gaze wandered inland, up past the bay, to the towering jungle foliage lining the sides of the massive indentation of coastline. The foothills of a great mountain range, with a forest of thick green and purple leaves, rose above the tranquil, settled waters of the wide bay. He could imagine being within the embrace of the forest, with branches extending up to the sky in all sorts of twisted patterns.

Nearing the headlands, where he could jump off with his board back into the fray, his eyes sought out the next pulse of waves. Time to focus. Sets were lined up in rows, like Earthish question marks drawn in the sand. The bluffs of yellow-stoned headlands were sliced by fractured segments of black ore, making for a splendid backdrop for their trusty spaceship.

Whatever binary starlight was penetrating the pall of Uehara's three moons was shining directly upon the next set of waves, illuminating their tunnel-like interiors. The blue bulges approached methodically from far beyond the mud flats, picking up more and more dark colors, as the fresh water from the sea merged with the sediment-laden waters at the river mouth. It was a particularly hollow cluster of rideable waves, and it was forming with intensity.

Probably a synchronous merging of the three moons' gravitational fields—the peak of the swell, literally, Max thought, as he leapt from the botcopter, board under his arm.

Once airborne, he turned on the anti-gravity and allowed himself to drift through the air into a calm patch of water close enough to the take-off zone for an easy paddle. A short rest was all he needed, his arms were happy back doing what they were most accustomed to, and he made haste to the oncoming set. Angling his board diagonally, he worked his way over so he would be in the direct line of the pulse of waves ready to explode onto the sandbars at the mouth of the river. Because of his exquisite timing, he was in perfect position, and caught the first wave of the set with ease. As always when dropping, he held his breath, even when wearing his helmet. Old habit. After making it around the first section in a flash, he settled into his riding stance and blasted turns all over the face of the wave—weaving and bobbing, slashing and carving, his board *literally* in tune with his mind. The revolutionary design, attached through focal points in his helmet, allowed his brain to communicate with his board, the AI adjusting the flexibility, tension and angle of his fins—while he rode.

Expensive, but worth it. Max relished the duality: just him and his board—the rider and the tool. *I'm a wave magnet! Algor be praised, what a life!*

***

Meanwhile, Mike and Claude had passed all the sections of the tidal bore, having the most fun at "the bridge." Right as they passed under the massive log they held their front paws together and stepped with their back paws onto the other's board.

"Double Carrot!" Claude yelled. If they were back home on Rabbit World, they would have earned a vegetable meal for the ages.

At the end, when their wave petered out into the open bay, they both snatched the safety bar of the botcopter, right at the exact same time, and were yanked out of the froth. A nanosecond after they lifted above the fray, a gargantuan-sized mud clump rolled past the place where they had just been. It would have crushed them.

"You didn't see that, did you, bro?" Claude laughed.

"See what?" Mike replied, fiddling with his surfsuit. "My epic turns? Yeah, I saw that!"

"Never mind." Claude shook his head.

Laughing and chattering on their ride back, Claude decided he was through surfing for the Uday. Usually the first to be back on the *Hopper*, Claude was ready to do a little research on hyperspace sheath emergency protocols. He took it upon himself to be the most responsible member of the crew, which meant sacrificing a few waves for the safety of the team. And the boys appreciated his dedication.

And they got to surf more waves. Win, win.

Claude flapped an ear at his brother. "Later, bro. I'm going to take a break and eat some gross synthetic veggies and get the hyperspace coordinates locked in. Have fun! Get a couple more good ones for me!"

Before Claude leapt off the botcopter onto the grassy bluff where the *Planet Hopper* sat idly, Mike shouted: "A billion out of a billion!" It was a reference back to their early surf competition Udays. Critics had given them no shot to win contests at the beginning of their pro careers. At one point a journalist put a holo on the Uweb claiming they had a one out of a billion chance of winning.

Claude called back with a wry smile, "You know it! Now get out there and tell Blob to get barreled... *and* to keep his suit excretion vacuum on during the bumps." He laughed and received a familiar grunt and nose twitch for a reply.

***

At the top of the lineup, Blob sat on his board in silence. Vern bobbed up and down next to him, also waiting for the next pulse, but he wasn't being very chatty, despite the epic session they were having. Of course, having a synthmetal mouth kind of curtailed that ability for his respected crew mate.

Blob's turn was next so he lay prone and paddled hard to catch the next aqueous offering from the Ueharan tidal bore. Pressing down with his chest, he clawed himself into the wave and made the drop with relative ease. Digging in with all four fins, the hefty alien came up off the bottom into a gaping barrel, big enough to fit him *and* the botcopter inside of it.

Blob pumped desperately for speed, hoping the wave wouldn't close out on him. For several Useconds he was completely inside the maw of the watery monster. As he was exiting with the spit, he went to claim his barrel to the guys and unknowingly crunched into a tree root that had been sucked into the impact zone. Blob cartwheeled off his board, turning into a projectile weighing somewhere in the neighborhood of two hundred kilos. He twisted helplessly in the air, his gratuitous boiler making him appear like a lopsided space barge in a spiral dive.

Dropping fast he had a split second to think of a way to avoid the dreaded hold-down. Suit and helmet aside, what creepiness lurked below? *If I make myself into a ball, get all my limbs tucked in...* He wrapped his forearms around his shins, bracing for impact.

Blob exploded through the whitewater, a sinking exoplanet probe. When his feet made contact with the bottom he pressed off the hard-packed sediment with all his weight. The momentum rebounded him back up to the surface in an instant.

"That was gnarly!" he yelled into the bot cam hovering above the fray and recording the action for posterity. He shook off the excess water collecting on his suit then gathered his board by retina scanning the return function on his mini-holoscreen projected inside his helmet. His board popped up like a cork, righted itself, and made its way to Blob as he tread water, trying to ascertain whether or not he was going to get out of the path of the next wave before it bowled him over. *Uh oh.*

At the take-off zone, Vern had no idea Blob had survived a close call, or that he was about to get plowed by the deadly tidal bore. He was too busy salivating over his next wave. *Yeah,* he thought, *if I could actually still produce saliva. Now it's my turn... to do some turns!* The pilot of the *Planet Hopper* would have grinned if he had a face. As he made his choice on which wave to go for, he stroked with his partially synthmetal arms to get into position to catch the oncoming bulge of brackish water.

Quickly, Vern was up and riding. He picked a nice medium-sized wave, but got lucky, for it was one of the rare kind, a "double-up" combining the power of two separate waves traveling at a different angle. Ahead, the sand bars and the miniature mud islands beneath the churning river were about to serve up a *very* tasty wave for the half-alien, half-android.

Vern stood tall, in his usual style: a narrow stance, feet close together, as he stayed high on the wave. He teleported across the swirling brown water, making it past one section after another, a seamless transition of fluid surfing.

Until whitewater exploded everywhere. Vern's mono visor became obfuscated, and he was temporarily blinded. Centering himself, he let his intuition take over. He was connected with his board through the AI neural pathways in his helmet, so he simply let the board do the work for him. A moment later his vision became clear again—in time for him to pop the tail thruster and catapult onto a conglomerate of foam chunks. For extra style points, he paused there on top of the pile as if it were a snow-covered mogul, then leaned over and re-dropped back into the wave and kept on speeding down the line.

***

Such awesome surfing! thought Captain Max, reviewing footage of the waves from earlier. *What a sesh!* All of his crew were satiated now. The feeling of being "surfed out"—to be physically, psychically, spiritually, and mentally drained from an amazing surf session—was something the guys longed for. It meant they were harvesting the fruits of their labors. They were getting results. Surfing places like Uehara Bay helped them believe they were, in fact, living the dream… surfing the best waves in the Milky Way.

Max gazed away from the holo, out of the cockpit synthglass windows. Uehara, during the one-star sunset, one-star sunrise, was a colorful sight from up on the bluffs overlooking the bay. It was an odd time of Uday, fractal light shone through a checkered atmosphere of carbon dioxide and argon, giving the surrounding hills a unique, glossy glow. The shadowing of the three moons drew odd shapes on the ground.

The crew settled into their reflexive patterns. Max was scanning the video footage of their session, per usual. Blob gathered all the surf gear and cleaned it. Mike was arguing with the AI regarding how to get the most power charge out of the old holding units on the *Planet Hopper*. Vern was plotting their next course, as it was sadly time to leave behind (possibly) the most incredible surf spot in the entire galaxy. Claude, meanwhile, was still pouring over data from a nearby pulsar burst, one so vast it had purportedly taken out pirate spaceships in the Outer Cygnus Arm, which wasn't too far from their present location. And no pulsar netting put up by the Ugov out here to protect them, either, Claude had informed Max.

As the shadows retreated and were sublimely overtaken by rays of a second dawn, Max disconnected from the Uweb and kicked his feet onto the dashboard of the cockpit. Out the synthglass window, beyond the coast, he perused a mountain pass in the distance. He traced a fissure in the rocks with his eyes.

Maybe that's not just a crack? he thought. After a few swipes with his thick blue fingers he found the screen he wanted. Zoom cameras affixed to the mini-drone flying in a silent orbit around their ship prevented any unexpected hazards. Surprises were no fun in worlds this far from help of any kind. Their ship had to be kept orderly and running at all times, and could not afford any physical or structural damage. If something were to go wrong with the ship...

There's no space garage out here, Max thought as he continued his survey, but this time with the bot camera as his eyes. *Ah ha! I was right! It's not a fissure, it's a trail.* Maybe it had been a massive crack at one time, but it was definitely being used as some sort of thoroughfare for the Ueharan peoples.

This posed a dilemma for Max. The Ugov was strict about interfering with Category C solar systems, where intelligent life was left to blossom on its own. Any contact with these types of "immature" systems was strictly forbidden. And, truth be told, his crew might have done it once or twice. *Or thrice. Forgive me Algor, maybe several times, but who's counting?*

Max had spent time at Galaxy's End, the notorious prison colony... *But that's all in the past,* he sighed, thinking of Rowdy Paul, his Istabanian large breed buddy, and the surf trip that went all wrong. Which, inevitably made him think of her, Gretta. He guessed he'd never find out what happened to her. *That was the darkest time of my life. And I'll never go back to Galaxy's End again.*

Ugov law notwithstanding, Uehara's infinite beauty was irresistible to Max. *This trail is obviously carved by the Ueharans,* Max opined. And natives needed to eat. He smiled impishly to himself before clicking the intercom.

"Hey, Blob!" Max called out. "You have any fresh produce for dinner tonight?"

Blob answered after a short static pause, "Yeah, right, Boss, just the same old GMOs. Synthetic sustenance, bro. Come on now..."

"Oh, I was just thinking..." Max's words trailed off.

"No, Max!" It was Claude now chiming in after overhearing the two extra-large members of the crew talking over the ship intercom. "I know *exactly* what you're thinking. That's what got us in trouble before, and as I remember, it landed you in the lockdown."

"An accident," Max replied. "I never meant to—"

"You never meant to what, Max?" Mike's voice came across the intercom as he joined the verbal fray. "Destroy the culture of the little planet with all those cute alien girls?"

"C'mon, Mike," said Max's crackling voice through the old-but-still-works-so-don't-replace-it intercom system blaring into every section of the *Planet Hopper*. "It wasn't that bad."

"Uh huh." Claude again. "And you're not the famous Maximillian of Algor? The one and only surf god with the big muscles?" The rabbit embellished the last part quite a bit with a mocking, high-pitched, feminine tone intended to further rankle the skipper. It wasn't all hands on deck... it was all hands berate the Captain.

Max was undeterred. "Well, I guess I'm speaking for myself, but I'm definitely hungry for something other than genetically-modified, hyperspace-grade carrot mush..."

The Captain's comment aroused Mike. "Yeah, great, carrot mush that grows from a drop of water and stinky Everlast soil." There was a thump over the intercom as Mike's paw whacked something. "It's revolting! I'll bet there's yummy berries on those bushes out in that jungle!"

"We have a crew member in favor!" shouted Max as he jumped up and pressed the release valve for the cockpit door.

"Are you sure about this, Max?" Blob sounded hesitant, but the possibility of fresh fruits, vegetables, beans—maybe even some local fauna meat—who was he kidding? He was already halfway out the door and loading gear for a "quick" jaunt into the jungle.

"Get your game faces on!" ordered Max. "Blob, Vern, Mike— you're riding with me. Claude, you watch after the *Hopper* and keep us notified on any native stirrings?"

"Uh, huh…" Claude muttered.

"The last thing I want to do is disturb *nature*," Max cackled as he clicked off the intercom and took a deep breath of fresh Ueharan air.

CHAPTER TWO

Natives of Uehara

Max loved adventure. He had a hard time comprehending the word fear. To him, danger was just another challenge, to overcome and defeat. Rules—ha! Rules were *made* for breaking. *As long as you don't get caught, at least,* he laughed to himself.

Thus, getting off the *Hopper* to explore and sniff around a bit, sounded like a great idea to him. Walking out of the exit hatch he observed Blob had loaded up the four-seat botcopter in an impressively short amount of time, and was ready to go. Mike and Vern arrived, with the rabbit putting his opposable thumb up. The foragers were ready to rumble in the jungle.

Once airborne and over the jungle, below them was only green… kilometer after kilometer of different shades of green. From within the incredibly dense under story there were an infinite number of arching darkened vines, intertwining with so many loops Max couldn't discern where one ended and the next began. The massive birds who fished at the great tidal bore were not to be found in this part of the steaming jungle—too full of tight corners. Instead, several other flying creatures zipped in and out of the dark channels that opened up into the forest, emerging and retreating from their nests with the vigor of a healthy biosphere.

Seems to always be a season of plenty here on Uehara. Max smiled. *What a bounty they have every Uday! Algor, I hope we can find something tasty out here...*

Floating along in their glinting machine—along the sides of the botcopter were hexagonal-shaped solar panels, and slotted wind retainers, which provided the botcopter all the power necessary to roam for Udays—the guys watched the terrain pass by with wide eyes and open mouths.

A droning buzz sounded as the organic tracking system clicked on. It had a decent range of a few hundred meters, and worked a lot better than eyes on the ground. When the indicator alarms beeped, the holoscreen flashed on and zoomed in on an image. The AI sensed possible edible organic material, although the best picture the scanners could produce while attempting to penetrate the dense foliage was cursory at best. And it was old technology. Each of the previous three times the indicators had discovered something, it had turned out to be nothing edible. *But this one looks promising.* Max squinted at the scanner. *Very promising indeed...*

"AI, take us in a little closer. There! Right there!" Max pointed to the screen.

"What in the Milky Way are those... what are they, four-legged... herbivores?" asked Mike, brows furrowed, squinting at the screen. "I haven't seen anything like those before. They remind me of those ancient Old Earth history shows with those big equines, remember those? The indigenous tribes would ride them."

"Uh, guys, I think we *are* going back in time to Old Earth—are you seeing *that?*" It was Claude, following them on the holoscreen back on the *Planet Hopper*. "You won't believe it when you do..."

"What is it, bro?" Mike asked.

"Well…" Claude chuckled before answering, "Those four-legged equines actually *do* have two-legged people riding on them!"

And it was true… through the thick, green fronds and plants, there they were, a group of Ueharan indigenous people, walking their steeds over and under, around and through the varied terrain. Their prowess allowed them to continue up the steep incline of the jungle at this part of the foothills with hardly a moment's hesitation.

"Whoa!" Max cried, spreading out his hands. "Vern, take over, go manual, and steer us in there… *quietly*. Turn off the main turbine, just use the glide stick."

When the Captain gave the orders, Vern obliged.

Max grabbed onto the hold bars and extended his arms to get a better view. *He better fly smooth… it's a long way to the forest floor.* Vern was curving the botcopter downward, getting closer by the Usecond. Max leaned further and further out.

"Captain, dude," Mike said, "what are you doing?"

Max didn't answer. When Vern had gotten him close enough, he assessed the terrain one last time, then leapt off the edge of the botcopter, landing on a soft, muddy bank. Ignoring the vehement protests of Mike and Blob, he broke into a run and burst up the hillside, splashing through deep divots in the mud as he went, pursuing the Ueharan natives.

Within five Uminutes of hard going, Max had covered the gap between him and the natives. The isolated sounds of snorting and whining from the mounts was barely discernible over the cacophony of avian and insect species buzzing and clicking all around them. For a Usecond, Max was nothing more than an insignificant fly stuck in an intense web of sound. *Great galaxies, this jungle is alive! Hmm. Not really any escape route if things do happen to go wrong.* He did a quick scan of the immediate surroundings before engaging the group. Facing him in every direction were identical, crisscrossing vines. He couldn't even guess which way was back to the botcopter drop spot.

"Max, c'mon now, you big Algorean nut, what are you doing?" Mike's voice came across his implant. "That's not smart. Ugov strictly prohibits getting in contact with—"

"Yeah, I know, Mike," Max whispered back in his com with annoyance in his voice. "I've dealt with those laws before. The Ugov isn't meddling with this solar system, we're on the far reaches of the Cygnus Arm. I think it's safe to say we are out of range of the scum lords."

Max's disdain for the policies of the Ugov was hard to swallow. There had been a lot of run-ins between him and the Ugov—a lot of bad history. The acrimony traced back to a time long ago, when Ugov military forces, immediately following the galactic war of the Cygnan Age, suppressed small rebellions on his home planet of Algor. It was a war pitting all nine alien races of the Cygnus Arm against the dominance of the Sun Peoples of the Orion Arm. If the Ugov wanted to prevent he and his crew from their mission to surf the greatest waves of the galaxy, they were going to have a hard time corralling this wild and fearless alien. *I've already escaped a prison colony once, never again.*

He was shaken out of his thoughts by Claude's voice. "Captain, monitors and heat sensors are showing they are slowing. At first the readings showed there were five of them, now it says six. I don't hear any emoting from them—just the damn jungle. Galaxies, it must be loud down there!"

Max crouched behind a gently sloping hill to allow him to continue talking in a low tone into his implant without being detected by the natives. "Dudes, I'm sick of the same old synthetic crap food… maybe they're friendly, let's see what kind of delicious vittles they have for us. Besides, I'll bet they have an artifact to trade. Remember how much that Beirstide mask and spear went for back on Ortal? We traveled on the bitcoin from it for a Umonth!"

Max broke through a last barrier of vegetation into the small circular opening in the jungle where the Ueharans had paused, for no apparent reason. As he cautiously stepped forward, he gaped at the astonished Ueharans.

The natives were a small species of humanoid, considerably smaller than Sun People, with odd patterns on their weathered skin, and very, *very* small, dark-colored eyes. One of the tribesmen made a loud exclamation, kicked his steed, and disappeared into the jungle—*mmm—that's probably not a good sign.*

Max turned his head around slowly. It was nothing but one big, confusing mixture of verdant foliage in every direction. He tried on his best smile and showed it to the remaining five natives, which… wasn't making a single bit of progress, Max judged from the consternation on the faces of the Ueharans. Their frowns twisted and were lost amidst their incredibly textured skin. They grunted and made agitated sounds to their fellows.

The Captain's next brilliant plan was to try to approach in an unthreatening manner, but that only succeeded in making the indigenous hunters brandish hollow-tube flutes from their sides.

Uh oh. Max ducked the first volley of projectiles. He attempted to dodge the second by sneaking behind a low-lying root bundle—to no avail. The sting of a dart entered his shoulder, his eyes bulged, and the darkness of his failing consciousness closed in from all sides.

✳✳✳

When Max awoke, he was lying in a puddle of brackish water, dazed and confused. It took a few moments for him to recall where he was, and his mouth was as dry as the deserts of Oreldychyne. He sensed he was underground by the humidity. Around him were four hanging vines, thick as tree trunks, each positioned beside one of his limbs. They entangled his entire body, and prevented him from budging a centimeter, despite numerous attempts to shake himself free from his organic shackles.

Then came the smell—a nostalgic scent of cooking meat. He was so used to breathing in the fumes associated with space travel he forgot how nice a good old fashioned barbecue smelled. *Yummy!* He was reminded of the countless hilarious nights he had spent with his crew mates, sitting around a natural-fired grill, talking smack to each other, eating local fauna, after another epic surf session. *I hope these natives have a good barbecue sauce!*

Light was dull where he lay, and the Ueharan creeping dusk was beginning to unfold. Max guessed it would last quite a long time because of the binary star system, but eventually it would be pitch dark. *Hmm. This wasn't a very good decision, Max,* his own mind scolded himself. *I don't think I've been invited to dinner after all—in fact I'm starting think I might be the main course!*

Living on the edge was one of Max's specialties, and instead of letting fear overcome him, instead he smiled inwardly and planned his escape. It didn't take long for him to run out of ideas. He prayed to Algor his crew were acting on his behalf.

There was movement in the cavern where he was being held captive, and he craned his neck to find the source of the footfalls. There were several of them, but his eyes rested upon one particular Ueharan. He was staring back at Max without lifting his gaze for even a nanosecond. *Must be a guard?* Max tried speaking to the unwavering figure, only to be silenced by a quick retort—a series of loud utterances in their crude language. This became a repeated chant, rising up all around him, although his position of restraint made it so he could not tell where the voices were coming from. *They seem to be calling back and forth.*

The voices broke apart, rose, and got louder. Clearly there was an argument brewing. It was between the man who had originally fixed his gaze upon Max, and another native with an equally-convincing voice. Gesturing, they took stock of Max as he tried to gauge who was the greater influence on the rest of the tribe.

Such amazing skin! He found himself wanting to touch it. Freckled and striped bulges formed unique lines on their faces. It was a dazzling type of natural camouflage that no doubt worked like a charm out in the jungle when they hunted.

A formidable male native, who walked up close to inspect Max, seemed to have a certain aura emanating from him. *Must be the main dude,* Max guessed. Next, a prestigious-looking female slid up beside the male, gesturing and groaning. Max tried his most accommodating smile—which surely would have melted a good Algorean woman. The smile didn't seem to go over quite so well here in Uehara. In fact, the male's brow furrowed. Others were now gathering around Max's prone figure, curious about the odd creature their hunters had caught in the jungle.

Max wiggled in a futile attempt to break the cords binding him. It was useless. Max may have been stronger than most aliens in the Milky Way, but he was incapable of lifting, moving, tossing or breaking his bonds. *What are these things made of? They've gotta be stronger than synthmetal!* They were thick, sure, but they shouldn't have had enough tensile strength to prevent him from breaking his wrists and ankles free. He had an inkling something else was responsible for keeping him pinned. On closer inspection, if he followed the path of intertwined sprigs—from his wrists and ankles, to their source a few meters away—their ends melded into a pool of pale turquoise sludge. It was feeding the vines, adding integrity to the fibers of his bonds. *Hmm,* thought Max, *the scenario gets even more sketchy.*

Luckily his wrist implant was still connected and a blinking orange light indicated the satellite marker was in use—the boys might still be able to find him. As long as he hadn't been moved too far, they should know his general location. *Which is... where, again?*

Lying prone, his perspective was obfuscated by the gesticulating Ueharan peoples, who were busy having their debate on what to do with their new captive.

Something occurred to Max: he *did* have the voice activation control on the metallic bitcoin holstered in his wrist implant.

"Bitcoin, *activate*." He choked the words out. His throat was still coated with a strange dryness, probably a symptom of the poison dart.

The bitcoin started to glow under a few layers of blue skin. A hush went through the group encircling him. *Okay, this is your chance, use all the tricks and gadgets.*

"Bitcoin, *illuminate!*" This time his words were louder, more forceful, more... *Max-like.*

The natives retreated a step back, all but the female elder, who was transfixed by the spheroid image now projecting from the bitcoin. She placed her hand into the light, gasping as it wavered.

The hologram first displayed the official Ugov motto in bright yellow—*From the Sun to the Stars*—flanked by a symmetrical pattern of numerals. A second image popped up, of Max's broad smiling face and coifed auburn hair.

"Bitcoin, *iterate!*"

As an AI voice droned, computer algorithms drummed up and exposed the dirty truth about the unmitigated credit disaster of the one and only... *"Maximillian M. Maxillion; Galaxy Address: the Cygnan Arm, in the Algor solar system, on planet Algor, on the continent Algol, within the city limits of Algas..."*

Max pondered the indenturing of the entire Milky Way through one simple device. It was quite genius. And malicious. Tucked neatly underneath the skin of each Ucitizen's wrist was their access to subsistence, and life without a bitcoin was untenable. It was the key to commerce, transportation, and the qualification to vote—not to mention the genetic updates needed to attain virtual immortality.

"...*Asset Level Four... zero balance. Asset Level Five... zero balance...*" The AI continued blathering in its standard, monotone Ugov voice. Unfortunately for Max's confidence, there weren't a lot of asset levels in his portfolio with *black* numbers—mostly red ones. *Sheesh, are we really in that bad of shape?*

Darkness had set in from the second Ueharan sun abruptly dipping to the other side of Yurt, causing a daily eclipse for the upper latitudes of the Ueharan continent. The dimness served to make a more dramatic backdrop for the hologram unfolding in front of the natives on a small screen hanging there in midair. *It's like magic to them,* Max smiled.

The indigenous people gasped at the light emanating from his bitcoin, and most of the tribesmen and tribeswomen had now retreated several steps away from Max.

"...*Asset Level Twelve... zero balance...*" the bitcoin droned. This prompted Max to finally say out loud: "I know, I know, c'mon, dude, give me a break! We're broke—don't rub it in! Bitcoin—*pulsate.*"

With the new voice command the small black sphere mercifully halted laying out the bleak state of the financial situation aboard the *Planet Hopper*. Instead a humming sound bounced off the walls of the cave, as the color spectrum of the hologram flashed in an irregular pattern.

A gasp matriculated through the Ueharans as they paced back a few more steps. Still standing close, however, was the brave female Ueharan elder, whose shifting skins seemed undisturbed by the miniature laser light show being broadcast from the wrist of the strange creature before them. She waved her hand through the light and the image broke up. Unafraid, she traced her fingers down the thinning band of colors to its inception point—the blue skin of Max's lower arm.

25

"Bitcoin, *rotate!*" This time Max hollered as loud as he could to make sure the woman understood it was *he* who was in control of this "magic." The little metallic disc responded by turning counter clockwise in its sheath.

The native woman's eyes widened, she yelled something back to the crowd, and repeated it. Again and again her shouts echoed off the walls of the damp cave. She raised her arms over her head and shuffled her feet while the crowd did the same. The woman's shouting was echoed not by the seeping cavern walls alone, but also by the people of the domain. Next to respond was the tribal elder who had first approached him, then another native to his side joined in the call. His voice was followed by another, until the entire chamber was blaring a repeated cry—the meaning of which was agonizingly vague to Max. Was he to be the sacrifice and subsequent meal for the tribe? Would they feast on him for the next few Udays? Or were they enthralled by the little talent show his bitcoin had put on? He sincerely hoped the latter was the case.

CHAPTER THREE

Ueharan Feast

"Yo, Claude, come in," Mike called back to the *Hopper* while hanging off the edge of the botcopter, trying to use a handheld, low-grade scanner to find their missing Captain.

"Gotcha loud and clear, bro, go ahead," Claude responded over the intercom.

"Are the ship's scanners getting anything on him?" Mike asked.

"Nah—nothing. Lost him a few Uminutes ago. What're those readings from your end? We don't have much time, Mike."

"Galaxy dust—still nothing here from the botcopter," Mike replied. "I can't get a beat on the Cap from just the heat trace and visuals—I need coordinates to crosscheck."

"Well," his brother replied, "try and piece something together—he couldn't have just… disappeared."

"He didn't just disappear!" Blob cried over the com. "He jumped off the botcopter into a jungle in order to make direct contact with alien natives! Once again, not thinking about the rest of the crew. He does this everywhere we go! It's ridiculous! We should be back on the—"

"Blob, get off the com, unless you're helping," Claude chimed back. "We don't need to hear you complaining, we need our Captain back. I know he burned you earlier and got the best wave of the Uday, but let it go, dude."

"Yeah," Blob continued his rant, "well, if he were thinking more about *us* than about *himself* we wouldn't be stalling out right now, risking our window to get off this planet. When that second sun goes behind the last of the three moons, the solar and lunar wind models don't look good..."

"Blob," Mike said, annoyed, "dude, stop stressing out, it's not helping. Claude will get the AI to run some models. We need to make that window if we can..." Mike tried to assuage his big-bellied friend.

"And if we can't?" Blob's question was unavoidable—like hyperspace nausea.

Mike rolled his eyes and shook his dreads back and forth, as if the answer was super obvious. "We get to surf the tidal bore again!" One of the biggest assets Mike brought to the crew was his ability to handle Blob's constant anxiety.

"Mike," Claude said as he multi-tasked, pulling up multiple holoscreens, perusing weather models, and scanning the geography of the coastal mountains. "Are there any visuals on a possible outcropping, or maybe... an indentation in the landscape?"

Mike checked before replying, "They must have hauled him into a valley or under a cliff. There is no way they would just have their village sitting out in the middle of the jungle, would they? Hey, wait a nano—is that, *smoke?* Vern do you have visual on that?" Mike shouted, pointing off the edge of the botcopter into the canopy.

Vern reacted by taking over the manual controls of the botcopter and making it turn sharply for a white column rising into the sky, a stark contrast to the primarily green backdrop of the jungle. The hum of the botcopter lessened as he eased off the throttle near the source of the emission.

"Not too close, Vern." Mike feared the indigenous people would scatter from the noise of the botcopter descending. *Then we'll never find him.*

Vern nodded. He pulled on the joystick and made a nifty back draft maneuver, bringing their vehicle down without using any engine power. He did it so smoothly Mike had to stick out his lower lip and nod his head to show how impressed he was with the piloting. Vern casually motioned Mike to the back of the botcopter with a twitch of his thumb.

"Claude," Mike asked as he readied to jump off the botcopter. "What do you have for body heat sensors? Got a lock on the location? How about a number on 'em? How many?"

"Uh, hold on, just a—"

"We don't have a nano, bro, I'm dropping in... yee hawww!" Mike hopped off the edge of the botcopter, gazing up at Vern's shrinking face. He activated his ankle boosters to soften his fall, descending through the air at a comfortable rate until his hind paws touched the jungle floor.

"Okay," Claude said. "That's it. Right below you... there, do you see that massive hollowed-out tree? I hope it's not a nest for some big-toothed predator. With all your fur and dreads you probably look like dinner, dude. Mike, try to be careful—there's soupy mud—the kind of mire you might not be able to get out of, and it would force your suit to activate its protection mode. Then you'll be stuck, and you'll have no choice but wait to be retrieved. Or get snacked on."

"Got it, bro." Mike replied. "Thanks for the visuals."

Mike found as good a landing spot as he was going to find amongst such dense brush. He made contact with the squishy ground, gingerly at first, to make sure he wasn't going to sink into impotency, as the sounds of the jungle fauna became overwhelming. It was one over the com, but for Mike, being right in the midst of it was an entirely different experience. *Good galaxies—my bro is right! I'm part of the food chain!*

A speckling of arboreal creatures eyed him lazily while they scratched themselves. Unthreatening to their core, the species had a reddish pigment to their fur, and possessed long tails, enabling them to hang and swing with ease. Piercing cries to each other intermittently broke their otherwise benign disposition, but they scrambled up higher in the branches when Mike came hopping by.

Serpent-like winged insects, the size of weather scanners, buzzed at and around each other in befuddling pathways. With impossible vectors, they flew up and over tall, flowering plants, curling and looping back around to suck their nectar over and over again.

The foliage and vines were all-encompassing. Similarly-shaped deep purple trees shrouded by a web of dark green vines. The symbiotic species formed intricate weavings, giving the whole place the impression of the sinewy fibers of bodily organs. In fact, everything around him seemed to be breathing in and out in unison—one gigantic lung.

Mike snapped out of his dazed state. He needed to help his main man, Max. Pressing a button on his implant he glanced at a mini hologram overview map. He assessed his current position coordinates and tried to gauge the distance between the 'copter and the *Hopper*. He moved in the direction of the smoke, which was easy to do, as the gray column was defined within the ever-blackening skies.

"Looks like..." Mike listened to his brother's voice guide him from kilometers away by using the ship's x-ray scanners. "Yep, straight ahead, Mike. Right under that overhang? It's subtle, but it's there."

Mike was disoriented by the potency of life all around him. Sounds and colors pervaded his senses. "Where? What overhang? All I see is trees."

His brother sighed at him, as if he'd done this a thousand times and it was taxing to his mellow vibe. "No, no... dude, *listen* to me," Claude said. "There is a little gap between a pile of boulders..."

Blood pumped through Mike's veins as he ducked under low-hanging vines. He scratched the fur on his head and cursed to himself. *Blob is right, Max needs to be more careful. Especially here on Uehara. I better not get put on the spit and roasted over the fire.*

Sentient beings were rumored to exist here, but no information about them existed on the Uwcb. Astrobiologist-sent drones had determined the geophysical characteristics of the various stars and the objects of their solar systems, which was how the boys had discovered the tidal bore of Uehara in the first place. Myths and legends of guys *actually* surfing the place were just that—myths and legends. *Until you get barreled in a tube there!* Mike had to smile.

"Claude, I still don't see it," Mike said, now panting heavily.

"Well, I can—and I'm a few kilometers away!" yelled Claude.

"Dude, calm down!" Mike activated his ankle boosters, chancing that the brief jolt of movement would reveal his presence. "It must be too far away." A quick burst, a hop, and another hop, and he finally discovered the spot where the smoke was originating.

"You getting this, Claude?" Mike asked, a mini-camera attached to the top of one of his dreadlocks sent a clearer live image to the *Hopper* mainframe holoscreen than his wrist implant, so he switched over.

"Yep," Claude said. "I think that must be the vent to their underground dwelling. It might be unstable. Make sure you—"

"Whoa!" Mike squeaked as his footing became unstable, and the mossy, wet ground beneath him crumbled away, revealing a makeshift staircase of tree roots and packed soil that disappeared into a dark abyss below. He took a deep breath and floated into the unknown.

***

Consistently awed by his surroundings, Mike made it to the bottom of the shaft and wobbled to his hind paws and tried to steady himself. He squinted and wiggled his nose at the dripping muddy walls facing him on all sides. Checking his implant for heat traces he half-mumbled, half-whispered into the com.

"Max? Max, can you hear me? Max, come in. Yo, Max, where ya at?"

Mike hopped along a muddy wall until he observed an opening. Sections of the branches and vines had been carved out manually by hand tool, forming a tunnel of vegetation. Despite the moist ground and the suffocating feel of the enclosed space, a large fire was burning somewhere up ahead.

"Max! C'mon, Captain, come in. *Please.*" Mike continued to try to reach his fearless leader.

When the large rabbit had nearly given up, convinced there was never going to be a reply and he would have to continue the search by paw, a static burst, followed by the sound of a familiar voice, came through the com on Mike's wrist.

"What's up, dude!" Max exclaimed, sounding as if he was chilling in a floating recliner on the beach. "Been waiting on you forever! Where ya been? You gotta come check out this funky palace down here. The locals are super cool!"

Clearly, the Captain was not in peril.

"You crazy son of an Algorean priest!" Mike said, shaking his head—half in disbelief, half in belief. "What in the Milky Way are you up to this time? Where are you? What kind of prank are you pulling on us, Cap?"

"Dude," Max replied, "no pranks. I'm just… you know, getting to know the local culture. You won't believe the fruit these people eat—it's delicious! Not to mention the herbal concoctions and the local jungle bush meat—it's incredible! Mike, you won't believe it!"

"Okay," Mike glanced around. "So… what's up, seriously now, dude… where can I find you? I'm in some sort of cavern. Not that you care, but I fell through a shaft from above. Am I even in the right spot? We saw smoke coming from near here. We were hoping to find you alive and well. I take it you're both?"

"Come on, Mike," Max chided. " 'Algoreans prevail.' That's my motto, you should know that by now!"

"I *do* know, because you remind us pretty much every other Usecond."

"Oh, please… I only bust it out when it's appropriate. Like when I save our butts. Remind me how many times I've done that, again?"

"A bunch," Mike conceded. "Now, where are you, you blue-skinned beast?"

"Uh, I'm just chilling out on a throne of branches, with the Ueharan babes feeding me their best grub. I'll send out a tracking beam. Punch me your coordinates."

Mike did so on the holoscreen of his implant, linking the two of them together invisibly. A flexible tracking beam popped out from both of their implants, despite being several hundred meters away, and the faint red beams searched for each other. Once they merged, a subsequent orange-lighted pathway formed, allowing Mike to hop his way through the maze of greenery. As Mike closed in on his Captain, the tunnels became less complex, all seeming to curve their way into one common, wider chamber. Sounds carried to his sensitive ears, sounds of grunting, chanting, and rabble rousing.

What party did Max invite himself to now?

Max had a propensity for engaging in social affairs, and as a consequence, the boys were expected to follow him into the frolicking—no matter what bizarre planet they were on, no matter what the bizarre customs might be.

Soon, a few of the natives approached Mike. Their incomparably distinctive skin and their beady eyes were mesmerizing. They waved to him and he hopped after them. Once he was closer, he was surprised by their stature, as they stood merely a head taller than Mike. The men chaperoned him to where the noise was the loudest, and, sure enough, there was Max, sitting on a makeshift throne of branches and fibers. Below him was a spread of local fare along with intricately-carved goblets containing sizzling potions. The smile on his face was ludicrously wide and a tad mischievous. The Captain had done it again.

"Come on, Mike, hop on over here and have a seat, I've got something for you."

Max fumbled beside himself and pulled out a twine basket containing a fancy display of root vegetables. They came in so many colors, shapes and textures it boggled the vegetarian's genetically-modified mind.

Mike picked up an orange, oblong vegetable from near the top of the basket and couldn't believe how dense it was in his paw. From growing up on Rabbit World, he had learned the denser and more colorful a vegetable was, the more nutrients were contained within. He smiled with satisfaction, biting into the tuber. It was one of the best perks of the mission the *Planet Hopper* had embarked upon... the exotic produce they got to taste on their travels. *Well,* Mike thought, *other than the perk, of course, of cruising through hyperspace sheaths all about the Milky Way, searching for the best waves to ride—that's pretty awesome too!*

"Dude, I'm going to start calling you King Max. This is too epic!" Mike cried out. Ueharans stood in a ring around their new god. A formidable species of warriors, despite their diminutive size, Mike guessed a modest group of them could probably take out an unarmed humanoid, even a buffed-out Algorean like Max. But the natives showed no sign whatsoever of animosity. They were transfixed on his Captain. *Especially* one of the older females, who kept creeping closer to his side.

"I think she likes me." Max winked at Mike, forcing the rabbit to roll his eyes, shake his head, and make a sound in the back of his throat.

"Not again. C'mon, Max. It's one thing to make contact. It's another thing to make *contact,* hear me?"

"I'm just saying... I think she's fond of me, what's the big deal?"

"Oh, nothing," Mike frowned, "only the breaking of several thousand Ugov laws. And our bitcoin is in the red, in case you forgot—we overspent to get out here."

"Will you stop worrying about the Ugov? Their creditors don't care what we do, as long as we don't do it *overtly.* Besides, we're on a planet in the Outer Cygnus Arm—almost five thousand light years from the Ugov Outpost. We're all good. Trust me."

"I guess you're right—and this *is* incredibly tasty! Epic veggies!" Mike finished munching on the orange root and grabbed a curved pepper with a twisted top of stringy fibers, the flesh inside speckled with crunchy nuggets, each with their own zap of flavor. "Man, these little crunchy things are good..."

"Probably larvae."

"Thanks, exactly what I wanted to imagine: bugs in my grub." Mike sighed.

"All organic food is bugs and microbes," laughed Max. "And I prefer microbes over GMOs any nano."

Mike giggled. "I hear you, I hear you. So, I'm glad you're enjoying your new little kingdom here, Emperor Max of the Ueharan Jungle, but the crew is probably pretty worried by this point, don't you think? Blob is probably popping through his vest by now. And you know my brother... galaxies! You think *I'm* a stress case? Claude has probably torn out one of his dreadlocks already. Let's get out of here and let the boys know we're all good. Isn't our take-off window closing by third dawn?"

"But Mike," Max pleaded, "this is fun! We've still got some time. I wouldn't mind staying a little longer." He nodded at the Ueharan beauty goggling at him from a few paces away. "Let's get the boys to come join the festivities! What do you think?"

The Captain asking the mate for permission? The irony was not lost on Mike.

"All right, all right," the giant rabbit said, "let me get out of this *cave of plenty* and go topside where I can get a signal. Although... I don't think Blob's going to be pleased we're doing this. *Again.* We've been warned not to meddle in Category C planet affairs before."

"Yeah, yeah. Just get Blob in front of this spread." Max waved his hand over the rows of bowls and cups spilling over with fresh goods. "I think he'll get over it pretty quickly, don't you?"

"True dat, cap. Now, how in the name of the Milky Way do I get out of here, anyway? It feels like we're stuck in a hole in the center of the earth." Mike glanced up and around the wide chamber—and the asphyxiating, slimy walls closed in on him. Occasionally, a little bit of star and moonlight filtered through a slight gap in the bowed matrix of vegetation where the smoke from their fires pressed its way through. There *was* a topside, after all.

CHAPTER FOUR

"Expedite Emergency Evacuation."

Twenty Uminutes later, Mike was ushering Blob and Vern through the tunnels and into the main chamber of the Ueharan's home. Mike laughed at Blob's facial expression as they mingled through the wild crowd. Calls and cheers rang out upon the arrival of the two new guests. The songs of the Ueharans grew stronger. Each member of the *Planet Hopper* crew had their own signature set of dance moves and vocalizations, performed by each Ueharan they passed by in their procession toward... the *king*.

Max's grin was visible from a kilometer away.

Blob rushed over and slapped Max on the back joyously, while Vern shuffled his feet to stand beside them.

"Didn't I tell you guys not to worry?" Max's grin somehow widened.

The boys shared small talk for a bit, until Blob's eyes caught a glimpse of the wide buffet of Ueharan delicacies, and a classic gorging ensued. The Boor put on an eating display so impressive to the Ueharans it inspired a new dance move. As they gyrated for him, they pushed out and retracted their bellies, with hands clasped behind their heads. Mike was dying with laughter and couldn't wait to tell Claude. He had a hunch they would be replicating the Ueharans' dance move to provoke their big buddy at some point in the near future.

Blob wasn't the only one getting the custom dance treatment, though. For Mike, the Ueharans joined hands around him and hopped on two feet as high they could. For Vern, they made a movement with their fingers across their eyes, closing and opening them, placed their palms over their mouths, spun in a circle, squatted, and repeated the pattern. And for Max, male Ueharans flexed their muscles, beat their chests, and shouted forcefully, this while the females rocked back and forth moaning. It was a clear effort by the indigenous peoples to communicate with the crew through their graceful body control, all while moving to the percussive beats ricocheting off the muddied walls of the cave chamber.

"This is radical!" Mike was ecstatic. The taste of amazingly fresh vegetables and the ritualistic prancing of the Ueharans made him wiggle his whiskers with glee.

"Can you believe this?" the Captain shouted above the din.

Mike waved his paw in the air. "If it weren't you who sniffed out this scene—I honestly wouldn't, no. Because it's you, Cap, I've come to expect this sort of thing."

"Ha! Yeah, Mike, and guess what else? We just surfed the Ueharan tidal bore!"

They hi-fived, Mike's tiny paw and Max's massive blue palm meeting in the air.

***

A bit later, as Max basked in their good fortune, a Ueharan woman walked up rhythmically to the beat. She mumbled and clicked and groaned and shook. He exchanged looks with his crew mates. Max took her offered hand, stood up, and they moved to the center of the chamber. Reacting to the odd couple, the main group of dancers split apart, opening up a space for them in the middle. He dwarfed her in size and lifted her easily off the ground, tossed her in the air, and caught her sure-handedly, causing a gasp from the natives, as well as a pause in the drum beat. The woman squealed with glee, and they danced together a while longer.

Max politely waved to his impromptu dance partner and worked his way back through the Ueharan men, now moving in a trance with shakes and shivers.

"Ha!" laughed Blob, when Max got back with a sheepish grin. "Check out Vern—he's doing the *Milky Way Shuffle*. He's a regular dance master!"

Even Vern was feeling frisky tonight. Which pretty much consisted of him standing in one place, rocking stiffly back and forth while a native performed much more—*flexible*—movements all around him.

The Boor let out a bellow, pointing at the Captain. "And you? Max, you're ridiculous, you know that? Every time we go anywhere, you have *got* to fraternize with the locals, don't you? Has there been any world where you *didn't* like eating and drinking and... entertainment?"

"Yeah, don't you remember Bairstoke?" Mike replied for Max, laughing with his familiar low-bellied guffaw.

Blob arched his eyebrow at Mike, as if attempting to jar his memory. "Oh... right. I remember now. Yeah, not a very fun trip. Those Bairstoke girls were about as mean a group of aliens as I've ever seen in that arm of the galaxy. Mutant sirens. Their songs had me practically bleeding from the ears! No fun. And the waves sucked too."

"Ha!" Max scratched his red hair. "The Bairstokes... I remember those girls! Nose warts and all..."

"Well," Blob sighed, "I'm kind of bummed to say it, dudes, but we probably should go." He frowned at Mike. "Your brother is probably wanting in on some of this grub. Shall we take a to-go order? Too bad we don't have drone flyby service, huh?"

Mike snapped his fingers. "Oh, galaxy dust—Claude! I forgot about *Claude*! He's probably freaking out right now! I'll bet he's about to send out sonic blasts to try to echolocate us. Let's get outta this underground maze. I'm glad I left the tracking beam on."

Max was having such a good time he didn't follow the boys to the tunnels until a few Uminutes later. He wanted to take it all in for one last time. *Oh, damn the Algor Almighty! I don't want to leave! This place is a VR fantasy hologame. Lush, green, life... the greatest organic foods and the nicest peoples—oh, not to mention an endless wave that breaks every single Uday at the same exact time.*

The realization punched him in the gut: *I'll never be back here again.* He tried to ingrain every sight, smell, and sound. He wished he had Vern's database to store it all, then he could conjure up the visceral parts at will, whenever he wanted to. *I guess it's just part of the journey... to get a brand new experience each time we surf a new world.* He stood up reluctantly and searched around for an empty basket to gather fresh vittles for Claude.

Max's dance partner/savior walked forward, squatted low, and made an unmistakably sad gesture. Her beady eyes fought back glistening tears. Max smiled, winked, grabbed a few more tubular vegetables, and exited the main cavern.

Illuminating the tunnels were the turquoise sludge pools used to keep him in bondage earlier. Robust vines crawled up the edges of the cave and interlocked with each other. The phenomenon made the vines form a thick, webbed structure that not only provided the framework of the Ueharan dwellings, but also formed their defense system.

Before Max left, he took a final survey of the magical scene. The speckled skin of the Ueharan faces watched him, no longer dancing. Remorseful moans echoed. He turned and walked out, pausing to use a small gadget from his wrist implant to take a drop of the slime from one of the turquoise pools.

Just a little sample for Claude to inspect. The Ugov shouldn't be mad at me, they should be grateful—I'm helping move the field of astrobiology forward!

***

"Where have you guys been?" Yes, Claude was perturbed when they returned. "This ain't right! This just ain't right! You guys don't care one speck of galaxy's dust about me, do you? I always get left on the *Hopper*. I never know where you guys are, or if you've been eaten alive! Didn't we all agree on certain rules? Team ethics?"

"Hey…" Max pulled out the Ueharan organic goodies and waved them in the air. "You prefer staying on the *Hopper*. And besides, at least we're not empty-handed, Claude, check it out!"

This prompted Claude to hop up and try to snatch them out of his grip.

"Not so fast, dude," Max said, snapping the vegetables out of Claude's reach. "I've got something you might like even more."

"Uh oh. What'd you steal, Max?" Claude shook his head knowingly.

"I didn't *steal* it," Max sighed. "I just… *sampled* it. A little capful of goo the Ueharans were using to keep me tied up… I mean, whatever it is, it has, well, let's just say it has *properties.*

Special sorts of properties. My guess is it somehow helps to strengthen organic bonding."

"Yeah, uh-huh," Blob snorted. "You were about to sample more than just the goo, dude."

"Uh… not true. Just because—" Max tried deflecting, poorly.

"Seriously, Max?" Claude pretended to admonish the Captain, flicking his dreadlocks back over his shoulder while munching on a scrumptious gourd. He was the last of the crew to sample the fresh goods. "Well, I'd say it was good idea to go explore… nice work, Captain!"

Blob groaned. "I think that's enough mollifying our fearless leader, who, by the way, nearly got us all captured and eaten, on a strictly prohibited Category C planet, just now… and, to make matters worse, thanks to his brilliant leadership, we might have missed our take-off window. AI, what's our countdown?"

Claude motioned to the holoscreen. It was going to be tight. The instantly-displayed calculations intuited from Blob's diction showed their window closing in less than half a Uhour.

There was a frozen moment where everyone in the cockpit shared a weary look.

Max nodded his consent and the crew broke apart in different directions. Each had to take care of their assigned responsibilities for getting the *Planet Hopper* ready for departure. A half Uhour was probably not enough time, but Max wouldn't have listened to protests, so no one even bothered giving them.

An alarm code whined in the cockpit.

Meteors, comets, and swarms of space dust came and went, but whatever set off this particular code alarm was something much more serious than amalgamations of rock, ice, and insignificant flotsam and jetsam. It was something *extremely* large.

That's not good, thought Max. *Not good at all.* On closer inspection, the hologram image displayed what had caused the alarm code to activate. It wasn't a hazard solely for the crew of the

Planet Hopper—it was a hazard for the *entire* Ueharan solar system.

"Claude!" Max cried over the com. "Dude, you're never going to believe this... the alarm code for a Persean Planet Ball tournament just went off!"

"What?" Claude yelped over the com. "Nah... couldn't be. They were defeated in the last Galactic War. The Udays of Planet Ball are over. It's gotta be a mistake. I'll double check with an AI simulation decoder, maybe cause we're so far out here, they haven't updated it yet through the Uweb..."

A moment later Claude's voice came back with the bad news. "Sorry to say, Captain," Claude said, "I even triple-checked. Get down here, it's better on the mainframe holoscreen. I could send it up to the cockpit, but you... you won't believe what I'm seeing."

"Vern, stay here, be ready for immediate launch." Max gulped, swiveled, and leapt from his co-pilot chair and raced to the mainframe compartment. *Planet Ballers? Here? That's impossible! The Persean Age was declared over and done with! It's gotta be a malfunction.*

Uweb history sites were overloaded with stories told of the vicious species of alien, who had been banished to the far side of the galaxy after losing a brutal war with the Ugov and their allies. Every Ucitizen could recite the words from the famous speech: "Planet Ball season is over, *forever.*"

But who could truly believe the utter decimation caused by the infamous game would never return? It was a deadly pastime played by the Persean elite, incomprehensible aliens able to hold a decent-sized moon in one hand. Giant Beings, as they were referred to in the familiar, had been competing against each other for eons upon eons—long before the Persean Arm of the galaxy was discovered to harbor sentient, technologically advanced life. Max blinked tears away as he imagined all the worlds, entire solar systems full of wonderful people, turned to galaxy dust through violent collisions. Entire legacies and cultures were incinerated, species disposed of like dark matter into the nothingness of deep space. Perseans were a most callous kind of alien.

Max scrambled through the air tube connecting each segment of the spaceship, and entered the control room where Mike and Blob huddled around Claude. The look in their eyes was unsettling.

"Max, this doesn't appear to be a false code." Claude interrupted the silence as everyone scanned the holochart listings scrolling at a pace they could all read. "The *Hopper* has pretty good code readers. This seems to be a legitimate, if not archaic code reading. I'm telling you, Max, we can't ignore this one. We have to risk missing the safety window on ascent and take our chances. According to these estimates... if we wait, we're not gonna make it out of range."

More high-pitched alarms wailed in the control room as one after another the medium-range sensors triggered.

"Yeah..." Claude shook his head. "Dudes, it's official—judging from those crude images—there are Persean spaceships coming in. Cursed galaxies! Uehara's binary solar system must be their chosen site to play a tournament! When this code shows, it means they're in range, and if they start stepping on planets while they're getting ready to start, well, we could be..."

Max pursed his lips, searched the eyes of his crew mates, sighed, and gave the order: "Expedite emergency evacuation."

The four of them scattered back to their tasks, this time having to shake off the urge to let themselves be paralyzed by fear. His crew mates were going to have to count on each other to get the *Planet Hopper* off the ground and safely out of range. No Utime to waste.

CHAPTER FIVE

Escape From Uehara Bay

Vern sat in the cockpit of the *Planet Hopper* multi-tasking. While preparing the engines for hyperspace travel he also calculated exit velocities from Uehara's gravitational pull, read local wind readings for initial ascent, and stored the data on his tertiary brain layer. He was compelled to do it. After all, Vern *was* an android.

But, in an absurd paradox, he was *also* an alien. Well, technically speaking, he was an AI symbiot. Or a cyborg, if one preferred slang, although, unlike those hybrid species, he never showed a speck of skin. He slept with his helmet, visor, and synthsuit on, and never took them off unless he was in total privacy. Not even his crew mates had ever laid eyes on his scorched and textured skin.

As the pilot, Vern had the most important job on the ship. But the bulk of his work didn't begin until take off, so he found himself daydreaming about his synthetic ancestry. *Ah, to be a mongrel,* thought Vern. *I'm a walking contradiction, for galaxy's sake!*

Claude's voice over the holo broke him from his meditations. "Yo, Vern!"

"How much time, Claude?" Vern asked.

"It's not looking good," Claude replied. "You may have to pull off some gnarly maneuvers to get us out of here… even if I *can* get the AI override to allow us to take off. Don't forget—I programmed our departure according to the window created between the triple moon system. The solar winds are so strong between the Ueharan triplets that if we try to shoot the gap—well, I don't really want to think about what happens if we don't squeak through."

"Dude," Blob chimed in over the ship intercom. "Getting pulverized by an errant moon thrown our way doesn't sound fun either. I'll take solar winds any Uday." He was always quick to point out obvious facts.

"Guys…" Max, who had entered the cockpit and sat in the co-pilot seat, tried to keep it together. Vern sensed the crew's emotions were running high. All this incredible flora and fauna being turned to plasma… not to mention the unique culture of the friendly Ueharan tribes—it was devastating to the boys. "It does no good to think about the negative possibilities. Let's focus on getting off this planet and out of range so we're not collateral damage—if the alarm codes are accurate."

Blob grumbled something.

"Dude!" Max's voice boomed over the com. "Close that massive maw of yours, Blob. Let's get focused here. Guys, we are all going to need each other to get out of this jam. Get back to your tasks—keep the com open for Claude's updates, okay?"

With Blob quelled, Vern swiped through one Uweb link after another, trying to find any helpful information on velocity maximization during a planetary exit. He was going to have to pull off a minor miracle here—but then what? The Persean ships were between them and their hyperspace sheath. A circuit buzzed, somewhere deep in the digital recesses of his modified mind, as he reached into the cockpit computer through his AI interface. There had to be something…

Up popped a holoscreen with the hyperspace specs on the *Planet Hopper*. Vern studied the data wondering how they were going to get around those Persean ships.

***

"Oh… no." It was the dread in Claude's voice that made a shiver crawl up Max's spine.

"What's up, Claude?" The Captain clicked the com link. "You get us a read on our escape route yet?"

"Negatory," Claude grumbled. "And guess who's just arrived in Outer Cygnus, a few systems over, and approaching, rapidly…" It wasn't a question, so he kept on: "Any other ideas for getting off this planet and through the launch window? We're reaching maximum index!"

"Relax, Claude," Max said. "We're going to get out of here. There's too many more waves in the galaxy for us to ride, praise Algor! Anybody got anything constructive?"

"Maybe." It was Mike. "Check the wind speeds at the top of that massive mountain range that runs north-south, looks to be… about thirty kilometers away!"

"What about it?" Max asked.

"Well…" Mike seemed to have been mulling this one over. "Maybe we take an aggressive line and use the air thermals coming up outta there to get some extra boost out of the atmosphere. We've got to shrink the time gap somehow."

Max nodded. "Great idea, Mike! We know Vern's up for the task, but… will it save enough time is the question."

"I think so, Captain," Vern replied, "According to my new projections, Mike's idea will probably work, but it'll be a bumpy ride…"

Max gave the order. "Do it! Vern, change heading for the mountain range. Everyone else get ready to buckle in till we're in the upper atmosphere."

Okay, one problem solved. Max frowned. *But what happens when we do get off Uehara? They're sitting there blocking our only way back to the Last Ugov Outpost…*

And suddenly the idea came to him.

"Hey, Vern!"

"Yes, Captain."

"There's a signature left in the wake of all hyperspace travel, a kind of demarcation line… the Persean ships, they'll leave an extremely broad energy resonance trailing behind them! It'll be humongous, considering the size of just one of their ships, probably super easy to pick up and…"

Vern guessed, "The *Planet Hopper* does have the technology—illegal, may I remind you—of energy resonance scanning. processing power, I could, conceivably, convert it to crude star map data."

"We could backdoor it!" Max cried. "Like surfing through a barrel section the hard way! Send it to Claude, Vern, have him check it out."

Vern leaned forward and held his wrist against the holoscreen input between he and the Captain and sent a short form of the concept to Claude.

"That's it!" cried Claude, the intercom buzzing with his loud shout. "Max, Vern, you dudes are geniuses! We trace their sheath, right as they are emerging from hyperspace, and try to follow it out of the collateral zone! Dudes—I think it's our only way out of here!"

"Whoa," Blob's inflection belying his doubt. "Guys, whoa. Slow your roll. Hold on a Usec. Tracing hyperspace sheaths ain't easy. I know the *Planet Hopper* has the apparatus… but it's a practice the Ugov used to catch pirates—not to calculate star maps. Those pirates have the shoddiest AI available. I wouldn't trust those sheaths, and neither does the Ugov. Why would we trust shoddy Persean sheaths? They're probably even worse!"

"Well," Mike threw in, "at least the *Planet Hopper* has the capability. Not many spaceships can trace resonance. Ugov elite and pirates have 'em—but they don't have Vern on their ship, like we do. No one else could make those computations in this short amount of time. But I'm on Blob's side, let's exhaust all possibilities before we go blindly following a hyperspace sheath—we don't even know where it leads."

"Yes, we do!" Blob protested. "Obviously it leads to the Persean arm. We'll be wiped away like mold spores. *And…* what if they don't want to be traced? What if they purposefully took off from a random, unpopulated solar system in Perseus, with no other sheath to trace? We'll be stranded out there! Forever!"

"There's probably a diversion," Mike agreed with Blob—it was a shaky proposition, at best. "There's no way they march into this little system and start throwing things around without provoking notice from Ugov rangers or the satellite monitors at the Last Outpost. Maybe they're just scouting—not playing."

Despite their reservations, Max tried to steer Blob and Mike toward the reality of the situation. "Mike's right. And Blob's right. If we get dropped off in the middle of dark space, in some Algor-forsaken place, with no sheath out—we're done for. We might as well surf one more session here on Uehara and take our medicine. I, for one, plan on *many* more surf sessions on *many* more planets.

Let's not forget. We swore an oath to each other. So if we have to use that Persean sheath… we have to."

"Uh, Max," Claude said, "we're gonna have to."

Max raised his eyebrows at Vern and clicked the com again. "What's up, furry friend, whatcha mean 'we have to?'"

"I mean," Claude replied, "we *have* to use the Persean sheath. Using the resonance-tracer is the only way to get far enough out of this solar system. I reran the projections. The debris event horizon—it's *going* to catch us. It's not a matter of *if* but *when*. We won't be able to make it back to the hyperspace sheath we came in on without being collateral damage. Even a pilot as epic as Vern can't dodge that much stuff for very long…"

"Okay, Claude, I'm convinced." Max swiveled in his floating chair. "Vern, get the energy resonance apparatus fired up and meld with the ship's AI. I'll get the dashboard configured for you, so when you're done you can take over for me behind the stick. Claude, go help Mike, we're going to need that wind boost if we're going to make it off this planet in time. Run a few models, find out how close and personal we can get with that mountain range without scraping the ship. Blob, get to the hyperspace chambers and start prepping the coffins."

***

Vern slipped off his floating chair and went over to the computer ports along the cockpit walls. He needed a hard cable connection; this was a matter of melding man and machine. *I hate letting it take over. Completely.* Whenever melding with the AI he became the proverbial "ghost in the machine," it was when he felt the least… *alien.*

He took the hard cable and hesitated with it in his hand. Once tethered to the ship's mainframe computer his consciousness would no longer be totally his *own,* and an energy resonance application took a fairly long time to process. The task required both Vern's and the *Planet Hopper's* data processors working in unison in order to be completed, and there was only one way to do that. He sighed and took the *Hopper's* AI hard cable with one hand and removed a section of his chest plate with the other. He inserted the cable into an auxiliary port built directly into his collar bone (or what was left of it) and a zap charged through his nervous system.

Beside the AI module an image popped up on a separate holoscreen, with a percentage bar alongside it. Each time new batches of processed data sifted through the algorithms—as the computer re-estimated the Planet Baller ships' arrival time—the bar changed.

Nothing more to do. Vern was linked in. From there on out it was a matter of crunching numbers. If he and the AI could trace a route to the Persean hyperspace platform before the resonance faded off into the ether, they might be able to pull this off.

***

Once Vern was linked in, Max checked on the others. "Mike, check the vector readings on those mountains. Which one is the highest altitude, and which one is closest to the window matrix?"

"Will do, Captain!" Mike's voice came over the com.

Max figured there might be a more efficient option. *Might as well be sure.*

Max squeezed his upper lip to the bottom of his nostrils. He glanced at the slumped figure of his pilot by the wall, before clicking the com link again. "Hey, guys, I'm monitoring Vern... the data processing threshold of the *Planet Hopper's* mainframe is being pushed pretty hard. We're using too many processors at once. Claude, you might have to hold off on the AI override. Vern has to get this sheath traced and locked in."

Claude bristled with a quick response. "Max... *dude*... if we don't get enough energy out of these turbo boosters we aren't getting through to the other side of the Uehara debris zone. The projections keep getting worse, I mean this is getting ridic—"

"Hey you big, mutant rabbit, settle down!" Max barked. "It's time to surf the solar wind and get out of here! Let Vern deal with the sheath, Claude, you work on getting as much transfer energy into the boosters as you can. Mike can prep our exit strategy. Blob, if the E-coffins are ready, get strapped in. I'll fly the *Hopper* till Vern is done downloading and ready to take over. Let's go! Look alive, boys, set wave coming, and if we don't catch it and ride it... well, there'll be no more rides for us to have. *Ever.*"

Max slid into his floating chair in the cockpit and started all systems with a few clicks on a mini holopad hovering on his dominant hand side. A lurching was felt throughout the ship as Max got them airborne in a jiffy.

Despite the imminent danger, Max found himself humming a song to himself, smiling and gripping tight on the console stick. He ramped up the thrusters and the *Hopper* reached cruising speed. *Just another Uday in the life.* He had convinced himself they were going to escape—*like every time*—and live to surf another Uday. His eyes narrowed as he observed the white-capped mountains looming ahead of them. They were impossibly wedged with massive glaciers and adorned with emerald green lakes, reflecting at him through the synthglass portals. The top peaks measured roughly thirty-four hundred kilometers in altitude, and they were getting impressively larger and larger on the monitors as they approached. Max was awe-struck for a moment. *Are we really going to be able to use those?*

The *Planet Hopper* lost fifty meters of altitude as the first of several wind bursts emanated from the nasty storm front clinging to the foothills of the Ueharan peaks. A cacophony of hard rain and hail smashed against her shell.

"Oh, yeah, now we're talking!" Max eased the crew with his seemingly unflappable demeanor over the com. "Give me some more, Uehara! Whatcha got?" His voice bellowed throughout the compartments of the ship.

Claude didn't sound keen. "Let's not coax her on, Max, we need all the help we can get. Good, Uehara, good. Be a good girl, now."

"All right, Max," Mike said. "See that triple spire up there? Two hundred forty-five degrees. Yep, aim for that, come up as steep and close to those cliffs as you can. I hope Vern doesn't get jealous when Max pilots us through this!"

Max focused on the front monitor, a drop of sweat slid down his broad blue skinned brow. The *Planet Hopper* was on a course it wouldn't dare take with the auto pilot running the show. Altitude sensors provoked alarms to go off inside the cockpit.

Max yanked on the console stick and the *Planet Hopper* narrowly avoided scraping the foothills. Spiraling upward, he couldn't waste a drop of thrusters, but couldn't overdo it, either. The ship shook and crackled and sizzled. A loud splatter hit the front portals. Followed by another.

"What in the galaxies is that?" Blob asked, after a thump came over the cockpit audio feed.

"Those cursed birds again!" Max growled, hoping they weren't big enough to clog any of the front sensor panels. "Remind me to never pass up a chance at hunting and roasting local birds at our next surf spot."

With the birds out of the way, they made it clear of the foothills, and the bizarre ice storm fizzled out. They were two-thirds of the way up the full height of the triple spire of peaks they were shooting for.

Once out from under the clouds, the wind changed dramatically. Instead of a constant resistance, with irregular bursts that threatened to shake the *Hopper* off its course, now it was all underneath her.

Yes! Projections guessed right—an updraft! Max thought. *We're going make it!*

"Nice call using the mountain boost, Mike!" Claude lauded his brother. "The models are changing every Usecond. This is the first time I've seen them turn around and improve our probabilities of making it through that orbital window."

"Sweet!" Max pumped his fist in the air.

In quite possibly the longest three plus Uminutes of Max's life, he listened in silence to the AI, waiting for Vern's meld to be complete. With an agonizingly slow and steady rhythm, the computer indicated it was still running the numbers, *beep beep beep beep beep beep beep...* Finally, a green-colored light flashed. A steady, droning buzz ensued.

"He's done!" shouted Max.

"Yes!" Claude cried.

"Let's get out of here!" Mike yelled.

"Claude—hit it!" Max ordered. "Everyone down to the coffins! Now!"

As they soared higher and higher, blazing through the various layers of Uehara's atmosphere, the planet became smaller and smaller on the view screen. Set against the backdrop of the blackness of space, it was no longer an all-encompassing canvas of color, now, Max could pick out the individual continents, the tectonics of the mountains, the systems of interlinked oceans, seas, and rivers.

The stoke—after having gotten safely off Uehara—dissolved away, as Max stared at the shrinking green ball through the monitors. This special place would cease to exist in a matter of Uhours. All of the glorious flora and fauna of the planet would be vaporized. And the unique, sentient, indigenous peoples they had met... they would be extinct for eternity.

***

Down in the hyperspace compartment, the black, oblong shapes of the Persean spaceships flickered on the open holoscreen. The luminescent quality of their sharp-pointed exteriors reminded Max of the phytoplankton in the Ueharan seas, swirling lights that had been visible when they were in orbit around the planet.

"Guys, here they come!" Mike pointed to the holomonitor.

Great, Max thought, *a last chance for the boys to fill their minds with potential nightmares.*

"Good Milky Way," Blob cried. "The noses of those things— they extend forever!"

"Is this really gonna work?" Mike stopped his hop.

"C'mon, bro, no time for second thoughts, get in there." Claude pushed Mike toward his hyperspace chamber, and boosted him up inside.

Blob's eyes were wide open, his monobrow shaped like an arcing rainbow, and he made loud grunts that echoed throughout the hyperspace compartment.

"Dang, Blob, you breathe loud!" Max scolded. He turned to everyone else and said: "Crew, get ready for either the ride of your life or the last ride of your life!"

"Nah, Captain," corrected Mike loudly, poking his head out from inside his hyperspace chamber. His dreadlocks were splayed on either side of his long, upright ears. "Getting sucked into a wormhole isn't my idea of the ride of a lifetime, especially when we don't know where it goes! It might close out!"

"Hey boys," Blob sobbed, the fine white and gray fur curling up around his cheeks. "If this doesn't go well, I just want to say…"

"Blob," started Claude, "spare us—"

"—we've heard it before!" all crew members except the big Boor said at the same time.

The AI voice drowned out the momentary distraction of laughter at the expense of their friend.

"Thirty Useconds, and counting. Twenty-nine, twenty-eight…"

Max pressed a button and his embryonic chamber doors slid open, revealing the malleable padding that would be his home for an amount of time that was either a nanosecond or infinity, depending on which scientific viewpoint one subscribed to. "Let's go, Vern. Let's go, Blob. We're past the solar winds, all we need now is to sneak past those Perseans ships, let the *P Hop* follow the trail of stardust and through the throat of that wormhole!"

"Fifteen, fourteen, thirteen…"

Once the other two crew mates were in, Max followed suit, immediately lying prone on his back and closing his eyes. The Captain praised Algor, struggling to retain his final thoughts before giving into the wicked anesthesia filling his E-chamber. His last realization was a troubling one: if the crew were indeed successful in this crazed attempt at salvation, and they were able to ride out on the Persean sheath, they would have the data to construct a star map that no one in the galaxy possessed—*other* than Perseans. Trillions of aliens had died in the aftermath of their apocalyptic matches of Planet Ball and his crew were inadvertently stealing perhaps their most precious secret. Max grimaced.

"Five, four, three…"

CHAPTER SIX

A Tradition of Destruction

Grand Master Stergis stood in his private quarters, arms folded, admiring the view on the wall monitor. His grin widened as the rest of his fleet emerged from the wormhole. One by one they popped out, dark, silvery shapes, sculpted from rare Persean metals. Their design was the same: a wide tail with long, rounded curves narrowing and converging into a needlepoint nose. As they exited the hyperspace platform their wavering motion belied the presence of a hole in the space-time continuum.

The grand master turned away from the monitor. The time had finally come! He could barely contain his joy as he donned his robe and left his quarters. Walking through the bustling corridors to the bridge, the ranks were in a mood of near jubilation. Each officer stopped and gave him a proper Persean salute as they passed.

Our time has finally come, Stergis mused, receiving a particularly emphatic salute from one of his generals posted up at the entryway to the bridge. The hyperspace sheath had worked, and now that they had arrived at the proposed solar board, preparation for the tournament would begin shortly.

All throughout the ship, screens showed the images of heroic scientists and engineers who had been working for Udecades to build a star map route that would allow them to slink into this far corner of the galaxy. It took two separate sheaths to get there from Persar, one to the edge of the Abandoned asteroid belt, and a much shorter one to Outer Cygnus, but they had done it.

By the time he had settled into his floating chair on the bridge, the entire fleet were lined up behind Stergis's flagship, locked into an approach vector for the outskirts of the Ueharan solar system.

The grand master shooed away assistants who offered him juice and snacks, he didn't want to be bothered. It was a Uday of reckoning for the Persean race, a Uday that Stergis had been waiting for all his life. According to the highest ranked Planet Ball officials, Uehara was the perfect system for the opening round of the tournament—with a complex and challenging solar board set-up. It was a good opportunity for him to shake off the space rust.

With a high level of unpredictability, the Ueharan solar board contained a laborious schematic of gravitational effects that would force mistakes from even the most experienced Planet Ball tossers. Errant throws meant even more collisions, more debris, and more energy milling about in the clear throw zones. With fourteen major planets and their combined thirty-nine moons, dozens of dwarf planets, two rotating asteroid belts, all moving in a peculiar pattern of clash and retreat, clash and retreat... no wonder it was so highly rated. And to add a fun little treat for the truly masochistic tossers, there was a pulsar wave zone: an area where it was illegal for a thrown planetoid to come to an orbital rest.

I know Chyrone will approve of that. Stergis smiled inwardly. *Years of bad press and divisive rhetoric, he'll never stop trying to supplant me. Let him try.*

His rival Chyrone was one of the most successful players in tournament history. Chyrone was a constant in his life. From childhood to adulthood, he was a rival of Stergis unlike any other on Persar. He was a peerless veteran player, with a top-notch pedigree, and *very* few defeats on his record. His family came from the most elite branches of the Persean Halls of Glory. A handful of sects even favored *him* for Grand Master of Perseus. All the media coverage predicted the incumbent would reach the finals of the Outer Cygnus tournament.

Stergis scratched the red stubble on the tip of his chin as he contemplated the strategy he was hoping to impose. Planet Ball tournaments were decided by the larger celestial bodies. The little objects—such as moons and comets—could be dealt with by a simple toss of a dense gas planet. Easy pickings. *Even an amateur knows: the larger the body you're left with at the end, the better.*

Gazing up at the main holoscreen on the bridge he saw that one of his technicians was running a slideshow of each available planetary body for the solar board. A close up image of one of the exoplanets manifested. It shone with a blue-green hue. He imagined throwing it. *All I need is the right holding gloves, the kind that allow a bit of extra grip—oh, the spin I could get on that thing!*

Stergis clicked on a holomirror to check his image. Dressed in the traditional maroon robes of the pre-tournament feast and address, his red shock of hair styled back, he searched his reflection for signs of weakness.

Not so long after his private musings in his quarters, he converted the words he had been practicing into a live speech transmitted to the formal attendees: "Planet Ball is a *right*, not a request, my fellow Perseans. Ever since the Sun Peoples spread like grotesque parasites across the galaxy, our way of life has been destroyed, subjugated to the will of life forms so insignificant in size as to be nearly imperceptible. Hatred for them burns in my core—as it should in all of yours!"

He took a pause to scan the audience with his fiery eyes. He was greeted with an equal fire from his attendees.

"We will have our revenge on the Ugov," he continued. "The audacious microscopic organisms think they can draw up laws to contain our stature in the galaxy? This is a new era—the new age of Perseus! We will rise and throw, as we have always done. *Always forward!*"

Applause and cheers echoed off the chambers of those who watched live. He quelled the noise by gesturing with arms extended and palms down. "We are unlike any of the other alien races of the Milky Way. Our star is the heart of the universe! *We* are the genesis. *We* are the synthesis of billions of worlds coalescing into one—our giant star. That's what they call our beautiful life giving orb, our Persar—a giant. What is a *giant*? According to what measure? These insignificant little cretins are the ones to decide what is large and what is small? They decide we are not allowed to throw planets? Not on our watch. We are the next generation of Perseans, we will bring Planet Ball back to the galaxy!"

Yelling and stomping ensued from the increasingly feverish crowd.

"*Always forward,* my brothers and sisters, that is our speak: *Always forward.* Our forefathers and mothers spoke these words. *Always forward,* we will perpetually advance in our dome walkers up to the next throw. We toss planets and we toss moons, not for sport, but for our very way of life. They talk about destruction— that we are destroying *intelligent* life—what life? The mold of squashed microbes on the tread of our boots? That is what these tiny beings are—nothing more than detritus. They talk about terraforming, spreading the way of Sun Peoples to all corners of the galaxy. That is how they create worlds, by injecting their poison into desolate rocks, mere specks of dust, and watching that poison grow into more of them! Increasing their ranks and attempting to choke us on their non-breathable gases. Perseans terraform not by poison but through the sport of Planet Ball. *We* are the ultimate creators! We build worlds through collisions, through accumulation of matter, and through gravitational pull. They think this is a game? A mindless destruction? We know the truth. That the Sun Peoples are afraid. So they banish us to the Persean Arm, drawing an imaginary line across dark matter, telling us: 'do not pass.' But what they haven't learned yet is that *our* generation is different. We aren't going to stand aside. We can—and *will*—relive the glory that our people have known, long before the slow sickness of the Sunish crawled across the galactic arms to us. I say *yes* to Planet Ball, and what say you all?"

The assorted crew on the bridge of the *Amalgamator*, and in the crowded chambers throughout, responded accordingly.

"*We* say yes to Planet Ball, to our traditions, to our very way of life. We say *no* to anyone or anything that stands in the way. Treaties be gone! There *is* no treaty. Merely a decree. The terms of the Sunish mandate say we are to never leave this corner of the galaxy, thereby limiting our access to the rare elements needed for sustaining life. They insult us and say: 'Play virtual Planet Ball, there's no difference, and no life has to die.' No life has to die? Is that what the Sun Peoples said as their fleets roamed space, systematically taking out every other alien species in their way? Did they consider the lives of the Perseans they bled to death with their viruses? Life and death are the sacred rules of our Persean world, we live and die, and so do the solar systems that we use to play our sport. Orion time is not Persean time. Utime is not our time. A moment for us is eons for them. They claim they are immortals because they genetically modify their own cells! But they could never compete with our longevity. We had to be patient. Wait for the right generation to reestablish our dominance of the Milky Way. Today *is* that Uday. This is our galaxy, make no mistake, fellow Perseans, and this—" he pointed at the monitor now cued to show the two Ueharan stars and its array of satellites—"is our solar system. These are the planets we will wield to determine the victor of the tournament. This will be the first tournament since the war, and the first of many more to follow. Our grand prizes will stagger the mind, as will the impressive style and grace of the players. And your grand master will be tossing the first stone!"

A loud cheer of approval erupted.

"I will challenge a worthy opponent, Tragull, to commence this historical Uday of celebration." Another cheer burst out, but a slight groan and maybe a few boos accompanied it this time, coming from a portion of the crowd highly loyal to Stergis. "So… we have talked and planned, discussed and organized—now it is finally time! Time to play… *Planet Ball!*"

A raucous roar emanated from his fellow Persean elite.

"*Always forward! Always forward! Always forward!*"

As the refrain crescendoed, the main monitor switched to a view from outside the Ueharan solar system, and the tiny green ball of the paradisiacal planet shined and flickered peacefully amid the darkness of empty space.

***

"Stergis, what's wrong? You seem distant. You seem preoccupied." His wife, Wella, a long, lean, bright-skinned woman, with curling locks of yellow hair cascading over her shoulders, spoke softly to him. She was one of the prettiest women on Persar, but her reputation as a cunning political advisor to her husband was her true claim to fame. She sidled up next to Stergis and stroked his forehead, parting his orange hair in the center, and planting a kiss on his lips.

"Ah, Wella, you read my soul. You always do." Stergis took her in his arms. "There never seems to be sufficient logistics… it's been so long since we have played a tournament, that, well, the historical records are just that—*records*. There are no living Perseans who have played a real, live tournament game. I want this to be a success, Wella, I—I want to create something for our people to build upon. But I don't want to be the one who unleashes the microscopic virus on us a second time."

"Dear one," she said, gazing deep into his amber eyes. Only the elite of Persar had the distinctive glossy tone of yellow. All the other Perseans had red and orange hues in their eyes. It was a distinct feature ripe for prejudice. "There is no doubt you are meant to be the one who returns us to glory. Your commitment to your forefathers' vision for the future of Persar is unwavering. I believe in you, and so do your fellow Persean Peoples. Ezran believes in you, as do the rest of the younger ranks coming up. *Believe* in this tradition… it is what we have been waiting for all of our lives. The parasite viruses cannot detect us here in Outer Cygnus, and we can play freely."

Stergis wanted to believe all was in order, but he had an itching suspicion that he could not seem to shake. "Yes, my dear. But I do have my concerns. Could there be spies in this area of Cygnus? Alien races cow down to their superior humans. They are willing to sit on the far side of the galaxy, waiting for nothing but an opportunity to gain the lauding of the Sunish. If they alert the scum to our presence…"

"Spies? Out here? Not possible," she said. "Although I did hear that Ugov organic detector beams have identified living humanoids in the solar system, most likely on the green planet, Uehara, that the system is named after. But they are a civilization far from the capability to send a message all the way back to Orion… or even the Outer Cygnan Outpost for that matter."

"Yes," Stergis grumbled. "I know that, I know that. But something in my intuition is warning me—"

"I think you are feeling the stress of this momentous occasion." The high lady rubbed his shoulders vigorously—*too* vigorously. "Try to relax, we have our final approach to Uehara, soon it will be time for you to lead the dome walkers to the throw zone. I'm sure the routes are being calculated right now as we speak." She didn't miss his frown. "Don't worry about the logistics. Hey—" She moved to face him, grabbing his chin with the tips of her fingers and drawing his head to her. "We should be starting soon, and you need to be at full concentration level. Go rest now, I'll wake you in a bit."

Before Stergis could retire a buzz came from the entry panel next to the door. An assistant named Buele was cleared by the AI scanner, and marched in with a purpose. The short man had golden droplets of sweat on his forehead and cheeks.

"What's the problem, Buele? A mechanical issue?" Stergis guessed.

"Always Forward! Sorry to disturb you, Grand Master, High Lady, but I'm afraid it's worse than that." The nervous assistant paused before delivering the news. "Our sensors have been showing an unusual energy source emanating from the green planet."

"What kind of energy source?" Wella asked, unprovoked.

Buele glanced from one superior to the other. "Something possibly indicative of a higher level of technology than we originally observed. There have even been uncorroborated readings that show an x-ray scanner has indeed picked up our wormhole resonance signal."

"What? How is that possible?" Stergis slammed his fist on a console. "We carefully selected this system because of its lack of communications technology. Those readings cannot be accurate!"

"Grand Master," Buele replied, "it's not an outpost, but we have reason to believe there is a spaceship with interstellar travel capabilities—and transmission receptors—somewhere near the vicinity of the Uehara exoplanet. It's possible they are an alien race. The bridge team is asking for you."

"Very well..." Stergis glanced at Wella with exasperation. Wella made eye contact with him, titled her head, and shrugged. "Tell them I'll be right up."

"Always forward!" Buele nodded, did an about face, and went out the slide door to the main hall.

Stergis turned to his wife and said: "I feel... this is an omen, a calling, I was alerted by my intuitive senses. Our forefathers are warning me from the other side. I don't think provoking the Ugov—as much as I would love to enact revenge—is prudent at this time. Maybe we should evacuate."

Wella closed her eyes. When she opened them she said: "This must be the moment of your first challenge in restoring order to the galaxy. You must find out who these aliens are and eliminate the threat of communication with the Ugov. We don't want the Persean elite to pick up any sign of negligence. Your reign as grand master depends on it. You cannot retreat."

Without a reply he kissed her on the cheek, and exited out the slide door, stomping his way to the air tube chamber that would bring him up to the bridge to meet with his captains and main scientists. He could not let this opportunity slip away.

I can't let this tournament be a false one. All faithful Perseans have been waiting for this Uday. What alien pirates would be lunatic enough to be flying around in a forbidden sector of the Outer Cygnus Arm? Whoever they are, they must have a death wish.

I can gladly grant them that.

The first explosive collision of planetesimals was a bit of a letdown for Stergis. Not because his throw was made with greater force than the decay parameters shown on the targeted gas planet, but that he left it too many degrees off kilter, and therefore gave his first round opponent, the capable Tragull, a passageway for him to sneak his second moon through. With a lack of displaced gases there was no gravity slip to alter the path of Tragull's two-moon, and he could capitalize on Stergis's mistake. Tragull would be in position to orbitize his three-moon, and have a clear advantage. It would be a blockade Stergis would have to dedicate resources to, and that would be a massive waste during the early stages of a match.

A signal call from the hyperspace ships to his dome walker sent an indicator beep.

"What is it?" snapped Stergis, hating to be disturbed during a match. He usually wouldn't bother acknowledging a call during match play, but there was the unresolved matter of the possible alien ship…

"Unfortunately it's not good news, Grand Master," the caller replied. It was Buele again, one of the new generation of tournament workers, who seemed to always be the one chosen to break bad news to him. "We've confirmed that there was indeed a ship, it was an alien ship, probably Cygnan-made. It received our approach transmission."

"What?" an incredulous Stergis screamed. "What approach transmission? You mean the ancient warning call? How is that possible? We have created our own hyperspace sheath to an unknown corner of the galaxy, was it not scrubbed of its Ugov settings?"

"Sir, the Ugov settings were impossible to remove from the sheath. Erasing the resonance in the stardust is too detailed a job.

And they were stamped with the Ugov restriction codes. As you know, in ancient times, before the war, when…"

"Yes, yes… back when they *allowed* us to play," he growled.

Despite the horrible news he continued his move, reaching his hand through the permeable layers of his dome walker to grasp a handful of asteroid ramble. He swung his arm back and forth and hurled the earthy bits to form a blockade. His intention was to deter his rival player from trying the move he feared most—setting up his two and three moons on the other side of Stergis's gas giant.

Buele observed the grand master's toss from the holoscreen. After the toss was complete, and all the shards and shrapnel had been pulled into stable gravity zones, Buele cleared his throat and spoke. "Grand Master, it gets worse. The ship is now on the move, on a direct track for the hyperspace platform. The generals think they're going to try to enter the event horizon of our wormhole."

"Never… They would never dare… Who in the name of Perseus are these scum of bacteria! They think they can escape their fate? Ueharan life is extinct!" he yelled, watching the results of his maneuver with a scowl, as the bits of amalgamated solid elements scattered into a web of flashing yellow explosions. "And that includes the Cygnan parasites aboard that ship—destroy them!"

CHAPTER SEVEN

Abandoned Among the Asteroids

Angus let his boots touch solid rock. The high-pitched squealing of the synthmetal bits boring into the ground was deafening. He might've been getting a headache.

Not hydrated enough, Angus thought. *Ariel won't be happy if I pass out again.*

His wife was always warning him that he was overdoing it, working too hard and not drinking enough water, and he regularly ignored her pleas. He had to provide for his people. If it meant headaches, so be it.

Today he was busy overseeing a drilling operation on an anonymous rock, part of a cluster within the southernmost portion of the Abandoned—the largest asteroid belt in the Milky Way. The massive conglomeration of rock and ice rendered a significant portion of the Outer Cygnus Arm inaccessible. *Just how we prefer it,* he thought.

Angus and his comrades—who fondly referred to themselves by the same name as the asteroid belt they called home—had been out on the fringe for more than a Udecade, eking out a living in one of the harshest environments in the universe: asteroids.

The rock they were drilling was a few kilometers in diameter, Angus estimated, and full of minerals. Its barren and pockmarked surface was the usual eyesore, but the piles of white ash strewn across the dark gray pallet of their mining site belied a veritable treasure trove of rare elements below. One of the rare elements being extracted from the drill site, silophane, was integral to their ability to live underground… inside an asteroid of their own. Devoid of oxygen, their hollowed out home they called the *Terrastroid*, required silophane as an oxygenator, fabricating the precious air circulating within its synthmetal halls.

Angus lifted up his head and watched a few mushroom clouds forming from the latest of a series of minor asteroid collisions, far enough away he didn't have to send out an EVAC transmission. He clicked his wrist pad holoscreen and conjured up his water function and a slow trickle of the precious fluid emanated from the side of his helmet and into his dry mouth. Water. There was a team working on that precious commodity, too. Those in charge of gathering water for the Abandoned had a rougher job than him. Usually it involved landing on a volatile comet, melting the ice off with heat scanners, and reclaiming the liquid into holding tanks. Each Uday, multiple stops—on multiple sites—were required to satiate the thirst of their hearty race of galactic misfits. Once the Uday's collections were complete, the water teams still had to transfer the spoils into a much larger reservoir back on the *Terrastroid* while mitigating evaporation.

"How's it going over there, Jonah?" Angus sent out a com signal to his friend working a half kilometer away from their dented and crusty short-range spaceship. To get close enough without risking further damage to the already blemished exterior of their ship, they had taken the land rover to the prospected site.

"Good, Ang. I think we're going to meet the minimum parameters for a Uday's work. If we can get a couple more kilos out of that brown section over there…"

"Mmm," Angus protested. "Do we have time for that much drilling? Won't we have to reset the plunger?"

"Yeah," replied Jonah, "but we can get airborne before that shower hits. The models are staying consistent with the arrival being about an hour. We can get it done, don't you think?" He was always eager to bring home an impressive haul.

Jonah wants to stay. Hard work is a tenet out here, after all. Angus understood oh so well how much everyone was counting on them. "Well, I'll have Ariel keep an eye on the system. She said it was supposed to be a pretty light one, anyway."

"See? No need to worry… your lovely lady confirmed it," Jonah replied, tempering his enthusiasm immediately. "Of course, you know how these things can go, though, right boss?"

One thing that peeved him about Jonah was that he often referred to Angus as *boss, boss man,* or *big boss man…* all of these antiquated pre-solar colloquialisms; it always got to him.

There aren't bosses in the Abandoned, just equals, thought Angus. *Someone has to run the drilling rig, and everyone knows I'm the best at the job. Doesn't mean I'm the boss!* He retreated to the relative calm of the land rover and took off his helmet inside. Long gray hair puffed past his shoulders.

"Hey, Jonah," he said into the com link. "Yes, my wife is lovely, and yes, I do know how these things can go. It's hard to predict meteor shower vectors, and that's why I keep asking you if we can get that brown section done in time."

He squinted at the monitor that contoured neatly to the curvature of the cockpit of their land rover. When his finger

71

touched the holoscreen map it came alive with a lustrous glow. He used his thumb and forefinger to zoom in on the brown section Jonah was talking about. When he did so, it lit up with an orange color indicating a jackpot of silophane.

"You got lucky, boss, when she found you," sang Jonah. "If it weren't for pretty Ariel, you'd be just like me—old, crusty, and not getting a lot of attention from the few unattached ladies of the Abandoned. What, with that mangled upper lip? And those black spots all over your nose…" he chided his friend.

"Hey, easy on me now, my non-subservient fellow—and will you please stop calling me *boss*? If you don't I'll have to vote you off the island," joked Angus. "And by the way, handsome bachelor, there's a reason why I'm with the most beautiful woman in the Abandoned and you are sitting in your domicile every night with the virtual stuff on your holo." His best friend Jonah had an absurdly long neck, with a tiny head precariously stacked on top. He always wore his dark eye goggles and he kept his signature mane of dark hair slicked back. It stuck there due to the lack of cleanliness.

"All right," Jonah said. "You might be more handsome than me, but you gotta admit, Ang, you moved up in class when you partnered with sweet Ariel."

"True, I'll give you that one, but—"

"No buts, it's the truth!" Jonah sounded exasperated. "You aren't that much prettier than me. I should have a gal like her, but nooo! All work and no play for the dull boy, Jonah, oh woe is me. Boo hoo." He talked in the third person quite frequently, another annoyance that Angus had to deal with.

Angus glanced over at the side bar control panel and scratched his poofy hair. *In all his efforts at poking fun at me, he turned off the manual overrides?*

"Jonah, check out your side bar, it's offline. Efficiency's suffering."

"All right, *boss man*, I'll check it."

Galaxies! Angus cringed at the moniker and swiveled his floating chair one hundred eighty degrees. He pressed a few buttons to adjust the angle of descent before engaging the drive shaft. The land rover lurched as it crept down the slope of the crater, approaching the drill site. Looking at all the gear strewn about he knew there wasn't going to be enough time to drill out that brown section, load everything onto the rover, transport it all from the drill site back to the ship, and get out of dodge of that impending meteor shower. He pressed the throttle a little harder.

The wheels of the rover were impregnable, they ground through the piles of ash and porous rock with ease, until coming to a stop a few hundred meters from the drill apparatus. He activated the drones, and they buzzed around the exterior of the apparatus, detaching various hoses and cylinders. Each one collapsed flush against hollowed sections on the outside frame of the land rover.

"Ang, I uploaded the logistics to the system," Jonah's voice came through the com, normal at first, but it quickly raised in pitch. "Hey! What gives, Ang? Why are the drones activated? No—no—wait! We're not done yet! Ang, that brown section is just chock full of the stuff. We might not get another chance on this rock. Projections show a major collision inevitable in the near future. If this little stroid gets pulverized we're going to be searching for a replacement source as good as this one for a long time. We've got to breathe, man. Your lady and kids gotta breathe too."

Angus turned on the holoscreen in the rover. "I know that, my friend, but they also have to have their husband and father back in time for that modified bean curd dinner that's on the table. Again."

Jonah laughed heartily. "It's not an Oreldychynean delicacy, Ang, you won't be missing much."

73

"Still, you never want to make the old lady angry, and if we get caught by that shower the AI weather module predicts—well, it could seriously affect the quality of my love life. You don't have to worry about that stuff though, now do you?"

Jonah made more of a moan than a sigh as he activated the closing beacon and got the needle into retraction mode, pausing for a few Useconds before pulling out the tip of the drill bit. Jonah motioned back over at the pile of brown clays one last time, shaking his head. All that potential silophane would sit there, unused, until pulverized into indifferent molecules when the next bang up happened.

With the glorified needle retracted, and containment tanks being loaded by the drones, Jonah was ready to return to the rover, but he stopped short and glanced upward.

Angus jerked his head as the first pieces hit the windshield of the rover. As he should have guessed, the shower came early, and was in fact *stronger* than predicted. Ravaging bits of rock, dust, and ice soon hailed upon their drill site.

"Get in here, Jonah!" Angus spat over the com.

The holoscreen image inside the rover became snowy, pixilated by the debris falling, but he could make out Jonah's figure: he had activated his boot thrusters and was making haste to get back.

Angus snapped his head to glance out the cockpit window. To the ship's right spinning clouds of gas were pouring out of steam vents. They were forming on the mini-asteroid in response to the crashing rocks and ice hitting the thin surface. Flashes of light, caused by sparks from the constant impacts of larger boulders, filled the sky with false daylight. Out in the Abandoned, there was no natural light other than energy created when two moving bodies bumped into each other. The bigger the combined mass, the better the light show. And it was starting to be quite a light show above them.

Jonah entered the hatch of the land rover wiping off a layer of dust from his spacesuit. Once inside, he slid into his co-pilot seat and helped Angus program the drones into their final holding positions.

Tanks loaded, crew on board, soon they were rolling across the relatively flat part of the valley. In the distance, their old ship sat on its stork-like stilts, docking lights on, and flashing to indicate its location.

"Phew, man," Jonah recoiled as a massive collision occurred overhead, the remnants exploding on the ground. "Whoa! It's getting pretty heavy right now. I'm glad *I* decided for us to bail out of here."

Angus shook his head, smiling. "Yeah, yeah... whatever. I better call home and get another update from Ariel..." but as he said the words, the holoscreen lit up with an incoming call. Her smile was enough to tell him there wasn't any real danger.

"Hey guys, how goes it?" she queried. "Any good haul today?"

"You betcha! Your loving man is coming home with the O₂!" Angus smiled back at the holoscreen, and flexed his biceps.

"Oooh, Angus, you are so strong and so sexy and so great." Jonah threw in his best Ariel voice impression, and reached over and squeezed his arm affectionately.

"Jonah, you're just jealous of our undying love," Ariel said. Her image on the holoscreen lifted her chin up in a sarcastic manner, as if the queen of a regal planet was shrugging off a beggar. Evidently she had been eavesdropping.

"No," said Jonah, "I disagree, my darling, as there's nothing undying about love, or anything for that matter. We're all going sometime. Love is impermanent. Love is—"

"How in the name of asteroids would you know what love is? Have you even tried to talk to a woman in the past decade?"

Jonah had a retort cocked and ready. "Of course I have—your *sister!*"

Feigning disgust, Ariel replied, "I don't have a sister, and even if I did, I wouldn't let her get within a kilometer of you."

"I told you, Ang," Jonah turned to complain to his friend in the land rover cockpit. "This is why I never get invited over for genetic bean mush—because *she's* trying to keep me away from her imaginary sister!"

"Will you stop it, Jonah, we still have to get off this ball of crud and fly past this shower. Ariel, will you give us an updated reading on this meteor shower? Are we good to take the same route back to the *Terrastroid*?"

"You're good to go, my love, it's projected to be light until much later. You guys fly safe, I'll have the *bean mush*—as your rude friend called it—ready to eat when you get in." With that and a quick smirk, she closed the holocall window and left the two friends to continue to trade verbal barbs—their favorite pastime.

It could get quite boring living in an asteroid belt in between the Outer Cygnus Arm and deep space. The people of the Abandoned had to find ways to entertain themselves. Usually, that meant demeaning each other to the point of either laughter or, in worst case scenarios, throwing punches, although it often depended on the amount of comet brewed elixirs they drank. Of course, the Abandoned colony forbade operating any machinery while imbibing the intoxicating beverages. But with the Uday of work over, there was one thing on both their minds, because they both spoke at once.

"I'm buying," said Angus.

"You're buying," said Jonah.

Jonah set up the AI transfer codes to allow the rover inside the hull of the spaceship. As they rumbled closer, the main doors slowly dropped to the ground, forming into a ramp. Angus ignored the AI settings and gunned the accelerator, pointing the land rover in a direct line for the entry point. The vehicle launched into the air over the uplifted edges of the craters they rolled over.

A Uminute later they came to a screeching halt, safely inside the ground vehicle docking bay.

Angus elbowed Jonah and said, in his corniest voice, "If you think I'm a good land rover driver, wait till you see me fly this ship!"

He had salvaged the spacecraft from a wreckage site near the Last Ugov Outpost. It was a piece of junk, his little asteroid hopper—its secondary thrusters were liable to fail at any given time, but it could still maneuver decently. It was an old fighter ship, used for localized extra-solar combat missions. Although the weapons were defunct, it still had a little spunkiness left in it. *Especially when I'm flying!* Angus smiled while imagining the barrel rolls, loop de loops, and zigzags he was about to do. It was a short flight from the drill site to their home asteroid, but he liked to make it entertaining.

Laughter filled the cockpit as they traded jokes while the generators warmed. Red lights changed to green on the dashboard so Angus switched off the protection energy filed and fired the primary thrusters. His dented spaceship lifted up and catapulted off the spinning asteroid.

Angus watched as the little rock disappeared in the rearview holoscreen. *Amazing that little ball gave us so much.* Mining and salvaging operations were the lifeblood of the Abandoned. If they wanted to be truly self-sufficient—meaning no deal-brokering with the Outer Cygnus pirates, and no borrowing from the Ugov cronies—that meant eking out a living on the edge of subsistence. A failed operation meant there would have to be two successful ones to cover the shortfall. Despite their nonchalance and careless laughter while under duress, both were hardy veterans of this type of life. Cold, dark, and ever-changing.

There was a lot of pressure on them to get the job done.

And, shortly after taking off from the mining asteroid and entering the fray, Angus had his opportunity to prove his wares.

Deftly maneuvering the ship through gaps between the asteroids, avoiding collisions of smaller particles that ricocheted in every direction, a gray mass loomed. He raced for it purposefully. The rock was four times the size of their ship, big enough to incite a large burst of pre-rubble, which smashed against their synthmetal hull. The ferocity of the blow created the effect of a cascading waterfall of sparkling light in front of them. Angus pointed the joystick for the space between the streams, hit the thrusters, and gave a whoop. As they flew through the bright curtain, emerging into a dark and spacious world on other side, they could relax.

It was time for food, water, rest, and—well, of course, some comet elixir.

***

Terrastroid, home of the Abandoned, was a large and irregular-shaped asteroid, a nondescript lump of mostly dark gray rock, other than a bit of a rusty red iron crust near the poles, and lighter-colored craters pocking the surface. Its exterior was nothing but endless small ridge lines of broken rocks with a layer of dust piled on top. Well, unless one inspected closer, when a pair of docking port doors opened to accept a spaceship.

Angus piloted his ship skillfully through the port doors near the equator of *Terrastroid*. A force field beam guided them from there and they entered a special haven. Their own world... carved out of sheer nothingness. The hollowed-out asteroid had fifty different levels, including mini-parks, entertainment gaming centers, portals, food shops, an elixir bar, as well as elemental and agricultural refineries. From the utter blackness outside to the bright white pseudo-sunlight, it was like going from night to Uday, literally.

By the time they had debarked and gulped down a few drinks at the elixir bar, Angus realized he was going to be late. He said goodbye to Jonah and rushed to the air tube that would take him through the various levels of the *Terrastroid* to his residence. He was going to have to take some flak. He would soon have to face Ariel, with her hands on her hips, pouting and carrying on. He didn't live on Utime, he lived on "Atime."

Low and behold, when he finally walked in through the portal to his family's chambers, she started in on him.

"Mortality is real here in the Abandoned, Angus. When you are whipping that old crusty ship through the clusters, it would be nice if you took a little more conservative route!"

Angus was not receiving his first lecture of the Uday, that came shortly after waking up.

"Think about your family." And she did have her hands on her hips. "Try taking the long way home—for once."

The comment necessitated damage control. "Dearest love, come on now! I'm the best pilot in this part of the galaxy. I flew attack ships during the last pirate uprising, I was—"

"Oh, we all remember..." she cut him off quickly. "You should have listened to my holomessage while you were out having an elixir with Jonah. You needed to stop by the food cooperative, so... out you go! We need something to go along with my *awful* cooking. I sent you a list."

"You heard him?"

"I hear everything, Ang."

"He's full of it... the only good meals he ever eats are at your table."

She pointed to the portal and scooted off to the kitchen.

"Dad!" a young woman's voice cried out from behind. "Seriously?"

Angus had a son and a daughter. His son Markus was perpetually complaining about something, but Angus loved him unfailingly. But he was *really* up against it now, because his daughter Murriel was in on the fussing. She usually greeted him with a smile and asked how his Uday was. Tonight it was pure whining. "Can you hurry up? We're hungry over here."

"Yeah, Dad, what were you doing out there?" Markus asked. "We watched a projection of your flight path, how many corkscrew turns do you have to make? It's not a long route home from the drill site! And Mom has the proof, because the tracking holo shows a twenty-minute delay—right next to port, where the elixir bar is located…"

"Well, I didn't want to make you wait!" he shouted. "That's why I drank it fast! And the longer you guys berate me, the longer it will take for you all to eat! So ease off papa, will you?"

He barged out the front portal and walked to the nearest conveyor as he opened the holoscreen window with a quick tap of his pointer finger on his wrist pad. He waved cordial greetings to a few of his fellow Abandoned making their way through the passageway from the space port to the domiciles.

Angus was easily recognizable—what, with his massive ball of black and silver hair, and centimeters long matching beard and mustache. He was also tall, and wore a spacesuit of the brightest shade of green—a color never worn in the Ugov territories. *But this is our home, not their home. We have our own colors.* Angus was a proud man.

His holocall screen made an odd alert signal, the type of signal he couldn't write off as nothing.

"Tower, what's up?" Before any reply a ship-wide warning signal went berserk, flashing on the circular monitors that wrapped along the length of conveyor passageways. He tried to make another holocall to the control booth, an underground tower that extended and retracted from the southern pole of their rocky home, to get the scoop.

"Angus," Randall, the tower control attendant, replied, "you won't believe this… there are sensors detecting an alien interstellar spaceship moving in an erratic flight path within the outer boundaries of the belt."

"What's not to believe? Pirates have to eat too, they're probably trying to find a few rocks to dig in to," Angus said, resting two fingers on his right temple. Another headache was coming on.

"No, it's not that, Angus, it's what's making the ship travel in such a way. There is also a Persean spaceship in the vicinity. The thing is so massive it's disrupting the natural gravitational flow and it's starting to effect the outer layers of our asteroid belt."

Angus had to clench his teeth to keep his jaw from dropping. "What? That's not possible! We're too far out... why would they come near this rock pile? We're just bacteria to them!"

"Nevertheless," Randall said, "these readings are undeniable... it appears they are *pursuing* the alien spaceship... Yep, Angus, the models are conclusive. We need to take action, maybe even send the call to evacuate."

"Not in this lifetime, Randy! I'm going to fly out to this alien ship. If I can eliminate its presence in the Abandoned, my guess is the Persean ship will leave. The giants probably don't want to be seen out here by any alien spacecraft that could alert the Ugov. Too close to the IDL. Will you call Jonah? Tell him to meet me down on the flight deck!"

"Are you going to blast them?"

"If I have to."

***

Angus was sweating and squinting, even behind his climate-controlled helmet. It was hot and steamy inside the cockpit of the recycled spaceship he knew like the back of his hand. His sidekick and best friend Jonah, on the contrary, had not a drop of moisture on his face, and with his hand hovering over a holoscreen, he was ready to press the right combinations of buttons.

"Hit it!" yelled Angus.

The ship lurched from the emergency launch, which blasted vapors throughout the landing port.

"No one hurt in our hasty take off, I hope?" Jonah asked.

"Well," Angus replied, "if we didn't do something quick—we might all be goners. Hopefully everyone got the alert to clear the platform."

They were tracking full throttle for the unknown ship when Angus heard the stress in his buddy's voice emerge.

"Well," Jonah asked, "what's the plan? Are we going to just veer into their flight zone?"

"We'll hail them when we're close enough to buzz them and get away clean. Let's get a sense of what we're after first. Any size readings coming in? It's obviously interstellar class… otherwise it couldn't be *here*."

"No insignia of any kind," replied Jonah. "It's not a Ugov sanctioned vehicle—must be our kind of people. Maybe they're renegades, trying to get away."

"Your short-term memory must be getting bad with all the elixirs. In case you've forgotten, Jonah, they are not getting away from the Ugov, they are being chased by the Giant Beings."

"Must be carrying risky cargo." Jonah said. "Maybe something useful?"

"Now you're thinking, Jonah. Let's save the Abandoned—*and* find out what it is."

Angus laughed as his buddy gripped tight to the sides of his headrest, the ship bouncing to and fro from the kinetics of his fancy piloting.

"Pretty soon they'll be showing on the holo—*there!*" Angus pointed.

Visible on the short range holoscanner was an odd-looking machine. Contrails of white gas streamed along the belly of the alien ship, a clear sign that it was slowing from post hyperspace velocity. Whoever they were, it was clear they were taking a track that would penetrate the outer guardian fields of the Abandoned. The guardian fields were the design of Wallace, the chief water miner of *Terrastroid*. He came up with the strategy to set up a field of minuscule rocks and ice, molded with blasts from a frozen electron beam. It was a first line of defense against larger impacts that could cause damage to the inner, more essential portions of the Abandoned.

"I want to find out what kind of pilot is flying this thing!" Angus growled as he took the manual control and forced the ship into a slicing roll. He set the code for Jonah to make a holocall and his partner got ready to make contact. Using the AI processor, his voice was instantly translated into the most popular alien tongues, even though it was more than probable they spoke Sunish. *Who doesn't anymore?* Angus thought. *Cygnans even take up human names.*

"Attention. Attention. Your ship has entered a zone managed by the independent people of the Abandoned. We've locked our blasters on your vessel. Reveal your intentions immediately, or suffer the consequences of broaching our sovereign territory."

After a short pause a slow, drawling, baritone voice said: "Yeah, hey, listen, dudes, this is Max, Captain of the *Planet Hopper*. We were hoping to hide among the asteroid belt. We had no idea this place was inhabited. By the way, I should probably mention to you, a Persean warship is headed this way, and they ain't happy with us."

"What is your status, Captain Max? Tell us why you're here—what's your true mission, and why should we allow you to have asylum among the Abandoned? You brought us Perseans? How do we know you're not Ugov spies?" While Jonah grilled the derelict ship with questions, Angus steered them into a holding pattern a short—but safe—distance away.

"Hey, dudes from the Abandoned, we have no affiliation with the Ugov whatsoever," the alien captain replied. "They want us worse than these giant freaks. Believe me, you... There's no love lost there!"

"So—let me get this straight," Angus had to chuckle. "You show up in *our* asteroid belt, out of an unknown hyperspace sheath, and you are not only bringing the wrath of the Perseans but also the tide of the Ugov upon us? They follow you to even this far outreach of the galaxy? Wonderful. Jonah, commence blaster alignment protocols. Lock on target."

The voice from the alien ship raised an octave: "Whoa, whoa, wait a minute there, fellas! Hold onto your spacesuit zippers! Give us a chance to help you. We have crude star map data you might want to have a look at. Maybe it can serve a... *purpose.* I am assuming you dudes aren't Ucitizens, living way out here, so y'all must be pirates. I'm familiar with the kind. Pirates love to trade. Therefore, by my logic, follow with me here, you'd be willing to make a deal to spare our lives? Help us help you. Our lives for our maps."

Angus shook his head in minor defiance and re-clicked the holocall button inside their old fighter jet. "All right, we'll give you a chance to show us what you've got—and if it's not something *we* need, then *you* aren't something we need. We have absolutely no room for new comers, so when you behold our paradise among the stones, don't get any crazy ideas, got it? Follow this heading and try to keep up with the best damn pilot in the rocks. Let's get out of here before those giants pick us up on their scanners!"

Angus hit the thrusters hard, veered over the top of the Planet Hopper, and buzzed past them leaving a wake of tangerine-colored exhaust for them to follow. Whoever was piloting was up for the challenge, and together the two ships dipped and dodged, swerved and curled, dropped and climbed their way over around, and through a myriad of crackling matter. Angus was impressed with the pilot's skill. The ever-changing pattern of hardened elemental rocks and ice would give the impression of a maze to the newly trained eye. The two ships—the larger one bulky and designed for cruising, the other one compact, sharp edged, and designed for attack and evasion—made an interesting pair, cutting single file through the darkness of the Abandoned.

CHAPTER EIGHT

Calm Within a Storm of Stones

We are going to be tortured until they shake the life out of our bodies, Mike thought during the final approach to the home of the Abandoned dudes. Closing in on the large asteroid, there was evidence of occupation in crude tunnel openings, shattered antennae and an exterior surface braised by pock-marked craters, spread throughout the waving contours. It reminded him of the stories and descriptions Max had told him about the prison colonies.

Is this going to be our fate? Beaten and imprisoned in the middle of nowhere?

After the most perilous and awesome escape from the most viscous and dangerous race of aliens in the entire galaxy, it was savagely ironic that they were about to be restrained and injected by truth serums and tortured with shock wands, in the bowels of some off-the-grid pirate's asteroid.

"Claude," Mike's ears were tucked as he blinked back tears. "I love you, my main hare. It's been great being your twin. The rest of you guys—you dudes aren't too shabby, either. I'll miss all of you…"

"C'mon, bro," Claude said. "We're fine. These Abandoned dudes seem totally cool with us. We give them the star map data, they give us a few supplies, and we're off to surf another Uday!"

"Yeah, right." Mike retorted. Claude was being unusually optimistic. To irk him, no doubt.

Max and Vern handled touchdown, while Blob and the twins nervously shifted in the cabin this way and that, preparing for the inevitable face-to-face meeting with their (supposed) saviors. The truth was irrefutable, Mike realized. Without these asteroid people taking them into their bastion, nestled deep within the Abandoned asteroid belt, they would have been turned to mush before penetrating even the farthest outskirts of the mass. It was a place so densely packed with matter and filled with so much debris there was a constant interaction of energy. Even a Planet Ball hyperspace ship would incur too much damage to make it worthwhile to chase them this deep.

There were rumors of permanent settlements among the Abandoned. Everyone assumed the people living out there were pirates. Uweb holovideos. Everyone assumed the people living out there were pirates. The crew of the *Planet Hopper* had met more than their share of those hanging around the Last Ugov Outpost, and had enough sense not to cross them. It was better to let their kind have the greater share of the deal, and be happy to get out with your spacesuits still covering your bodies.

After touching down bumpily, the *Planet Hopper*'s hatch doors opened, revealing a massive chamber carved from dark gray rock, with a sophisticated lighting system lining the entire surface of the roof. Mike guessed it was a method of simulating Uday and night, regulating body cycles while living in a place so dark and devoid of solar energy.

Despite his reservations, Mike resignedly jumped out first, figuring he should be first to "take the shocking wand for the team," landing on his hind paws with an echo on the light gray metallic material of the flooring. The crew popped out after him, one by one, immediately undergoing the same revelation: *Hey— this place is pretty cool!*

An Earthish man with a long neck and greasy dark hair stomped up, with others wearing similar tight fighting well worn spacesuits gathering up behind. "Yeah, pretty cool... and pretty *off-limits* for the likes of you guys. Don't you strangers go getting any ideas of remaining here. Where are you from and why are you in our neighborhood?"

Another voice, in an Earthish dialect Mike could understand, spoke out of the small gathering of ten or twelve Abandoned men. "We don't take kindly to strangers."

Despite the obvious size disadvantage, the less-than-pleased greeting party were finding strength in numbers. After scooting forward onto the landing pad area with scowls on their faces, more than a dozen of them had the boys boxed in against their ship, with a fifty meter sheer drop-off adjacent to them on either side of the docking bay floor. Most of the men crowding up clearly weren't keen on the idea of having outsiders standing inside the asteroid, even for five Uminutes.

"Why are you alien freaks here?" another voice demanded.

"Those weird animals look like food—not humanoids!" another said in reference to Mike and Claude, who winked at each other.

Not the first time we've heard that one, Mike thought. It didn't even faze them anymore they were so used to hearing it.

"Maybe we can use them in the quarry or as mining labor," an Abandoned man said.

Nor the first time we've heard that one, Mike stifled a laugh.

The one with the dark goggles, addressed the tall black and silver haired man standing beside him, "I'm telling you, Angus, this is a bad idea. You shouldn't have brought these guys here."

"Yeah, Angus, what is this? Nobody voted on this." A riled-up Abandoned man shook his fist at the intruders.

Several of the Abandoned men drew out compact, synthmetal staffs from straps on the side of their legs. The small mob edged closer.

"Quiet down, everyone! Quiet!" the man named Angus shouted, clearly annoyed with being questioned. "This isn't some damned Ugov court council! This is our home, and I'm one of the most respected elders. You know me well enough—I would *never* jeopardize our home. They have valuable information that we need. They've seen Planet Ball tournament spaceships."

A loud grunt echoed through the landing pad area, elicited by his last comment.

Their leader spoke again, much more slowly this time, and with their full attention. "We *could* end up being collateral damage. These strange folk know of these tidings and have expressed a willingness to help inform us. Bringing them here *is* the best course of action. We need this intel for our survival."

After he finished delivering the grim news a silence ensued, broken by the hum of generators and air processing machines that constantly groaned from every corner of the wide chamber. The Abandoned men stared wide-eyed at each other. Finally a young man broke the silence and spoke.

"Father, let's bring our guests back to our quarters, they must be exhausted after their brave escape from the Giant Beings."

The leader regarded the young man who had broken the silence with a frown, then turned back to the small mob. "Fellow

Abandoned men, I'll arrange a meeting with the other elders shortly. After interrogating—" Mike jumped a little bit. "*Parlaying* with the strangers?"

Mike nodded happily. Much better word choice.

The leader's big ball of shimmering silver hair waved back and forth as he continued: "Then, together, we can come up with a strategy to protect our homeland from this new threat. Agreed?"

It wasn't a query. The Abandoned men grumbled as they walked away, throwing more than a few disdainful glances at the crew.

"Hey!" Mike tried to take advantage of the momentum, channeling his inner Max, addressing the young man who had spoken up for them. "Thanks, kid! That's a great idea! We'd love to take you and your father up on the invite! What was your name? Mine's Mike, this here is my twin brother Claude—dumb as a stump; to my left, that's Vern, he's stiff as board, but for a reason, he's a Gen-3er, well, kind of, anyway, that's a long story …but a much shorter story is the name of my buddy over here, Blob—can you guess how he got that moniker? Last but not least, may I introduce Captain Max, he runs the show when I finish blabbering—"

"Which…" said Max nudging past Mike, "would be right now! Angus, is it?"

In a snap Mike was back of the pack again, his gregarious leader schmoozing their saviors with every platitude known to the Milky Way. *That's why he's the Cap!* Mike shrugged, hopping after them.

***

Mike couldn't help but overhear them banter. *Well,* he thought, *it's not my fault, I do have these…* He kept his ears curled for the father and son as they talked.

"What?" said Angus's son Markus with an innocent shrug, avoiding his father's furious stare.

"You shouldn't have come down to the flight deck, you don't have permission." Angus grunted, pacing back and forth in the antechamber to their home. Mike and the boys stood back waiting for them to have it out.

"Oh, Father," Markus cajoled, "I was curious about the thoughts of outsiders, what I could glean from them, so I decided to tube down there. I couldn't resist the opportunity, so I came closer to listen in. Can you blame me, Father? This is the most exciting thing that has ever happened on the *Terrastroid!*"

"Markus, I…"

"Father, I can sense goodness among these strangers. You must too?"

Angus sniffed, straightened up his posture, and made the grunting sound again. He marched them to an air tube and a few hallways later they were in the greeting chamber. His wife Ariel was standing there, arms crossed, and he suffered a berating unlike anything Mike had heard before. *No wonder he was nervous to have us over,* he had to laugh, despite Angus's face turning bright crimson.

But thankfully, a little while after Ariel's initial tirade on her husband, quelled only by their daughter Murriel's soothing touch, Mike sensed the matriarch was loosening up. Once she had figured out he and the boys were innocuous, she was settling down.

Angus finished introducing them, and Ariel had them sit in uncomfortable floating chairs. Murriel served them some sort of traditional Abandoned drink—it was a blue-colored liquid, with chunks of something bubbling around inside the synthglass flutes. Mike couldn't help wiggling his nose and whiskers at the smell.

"Not exactly earth elixir, eh bro?" He elbowed Claude in the next floating chair.

"That's for sure." Claude giggled.

Blob threw in his unwanted opinion. "You don't need any more elixirs, you rabbits drink too many of those already..."

"What's a rabbit?" asked Ariel, overhearing every word spoken in her home.

"Well," Mike said, a twinkle in his dark eyes, "that's a long story..."

***

After a meal as foreign as any he had ever tasted—*Hey,* Mike thought, *at least it's vegetarian*—he searched around for a holocomputer outlet and asked his hosts if he could use it to browse the Uweb. Ariel gave the "that's fine," nod to him, so he hopped over to the corner of the antechamber and activated the screen with a wave of his paw. Even though there was no connection to the Uweb way out here in the asteroid belt, Mike had access to the historical data through his wrist implant. The glowing screen was an antique model and the contrast took getting used to, but, after some trial and error, Mike was able to navigate his way to the search engines. He wanted to glean information about their location and there was something he needed to look up.... he had a premonition brewing... *But what?*

While Mike browsed the Uweb, he listened to Angus's family share stories with his crew mates. The *Hopper* dudes were educated on the hardships of a life carved out of asteroids, and the *Terrastroid* family was learning what "galactic surf safari" meant.

"Well, the energy part is simple," Angus said. "We use rare elements mined from within the rocks themselves. Mining is our main source of energy, although we do use solar, wind, and tidal motion at times, when possible... we convert the REs into pure, clean energy and pipe it to every millimeter of this place." His arms went up into the air, waving to the ceiling, but in a definitive circular motion, belying the structure's true shape beyond the rectangular confines of their domicile. "There's always more rock—if you don't overpopulate, at least. Our peoples have very strict parameters regarding our growth. Living out here is sustainable because of our collective understanding. We share *everything*. There is no profit here, no proliferation. Only a united consciousness, bent on keeping our families alive, while keeping our affairs free from the Ugov's interference. Everyone here has been abused by the rigged systems of Ugov law, and that's why we fled to this far corner of the galaxy."

"What about food?" Blob changed the subject, sounding curious enough, the tips of his pointed monobrow soaring up and out. "Do you have other kinds of food than what we ate at dinner?"

"Blob!" Mike hissed at him.

"What?" He shrugged and turned his palms up, flexing his four fingers.

The rest of the crew joined Mike in giving him the "Really, Blob?" look.

"What do you mean?" Ariel stormed across the chamber to confront the Boor, who scrambled up from his lounging position to sit upright.

Too late.

"What's the matter, Mr. Blob?" she pointed at him. "You didn't enjoy your meal? Then you don't have to eat here. You can starve for all I care… ungrateful outsiders. No wonder you aliens are stranded way out here trying to…"

"No, no, hold on," Max tried to curb her ire while motioning and pantomiming to Blob that he should make amends—*quickly*. "Ariel, Blob means no offense. He was just wondering where you get your food from, how it's so finely produced? He's a former Cygnan Eating Contest Champion, so he is *really* into food. It's delicious—*isn't it, Blob?*"

"Ariel, I—" Blob tried to speak but slobbered all over himself. "No, I mean, yes, I mean—it's true that I liked it!"

"What's not true?" Ariel continued to pursue him, acting as if the eating champion alien had better not be the critic out of this bunch. "So your Captain Max is lying? You *didn't* like it?"

Blob's jaw dropped. "No, that's not what I meant. I meant that I liked your food, that—" he stammered, unable to sweet talk his way out of his unintentional effrontery.

"Sure, sure… just don't expect too much. Got it, Eating Champ? I can give you a smaller portion next time…" She eyed his massive belly. "And don't forget you're in the Abandoned— the meal I prepared for you might be your last." And with that Ariel trampled on his toe purposely on her way out of the antechamber.

"Ow! Hey! What's that for?" Blob grabbed his toe and pouted. "I always get blamed for everything. Thanks a lot, Max!"

"Dude, you got into that one all by yourself." Max shrugged. "Caught inside on a big set wave closing out on your head—a rogue wave named Ariel!"

"It's all right, Blob," Angus comforted, "Ariel is *very* sensitive about her food preparation. She takes it seriously. She acts that way with everyone, believe me. My best friend, Jonah, he takes the abuse every time—and he loves her food!"

Angus reached over and activated the holocomputer, clicked a few buttons, and a three dimensional hologram model of *Terrastroid* hung in the space above their floating chairs. "Check this out, you'll love this…"

"Whoa—that's really cool." Blob's smile was broad enough to fit the twins' heads inside it. "How do you keep this place safe, anyhow, with stuff colliding everywhere?"

"Oh, we've got a multitude of features that help us keep from being struck by random matter, believe me. It's even more important than keeping hydrated and getting nutrition."

Mike hopped over and pointed to a portion of the holoimage.

Angus smiled. "Ahh, yes, those are dual-purpose protection shield emitters that are aligned with remote operated mini-asteroids in tow. By rotating the orbits of our triad of accompanying satellite rocks, and activating the protection shield, it creates an event horizon pulse of energy that wraps around the entirety of our asylum. It's a *very* powerful force field that can repel most of the little debris—the size that's undetectable and unavoidable. As for the big boys, the crushers, the game enders, those rocks don't come around too often, but if they do..." Angus swiped on the holoscreen and the image of the *Terrastroid* seemed to—*move*.

"Hey!" Mike exclaimed, pointing. "You've got thrusters on here, don't you, Angus? There's slots for them on the poles!"

"That's correct, Mike! Excellent deduction. Our big rock is a spherical spaceship—*disguised* as a large asteroid."

He rotated the image of their home planetesimal to show a replication of the force field, zooming back in to the surface and highlighting subtle shapes of darkened jet thrusters waiting in hibernation until called upon.

"You mean, this... entire asteroid? It actually flies?" Max was in disbelief.

"Yep," replied Angus. "And it has two gears. One for cruising long distance, the other for immediate evacuations." Angus laughed at his guest's contorted faces. "Oh, no, not to worry, crew, a collision worth jetting away from doesn't happen often, and we get alerts far ahead of time. More commonly, the need for us to evacuate is when a ranger strays this far into the chaos trying to bust pirates."

"Rangers?" Ariel called from the com in the kitchen, obviously half-listening in to the conversation in the antechamber. "What rangers?"

"Nothing, dear…" Angus clicked a few more times to provide a live cam view of several areas on the interior of the *Terrastroid*. "This is our home. Our paradise, guarded carefully inside the darkened shell of our custom-built asteroid. All processes related to food creation and atmospheric regulation occurs here." He swiped and tapped the holoscreen. "Every speck of food and water are continuously subjugated to the cycle… our cycle of life. From synthesis to extinguishment, every single organism—down to the individual cell—is utilized for a specific purpose. We live out here with nothing, strangers. No wrist implants, no services rendered for charge, no reliance on a bitcoin system of oppression and greed. Among our people we can't assume there will always be more, we have to make sure we save for the future. And the future of our children. That's why we have two children, maximum. There is no three, you replace yourself in this asylum, no one gets extras."

"And then there's the pirates, of course…"Angus put his hand over his mouth, his head turning to the kitchen.

"Pirates?" Ariel's voice came across the com. "What pirates?"

"Nothing, dear…" he monotoned in reply, then continued talking to the boys. "Yeah, they're out here, too. But we do not associate ourselves or align ourselves with them in any fashion. Naturally, there are exceptions and there are… *agreements*."

"What kind of agreements?" asked Mike.

"You mean a truce?" guessed Max.

"Let's call it a necessary *arrangement*," Angus responded. "We don't reveal their location, they don't reveal ours. We both understand that drawing attention to the other will have repercussions, and neither of us want to deal with the Ugov. Occasionally, we have to meet with them and ratify certain aspects of our mutual pact. And we do exchange mined goods for spices and seeds, but this is closely audited to make sure we receive no stolen goods."

"Ah, I was sure I tasted *some* kind of spice!" Blob blurted out.

Ariel's voice came over the com so fast she must have been hovering next to the talk button: "Hey one with the big belly! No! I didn't use any foreign spice! That was my *own* recipe. So if you really didn't enjoy it, I can send you to a restaurant two hundred and fifty thousand light years from here—they serve *your* kind."

The conversation came to an uncomfortable pause for a moment, but then everyone burst out laughing, unable to stop for half a Uminute.

When the laughing fit died, Angus cleared his throat and showed no signs of eschewing his diatribe on the virtues of their holy asylum, when his daughter Murriel happily took over the reigns. Her high-pitched singsong voice made an interesting contrast to her father's hoarse one.

"What my father is trying to say is… we are special. This place is a miracle. Nowhere in the galaxy is there a life more sturdy or a people more passionate. Mark this design…" She swiped a few times on the holoscreen to revive the glow that automatically dulled on a timer. "Here, if you examine the secondary level a bit closer… the genius of our architects and builders is evident. This orange coded section…" She zoomed in, tapped a few times with her index finger, maximizing a detailed information box. "This is fortified to handle anything that manages to penetrate our force shield and the top layers of crust. We made it from a substance mined from asteroid clusters nearby. I promise you… it's as strong as any Ugov grade synthmetal." The screen showed old video footage of Abandoned scientists crafting a massive cylindrical tube. "The strength of this interior layer is nearly equivalent to the lining of a Ugov interstellar trawler. It allows the outer crust to become pliable, to bend and absorb the impact of an asteroid collision. Pretty amazing, no?"

Mike, for one, was impressed with the level of technology these people had, considering how far they were from anything.

A signal flashed on a wall monitor. Ariel reached for a nearby device, engaging it with an eye scan, and with a flicker, a second holoscreen opened. On it hovered the image of a tall brown-haired man, standing erect, with hands behind his back, shuffling his feet.

"Rymon?" The hostess greeted the holoimage. "To what do we owe this honor, oh great wizard of hyperspace?"

"Greetings, Ariel. I have been notified of the existence of strangers among us—invited to your family home?" Rymon queried.

Ariel stepped back from the virtual screen to reveal the entire chamber. "You mean these guys?"

"Yes, well, I, uh…" Rymon stuttered, clearly embarrassed they had overheard him.

"They're our guests," Ariel posited, "and they're completely harmless. In fact, they possess a wealth of information from the outside world that could be *crucial* to our survival."

Rymon made an odd grunt sound, expectorating. *No genetic plug-ins,* Mike thought, *these people can get sick and die—like everyone used to.*

Rymon's face moved closer on the holoscreen. "I would like to meet with these outworlders, if it please you."

Ariel made a pip sound to Angus who grumbled his consent.

"That's fine, Rymon," Angus said. "But *just* you. Please don't bring your brothers. We won't have enough space, our new friends are… well, they're rather large."

"No problem," Rymon replied. "They are otherwise engaged, helping keep our realm safe I imagine…"

"I'm sure they are…"

Hyperspace wizard, huh? Mike was pondering how he was ever going to surf a wave again, stranded way out in an asteroid belt. *Maybe I can glean a little info from him…*

***

Soon Rymon arrived, with his two brothers in tow, despite the protests of Ariel and her family. Sharing similar features, the brothers also wore their hair in exactly the same fashion, a reddish blond, curly and unkempt, the kind that could harbor an avian nest. Even their eyebrows were bushy. *Geez*, Mike thought, *these guys might have fluffier hair than me and my bro!*

"Rymon!" Angus exclaimed, his smile disappearing when his brothers walked in after him. "Lymon. Symon."

Their host ushered his comrades into the greeting chamber where Mike and his crew were lounging. By the way their eyeballs were hanging out of their sockets, Mike figured the new guests had never met aliens or mutants before, so he hopped over to break the ice. But (of course) before he could speak, Max took over the introductions, which soon developed into laughter and story-telling. *This is why we haven't been left to die,* Mike thought. *Cap just seems to have a way...*

"So you guys are hyperspace scientists?" Mike asked the brothers, as the conversation settled. His surf-first mentality was barking again. "Where can you take us? We obviously can't stay here. So we are going to have take off pretty soon. We don't want to burden your wonderful hospitality or put you in any danger..."

Lymon was first to answer. "Our star maps can get *us* anywhere we need to go... we've got sheaths to every arm in the galaxy." He emphasized the *us* plainly.

"Yes," continued Symon, a grin plastered on his face. "But there is no way of assuring a safe arrival. Either direction. The cronies at the Universal Government Hyperspace Transportation Council have the resources to do quadrillions of trials. They can do all sorts of risk-assessment with drones. Travel through sanctioned Ugov-built sheaths is nearly one hundred percent fail proof."

Rymon, the eldest, had the last word. "Don't get me wrong—our sheaths are good—but no such guarantees exist here in the A-belt."

The brother's comments made Mike consider where they were at that moment. *We took a pretty iffy star map to get out to Uehara, we used an even sketchier one to escape the place. And here we are, in the furthest doldrums of the galaxy, with zero liquid moving water, much less the tidal influence of a large stellar body, much less an ocean, much less any waves to ride. We're about as far away from waves as we've ever been in our lives right now. This is pretty grim.*

Mike mentally checked out of the conversation in the room as his frothing increased to a dangerous level. Being a landlocked diehard surfer was hard to take. Whenever Mike and his buddies were deprived of good waves for prolonged periods of time, depression set in. *What are we on the run for, any way? Why are we risking our lives in the first place? If we're going to be surf outlaws, we should be getting waves all the time! That's what this whole thing is about!*

The mutant rabbit's light gray-colored fur rolled up and down as he unconsciously scratched at the clumps near his haunches with his back paw. *Itching myself—a part of my rabbit brain that Dr. Kane couldn't scrub out of my genes, I suppose.* His mind wandered back to its perpetual destination—surfing—conditioned into him over years of watching addictive surf videos on the recommendations of AI algorithms. *Riding waves in exotic places, ahh, what a thrill! Uehara was unbelievable. Nobody will ever believe us when we tell them about the tidal bore, because the place straight up doesn't exist anymore.* Surfing the tidal bore made him consider what other kinds of waves were out there. Oceanic, tidal, what else …? What galactic arm hadn't they surfed? *Perseus is out of the question, obviously. Giant Beings are best to be avoided. Sagittarius Arm? We knocked that one off the list already.* Mike continued to catalog past surf experiences in his mind. *We've all surfed the Sun Planets, and Max, Vern, and Blob have scoured every surf spot in the Cygnus Arm. What about a different arm? Centaurus—that's it!*

"I wonder if there are any waves to surf in the Centaurus Arm," Mike asked out of the blue while the conversation had ironically drifted toward the mission of the crew of the *Planet Hopper*. Max had been embellishing their exploits in Uehara, and while doing so he couldn't help but describe the sport of surfing. It was their lifeblood, he exhorted, why they risked it all, why they continued going out into the abyss. It was the search for and the thrill of riding energy waves with their surfboards that kept them alive.

Rymon responded to Mike's question, "There's waves of energy in every solar system in the universe—of course. There's waves everywhere, even in this room. Light waves, sound waves… but waves to ride on with your surfboards? No."

"That's insane!" Murriel cried. "Why would you want to travel to Centaurus in search of waves? What waves could there possibly be in a part of the galaxy that more than likely has no oceans, no bodies of liquid water. Board riding occurs on oceanic waves, or— rivers, as you described the Ueharan tidal bore."

"Murriel is correct," Lymon extrapolated for her. "That arm of the galaxy is mostly a realm of fire. Heat. Volcanoes. Non-stop exploding viscous materials. There's nothing but decimation out there. No sentient organic life forms whatsoever. *Definitely* no oceans. Unless they're made of molten lava…"

"Well," Symon butted in, "that's not confirmed, Ly, it's a relatively unexplored region of the Milky Way. Just because the Ugov census indicates lack of intelligent life doesn't mean squat. And there could be liquid water on the far outer sub-arms, couldn't there? It can't be that hot all the way through."

"Yeah, but Symon," his brother countered, "our forefathers did travel there on a mining mission. Believe me, if they had found any kind of life, or any kind of water they would have reported it. It's a place so hot, with so many erupting volcanoes, it melted most of the outer shell of their spaceship. Primitive designs, like those, were barely hyperspace-travel-worthy back then. There was nothing in the Centaurian Arm but fire and ash."

"Symon is correct," began Rymon, who seemed to be the most respected voice among the brothers. "It *is* a land of fire and ash, as you said Lymon, but it is more than likely inhabited. How could we predict otherwise? Every arm has its own distinct life forms born of an unimaginable combination of elements. Maybe there is a kind of physics that we can't quite comprehend yet? A specialized metabolism honed to its own environment, meant for running hot. You never know. There are many incredible life forms discovered in the past by the astrobiologists. That Cris Crane and his protégé daughter, Piper, they really pushed the boundaries of what we thought was possible…" Rymon's voice tailed off as he reminisced.

Mike finally got around to answering Murriel's question. "The reason why I'm curious if there's rideable waves on Centaurus is geophysics, more specifically, volcanism. I'm pretty sure waves of magma are created by constant earthquakes from the core of these super-heated planets, the closer the proximity of the earthquake to the slope of the mountainside, the better the chance of creating waves of liquid magma. Theoretically, if the conditions were right, you could ride them from the top of the caldera where it shoots out, all the way to the dried magma fields that extend out from the base of the volcano. I researched this stuff at the University for Mutants when me and Claude were little groms. I was pretty much obsessed with trying to identify every possible type of non-synthetic wave. Oceans, rivers, avalanches, calving icebergs. And lava flows. The bigger the volcano, the bigger the earthquake, the bigger the…" he waved his stubby arms for emphasis.

"…waves!" everyone in the room finished for him.

"Well," Lymon said, "if big volcanoes are what you're after, the biggest in the galaxy are on the planet our elders dubbed the Orb. Its parent star is so bright and glows with such ferocity it outshines other stars that are several light years closer. The plumes from volcanic eruptions on its surface were reported to extend far out into the Orb's stratosphere. Our great ancestors traveled there in the hopes of locating rare crystal gems, forged in the hearts of the calderas—gems that supposedly allowed the wielder to harness energy as strong as a billion stars. Supposedly, they returned with a few."

"Or *so* they say." Ariel growled at Lymon.

Mike hopped over to an interface on the wall and accessed the holocomputer matrix that he had been inspecting earlier while the group had talked story. "So," he said, "is this where you mean?" He pointed his paw to a map and accompanying matrix graphic that showed layers of the Centaurus Arm. He sifted through the minor ones until he found an anomaly. In one particular portion there was a very, *very* bright emanation in comparison to the rest of the stars that made up the bulk of the celestial bodies there. "This must be where the Orb is located, right?"

"It is," said Rymon. "There is no mistaking a place so incredibly colorful. Every fraction of every color in the wheel is represented in pebble form, among the cooling sands of the Orb. Another myth or legend or fact, depending on your point of view, the light from its star is a wavering kaleidoscope of wavelengths—it has to be one of the most stunning collections of shades and hues in the galaxy. Even more spectacular than the crashing pulsars of Bridgegone."

"Well…" Symon interjected. "Most of the main entries on the Uweb are dedicated to the Orb's unique tectonics and geological processes. But what's trending beneath is the unparalleled volcanism that goes on every Uday on planets all throughout that specific solar system. I think you're right, Lymon, the biggest and most prone to earthquakes must be the volcanoes there." He pointed to a hologram of a planet floating in the middle of the chamber, visible from all sides. It spun slowly around as if it were an animal showing off its colors proudly to a potential mate.

This is what my subconscious was telling me earlier, thought Mike, *what could be more epic than surfing lava waves?*

Max's face opened into a bright smile. "Well, boys," said the Captain. "I think we need to do a fair trade. Rymon and his brothers can give us the star map data that will get us to our next surf destination—*and* back, right? And we can give them the star map data from Outer Cygnus to the hyperspace platform at the edge of the Abandoned."

"What?" shouted Symon, jumping up and gesticulating. "We have been searching for that for eons! That's one of the few places we had trouble making a new star map for. There are access points that we need in Outer Cygnus. Food. Resources. It could help our cause immensely!"

Angus raised an eyebrow at Symon.

Max cleared his voice. "Did I hear you say you had access points you needed in Outer Cygnus?" Max didn't wait for his question to be answered. "We... umm, have some bad news for you, in that regard."

All those present turned their gaze on the Algorean.

"I'm sorry to say," said Max, "the Ueharan solar system is gone. The Perseans crushed it playing their game. There is a similar solar system not even a parsec away, but Uehara..." He made a flick with his hand into the air.

It was quiet for a moment before Angus spoke. "So the Perseans *are* close. Why near the Abandoned? Why near *us*?"

"Because," said Rymon, "they are stitching together their own rudimentary hyperspace sheaths. But, obviously, Perseans aren't as bad at science as they are reputed. Especially if they made a sheath of their own from the Persean Arm to the platform near us.

They must have needed a platform somewhere nearby in order to make the jump to Outer Cygnus. If they were building it with old Ugov specs and technology that is nearly defunct, it would stand to reason they couldn't build one all the way from Perseus."

"I agree," Lymon put in. "And they probably put it near the Abandoned because what Ugov ship is roving around out there, save for the occasional space ranger? They needed a low profile spot to unload materials and relay equipment."

Rymon raised his eyebrow at Angus. "What do you think?"

All eyes in the chamber fixed on the elder Abandoned leader. *The dude sure looks like a renegade,* Mike laughed to himself. *If Uweb producers could get their crews out here they would make reality holos documenting "the extraordinary life of the Abandoned."*

"Of course," Angus said, pausing to clear his throat, while wrapping a hand around his neck to suppress his cough. "We can arrange that. Sending psychotic surfers to the volcanic waves of the Orb in exchange for a new route to Outer Cygnus? I'm pretty sure the other elders will ratify that."

Mike was not a religious rabbit, but he was convinced that serendipity existed, and that their mission to surf the Milky Way was a "holy" one. What else could explain where they were right now, and the amazing trip they were about to take? It was as if the crew had no control over where they would go next—the waves beckoned them and they dutifully followed.

CHAPTER NINE

Waves of Magma

After the cooling period of post-hyperspace flight conditions subsided the *Planet Hopper* kicked into gear. As its name suggested, the spaceship was great for cruising from planet to planet, and satellite to satellite, within a given solar system. So, while Vern piloted them into a circumnavigating flight pattern around the Orb, Claude prodded the AI mainframe computer. He had already charted the *Planet Hopper*'s route to a landing zone nestled among the spacious and crisped golden lava fields, far from the hectic activity. From there they would take the botcopters to the first volcano that met the proper criteria to pull off what they were trying to do. Surf magma waves. *We must be the most die-hard surfers in the galaxy to be where we are right now.* Claude smiled with pride, so wide his whiskers hurt at their roots.

A few Uminutes later, with the *Hopper* in stasis mode, the boys loaded into two botcopters and popped out the hatch doors, Vern flying Claude and his brother in the first, and Max and Blob in the other. As they floated up the steep slope of the volcano Claude held on tight as Vern had to maneuver a few times in order to avoid steaming geysers shooting up at random intervals. To make it an even more harrowing lift to the top, visibility was non-existent at certain points—without radar they would have been flying blind.

Nearing the top, both botcopters dipped below a rainstorm of fragments, the largest chunks crashing hard into the synthglass windshields.

"Right there, Vern!" Max shouted through the com.

Vern dropped the botcopter to the edge of the caldera and came to a bumpy, rock-grinding stop, causing Claude to press with all his might with his forepaws so he didn't face plant against the interior of the botcopter.

A Usecond later, Max landed much more smoothly, and that of course spawned a reaction over the com from the Captain.

"Aren't you the expert pilot, Vern? Half-man, half-machine, no mistakes, no errors, am I right?" Max chided, sending a holomeme of a stiff Gen-2er trying to move its arms which projected into the cabin of their botcopter. Claude laughed as Vern quickly swiped away the image.

Max didn't quit. "How did I land mine better than yours? I guess that's why they call me Captain, eh, Vern?"

Vern linked with the AI voice simulator and selected "banshee" setting for a loud and simple response: "Shut up!"

Even Vern's nervous right now, thought Claude. *Max is more fired up than usual... that's his way of showing it. He would never admit as much, too proud, too strong, too tough. Algorean men like Max don't cry... probably never have.*

Claude surveyed Mike. His brother was flicking his braids back and forth with his forepaw. *Another sure sign.* Mike had his own butterflies fluttering in his tummy. And Blob? *Uh, yeah, him too.* The big Boor was rocking back and forth in his seat, panting because his species wasn't able to sweat, stretching out his arms with big circles from the shoulder joints.

"All right, boys, look alive!" Max yelled. "Time to see what this volcano surf thing is all about, let's go!" Without hesitation he grabbed his board, leapt off the side of the botcopter, and stomped to the rim of the caldera.

When the entire crew was peering over the edge, boards grasped under their arms, the com went silent. A reflective glow of orange was cast off their visors, making it so Claude was unable to survey his crew mate's facial expressions, but he guessed there were a few jaws dropping inside those helmets.

A belching, growling sound came from far below and an ejection hurled up a towering spray of orange lava. *This might have been my bro's idea,* Claude thought, *but I'm the one that figured this whole thing out, I better not have screwed up the numbers.* Claude had timed it so that when they touched down near the edge of the volcano they could suss it out a bit, get comfortable on their boards, and make sure their suits were in working order before the eruption. He tapped his wrist implant and went over the readings again.

Everything was copasetic, so Claude activated the AI auto pilot function, and sent the two botcopters back to the *Planet Hopper* to await their command for pick up.

"All right," Claude said, peeking at the display inside his helmet. "The timer is ticking… this thing is going to explode in a matter of moments. The simulators show the lava flow spilling over the bulging side of the caldera. It's gonna tumble down in one big old honking oscillation… oh, did I mention we can't miss the window, because if we do…"

"What, Claude, we're burned alive?" Mike asked, probably trying to be sarcastic to improve morale. The sentiment backfired on him.

"No, not really," replied Claude. "More like sizzled into liquid…"

Of course, Blob had to toss his description in there: "Nah, more like boiled into charred magma dust."

"Mmm," Max understood the game, "I'd say more like being instantly pulverized to ash."

Vern simulated a message to the crew, "Technically, it would be a nanosecond of extreme pain, followed by a coagulated matter 'reinfusion,' with our bodies, suits and boards becoming a single entity."

Claude grunted after reading it. "Uh, thanks for the input Vern... anyway, successfully making the window means that we are riding on *top* of the pyroclastic flow. This is an effusive-type exploder, it should produce an avalanche. Galaxies, that's a steep slope..."

They all glanced over the brink again. The reflected orange off their visors identified the energy source for the wave they were about to ride. Toxic gases formed a confluent stream, rising ever upwards, obfuscating the cone.

Blob, meanwhile, had turned around and was considering the drop-in. He reverted back into concerned mode. "It's pretty steep, Claude. You think this is even doable?"

When he saw how far it was to the plateau Claude internalized the fact everyone was counting on him to safely surf these lava waves. Mike came up with the concept and did the initial research, which spawned the mission in the first place, but without Claude's calculations and detailed planning... there would be no sesh. The enormity of the moment, the sheer trust they were putting in him, it was all a bit much—*especially* considering he needed to be on his game and focused. Mistakes—such as pearling the nose of your board—in these kind of extreme conditions came with dire consequences.

"Yes, it's doable." All positive, Max was a calming contagion. "That's why we came all this way, dudes. It's on. Claude—we trust him, I trust him. We've got this. We're going to shred this! What's the count, my furry friend?"

"T-minus three Umins!" Claude checked his helmet holodisplay and shouted. "Let's brace ourselves against the edge of these dried magma boulders. The earthquake is going to be a massive single jolt. Big enough to bump us over the edge when we're not ready, let's get away from the side a little bit…"

Claude backed away from the caldera drop-off, but before retreating all the way, he took one last look at the molten lake a kilometer below. There were an array of noxious gray clouds partially concealing the bright crimson swirl. The terminus of their epic ride.

"Anyone want to go for a swim after? Pretty colored water, eh?" Mike joked as they strapped into their boards and linked themselves to festooned boulders scattered on the narrow plateau. Magnetic synthmetal clasps allowed them to attach their boots to the decks of their boards and avoid any displacement—up to a specific kinetic threshold, of course, when they automatically loosened to avoid snapping a tibia.

"All right!" Claude said. "This is it! When this quake jerks, it's going to be fast. We launch over the edge with foot thrusters on alt mode. Once we get above the lava flow we drop-in and ride it to the bottom!"

"Lava boarding and lava surfing, all in one!" Blob cried.

Mike chased Blob's yelp with one of his own. "I'm fired up, ha ha ha—*literally!* Get it? Do you guys get it? I made a pun!"

"Ten, nine, eight…" Claude counted alongside the relative time ticker within the view screen inside his helmet. *These projections better be right. AI don't fail me now.*

"…four, three, two…"

***

Before zero, Claude felt an incredible pressure below them. An intense, but short-lived, wave of heat and power passed through the ground.

The prodigious jolt of the earthquake was their cue: one by one, in order of who was closest to the edge, they hit their thrusters, aligning with the flow of lava bursting over the side. Max was first to make contact. He hit tail first, his fins slicing into the lava, a splash of reddish, oozing slime projecting from his board.

Blob dropped in next, screeching in classic Boorish fashion. He followed Max's line, although the orange lines disappeared immediately, the colorful gaps drawn by his fins sealing with a hiss.

Claude gave his brother a familiar nod. *Go for it, dude!*

Mike hooted. He stomped his back paw on the thrusters of his board, launching over the hardened gray lip of the caldera. Spinning counterclockwise through the air, Mike grabbed his rail and turned a full three hundred and sixty degrees, landing in the pyroclastic flow in time to ollie over a large chunk of material not yet disintegrated by the heat. Claude grinned. *Sick move, bro!*

Vern was ready to go, so Claude gave him the paws up sign, and their half-android pilot launched over the edge into the fray.

"Woo-hoo!" Claude called out as he followed right after Vern, the familiar weightlessness overcoming him as his board succumbed to the steep pitch of the talus slope.

Instead of carving, Claude went into a tuck so he could get a good view of the Captain, who remained in front. The skillful carving of Max was awe-inspiring, he drew huge curved arcs in the tumbling flow, with each front side turn he seemed to get his body lower and lower, bending the rail of his board, so low he could have kissed the melting fluid with his visor.

Claude watched Blob try hard to catch up to Max. Blob's surfing lacked the same luster, but he was amazingly effective. He had so much mass in his core he would never draw as pretty a line as his Captain. His belly literally prevented it through physics. That he could surf at all was a Milky Way miracle, much less the fact he was a former contest winner on Boor. Blob skipped a few turns, straightening out instead, trying to catch up to the Captain. Max must have sensed the heavyweight's presence over his shoulder, or maybe he glanced at a rear monitor within his helmet, because right when Blob was about to pass him, he stomped his thrusters and jolted ahead a few meters.

Claude rode up next to Mike and they went into doubles mode, harkening back to when they used to surf in competitions back on Rabbit World. They maneuvered around each other deftly, each turn a near collision, as their boards passed within centimeters. Curvy indentations on the lava trailed behind them like insignias. A few Usecs later they split apart and continued shredding through the lava, drawing their own lines for awhile, synthmetal fins digging in deep.

Claude made sure to keep his focus on a green tracking beam emanating from the nose of his board. The tracking beam scanned and designated an obstacle free path for the boys to follow, as well as outlining the inertia resonance of their buddies who rode ahead of them. This provided everyone with a good idea—in real time—of what kind of lines everyone else was drawing with their boards. Vern did uniform, machine-like S-turns, mostly, with his board rotating from rail to rail. Max's lines were perfect equidistant loops, but with huge indentations in the surface material from where his fins gouged. Blob's were irregular and jagged at first, then pointed straight down, as he tried in vain to keep up with the Cap. Claude and his brother, of course, had the perfect double parabola shape.

"Eh, boys!" Claude's voice projected to the other four's helmet coms as he watched the virtual pathway mini-monitor in his helmet with his peripheral vision. "Let me get in front!"

Max slowed, allowing Claude to pass him. He guided the boys to the final section before their ride turned into a vertical drop-off. The lava rock bars were looming below. Circular, oval-shaped, blackened rolls of dried lava stretched out before them, made of perfectly smooth, sculpted volcanic rock—they were laid with purpose and precision, as if constructed by a wave pool designer. Each of the onyx rolls were identical. And large.

Holy Galaxies—they look taller than on the recon images the AI fed us! Claude began to fret the closer they got to the point of no return. *Those've got to be fifty meters high!*

"We are about to hit the ledge, we need to get behind the flow and let it hit the rock bar first—*before* we drop over! Everyone got it?"

"Yeeeeahhhh!" Mike shouted.

"Boor's tears, this is gnarly!" Blob proclaimed loudly.

"Tear it up, Blob!" Max urged.

As Claude had predicted, an enormous flow of gurgling orange and red lava cascaded over. They followed Claude's line and set their boards on hover-mode, bobbing a few meters above the volcanic material—which had transformed from hardened rock to snaking streams of fast moving liquid molten lava. The wave was startlingly colorful; the neon orange and muddied reds gave way to a mixture of yellows and dark greens. Nuggets of dried rock crackled and popped this way and that, revealing a jade-colored interior. The rocks were polished underneath, when the crisp dark outer layer melted away.

"Okay, guys," Claude cried "this is it! Get ready for the ride of your life!"

He was about to surprise Max and be the first to go, when a tremor came on in earnest. It was one of Claude's worst fears about their session—rogue phreatomagmatic explosions. Projections he ran back on the *Hopper* showed a slight possibility of them developing. If magma from the scalding reservoir of metals came up from within the planet's core, meeting the sub freezing temperatures of the surface atmosphere, unpredictable mini-eruptions could occur. *Anywhere* on the caldera.

"Everyone—get down!" Claude called over the com.

The crew took his warning seriously, all five dropping prone on their boards and covering their helmets and visors.

Luckily, the bulk of the blast missed them, but it left their suits splattered with sizzling material.

"Press your exhaust function!" Max ordered. "Get all the burning chunks off your suits before they do any damage to the external synthfibers!"

Each of them activated the correct holobutton and they were cocooned momentarily in a cleansing spray. They inspected each other after the cloud faded, Claude wiping off a few embers from Mike's back.

"Close call," Claude said. "There could be more of those, let's watch out for them dudes. Oh, and by the way… catch me if you can!"

He abruptly stomped the thruster pad and jolted over the edge of the red waterfall. *I'm free—free falling!* Claude sang to himself. His board compressed as it made contact with the flow. He leaned way back on his tail, feeling his fins dig in, and control came back to him.

With full balance restored he pumped his way along the bottom of the trough, waiting for the right moment to pounce. It came. He leaned hard on his inside rail, whipping up into the throat of the beast, then tapping the brake pedal with his toe, stalling his board within the face of the wave. The orange lip covered him from sight.

"Claude just got barreled!" The intercom went berserk with hoots and hollers.

"Still am!" the giant rabbit yelled from inside the molten cavern.

One by one, they followed Claude, lined up like gliding sea birds, each getting their chance to enjoy the view from inside the tube.

"Yeah!"

"Epic!"

"Wooo!"

"Unreal!"

Now, this *is surfing the Milky Way!* Claude thought, emerging triumphantly from the barrel, his paws high in the air.

CHAPTER TEN

Blob's Big Drop

What is my real name? I can't even remember. I've been answering to that damn nickname my whole life! Blob was ruminating about his past, as was oft the case when working on menial tasks assigned to him by Max. He caught himself staring out at the rugged landscape of the Orb through a portal in the *Planet Hopper*'s cargo bay.

Blob was a big alien. To put it mildly. A humanoid with an impressively large stomach, the Boor was capable of eating galactically-renowned quantities of food. Setting records in eating contests when he was in his youth, he had driven his family out of house and home from the sheer cost of keeping him fed. Painful memories of those early years riddled his dreams. His home planet of Boor had been decimated by a nearby Persean attack during the war—not surprisingly for the race of Cygnans and their Boorish ways, the survivors fought over food and water resources. Like all the large breed aliens had too.

His past was checkered with strife, he and his family were part of a Diaspora to a local moon, forced to live in a "temporary safe place"—it wasn't—under a dome where they lived a completely artificial life. It was the only way a barren moon could sustain such a large influx of refugees, by simplifying life to the bare minimums. They dubbed it "the free prison." You could go where you wanted to go and do what you wanted to do, but there weren't many choices of things *to* do. And, regardless, each Uday you returned to your domicile. Blank gray walls of nothingness. No holoscreens or VAR. Depression made his mother ill, and she soon passed on. Despite the Sun Peoples sharing genetic modification with the alien races, not everyone was fortunate enough to be inoculated expediently. There were Boorish people who perished not by mortal combat, or collateral damage to the war, but from sheer heartsickness. Boor was a beautiful planet before the war, and had yet to retain its original state, many Uyears later.

But living in those artificial conditions in that disgusting dome became beneficial for Blob in the long run. He became self-sufficient and motivated. His diet changed. No longer was he able to patronize the all-you-can-eat parlors of delicious Boorish delights on the planet below. Instead, his food was artificially engineered, nearly tasteless, extremely nutritious, and very filling. All of this despite a full meal being no larger than what would fit in a Boor appetizer bowl. His propensity for eating large quantities tapered into a uniform meal ingested at exactly the same Uhour every single Uday. He lost kilos of weight, but never shed the nickname Blob. He may have lost the weight—but he *hadn't* lost the appetite. He simply surfed more to burn off the calories.

Blob clicked the intercom to notify the guys their surf equipment was ready. "Gear is checked. We getting close yet, Max?"

"Check that, Blob," Max replied after a slight delay. "We are a go, I repeat we are a go."

"Blob!" Mike popped up on a mini holoscreen over Blob's shoulder with extra high volume. "Have you checked this out, dude?"

Probably to annoy me, thought the big Boor. *He always cranks the volume up, that little rabbit mongrel!* "What's up, Mikey?"

"Dude, this is the craziest... I mean, it's... it's," Mike stammered on, trying to describe what he and the crew were jaw dropping about. "It's humongous! Blob, you are going to rip this up! I can't even picture how hard you are going to charge this thing... I mean, it's got to be a hundred kilometers high!"

Rising off a plateau of recognizably symmetrical lava mounds was a conical stratovolcano, not dissimilar from the first volcano they surfed earlier in the Uday, except on a much grander scale. *I guess surfing one puny volcano isn't enough for our crew,* Blob snorted.

The tip of the monstrous, fiery mountain disappeared among seeding methane clouds draping its summit. A belching stream of exhaust stretched far and wide, encircling the entire planet. Staring from the bay portal Blob tried to take it all in. There it was, the king of all volcanoes, boiling with countless billions of cubic liters of liquid magma. And by staring at it, Blob was internalizing the utter insanity of riding lava waves the AI on the ship couldn't calculate the size of.

Plus we're gonna get tubed, thought Blob, *those waves are going to spit the biggest barrels!*

He air tubed up to the cockpit and raised the number of crew staring out the synthglass of the front portal to all five of them.

"Well, thanks a lot for finding this thing, Claude," Mike joked. "We're all going to die today."

"No, Mike," Blob retorted excitedly, leaning down and slapping him hard on his furry back. "We're all going to get the biggest barrels of our lives today!"

Mike shrunk away from the well-intentioned blow that left his shoulder throbbing. "Easy, big guy, don't get too excited, did you eat your energy goo already, or what?"

"Get us in orbit, Vern," Blob yelled, far too loud for the narrow confines of the cockpit. "We've got more riding to do on this galactic gem of a planet!"

"Aye, aye, Captain Blob," Vern replied, using the sarcasm accentuation setting. "I'm so glad to be of service—to the mess and gear guy. Hold on to your eyeballs, we're going in…"

The *Planet Hopper* swerved upward, causing everyone to grab the closest thing to hold on to. Vern used the updraft alongside the edge of the sloping saddle, pointing for the caldera, not yet visible through the cockpit portal because of a shroud of gray and black gas clouds. A hard acidic rain fell, pelting their spaceship with a thudding sound, followed by a definitive hissing, as the liquid sizzled on the synthmetal shell.

Max was quick to direct, "Better put the low energy shields on, Vern."

On Vern's touch a yellow flicker surrounded the *Planet Hopper*, and the thick acidic drops became flashes against the force field.

Blob read the shield indicator light. It was at thirteen percent coverage—unsettlingly low. As if to make the point, a larger chunk of dried magma broke all the way through, and banged into *Hopper*'s shell with a hollow thud.

"Make it seventeen percent, will ya?" The Captain ordered the adjustment in response, as the volume of the hot precipitation increased. The higher the ship went, the harder the thumping. One of the downpours jolted Blob clear off his seat.

Wow, thought Blob as he bit his lip, *feels kind of like those little chunks of asteroids did, out in the Abandoned—but these are way hotter!*

He retreated back to his post in the bay of the ship, with Mike accompanying him, without Max's prompt. The two quickly clicked and swiped on their holopads, and activated the botcopter warm-up protocol.

This is crazy, Blob gulped, his massive gray tongue sliding over his lips. *But this is why I'm here with my buddies, surfing the Centaurian volcanoes. For this moment, right here, right now. I'm going to go so big!*

Blob was having an epic session, but within a nanosecond, that all changed. A tiny alarm tone and a flashing red indicator popped up on his helmet's holoscreen.

He had been last to drop-in off the caldera, taking a few extra Usecs to admire the view, and to watch the first few turns and maneuvers by his buddies, before taking the leap himself. Halfway down the gushing talus slope, digging his fins and rails deeply into the orange soup on each S-turn, his wide mouth went from a grin to a long straight line.

Oh, no! Blob was panting—even with the climate control of his suit—because of the intense heat radiating up from underneath his board. *There must be something wrong with the cooling system!* Boorish men were known not only for their unbelievable capacity to eat and drink, but also for their capacity to breathe deeply— along with other prolific bodily functions.

Condensation was building up inside his helmet, and his visor was getting blurry, so he came to a carving stop, off to the edge of the flow, with his board perpendicular to the bottom of the volcano. Before he could click the holo to tell the guys what was happening, a feeling of vertigo overcame him. *What the...*

He was falling!

Unable to reach the control panel on his rail, he plummeted through a fissure in the crust. With his boots magnetically locked, Blob's feet remained attached to his board, but he had to wave his arms frantically to keep from flipping over in midair. Finally, his fins and tail made contact with a sloping pitch of tiny rocks, and he regained traction on the solid talus. Slightly less fine than sand, the little pebbles beneath him were glowing with a multitude of colors—a billion variations of the light spectrum, from bright pink to the darkest purple. Blob's mouth opened wide. Even through the partially obstructed view through his foggy visor, he was amazed at the vast, glistening swales of miniature gemstones.

Holy Milky Way! That was gnarly! Whoa, where am I?

He looked up in vain, trying to spot where he had fallen in. With no other choice he started a downward-angled traverse, carving S-shaped turns slowly and smoothly over the talus. He could feel his board under him, and could have closed his eyes and surfed merely by the interplay between his riding machine and the dazzling display of fine, round stones.

Are those... nah, couldn't be.

He leaned back on his heels and did a quick slide out, coming to a halt. He reached his glove into the sands. Rounded and oblong gemstones rolled in his palm, the likes of which would cause a gemologist to faint. Shimmering with reflective crystals of orange, yellow, aquamarine greens and oceanic blues, each one pure and smooth to the touch. He tried his inner-helmet holocall, seeking to show the crew his big discovery. The reply was nothing but a fuzzy, crackling noise.

Hmm. Maybe heat interference. How deep am I, anyway?

Blob tried to get his bearings; a kaleidoscope of colors removed all sense of direction. From Claude's debriefing he recalled that many volcanoes created magmatic gemstones. Gas bubbles, formed during the magma events, when they had a chance to cool off, turned into this mother lode of treasure surrounding him in every direction.

Something especially bright caught his eye. A purple glow emanated from within a certain patch of pebble-sized gems that drew his attention. Blob slid over to the gleaming beacon with a tap of his heel on the forward thruster of his board, and reached into the pile, extracting a gem about the size of one of his eyeballs. But when he held it in front of his face it was so bright he had to avert his gaze from its lustrous beauty. He didn't want to discard it back among the pile, so he placed it in his leg pouch, turned his board around, and searched for a way out.

Finally a crackle of a reply came over the holocom.

"Blob!" Mike squeaked. "Where you been, big alien? We were worried, dude!"

"Oh, nothing much…" Blob said. "Just admiring the view—from *inside* the volcano!"

He checked the humidity setting on his suit. The time he spent under the crust had equalized things—no moisture was coming from his mouth because he had stopped panting.

Once he was able to line up Mike's com location it didn't take long for Blob to find the same crack he had fallen through. Using the hover function on his surfboard, he ascended back topside.

Phew! He spotted Mike, standing on his board not too far away. The rest of the crew were hovering in a cluster further down the grade. Blob pointed his board downhill. Glowing balls of ejected lava sprayed in the air. He ducked one fragment, but a few other specks sizzled on the outside of his suit as he made his way to the mutant rabbit.

Mike chastised over the com, "Hey, big boy, you've gotta keep in contact!"

When Blob got close enough Mike's whiskered smile was visible through his faceplate glass. But Blob zipped right past him with a hoot, wiping the smile right off the rabbit's face as he stepped on his thruster pad and lurched after him. Making quite the pair, the big Boor and the little rabbit sped to meet the rest of the crew, who were idling their boards on the darkened, unmoving crust adjacent to a wide orange river. Blob and Mike bombed the final portion of the slope without turning, getting as much speed as possible in a low tuck. Blob spoke into his helmet com. "Sorry, Max, sorry boys… couldn't be avoided. A crack opened right under my board!"

"What?" Max bellowed.

"Yeah," Blob said, "it was *so* gnarly! I free fell a hundred meters, into this incredible stuff, like lava sands or something. Really, *really* cool colors. A trillion smooth marbles. Sparkling everywhere. I was inside a cavern, some kind of... of mineral deposit or something." He fiddled with his leg pouch that contained the deep purple gem, the thousands of perfect edges sliced across its face still prominent in his mind. He considered saying something about it, but refrained, taking his hand away from the pouch. *No time for that,* he told himself.

Max jerked forward on his board. "Come on, boys—let's surf! Our window is closing, once this flow stops, that's it."

Claude got them on task. "I didn't do projections for the next eruption. Long period lava swells don't last for a Uweek, like on a body of water, they decay quickly here on Centaurus."

The crew followed Max to a sliding stop and together in a line gazed over the cornice of black rock, the last hurdle for the lava to get over before it dropped precipitously to the awaiting lava bars of the plateau. The curvature of the catchment swale spread out to the horizon.

"I'll go first!" Claude promptly dropped over the edge, ricocheting off the waterfall of lava, his fins digging in and sending an orange spray up into the air. Once he made contact with the flow, he pumped his board from rail to rail to gain speed. For it to become a rideable wave, the energy of the moving magma had to tumble over itself the moment it passed by the trough of dried magma bars underneath.

One by one, carving a turn and stalling on the scalding waterfall exactly as Claude had, each of the crew followed his line, and dropped into the lava wave—a bright orange canvas to draw their fancy lines.

At the far end of the flow, where the magma had finally petered out, becoming merely a trickle, it had formed a bulge of hardened, black talus. Up on top of the crusty rise Blob stopped his board next to Claude's with a power slide. Max, Vern and the twins followed suit. Standing tall on his board, Blob estimated how far across the lava sea flats they had surfed. The darkened lower slope was barely visible now. A shroud of acid rain clouds enveloping the horizon in a blue-gray deluge. They were perched on a kind of organic demarcation line—the place where cooled earth finally stood its ground to the sizzling river. It was poignantly clear they had come to the end of one of the greatest waves they had ever ridden. They had reached the termination of an incredibly powerful energy burst, taking them from the top of a fifty thousand-meter volcano, and across a plateau of several kilometers, in a matter of Uminutes. The crew's galactic surf safari was back on track—in a *big* way.

***

"Uh, guys," Max said in a hushed voice. "Are you seeing what I'm seeing?" He orally commanded the magnetic release on his feet, and jumped off his board, which had been hovering a meter above the ground. As the adrenaline from the crew's surf session was beginning to subside—it jumped back up to an even higher level.

Humanoid *figures* emerged from the vapor drifts, a few meters away, posturing from an ashy gray escarpment of dusty marbled black stone.

Blob gasped, "You've got to be kidding me!"

Claude had a proposition that made sense, "We're delusional from the ride."

"We're... they're..." Mike stammered. "Are—are they moving?"

Vern disconnected from his board and stepped to Max's side, clicking open the holoscreen on his wrist. He tapped on a virtual screen. "I'm analyzing them through relay with the *Planet Hopper* AI mainframe. They are definitely sentient humanoids! Judging from the sensors, they must be able to breathe noxious gases, and exhale others of equal potency."

"Gases?" Max was equal parts quizzical and shocked. "What do you mean, Vern?"

"It's confirmed, Captain," Vern replied. "They seem to be exhausting intense vapor gases—through their skin. There's eight of them. With a sort of extremely powerful radiation coming off them. They're advancing our way, guys…"

Max gulped. It was a group of aliens, no doubt about it, each wearing a dark, metallic cloak, draped across their shoulders and hanging behind them all the way to the ground. As the odd creatures drew closer, the rest of the boys unstrapped, and huddled together, their boards floating behind them.

A moment later, into focus came the first ever observation of a novel alien species in the Milky Way. Their skin seemed to consist of a crusty exterior broken open in parts to reveal an incredibly smooth under layer, with saurian green and brown patterns woven throughout. The seams around the patches of skin vented gas in small wisps.

We've made Uhistory, Max chuckled to himself. *Again.*

Each of the eight figures moved forward in slow, deliberate steps, small red flames burning in the palms of their three-digit hands. One of them showed off the potency of those hands by sending out a burst to the ground in front of them, sending up rock and crud into the air.

Max shuffled and herded the boys closer with tentacle arms. He whispered, "Stay close. If we have to bail, we jump on our boards and head back to the volcano."

"Dudes," Mike said in a hushed tone, blinking. "They are going to incinerate us."

Max disagreed. "They already would have done that if they wanted to…" He had another guess: "I think they want something from us."

"They have a form of energy that is off the charts," Vern informed them from the AI interface scan displayed on the inside of his helmet holoscreen. "It's emanating from the crown of their skulls."

Each of the aliens had an oval indentation on top of their head which holstered a sort of... gemstone. All eight were adorned with a uniquely colored gem. They pointed their triads of fingers at the largest member of the crew. Max cocked his head at Blob. *Yep, they're definitely focused on Blob.*

The aliens continued forward, still using carefully measured steps.

"Whoa, guys, should we bail?" Mike hopped back. "This doesn't seem like a friendly greeting. More like a friendly warning."

"Not yet." Max was solemn, studying the otherworldly locals with composure.

"I agree with the Captain," Claude said. "I am not sensing aggression from them. I am sensing something else, a different emotion... *recognition*, maybe?"

"What?" Mike didn't seem to buy his brother's assertion. "How is that possible, Vern?"

"Max and Claude are right," Vern replied, "it appears they are appealing for something. At least according to my AI body language interpretation app."

"That's weird!" Blob said, too loudly, drawing Max's stare. "I wonder what that could possibly be?" Blob's massive monobrow tilted over his eyes and stretched up and past his ears on the other end.

Max narrowed his eyes at his hefty crew mate. *No, Blob... don't tell me—*

The pouch on Blob's leg containing the purple stone began to emit a radiant light. It was so bright it penetrated the material of his suit enough to be visible by all present. With everyone now staring at him, Blob had no choice but to pull it out.

As soon as the purple gemstone was revealed the Centaurian aliens hushed their hissing and stood motionless for the first time. Gray exhaust matriculated from their limbs into the dark, thin atmosphere. The leader stepped forward and motioned to his head, then pointed three fingers at what was in Blob's outstretched hand.

The crew sounded off, Max first: "You've got to be kidding me…"

Mike squawked next: "Dude, you cannot be serious! What have you done? Did you steal that thing from these guys?"

Claude chastised in his calm way: "Not a smart move, Blob."

Vern folded his arms across his chest sternly.

Blob's broad shoulders slumped and he sighed. "I… I was *going* to tell you guys. I just… I didn't have a chance to… I was going to surprise you guys! It's a rare treasure! It could be worth… who knows how much black bit, we'd be rich for years! We could surf anywhere we wanted in the galaxy!" He was practically shouting now, his thick Boorish accent making every Sunish word seem to reverberate.

"Hey, Blob," Claude said, "do you mean *we'd* be rich for years, or *you'd* be rich for years?"

"No! I…" Blob tried to fend off the scorn of his friends. The Boor deferred to his superior.

"Blob, you're going to give it back to them… right now," Max calmly ordered his longtime friend.

Max nodded and Blob moped toward the leader of the Vapor People. He towered over the lead alien and must have weighed as much as all eight of them combined. The creature was regarding the big Boorish alien with curiosity, the regularity of its heartbeat indicated by each pulse of red from within recessed eye sockets. A ragged arm extended from the dark cloak that hung from its shoulders all the way to the blackened surface of the dried lava below its feet. Blob took the stone and turned his hand over, dropping it into the flaming palm of the leader. As soon as the gem made contact with its skin, it let out a loud hiss of vapor. The other seven came forward and straddled their leader, hissing vociferously, as the purple gemstone levitated above his burning hand.

Vern stated the obvious, "I'm sensing they're pleased."

"Good call, Max!" Mike cried out. "I think giving them the gem made us heroes!"

The Vapor Peoples motioned to the crew, beckoning them to follow in their direction. Apparently, they wanted the ragtag group of surf safari heathens to follow them. With no further hissing, the cloaked figures departed off into the barren wasteland. The dried lava field around them seemed to know no boundaries, other than, of course, the base of the mega volcano tapering off into dark clouds.

"Well," Max said as he stepped on his surfboard, still in hover mode, and scooted along after their odd hosts. "What're we waiting for? Let's go!"

The rest of the crew got in line and hopped up on their boards. As was always the case, resistance was futile when the captain made a call to action.

***

Within a few Uminutes they reached their destination. It was a shelter, dug into the rock, and they arrived at the perfect time, as acid rain clouds gathered above, ready to turn the exposed lava beds into a sizzling quagmire. The boys followed their mystical hosts to the shelter, unable to expect what was to come. One thing was clear: these were spiritual people, and they worshipped the gemstone that Blob had discovered.

Once inside the dug-in shelter, Blob could tell that it had been forged from glazed volcanic clay. Insulated and protected, it was a perfect nesting place from the harsh conditions on the exterior of the Orb. But, on closer inspection, he guessed it was more than merely a shelter. It was a holy place to them. There was a ritual about to unfold—and whether or not he liked it, he was going to be part of it.

As he intuited, the Vapor People hailed Blob with hissing and waving. Each of their gemstones sparkled atop their uncloaked heads. They guided him to an onyx throne with gentle prods on his shoulders and back. Too small for his bottom, he crouched on the smooth black rock just the same. Adjacent to the formal seat was an orange-colored hot springs pool—boiling, bubbling, and steaming gas into the stuffy confines. The leader from before was there. It ladled out some of the hot liquid, pouring it with care into a small triangular cauldron carved from pyrite rock. Once full, the Centaurian set it in front of Blob.

"Should I be nervous?" he asked, turning to the guys for moral support.

"You're all good, Blob." Mike laughed. "Just go with it. Ha—this is so awesome! For once you're the laboratory pet, not me and my bro!"

The leader now wielded the purple stone that Blob had found among the rainbow lava sands of the giant stratovolcano. The creature plunged the gem into the cauldron, pulling it right back out. Blob couldn't stop staring at it, no matter how hard he resisted. His eyes glazed over, and his head slumped forward slightly—as if he had nodded off—yet he was fully cognizant.

"Whoa, guys, this is crazy…" Blob narrated the surreal out of body voyage he was undergoing. "I'm back in the volcano again, riding on the rainbow sands… there are so many colors!"

What is that shine? Ahh, the gemstones. I'm going back in time.

"The purple stone!" Blob blurted out to the guys.

Next, came select images of the past few Uhours, fast forwarded. The triumphant surf session went by in a flash. Blob was privy to a three hundred and sixty degree view, as if watching footage from a bot cam. There they were—the crew of the *Planet Hopper* following the Vapor Peoples into the hovel… but a swirl of vertigo came over him, and his head dropped. In his mind's eye he was now somewhere else—far from the Orb. It was familiar to him… *I'm back in the Abandoned asteroid belt!* Colliding meteorites and looping debris clouds, lit by the energy of their explosions, were visible in every direction. *Terrastroid,* the portable planet disguised as a large asteroid, gently spun in dark space. There was Angus. And his lovely family. His friend Jonah and the three brothers. Smiling and laughing. But the vision flickered, and their faces twisted into consternation and horror. A massive translucent bubble, rolling through the blankness of deep space with pace and purpose, appeared next. Dozens of others came into Blob's dream, each one a hundred times more massive than his native planet of Boor, and each one containing a sinister-looking alien being with reddish hair and yellow skin.

Planet Ballers! The last image was the most frightening of all, a Persean spaceship firing a dark weapon. He tried to cover his eyes, but the vision was compulsory. A tiny black hole formed in the space where the weapon was fired, and one by one, asteroids succumbed to the awful backward motion—toward the event horizon.

Blob snapped out of it, shook his head to and fro, and found his amused friends regarding him. They giggled while mimicking his physical state while he had been undergoing the visions, making exaggerated movements of their heads and rolling their eyes.

"Dude…" Claude laughed. "You look like you swallowed several liters of Boorish beer."

"Yeah, Blob," Mike joked, "no drinking and surfing, that's the rule!"

Max stopped the charade, a bit more concerned about the welfare of his mate than the rabbits. "He's not drunk, he's hallucinating. Blob—you all right, dude? The Ri-Ri cactus dust supply was empty, I thought?"

Blob was still dazed, but managed to answer, albeit in a meek voice. "Yeah, I guess so. I *saw* things. Guys, I think I may have... I was transported into the past, I was here, and then, I think... maybe I traveled into the future."

"Oh, yeah." Mike was the most sarcastic of the bunch. "And how did you mange that? Wait—don't tell me! You've discovered the secret of the space time continuum? Ha ha, yeah right!"

"Shut it, Mike," Max warned. "Let him speak."

Blob snorted at Mike. "I was on the volcano surfing. I could feel myself fall through into the chasm. The purple gem I found was there—much brighter than I remember it—and I grabbed it. Right after, I had a vision of the Abandoned, and of Angus and his family and friends."

"Cool!" Mike teased. "How are they? Did you say hi for us?"

Claude laughed and slapped paws with his brother's heckle. "Tell those brothers they hooked us up with the best waves ever!"

"It wasn't like that." Blob whined. "I wasn't *there* there. I was, like, watching it all from above..."

"Huh?" Max squinted.

"*Listen to me!*" Blob's tone changed, "I saw something else. The Perscans!"

Max stroked his chin. "What do you mean you *saw* them?"

"Well..." Blob turned away from his friends. "There were lots of them, rolling in these clear bubbles, Planet Ball regalia and all! Remember that same massive spaceship that chased us back at Uehara? It was flying in space, but I swear, dudes, it was cruising right at the edge of the Abandoned. Hundred percent for sure."

The boys fell silent. Blob continued, "There's more… this is gonna sound really weird—but there was an itty bitty black hole sucking up asteroids! The *Terrastroid* was nearby."

It grew so quiet in the Centaurian hut the only sound was the noxious breathing of the Vapor People.

"Guys," Blob said, choking back a tear. "I think the Perseans are going to endanger the Abandoned's home."

Claude continued to quiz him. "How do you gather all that, Blob? Just from this—this *vision*—for lack of a better word?"

Blob shrugged before answering, "It's hard to describe, it's just a feeling. I … *know* it's all real, somehow."

"Hmm," Max purred. "That's not good. That's not good at all. We already had to watch one epic world get destroyed by those jerks. We can't let them to do it the Abandoned. They're our friends! We have to warn Angus somehow. Come on, let's go! Let's salute these vapor dudes and get back to the *Planet Hopper*!"

The leader of the strange Centaurians took away the purple gemstone. Its three red eyes glowed as it reached over and placed the gemstone back on a makeshift altar. The big Boor stood up, and before joining the boys, he smiled and bowed, locking eyes with the leader. They were a fiery red, as if pulsing with the very blood of the mega volcano.

All of this has happened before, Blob thought. *Must be a space-time continuum thing?*

He gazed over at the purple gemstone on the altar, shrugged, and turned to go. Something made him glance over his shoulder one last time to regard the odd aliens. Their red eyes and flaming hands were something out of a story Blob's mom would recite to him and his siblings back on Boor when he was a child.

***

Riding their boards on hover mode to the appointed rendezvous location Blob was relieved when they made it over the final rise and the *Planet Hopper* was there waiting for them. Behind their spaceship was the titanic dark gray outline of the slope of the mega volcano. Lightning strikes illuminated the silver clouds that shrouded the caldera in an uneven pattern. The long slope of the mega volcano was a pure black sheet, other than a tiny orange beacon of light at the top, breaking through the clouds. One last flare of lava to mark the pinnacle of their achievement.

CHAPTER ELEVEN

The Argument for Life

Why is there always so much resistance to every single project I bring before them? mused Piper Crane, Chief Executive Officer of the much-maligned Terraform Division of the Ugovernment. She was beyond frustrated, and things were coming to a head that evening.

It seemed as if the unthinkable was about to happen. After Udecades of trying to get an increase in funding from the Universal Government hacks, she and her team of astrobiologists were facing a drastic *decrease* in resources. Without Ugov support, there wouldn't be enough privately sourced bitcoin to make the millennia-old tradition of terraforming viable any longer.

My father didn't work his whole life to create this division to have it get voted away. She grimaced at the cityscape from a vast open air sky deck overlooking the hubbub. She *hated* having to travel to Sun City. Fumes from between moonscrapers streamed ever upward in a white spiral to the sky, nauseating her. Off in the distance, the dark green mountains basked in twilight. She imagined being up there, walking on a trail, breathing in the fresh air from the Corwin Trees, but the chemical stink of the city ruined the sentiment.

Thus far, no matter what excuse they brought to her regarding the need to cut back on funding, she had been able to distract them with data-supported arguments. Her rationalizations pointed to the possibility of bitcoin profit as a bonus for funding terraform missions. Piper and her team wanted to use astrobiology as a tool to provide sanctum for those displaced by disasters like war, interstellar turbulence, such as solar flares and supernovae explosions, overpopulation due to virtual immortality, or even the utter decimation caused by Planet Ball.

With Sun City as its galactic headquarters, the Ugov made sure that their moonscrapers overwhelmed the skyline she gazed out upon. They hired the best architects in the galaxy to make sure theirs were taller and more modern than any of the Blackons' privately funded spires.

Piper was overwhelmed for a moment with the frenetic pace of it all. Peoples of all races, all sizes, shapes, descriptions, going about their business, zipping around in air cars or riding string chairs from moonscraper to moonscraper. The capital of Orion was where all aliens in the galaxy had to come to get their authorization to do practically anything, and it was no different for the Chief Executive. Every project she presented had to be ratified by high councils as if she were an ordinary Ucitizen. But it wasn't always that way.

Piper's predecessors, the original terraforming heroes that included her father, the esteemed Cris Crane, managed to meet the demands of the refugees of the first Galactic War. Every last request for resources was granted during that dark time, and for that she had to be thankful. Without that bitcoin from the Ugov high councils, there would have been no future for trillions of sentient beings that would have had nowhere to go because of the destruction of their home worlds.

That used to be unacceptable to the Ugov back then. They would never let aliens just... die. They cared for their fellow Ucitizens, and made sure they had planets to live on. And that's how it should *be now!*

But it *was* acceptable now—and there wasn't much she could do about it. Except trying to push more projects forward, using her team's expertise, and continue to hope that the Ugov officials who inspected her proposals found a rare element integral to synthetic manufacturing.

Isn't it an odd coincidence, she thought, *every project they approved in the past Udecade just* happened *to have the right combination of elements they needed for some other purpose? Something that, ultimately, would make them more black bitcoin than it would cost to fund our trip in the first place?*

An indicator light flashed on her wrist implant with a familiar accompanying beep, followed by the projection of a small holoimage of her top security officer, Royce Knox. His face was chiseled and scarred, but his expression confident and composed. Since her father had passed, Piper relished the paternal relationship that she had developed with Royce, and was always eager to talk to him.

"Knox!" Piper cried. "How are the preparations going? Will we make the launch window on time?"

"Yes, Chief Crane. All is on schedule. Have you finished your meeting with the high council?"

"Nope. Still waiting... out on this cold sky deck, if you can believe it. The Ugov, late for an appointment, what are the chances?"

"High percentage," Knox replied. "But I believe the council will ratify our project, especially if we reveal the rare element data. But if they don't—"

"Uh-huh," she interrupted him frequently. "Let's hope we don't have to go there. Meanwhile, I'm stuck here in this noxious, post-urban gas hole—" she gestured around her as if Knox could smell it too—"when I could be in the lab with Melia, doing actual *work*."

"This *is* work, Piper," Knox lectured. "It's part of the job."

"It shouldn't have to be!"

Royce Knox always kept a composed tone to his voice. "Well, everything takes black bitcoin, without it, the work of your father—his genius—will be wasted. We've been over this before, Piper."

She sighed. "Well, I guess I just needed to hear it again." *Oh, my dear father...*

A contingent of Ugov employees milled about near the air tube entrance to the council rooms. All wore cheek plates and bore the same white terrestrial suits, with the easily recognizable signature blue planet graphic emblazoned upon their sternums. Blue sashes rode down each pant leg to accompany the graphic. It was, without a doubt, the most popular wardrobe in the galaxy.

"All right, Knox, they're here, gotta go, make sure you talk to Melia and make sure that—"

"She gets the new synthetic fertilizer numbers. I already uploaded them." He smiled wryly. He was first to click the off button. She was left staring at empty space for a Usecond.

***

Once all had arrived in the meeting chambers, one of the councilors motioned Piper to a floating chair. There were supposed to be fourteen of them in attendance, all but one of

140

which would have the auspicious sensor port inserted into their left cheekbone. Piper found it puzzling, *we win a war against androids, banish them to the Sagittarius Arm, and our elite leaders look more and more like them every Uday.*

"Councilman Shuler, Councilwoman Martins," she addressed the elders of the group first, as was custom. "Thank you for taking the time to meet with me." She hoped it wasn't too sarcastic a tone. She didn't want to start insulting them—*yet.* But she couldn't help herself, they were over a Uhour late.

Shuler spoke first. "Chief Executive Crane, sorry for the delay. We are interested in learning about your project to explore the Outer Cygnus Arm. Tell us more."

Piper surveyed the other councilors present. "Councilman Adonis was not able to attend, I deduce?"

"No," Martins replied. "He wasn't. But he did send a message..." The councilwoman had already activated the screen, otherwise Piper would have shrugged it off and begun the meeting.

Popping up in crisp, clean resolution indicative of Ugov technology was a man's face. His dark eyebrows and short beard of the same color framed a handsome face. Adorning his head was a small crop of black hair, with silver strands woven within. He never wore the traditional white and blue suit of the Ugov councilors—nor would he ever submit to a cheek plate.

"Executive Crane," his phlegmatic voice came on. "Thank you so much for making the trip to Sun City."

Uh, excuse me? Piper was quickly annoyed. *I wasn't on a project deep in outer space,* she conversed with him internally. *I was at the main lab here on New Earth. It's not a very long trip on the lev-train, Councilman.*

Adonis's holo continued. "I am so sorry I was unable to attend with the rest of the councilors. I had to tend to matters over in Sagittarius. Rowdy androids, you know the deal... But I will make sure Councilman Shuler and Councilwoman Martins update me on all the proceedings. Until next time." He bowed his chin slightly to the camera, removed eye contact, and the hologram screen flashed off, but for Piper, his presence still lingered in the room.

"So," the councilwoman floating across from her said, "Executive Crane, shall we get down to business?"

Nice choice of words, Martins. It's all about business for your kind, isn't it?

"Has it been confirmed you have discovered traces of rare elements in the rotating metal core of one of your exoplanets? Can you corroborate?"

"Well…" Piper said, holding her breath for a moment. "Right to the heart of the matter, eh? Yes, Councilman Martins. To answer your blunt question, there is a surplus of modular data from our initial flyby scans. One of our drones picked up irrefutable readings. There *are* rare earths present. In which case, we could help to pay back the funding we so desperately need. It's not a mystery why I'm here before you, councilors." She floated up in her chair and waved her arms at the procession. "It's not *our* mission to recoup precious metals for the Ugov. There is a whole other division dedicated to that pursuit, no?" She fixed her gaze on one specific man out of the fourteen councilors present, a bald-headed, cantankerous elderly man, Executive Zander. Her pause in speech and abrupt head jerk made it clear she had identified him for who he was: the Chief Executive Officer of the Mining and Recovery Division of the Ugovernment. Her foe. "Executive Zander is in attendance, I see. Greetings, Councilman."

He spat a fake courtesy back her way, avoiding her piercing almond eyed stare.

"And," continued Piper, gesturing back to the other councilors, "I'm sure he'll be more than pleased to take care of all the extractions. When the time comes. So, yes, we can help scout the systems, send some initial probes down to the surface of viable exoplanets within our search list. We will gladly provide that data, and Executive Zander can do as he wishes—*with* the understanding that he will abide with Ugovernment law, and won't interfere with terraforming operations. It's got to be clean cutting, Councilman. All emissions matter when we're crafting a biosphere."

She smirked at the bald man: his neurolink cheek plate registered several dim green lights, one flickering on and off in a seemingly random pattern. His floating chair drew back, allowing one of the other councilors to form a slight buffer between them. He always stayed behind his curtain of protection, keeping Piper at bay with his cronies.

Another councilor spoke, a young man she did not recognize. Councilman Lawrence his title glowed above him. "With all due respect, Executive Crane, the wars are long over. There is no need for filling these uninhabitable worlds that you have planned to birth. Terraforming was designed as an experimental technique to meet a demand for refugees. Ucenturies ago."

Another Zander clone. The young Ugov Councilman was slobbering as he spoke; as if he could taste the spoils of the prospected digs to come. Piper stared at Lawrence's eyes until he averted them and floated back.

Martins confirmed Lawrence's notion. "There are no more refugees, Executive Crane. There are no more wars. Therefore, there is no clear need for creating habitable worlds. We have no aliens to live on them."

Piper rose her voice an octave or two. "Councilors, we are trying to do the Ugov a favor. There are so many different ways that our terraforming projects are beneficial to the overall bitcoin black line for the Ugov. It's not a matter of refugees alone. Let me lay a few of them out for you, just in case you may have forgotten since the last holo I posted..."

"For one, there is *always* going to be the overpopulation issue. With our genetic modification methods and AI wrist implants, the Ugov citizen has become virtually immortal. This means living an indefinite period of time. Which in turn leads to large progenies eating a lot of food, drinking a lot of water and using, in general, enough resources to cause intergalactic instability. The Ugov will need places these excessive consumers can go to buy up all the products the Blackons are selling."

She scanned the small congregation in front of her for signs of affirmation. A couple of the councilors might have nodded, but she might have been looking too hard. She continued, regardless of the reception. "Then, of course, there is the frequent interstellar turbulence that takes out many of our fellow Ucitizens' home worlds. Supernovae explosions, black hole gravity pull zone extensions, solar flares, rogue asteroid belts... this is another huge source of displacement. *We* can accommodate them. *We* have the means to create enough worlds to stay ahead of the problem, to reduce suffering among our constituents. New worlds can be self-sufficient within a few Uyears, therefore recouping the investment at that time... all the while making sure Ugov bitcoins are in the black."

She paused for emphasis, before spurting: "And what about the Planet Ballers? The giant scourge have destroyed so many worlds and put so many others at risk, spawning periods of mass Diaspora, and when they next throw planets around, Ucitizens will be forced to flee—"

"Executive Crane," Councilman Shuler interrupted, "there haven't been any Planet Ball tournaments in half a Ucentury, it was part of the treaty the Perseans signed off on. The Giant Beings have been neutralized and remain banished to their arm of the galaxy. All the hyperspace sheaths to and from the Perseus Arm are permanently blockaded. They don't factor into this—*whatsoever.*"

She ignored him. "I, myself—like any rational Ugov citizen—know full well the Persean truce is merely a temporary abide, and that those despicable giants will be back at their hobby invariably."

There was a grumbling among the fourteen. Piper used her most impassioned voice to slice through the low voices. "Terraforming has brought goodness and sanctity to the galaxy. My team, we are astrobiologists. We do so much more than create havens for displaced Ucitizens. We also discover new organic life, with advancements to science that are *invaluable*. The unique chemical processes that we use while making life work in different modes than ours have resulted in many, many breakthroughs in bioengineering. Helping food production. Medical advancements. It's not exclusively materials for hyperspace sheaths, IG spaceships, and moonscrapers you're acquiring from these worlds we discover for you. Think about everything else the Milky Way gains with the bitcoin funding we are asking for. It's not for building expensive planetary oases for displaced Ugov citizens... it's for the discoveries that propel Sun People into the future. My division holds that key. Give us the means to wield our skills. Choose life over death."

The meeting chamber was silent for a moment.

Martins broke the silence. "Let us deliberate for a few Uminutes, Executive Crane. We'll holo you on the sky deck as soon as we have decided. Thank you again for all your efforts." Martins nodded to Piper before swiping lightly on her cheek plate, obscuring her expression.

The thirteen councilors floated together into a flock, withdrawing to confer in small groups.

***

What rational argument could shoot down such passionate proselytizing? Piper smirked and shook her head. *Yeah, right— nothing is sacred among the moonscrapers of Sun City.*

She went out and strolled the sky deck adjacent to the meeting chambers, gazing up the length of the building that housed the seat of Universal Government in the Milky Way. Because Sun City was *the* major hub for all governing procedures, many of the moonscrapers within her view housed important divisions of the Ugovernment. They were probably holding their own caucuses, within their own meeting chambers, at this very moment. Ad infinitum. It was happening all around her—politicking at an exponential level.

But each moonscraper was more than simply a place to legislate; it was practically a city within itself, complete with residential floors, entertainment centers, restaurant services, markets, and virtual reality centers. It gave her a measure of peace to see ordinary humans and aliens milling about, blissfully ignorant from the constraints of Ugov politics.

Ambient lighting from the rail glowed through her hands as she grabbed and leaned outward over the edge of the sky deck. Wafting in the air was the smell of turbine emissions mixed with the ether exhaust coming from the sky cars zipping by in patterned routes. Reddish streaks were left in their wakes. She stared at one of the streaks until it dissipated.

This is why we need new worlds.

She pictured the faces of her exploration team, no doubt they were busily preparing the *Lifebringer* for their mission to Outer Cygnus. They were her best friends, her allies, and her trusted colleagues. They were the carriers of her and her father's dream: to advance the field of astrobiology and create habitable worlds— thereby generating the means of salvation for trillions of aliens.

Melia, her first officer, was the other half of her brain. They completed each other. They even looked alike, although, Melia was shorter than Piper, had green eyes—not dark brown—and was…well, if she was being honest, more well-endowed. Their leadership styles differed, however. The chief was bossy and conservative, the chief's mate was obliging and liberal. Friends for Udecades, they could recite each other's stories, all the love and loss, all the jobs and education, all the travels and adventures. Piper treated Melia more as a peer than a subordinate—whereas, with the rest of the crew, although she adored them, she wasn't shy on giving them a good tongue lashing, when warranted.

Nala and Carrysa were her most devoted workers. They ran the lab and had to listen to orders from Piper in a gruff tone (and Melia in an amiable one) pretty much all Uday, every Uday. Marjorie, a mixed-race Algorean, was in charge of robotics. And then there was John, the lead pilot of their IG spaceship, and her unofficial advisor. He was the oldest member of the group, and the only male crew mate, living a few Udecades longer than the rest. He'd never reveal exactly how old he was, but he was a part of the division even before the legendary Cris Crane, Piper's father and founder of the modern incarnation of Terraforming.

"Executive Crane?" a voice interrupted her thoughts, she turned to be greeted by a cheek plate glowing with a pale green light. It was one of the councilors come to retrieve her. "We are reconvening now. I think you will be pleased with our findings."

***

Shortly after the council notified Piper her division would be granted the funds to pay for the Outer Cygnus project, the meeting adjourned, and while councilors lingered to discuss details with Chief Crane, one of the thirteen attendees excused himself right away and left the room. He descended several floors by air tube, passed through a hallway of impeccably black synthmetal, and entered a large business park by activating a portal.

Every few steps he glanced over his shoulder.

Because of his formal appearance, he mixed right in with the crowd, as most of them were wearing the same white and blue lapel coat, with cheekplates covering a portion of their faces. People were milling about at their leisure, conversations rising and falling. He sought a place providing enough background filter noise to make a private holocall. All it would take is one Ugov official overhearing the conversation he was about to have—and he'd be on his way to Galaxy's End.

His opportunity arose. A giggling couple vacated a private floating bench, walking away arm in arm into the flow of foot traffic. The bench was separated from the main thoroughfare, and had a view in all directions. No one could sneak up and eavesdrop on him there. He slumped on the bench and clicked the holocall button on his wrist implant

The call bar loaded on the mini holoscreen projected above his wrist and he took the small cube and made it larger, but still small enough to snuff out quickly if need be.

A face materialized with a dark, manicured beard, with long silver streaks, outlining a pointed chin and deep inset eyes. He wore a traditional black suit of his ilk, skintight with a golden circle on the breast. He was one of the group of hyper-capitalists that received the moniker "Blackons" because of their singular purpose: adding black to their bitcoins.

"Councilman Dorayne."

"Myrtel Hemperley."

"What news do you have for me?"

"Important. The council met with Chief Crane moments ago."

"And…?"

Dorayne gulped nervously before he relayed the news, fearing the powerful man's reaction. "Councilman Shuler and Martins were in favor and swung the majority vote to approve funding—they are going to extend the terraforming proposal zone. It will now include Outer Cygnus and the Uehara solar system. And all of its neighboring systems." He delayed for a Usecond before saying: "It's in the general vicinity of the Abandoned asteroid belt... "

"I know where it's located, Dorayne!"

"They are going on a mission within a few Udays to scout the area. Executive Zander got on board as soon as Piper Crane flaunted the possibility of rare elements being present in the Ueharan solar system."

"Galaxies! That greedy bastard!"

"I think we should contact our mutual friends and alert them of the proposed Ugov activity. Isn't that the location they are planning to use for their next—"

"Of course we should, Dorayne, don't state the obvious. Do you have anything useful to add? Any other intel that makes this conversation necessary?"

"Well... I..."

Before Dorayne could muster a reply, the holocall blinked off. He sat in silence with his thoughts for a moment. When he got up off the floating bench and merged back into the crowd, he had to wipe the perspiration from his forehead.

CHAPTER TWELVE

A Black and Red Galaxy

The loud shout of the rider blurted from the sound monitors, setting off a cry of dismay throughout the crowd. Myrtel Hemperley grunted at the visceral reaction, leaning forward in his personal luxury viewing box to spy on the action.

The Ratite Arena on Myrtel World had a full capacity of a hundred thousand mostly Sunish people, each and every one of them standing on the floating bleachers, cheering louder and louder each time a rider made a dangerous move on the muddy racetrack. One particular rider was stuck in place, unable to move, right on the corner of a sharp turn. The poor rider was wedged into the gap below one of the low retaining walls, and a stampede of riders and their beasts were charging directly at the unfortunate athlete!

The elite patrons in neighboring view boxes started shouting. "Oh, no!"

"That rider is going to die!"

"Good galaxy, no! The stampede is going to run him over!"

"Watch out! Watch out!"

"Somebody help him!"

"I can't watch!"

Myrtel had promoted the event for Uweeks, and this was an important race, one of the biggest of the Uday, and it was shaping up to be the most entertaining of the Uday as well. He loved watching the competing riders. It was a true contest of agility and control, bouncing up and down on their two-legged, flightless bird mounts, all of them attempting to reach the finish line before the seven other riders. The over-sized birds weighed more than three hundred kilograms, but were still able to get off the ground by performing little leaps, their impotent wings fluttering in a futile attempt to stay airborne.

All of the holoscreen monitors in the arena, including the oppressively large one hovering over the maze, projected a close up of the action in high resolution.

A communal gasp breathed through the arena—would he be able to free himself before he and his mount were trampled to death? Donning a laser whip, the trapped rider attempted to zap the big bird in its rump. It was one amazing specimen of a mount, all legs and puffy gray feathers and eyes, furiously twitching and shaking while trying to free itself.

The rider's leg was pinned tight under the weight of the ratite. Any longer and it would certainly mean... The bot cameras zipped in to give a close-up shot to the fans, revealing it was a woman, *not* a man, as most of the crowd had assumed, who was trapped. She wore an all-black uniform and protective goggles over her eyes, the red lenses glowing intensely. At the last moment, the rider managed to wiggle her upper body loose. She reached out, scooped up the laser whip, and provided her mount the gumption to push itself free of the padded corner. The competitor leapt up acrobatically from the dirt and slid onto the saddle of her steed, snapping the reigns hard. Within an instant they were skittering along behind the rest of the racers, who passed them as they were reaccelerating.

The crowd loved it—exhorting the Red Lens Rider to get back into the race. Myrtel guessed that even those who had bet against her couldn't help but cheer for her now—such a dramatic escape garnered support. It was not a foregone conclusion riders would survive a Uday of racing at the Ratite Arena. Causalities were not out of the ordinary. Once every few races, a rider or mount (sometimes both) was crushed or battered by the laws of physics—or the law of being in the wrong place at the wrong time.

This might be one of those races, Myrtel thought as he checked for a message. Again. As he had already done several times. Waiting was not one of Myrtel's strong suits, and he was ready to throw a fit when the man finally showed up for their meeting. *Where is this imbecile?*

Hemperley's appointment was with Dmitri Stack, a man who came from the same elite class dubbed the Blackons, and he was unapologetic when he came stomping off the conveyor into Myrtel's personal viewing box. Not many had the audacity to come to another Blackon's *personal* solar system, be late, and complain about the hospitality—but this was Dmitri Stack, broker of state of the art "defense" systems.

"Hemperley," Stack whined, a short hunch-backed man with thinning gray hair, "it would be so lovely if I could have an elixir in my hand. I have a miserable headache, and this crowd noise... can't you enclose your view box and we can watch on the holoscreen? I mean, really..."

The man had an annoying voice, and his non-stop diatribes were unbearable. Myrtel would have to interrupt him if he ever wanted to get a word in.

"... and by the way, these aren't that good of racers, I was watching the holo on the air limo over to the arena, I've seen better over in the Orelyd—whatever the damned galaxies you call it—systems." Stack kept blabbering. "... where did you get these mongrels anyway, Hemperley? I wouldn't have any idea on who to bet on... you're going to have to show me current rider statistics..."

Myrtel feigned a genuine salutation. "Dmitri, welcome to—"

"Hemperley, again, Good Galaxies! Where is my elixir? I can't do business without a good tasting..."

Myrtel responded by waving his hand over his head. An attractive female attendant picked up the command immediately, and a tall green glass of elixir was set on a floating beverage holder within reach of his maligned guest. Myrtel despised dealing with most of his Blackon peers. *Look at him, absolutely no sense of decorum.*

"Ahh," Stack said, putting his dirty boots up on the floating table between them. "Now *this* is more like it."

Myrtel's open-air private seating box provided the best view in the arena, dead center and halfway between the lower bowl and the upper bowl. A general admission ticket to Ratite Arena cost enough black bit for most Ucitizens to live off for five Uyears, and the front row seats—where you could feel the dirt kicked up into your face, and could smell the breath of the ratites as they raced past—well those could cost more than buying a small moon.

"There's that Red Lens Rider again!" Dmitri exclaimed. "There she goes! Does she race again today? I want to place a bet, even though she wears red glasses, and I rarely bet on red, there's something about her... she must be..."

Myrtel forced a laugh. "She's the great granddaughter of the infamous beast trainer Jakob Klaberkiss... and she is considered the best rider in the galaxy. She descends from the Great Purple Rider clans."

"Oh, please," Dmitri replied. "I don't believe that for a Usecond. She can't be that good?"

Myrtel raised an eyebrow sensing a chance to put more black on his bit. "She'll win this race. I guarantee it."

Judging by the circumstances of the race, it was inconceivable she could be victorious: there were two sections left, and the young woman was a full ten lengths behind the main pack. In addition, ahead of those six riders, running on his own, was a veteran rider on a brown-feathered steed. Long, thin, stilt-like legs pitter-pattered across the track. The veteran was so far ahead he couldn't be caught by the pack, much less by the Red Lens Rider.

"I'll take that bet." Dmitri smirked at him.

Myrtel raised his other eyebrow, spinning his web further. "The betting bots are closed until after each race."

Dmitri's smirk grew. "I'm not talking through the system, Myrtel. I'm talking a personal bet. You and me. A friendly bet between fellow Blackons. The girl loses this race."

Myrtel locked eyes with the diminutive man. He was dressed in all black, with a golden coin lapel on the right breast, the signature symbol of their dark cult of financial moguls. Myrtel, conversely, was a tall man, with a triangular gray beard covering a chin that jutted out from his rounded face. His eyes were a fierce blue, squinting ever tighter as Stack drew his ire.

"What? A man who owns the best gambling planets in the galaxy is afraid to make a bet? C'mon, Hemperley, put your bitcoin where your mouth is!"

Without a word, Myrtel pressed on his mini-holoscreen and tapped in the details. Seven trillion bit. Straight bet. Lady Red Lens to lose. Dmitri (for once) did not speak, but nodded his agreement to the terms, and they settled back into their floating seats.

Myrtel watched the maze with his naked eye to get a better perspective of how much ground Lady Red Lens had to make up. The main holoscreen above the dome showed a close-up view of the action, filmed by floating drone cameras posted in every possible location of the race track, so most of the spectators in the viewing boxes had their heads craned upward, away from the action.

As if on cue, Lady Red Lens's mount accelerated, leaping completely over sections of the racetrack designed for traversing up, then back down. The gap closed. A stumble in the lead group caused a minor collision, and the two steeds and their riders jostled a bit, having to slow to avoid tumbling off. This allowed her to catch and pass them easily, hurdling over one of her opponent's ratite, and landing on top of the other, before bouncing into the clear. A few swings of her laser whip kept her momentum going, and before the section was complete, Lady Red Lens and her three hundred kilogram bird were leading the main group.

Jump by jump, she was reeling in the leader.

Dmitri's lips were pressed together tightly as he clicked the kilometers per hour estimates to track the speed of the two finalists. His screen showed the two riders as color arcs; the trailing arc was gaining on the lead one. Myrtel clicked a button on his wrist implant nonchalantly. A Usecond later the veteran rider on the lead bird, who assumed he was in the clear for the last lap and was going to be able to coast to victory, was bucked off his steed. Spinning and twisting in the air, a full five meters up, the surprised rider landed with a splat—right in the path of the charging Lady Red Lens. *Crunch!* Her ratite trampled the veteran as he cried out.

On she sped, never looking back again, all the way through the finish line for the victory.

The roar of the arena was deafening. A hundred thousand limbs were shaking in the air at once. Myrtel smiled. Genuinely, this time.

Stack wasn't smiling. "Hmmph. Well, well. I guess you know your riders, Myrtel. I should have expected it. But I enjoy wagering... *against* long shots. The pay off is much more... satisfying when I win. I'll have my bankers credit your bitcoin."

As Stack tapped a few buttons to make the electronic transaction he went on a signature rant. "So, Mr. Hemperley, king of your very own solar system, other than the privileged Sunish attending this race—how elitist of you, by the way—tell me now, why is it you invited me here? Not to take my seven trillion bit on a sucker bet, I'm quite sure. You sneeze seven trillion bit. What is it? Let me guess, this will be so much fun... I know! You need credit for a new project, a new moon, perhaps? An elixir-manufacturing planet? Maybe I can recoup my losses by overcharging you. Ha. Ha. No, that can't be it... my bitcoin *is* blacker than yours, of course, but..."

Myrtel fixed him with a cold blue eyes. *How nice it would be to have you sizzled in a laser sauna... on a slow setting.* His menacing stare was rendered impotent by Dmitri, who was busy staring at the glamorous attendants as they did their best to appear busy. Myrtel snapped his fingers, and the women left, much to the chagrin of his guest, who pouted as he watched them go.

"Dmitri," Myrtel said, "the Milky Way is ready for a change. Peace has brought less freedom and wealth to *our* peoples, but improved the lives of aliens and mutants and androids, living thousands of light years from us. There is no equity in that. What do aliens in another arm of the galaxy really mean to Orion? The Ugovernment laws decide how much black to red ratio any of us truly have. With my new system in place I can offer you no limit on solar system expansion, no limit on gambling profits, hands-off all of your illicit investments. We would have complete control over the finances of the galaxy."

"Ha!" Dmitri laughed, hamming it up by doubling over with self-amusement. "That sounds great, for us, all this 'hands-off' governing. And what makes you think we don't already have complete control of most of the black bitcoin in Orion? And you?

What about you? What is it that you personally get from this great, new, shiny and wonderful system of governing? To be king? To rule by sitting on a golden throne in Sun City?"

I will kill this man someday, Myrtel thought, imagining how good it would feel to throw him from his viewing box—the satisfying sound of the thud when Stack's body hit the ground one hundred meters below.

"Dmitri," Myrtel continued to control himself from erupting. "You and I both know that the Ugov has its tendrils in every last transaction you make, or any Ucitizen for that matter. Their mainframe system is indefatigable. Their tracking systems unavoidable. If they have the military to keep that virtual net in place—"

"That's no dopamine stimulating holo newsflash, Myrtel. The Ugov has always tried to prevent Blackon solar expansion projects. And so—what? Your new system will allow us unfettered access? That's great in theory, but what possible coup could displace a military as potent as the Ugov's? Even my droid mercenaries have their limits."

"I cannot reveal my methods yet. But suffice it to say that I have a powerful ally, an old nemesis of the Sun Peoples dominion, who possess a tremendous weapon."

"Perseans!" Dmitri deduced, clapping his hands together as the idea came to him, infuriating Myrtel. "I should have guessed that's what this meeting was all about! This is about Perseans, isn't it?"

"Listen to me, Stack," Myrtel wheezed. "They are on the rise, as is their slogan: 'Always forward.' There's no stopping them. It's a matter of time. They are poised and ready to resume Planet Ball play and will defend that right at any cost. Even if that means starting another war."

"Great, and you want me to be complicit in beginning the next galactic war? I should be so privileged! Really? Even for you Myrtel, this is crazy! You must think I'm a—*arrgh!*"

The little man was cut off mid-sentence as Myrtel snapped out his arm and snatched his neck firmly within his grasp and brought the cowering man's face inches away from his own. "Listen carefully, you sniveling fool. I'm not *asking* for your bitcoin and droids. I'm *telling* you that you are going to help finance and protect my plans. In return, I will *not* snuff the breath from your lungs for the very last time. Remember this, Dmitri: immortality exists only when you have oxygen in your lungs. I will pay upfront for rental of the droids, and pay back any borrowed bitcoin with interest. You will see that it's not the myth of inexhaustibility that the Ugov lobbies against, it's the promise of continuous progress. To move the galaxy forward, we Blackons have to allow it to grow—*without* limitations. We must eliminate the Universal Law that binds us. We must allow Perseans to play their game." Myrtel lessened his grip. The twitching man finally breathed in a gasp of air.

"Now… you *will* get your investors to lend me the black I need on my bitcoin and prepare the droid army. I will lead the overthrow of the Ugov with the assistance of the Perseans. The Giant Beings will be free of constraints on their traditional way of life, and in return will not bother with our side of the galaxy again. It is the best way to have peace *and* progress. Now," he turned the frightened man around, grabbed the nape of his black cloak and leaned him out over the edge of the view box so he could get a real sense of how far down it was. There were jagged railings, posts and other obstacles, each with the capability of impalement, looming below.

"All right, all right!" Dmitri shrieked. "You'll get all the support you want! You can use my droid army for half cost! Put me down, please, put me down!"

Myrtel slowly dragged him back into the view box. He was a bit disappointed that Dmitri gave in, watching him fall would have been much to his liking, but this was a necessary part of the deal.

After all, every coup needs financial backing. And Stack also happens to have a formidable army of drone mercenaries. That will come in handy at some juncture, I'm sure.

***

In Science We Trust, read part of the inscription, beginning at three hundred and sixty degrees, on the obverse side of the bitcoin in Myrtel's hand. More symbols continued on after the Ugov signature slogan, wrapping all the way around to meet it. The next part read: *Ugov Standard Bitcoin,* which was followed by a list of the arm, star, and planet where it was coded. His read: *Orion, Myrtel, Myrtel World.* Inside the ring of inscriptions was the slate black synthmetal comprising the mass of the device. They were used by every Ugov citizen in the galaxy. Without a bitcoin, a Ucitizen had no way of buying or selling anything of value, forced to barter foolishly, like a miserable, low-tech species living on some galaxy-forsaken planet.

He put his bitcoin back into its slot within his wrist implant and walked toward the starship docking bay. It was laughable to him that the shiny synthmetal disc—that held so much proverbial weight—in actuality was as light as a synthfoam fiber.

His mind turned to the meeting with Dmitri Stack... *That flittering little insect. And these are the kind of people we have managing all the bitcoin of the governed galaxy? It's amazing they're still functioning! Spineless. Not a thick bone in them, whatsoever.*

Stomping up the walkway to the air tubes, he ignored the gaping by those he passed, all of whom immediately recognized the face—literally—of the planet they were visiting. There were no residents in this private solar system, you were either a tourist or an "inhabitant," the latter there to perform one function or another to operate an eight-planet solar system. Ironically, it was terraformed by the best in the galaxy, none other than Piper Crane herself.

That woman will be trouble, no doubt. He recalled how hard it was to get her to cooperate with the builders and contractors when putting together his world for him. She was always pulling the Ugov card. *And now she's meddling in the Outer Cygnus Arm? This is another job for Councilman Dorayne.*

CHAPTER THIRTEEN

The Green Twins

"Hey Melia," Piper turned to her best friend, who was busy fiddling with mechanical gear. It had only been a few Uhours since they popped out of the hyperspace sheath in Outer Cygnus, and already she was hard at work. "Did we ever find out the cause for the drone blacking out yet?"

"Um, no," Melia replied, snapping a module into place. "I don't believe so. Kennedy takes all that data from the outpost receptors and compiles it back at the GTC. It takes awhile. I'm pretty sure he didn't have anything definitive before we left."

"Hmm, that's strange." Piper sighed. "We should be grateful for what data we *did* get, I guess. Without that last flyby, we never could have gotten the black bitcoin ticket."

"You mean finding a rare element in the spinning core of Uehara helped persuade them a little?"

"Yep."

"Ugh, I *hate* those councilor cronies. They take your genius and force you to use it for their purposes."

"Well," Piper shrugged. "I guess it's just part of the deal. I should be used to it by now, if I'm being honest…"

"It's pure corruption, that's all it is." Melia's eyes were filled with ambivalence as she walked over and reached out her hand. Piper took it and hauled her in for a long hug, then extended her arms so they were standing eye to eye.

"Don't worry, Melia." Piper smiled at her friend and touched her cheek gently. "I'll never let them get their mitts onto one of our pet planets unless I'm absolutely sure it won't meet our criteria. If we can't terraform it—well, we might as well give it up to Zander and his drill rigs. What other choice do we have? We can't go rallying funds from the Blackons. Then we'd *really* be on a leash."

The intercom buzzed with alarm frequency, shattering their heartfelt moment. The holoscreen popped up without either of them accepting the call—indicating an emergency call override.

John's face came up on the holo, and the dismay in his voice was palpable. "Piper, Melia—come up to the bridge, now!" The low-resolution image on the holoscreen couldn't hide the grimace on his face. John was a short, mostly balding man of mixed complexion. He was one of Piper's favorites, particularly devoted to Terraform protocols, and he would give his life for the safety of the crew aboard.

What now? Piper pushed off the interior compartment wall and floated to the terrestrial gravity chamber where she could stand on her feet. She slammed her fist on the open button and the slide door whooshed aside. Piper waved her arm at Melia following behind, and they ran up the narrow passage to the bridge.

When Piper and Melia rushed onto the bridge they found John staring out the front portal, jaw wide open, blinking his eyes in disbelief.

"Piper, Melia, I—I can't believe I'm saying this, but… Uehara is gone!"

"*What?*" Piper cried. "That's impossible. We got the readings back from that drone, what—two Uweeks ago?" This was one of Piper's prized site locations! She was sure it would pass the criterion. Disappointment hit her like a punch in the gut.

"That must be why the drone stopped giving transmissions!" Marjorie's deep voice bellowed from behind as she stomped onto the bridge. Marjorie's deep voice bellowed from behind as she stomped onto the bridge. With her hefty physique and tattooed face, Lifebringer's robotics engineer was a force to be reckoned with, but her normally buoyant personality was subdued by the view through the portal of the ship.

It was pure chaos. Meteoric collisions abounded. Sparks of energy from the collisions flashed in every direction, causing Piper to speculate whether the fiery mass might come close enough to endanger their spaceship. She focused on one particularly large, ovular-shaped planetesimal. It appeared to be a dark green flower, one that was losing its petals, piece by piece, slowly separating, as if the wind were blowing it apart. The planet once called Uehara.

All that flora and fauna, unique to the Milky Way, gone forever. Piper shook her head over and over.

"What could have caused it?" Carrysa asked what everyone else wanted to, breaking the stunned silence in the cockpit, as she and Nala had made it up to the bridge to witness the holocaust with the rest of the crew.

"I'm not sure," John conjectured. "Maybe the Abandoned asteroid belt has an outlying field of asteroids, arcing with long, irregular orbits?"

"No, John, that can't be right." Piper had to strain to hear Nala's voice every time she spoke. The dark featured Earthish woman was a delicate creature, but oh-so-nimble and quick, standing merely one and a half meters tall and slim as a laser beam.

She was so discreet she could usually come and go as she pleased without anyone noticing. A bonafide wraith. "The other planets seem to have been vaporized, or… at the very least, shattered into trillions of pieces."

John mumbled something under his breath as he clicked to long range scanning. Indeed Nala's observations were confirmed: every last one of its nineteen planetesimals were simply reduced to dust! It was as if everything in the solar system. The view on the holoscreen produced despondent faces on her crew. It was as if everything in the solar system was being… sucked up into the star.

Piper was inclined to address the team. "Hmm. Well, this is a major let down," she verbalized the crew's sentiments. "What's left but to take a few measurements, try to gather as much data as we can, and maybe the AI mainframe can come up with more answers?"

"Piper, shouldn't we—" Marjorie gasped in the middle of speaking. They witnessed a collision so fierce and bright that everyone shaded their eyes, even behind the protective layers of the front portal.

"Get the heck outta here?" Piper finished for her robotics engineer.

"Are those within striking range, John?" Melia asked.

"No, no." John tried to quell everyone's worst fear—a rogue chunk of debris hitting the ship. "It's all right, we're safe—for a bit longer. The models show the mass will not penetrate this far into space for a few more Uhours. The lighter projectiles might make it earlier, but *Lifebringer* can deal with those easily."

"All right!" Piper barked out. "That's enough time for a few receptor scans. Carrysa, can you take care of that? I'll go help Nala in the lab. Melia, you will finish up with the log for Uehara. John, once you're sure we're in a safe zone, start researching that unnamed system. I propose we'll call this next one 'Uehiron,' an ode to its fallen neighbor."

"Cool name, Piper," said Carrysa. "There must be a reason we are being diverted to Uehiron. Imagine what could possibly be waiting for us there. Maybe that's where we were supposed to go in the first place. Like fate, or something?"

Another bright explosion forced them to jump back. It might have been millions of kilometers away, but this one was still closer than the last.

"John." Piper motioned with her hand. "Speaking of fate... I'd prefer ours has nothing to do with those explosions—take us out as far from that mess as the receptors can still get an adequate scan going. Whatever sparse readings we get from this deceased system isn't more important than getting a hole punched into the side of *Lifebringer*."

"On it, Chief Crane," John responded, closing one holoscreen and grabbing onto the joystick.

Piper waved her arms at the girls. "Well, it's on to the next best prospect on the list. Uehiron, here we come. Let's do our jobs. This isn't the first time we've had a disappointment. Chins up, ladies!"

They all left the cockpit, but the glumness in their step was hard to ignore. Piper was left standing by herself for a moment as John fired up the thrusters.

***

Piper poured over the Uehiron data charts in her private chambers.

No matter how many different models she ran, they kept projecting that there was a good chance that sentient life had indeed developed on one of the planets of Uehiron. *That probably means the Ueharan system was populated with sentient beings as well, considering the mutual characteristics they shared.*

She reached for the Uweb button on her holoscreen, compacted into a window for easy sifting. Flashing on the screen one by one, she scrolled through images and text about the multitude of ways that terraformers had used over the millennia to create habitability. It didn't matter how desolate or cold, they had found at least marginal success. Even hot worlds, racked with carbon monoxide storms and devoid of any life, were game for the terraformers.

Cristopher Crane's Golden Age of Space Exploration made significant advances in astrobiology... Piper read—for the one-thousandth time in her life, she guessed.

"It's all about galactic archeology, my pretty little bird," Piper recalled her father saying to her. "There are a finite number of conditions we can adjust."

If a targeted solar system was in "too-young-of-a-stage," she had learned from him, the chaotic nature of bombarding particulate matter would render the prospective site untenable. Conversely, if the given solar system was in an elderly stage, it could be similarly futile to try to create there. It would be a dark, cold place, with a white dwarf slowly contracting into a potential black hole.

"New School" terraformers tried a variety of other techniques, including out-gassing from the core, effective for planets right on the verge, ones only needing a little kick start. But as for Piper, living in the shadow of her father's greatness, she preferred a mixture of techniques, old and new, and insisted each project first needed to be evaluated by the contemporary criterion... then individually-based methodology could be applied. His words played in her mind as if they were speaking on a holocall.

There was only one thing more exciting than building worlds—the possibility of discovering *special* beings. New, carbon-based, sentient life forms. Astrobiologists were innately altruistic; they wanted to help the helpless aliens of the Milky Way. But, it could be argued, that what was even more important for the welfare of Ucitizens was discovering new life, studying it, and finding unknown processes that allowed technology to evolve.

"Maybe you're the next big thing!" Piper said to the holoscreen. The AI rendering of the exoplanet Uehiron floated there peacefully; she wondered if it felt sorrow that its green twin had been destroyed, a few light years away.

CHAPTER FOURTEEN

The Giant's Game

It was an auspicious time for Persean culture. The Giant Beings stood precariously on the brink of no return. When they openly flaunted a Planet Ball tournament outside the Perseus Arm, it was a proverbial ion cannon blast across the bow of the Ugov. It was a provocation sure to draw retaliation. Perseans had to be confident in their powers and come together as a race if they wanted to defeat the Sun Peoples and turn the galactic order upside down. And no one understood the importance of the moment better than Wella.

The high lady stood in her chambers, squinting and staring into a set of holoscreens positioned in columns throughout the open air space. She wasn't focusing on any one screen, instead synthesizing the information from all the various pages. Among them: historical war documents, Planet Ball tournament guidelines, Persar general news, agribusiness data, new galactic archeology, cultural propaganda, and such. She liked to meditate while multiplatform mind tasking. It helped her tap the cognitive potential of her brain.

I'm going to need all the functional capacities I can get when I present my arguments at The Arrangings today.

"All close." She shut down the screens and opened a virtual mirror. Immaculately dressed, tucked into a gown of woven Persean bovine fur, the wife of the grand master also wore a traditional necklace of misshapen turquoise stones. She wore matching combs of the same blue-green shade perched into her long yellow hair. Putting on a fake smile, she tugged at the edges of her white gown, attempting to adjust what was flawless. But she had to be fastidious if she was going to make an impression in the Dome. And with so much at stake...

The Arrangings were a biannual forum attended by Persean elite. Although the event had been modernized over the centuries, much remained the same as when their ancestors would gather to drink, eat, dance, and parlay with each other (in that order), until all the "arrangements" necessary to keep peace among their peoples were agreed upon.

Laborious affairs, that sometimes lasted more than a week, the Arrangings commenced with the innocuous portion called Mingling, where the constituents spent time drinking elixirs and sharing informal pleasantries with each other. Any talk of business was frowned upon during this initial phase.

Next came Gorging—aptly named for the incredible amount of food the group would ingest, in a comparatively short period of time.

Later came Moshing, a form of physical dancing with body parts making contact with other body parts.

And lastly came the part they called Quarreling. The singular portion of the evening Wella was concerned about. In fact, she could do without all the other traditions, but that wasn't the case with most of the elite in attendance.

"Pathetic herd mentality," she hissed to her image in the holomirror. But at least the hardline traditionalists weren't being swayed to give up on galactic hegemony.

A cowardly generation of Perseans, these new ones, she thought, running her fingers through her yellow hair. The high lady feared the juveniles were becoming docile, and were willing to leave ownership of the Milky Way to the Sun Peoples indefinitely. She was determined to keep that from happening. *And it begins now!* She closed the holomirror and headed for the door.

***

When she arrived outside the Arrangers Dome Wella sought her allies among the swirl of the ladies' white gowns and the men's flapping red cloaks. She cast a sour gaze upon a group of younger attendees. Loitering about the entryway, they all seemed to be smiling at once, touching each other's shoulders and embracing— as if they were attending a pagan festival. Wella narrowed her eyes and shoved back her nausea. *It is an embarrassment to Persean culture! Arrangings aren't a celebration. They're administration. These youth feel entitled to live a life of constant ecstasy—they've absolutely no regard for the suffering the elders have endured in the past.*

One of the boisterous adolescents recognized her elegancy and, attempting to live up to the name of the initial portion of the grand procession, came over to mingle with her. *Hmm. Maybe not all of them?*

"Greetings, High Lady! Wella the Wise, I am so excited to be joining the Arrangings. I have much to—"

"What is your name?" Wella demanded.

"Bijr, third of my family line, born during the time of—"

"Listen carefully, Bijr." She worked him with her eyes, as if scanning a garbage processor for any signs of malfunction. She finished the assessment with her amber eyes locked on his. "I don't care what family line you come from, I don't care what era you were born in, you are merely the offspring of the wealthy and exalted, someone who has access to these holy proceedings by way of status, not through merit, not through your efforts to further the Perseans' rightful place in the galaxy…"

"But, my eminence," the look on his face was priceless as he tried to recover his dignity. "My wish is to serve the grand master and—"

"We don't care about your wishes. The Arrangings are not about the wishes of the younger generations. But you are obviously here for another reason. Go smile and enjoy the proceeds." She gestured to the slight bulge of his belly pressing against his shirt. "Especially the Gorging."

Wella pretended to turn and walk away, waiting for him to bite the lure.

"High Lady, please, I—"

Slowly, she turned back to face him, making sure to twirl her skirt. "Bijr. If your generation are going to be part of my movement, if you truly care about the traditions of Persean culture, you need to support me when I quarrel later. There are weak Perseans among you—" she motioned with her hands in small circles at the small clusters of young arrangers talking and drinking elixirs—"willing to bow down to the Sun Peoples. They want to avoid conflict by prohibiting their own people from Planet Ball tournaments." She stared into his eyes even deeper, surprising a smile as he twitched and took a small step back. "You and your little juvenile friends over there aren't those kind of people, are you?"

"Well, no, of course not. We… we support the grand master and his cause," came his automated reply. Her frown made him quickly add: "And we support the high lady."

174

"That's good." Wella smirked. "That's *very* good. Because we are ridding the Persar solar system of those dissenters. They will be viewed as a threat to security. As traitors. You know what happens to traitors of Persar?"

"Never!" cried Bijr. "Never, my lady. We will always stay loyal to the cause." He glanced over at the group of friends he had been consorting with. They had stopped their gay affairs, and were glancing his way with curiosity. "We may be juveniles, but we are supporters of the Persean traditions. *I'll* make sure of that."

"Good!" Wella said, folding her arms across her chest. "This next generation of players being trained, they need real Planet Ball, not models and virtual gaming. I want you to keep a close eye on Jhorken and Phellen, they are two up and comers, with passion for the game."

"And the grand master's nephew, Ezran, High Lady, what of him?"

She grimaced. "No. Leave him be. I want you to focus on the other two. Make sure they have true Persean ideals. Do you understand?"

"Always forward." Bijr saluted her with the gesture of their people: a hand made into a circle, flicked forward into open fingers, signifying a dome walker rolling through space, and the art of tossing a planetesimal.

She watched him retreat back to his cluster, peeking over his shoulder to see if she was still standing there regarding him. On his last turn she made sure to slip into the crowd, intermixing with a cluster of more esteemed arrangers, and took pleasure in watching his head jerk around trying to spy her again. Oh, yes, she had definitely made an impression.

In fact, their conversation affected Bijr measurably, because a little later on that evening, during the quarreling, he stood up in support of Wella's "Grounds for Play," a vindication speech in defense of upholding the great tradition of the sport the elders had loved so much. Bijr was reputed to be trustworthy and his passionate shouts elicited a similar response from several juveniles. They floated their chairs into the open air of the dome, one after another, in accordance. As the clamor rose, Wella made eye contact with Bijr. He beamed, seeking her approval.

She nodded and smiled, ever so slightly.

***

She was in a foul mood when I left her. Stergis pictured Wella at the Arrangings. *I can only imagine the fervor she is drumming up in the dome.*

He stood in a logistics chamber, waiting for a meeting with his top general, trying to ignore the holoscreens showing replays of the Ueharan tournament. He'd already watched the footage three times, and it merely served to remind him of the breach in security with the alien ship. Buele let them slip away…

He turned his mind away from the Outer Cygnus dilemma and called up a holovideo of Wella from one of their trips to the countryside. She was positively glowing in the image, twirling her skirt, her golden hair sparkling in Persar's glow.

He loved his wife, but they played such different roles. She was the spiritual and political figurehead of Persar, while he was more focused on Planet Ball and industry. They had been spending less and less time together since his rise through the ranks to the mantle of Grand Master.

Then, of course, there were the rumors about her… faithfulness. But he had never given them heed. *Pathetic attempts by dissenters to undermine me.*

But she was so lovely, and he was… well, not. He shut off the video and activated a holomirror. His reflection told the truth. The lines of aging were carved into his forehead and cheeks like dried canyon beds through a desolate moonscape. He sighed and walked over to the synthglass windows of the chamber. Below was a view of the hangar. The *Amalgamator* was on full display from his perch, the pale lighting of the hangar bay glistening across the polished black synthmetal. Now *she* is lovely.

"Grand Master…" His contemplations were broken as the General slid through the hissing of air valves on the entry door. Lorne, who had been in charge of eliminating the Cygnan alien threat back at the Uehara tournament, stepped in glumly. "Always forward. You wanted to meet with me?"

"You failed me."

"I did, Grand Master. I loathe the Uday."

"What were your commands?"

"Eliminate the alien threat."

"And why did you not follow through with those commands?"

"The spies managed to enter the depths of the Abandoned asteroid belt. Not even our starships could penetrate through the dense matter. We had to give up the chase or risk destroying a precious Persean warship. I made the order to enter the hyperspace sheath back to Persar."

"And, General Lorne, why was it so important to the Persean cause to eliminate this threat?"

"To avoid letting our enemies gain information about our ambitions."

"Yes, yes. That is indeed the case. We cannot let the Ugov tiny peoples have any reason to be looking in the far Outer Cygnus Arm. To them it is a wasteland. To us it is the collection of the most prized solar hoards that could ever be imagined."

"I highly doubt that the alien ship could have survived in the asteroid field, Grand Master. Even if they managed to escape temporarily, how could they have traveled back to Uehara without detection? My guess is that the threat eliminated itself."

"Your guess?" The grand master wasn't appeased by guesswork. He desired certainty.

Lorne shuffled his feet. "Our recon team is searching for any sign that a ship made the hyperspace journey anywhere near the Intergalactic Dividing Line. Thus far, Grand Master, there has been no indication that this is indeed the case. If they tried to go out this way, we'll find out soon enough. If they didn't, well, they are either stranded in deep space, or smashed into galactic dust."

"You'd better hope so, General."

"Grand Master, I have other news. Our tiny champion has been trying to contact us."

"What? Now?" Stergis shook his head in frustration. *That little Sun man better have good news for me.*

"It must be urgent. There has been a crescendo of pulsars near the galactic core; any communication through deep space from the Orion Arm has been shredded. However, there have been confirmations of attempts to come online with us."

Stergis hummed to himself.

Lorne observed the consternation on his superior's face. "Grand Master?" the general asked. "Will we be installing the new stellar stimulator technology?"

"We may be forced to, General. Get down to the com center. Alert me the moment his message is ready to be decoded."

CHAPTER FIFTEEN

The Prodigy and the Weapon

After meeting with his generals, Stergis took a lev-train to another part of the high latitude continent to visit his nephew Ezran at the Planet Ball Scholarship Hall. His young relative was his prodigy. Without a son of his own (Wella claimed her role in Persean politics was more important than providing him an heir), Stergis hoped that someday he could replace him as Grand Master of Perseus. Until then, the young man remained in the Scholarship Hall, Uday and night, hoping to become the next star of their sport.

This was one of the few duties Stergis enjoyed as grand master. A group of attendants greeted him cordially upon exiting the lev-train and walked beside him to the halls' entrance. Whenever he made his visits, both scholars and professors alike immediately spurted out a shell-shocked, "Always Forward," along with the appropriate hand gesture. As he sauntered through the long corridors of the institution, they stood and made the obligatory salute, without eye contact, then sat, returning to their duties with haste, as if the all-powerful grand master would sense if they were toiling efficiently.

Each chamber he passed had rows of holoscreens flashing brightly or dimly, depending on the content of the page the student was using. The screens were the solitary light source in the working chambers, causing a sporadic kaleidoscope of colored beams to splay throughout.

With an approving nod, Stergis and his entourage made their way to the air tube that would connect them to the practice facilities. *Time to survey the future of the sport, oh how I pray Ezran can hold the mantle.*

A familiar voice greeted Stergis with enthusiasm as soon as he entered the broad chamber where scholars were engaged in scrimmages. The Grand Scholar of Planet Ball must have been waiting right by the door for his arrival. "Always Forward! Good Uday, Grand Master! It has been too long since your last inspection. Thank you for coming, I'm sure our pupils will not disappoint you."

"Good Uday, Perk." He made the gesture. "Always Forward. Shall we start with my nephew, since he will no doubt convince me of your claims?"

As they walked, Perk expounded on news from the hall. "Ezran has been the top of his class, as usual, and he has been forming a cluster of potential Junior Planet Ball tournament entrants. Jhorken, Phellen, and a few others. Of course, before they can qualify, they must get past the pre-tournament scrimmages, which have become increasingly more challenging. Per your request. We want our future tournaments to bring Planet Ball to a new level that has never been seen before."

There he is! Stergis gazed upon the handsome young Persean man, ensconced in his private study chamber with several holoscreens open, and small icons floating in the air like virtual clouds, awaiting the touch of a finger to enable them. A resting vestibule, designed to replicate the hyperspace compartment of an intergalactic spaceship, was fixed to a wall of the chamber. *The young man must sleep here.* Even Stergis was impressed by that kind of dedication to the cause.

His nephew sensed the movement behind him and turned and smiled at his uncle. "Always Forward! Greetings, Grand Master."

"Ezran—Always Forward—so good to hear of your progress." Stergis pointed at the closest screen. "Ahh! You're working on variant toss outcomes. Quiz time. Please describe each, and provide an example."

Ezran beamed, eager to show off his knowledge. "Of course, Uncle. There are failed outcomes, providential outcomes, and preferential outcomes in any given toss. Failed outcomes are when a player creates a strategy that subsequently fails during round play, leaving the player at a disadvantage. Providential outcomes are when a player does not meet strategy objectives, but nevertheless retains an advantage related to the toss. Preferred outcomes are when a player meets strategy objectives and creates the specified advantage sought after.

"In the example on my holoscreen, I have been doing projections using *this* scenario: a player tosses their solar stone at a gap between one of their opponent's average size planets and its singular moon, with the objective being to curl the opponent's moon, so that it becomes dislodged of its orbit, and is pulled into the gravitational field of the parent planet, inducing a massive collision. A pretty simple toss objective.

"For the failed outcome scenario that keeps coming up on the computation diagrams, right there, yes," Ezran pointed to a smaller holoscreen. "It shows the action of the solar stone, and how it doesn't cause the intended collision to take place, but instead grazes the side of the singular moon, rendering the player's stone a pile of dust and rocks—a distribution that is clearly below the regulated size standards that a solar stone must meet in order to be useable by said player. Once the inter-solar sweeper comes through at the end of the round, and all the smaller matter is brought forward, there will be nothing left of the player's stone. A clear loss—and a toss I never would have taken."

Stergis raised his eyebrows and exchanged head nods with Perk, who had been listening intently off to the side.

Ezran smiled, basking in his uncle's obvious delight with his answer to the impromptu quiz. "All I have ever wanted," the young prodigy said, "since I was a little boy, was to keep the tradition,"

"Mark me, Ezran," said Stergis, ignoring the interaction. "We need high quality scrimmages before we can even *think* about filling the ranks of the professional divisions. We need young players who can hone their skills without the pressures of competing in a major event. So, Ezran, it falls on your shoulders. You *must* continue to challenge them to improve."

The grand master turned to regard Perk. "My sources tell me that Jhorken and Phellen have scored high enough on their virtual games that they could be promoted before the grand tournament in Outer Cygnus. Is this indeed the case?"

"Yes, Grand Master," Perk replied. "I believe I would promote them. They have defeated most of the solar board renderings that I can come up with. Usually, new recruits are below fifty percent success rate. Jhorken and Phellen are around ninety, ninety-five percent. But they are undisciplined. They take chances. That being said—"

"Yes, well," Ezran cut in, "I know another great player who has a similar style." He nodded to his uncle in a clear attempt at placation, which was fully and heartily gobbled up by the Persean leader.

"Ha!" laughed Stergis. "I suppose I *have* been known to gamble with an angle of decay here and there. On occasion…" It was part of the reason Stergis was such a fearsome Planet Baller—opponents had a hard time figuring out if he would gamble or play conservative.

"Uncle, I often wonder, what could possibly compare to the thrill of winning a tournament. Just taking a single round by clearing a zone—even a small victory within a game—what an incredible experience to have," Ezran waxed. "Oh how I wish I could feel it—to be in a live match, using good technique mixed with intuition…"

Stergis regarded his kin, blond hair, speckled yellow skin, eyes perfect white ovals containing piercing green pupils. *What noble features! He is a special one. Could he be the one to succeed me? Best not to even think of it—yet.*

"Uncle, may I make a request? I've proven my worth, haven't I?"

Stergis raised his eyebrows and put out his palms.

"Take me with you for the inaugural tournament."

The grand master slowly nodded to Ezran, giving him a quick squeeze on the shoulders. *The passion of Planet Ball burns white hot in his veins.* He did not want to risk putting his prodigy in danger, but how could he keep him from his destiny? Ezran would be aboard the *Amalgamator* to witness the inaugural first throw.

***

After finishing his tour—during which the grand master again elicited the wave-like up and down response of the underlings of the study hall, the words and hand gestures melding into each other as he walked past—he proceeded to the Grand Scholar's private chambers. It was time for a meeting that wasn't on the record.

Inside, Perk offered him a floating chair. Stergis examined the elder's domicile while settling in. Perk kept the place immaculate. An array of fine art and exotic plants gave his quarters a distinct decor, but also made it overcrowded and stuffy. Located in the recesses of the hall, below the boxy synthmetal edifice that housed the future stars of the sport, Perk's quarters were as private a location as you could find. Even so, upon entering, Stergis had secured the chamber door and had clicked on privacy settings so that anything spoken would be rubbed out with high frequency barbs. There was no possibility of recording and hearing the words that would be spoken.

"Where is it?" Stergis was eager to find out how much progress Perk had made on a prototype he had been working on. Perk reached up to a holocloud icon, pressed it, and entered a cryptic password that dissolved a nanosecond after activation. The room dimmed, adjusting for the image on a large holoscreen that opened up when Perk clicked a second time. The screen showed a solar board from afar, rotating the view three hundred and sixty degrees for the viewer in order to show every angle. Perk pressed a few more buttons and a sped-up version of the virtual tournament game progressed on the screen. Eventually, the last tosses are thrown, and all matter ends up shown burning up in the outer corona of the host star.

"Grand Master..." Perk tapped a few times and a new image appeared. "Here is the prototype unit. But the proximity it needs to be deployed from... it's relatively close."

"Ah ha," said Stergis, noting the ships evacuating from the solar board on the screen. "That's why they're making a quick getaway."

As the models played out, Stergis observed that the tournament award ceremony, usually held in close proximity of the host star, did not occur in the virtual rendering.

"Yes," Perk replied. "Astute observation, Grand Master. Our designers have not found a way to initiate the black hole triggering process without necessitating immediate retreat. Thus far, manufacturing a permanent buffer has eluded our engineers."

"Hmm." Stergis frowned. "That's of the utmost importance, Perk, although I'm sure you know that. If we can deploy the solar death sequence from each and every solar host, we can clean up the evidence of any tournament. When Ugov bacteria snooping around can't find any proof, well, that would change *everything*. We wouldn't have to go to war. Lose millions of Persean lives."

After a brief silence, expecting a prompt comment from the high scholar, Stergis raised his eyebrows. "Perk, do you need to say something?"

"Grand Master," Perk said, his voice wavering. "You inquired on the timing. And of the alternate usage. As a... *weapon*."

"And?"

"We believe we will have a prototype ready."

"*What?*" Stergis exclaimed, wide-eyed—this was an unexpected boon. "In time to use for the tournament?"

"Yes, hopefully. My team thinks we will be able to initiate a black hole sequence with a temporary buffer, giving us time to escape through the hyperspace sheath back to Persar."

Stergis narrowed his eyes—oh, the power he and his team would possess! They could literally erase the tiny viral scum, star by star. But could he truly defeat them, even with a weapon as powerful as this?

"That is excellent news, Perk. Tell your team they can increase their compensation. This is a significant accomplishment!"

Perk smiled meekly. Despite his loyalty, the older man was far from ignorant. He fully understood the ramifications of unleashing a black hole upon an ordinary solar system—it would remove every last trace of it, negating the existence of matter, while opening up the possibility of losing control of the sequence. A rogue black hole without a permanent buffer could mean...

Perk seemed flustered when he said, "But, Grand Master, I want to caution you. We haven't figured out a way to close the event horizon on a long-term basis, so even if we were able to activate the prototype unit—"

Stergis's stare halted him mid-sentence.

"Perk, you and your team have a job to do. Get me that buffer, with increased range. There's not much time. Don't disappoint me, or the Persean race. When Wella returns she will confirm that the Arrangings have ratified the location of the next grand tournament. We will unleash our stones on the neighboring system of Uehara. Soon, we are going to have to fold space and time to get to Cygnus Arm, and I want us to bring this technological capability with us. General Lorne will be checking in on your development team periodically. Understood?"

It was understood. Perk mumbled the creed and dismissed himself from his own quarters. He was trained to vacate after his debriefing whenever Stergis visited. The privacy bubble in his quarters was going to be utilized by the grand master to contact a special ally. A tiny being, far from Persar.

***

"Myrtel."

"Stergis."

"I take it our plans are in order?"

"No, not exactly. There is an issue."

"What issue?" Stergis's voice rose when the little alien spoke.

"A security issue. Your prospected host solar system for the next tournament has come under the attention of the Ugov. They have sent a terraform team to the Outer Cygnus Arm to explore the area for rare elements and signs of sentient life. That includes the twin system of Uehara."

"I see."

"You may have to rethink the timing of your next tournament."

"Rethink? Ha! Myrtel, do you really take Perseans so lightly? Our race is always moving forward, in case you haven't heard our saying. If Sun People are in the way when we play... they will be incinerated, befitting the bacterium that they are."

Myrtel growled, "Remember, Stergis, you are talking to a Sunish man. We have agreed to help each other, don't forget your side of the bargain."

Stergis's reply was similarly frosty. "And how could I possibly forget the fact that you are a Sun alien? We have to talk to each other through a translator program that takes half a city's worth of digital storage space."

A silence between them manifested.

Myrtel broke the silence. "And the new technology?"

"My team has the first prototype made. The range seems consistent with our needs."

"So—your team has found a way to kick start a sun into the dying process?"

"Yes."

"Have you wielded it yet?"

"Obviously not. The buffers are not in place. But they shall be soon."

"Well, other than this terraforming operation setback, everything seems to be progressing as scheduled... together we will be able to usher in a new galactic era and eliminate the Ugov elite."

"Those microscopic terraformers searching for their even smaller forms of bacterium on these distant solar systems... the absurdity of it! They will be the first casualties of the new war." Stergis made the Always Forward gesture and clicked off the ragged image on the holoscreen in Perk's quarters.

CHAPTER SIXTEEN

The Special
Spaceship

Max stood in the cockpit staring out the synthglass window at the Orb, a red glowing ball against the black backdrop of space. The Vapor People and their home of exploding volcanoes had to be a one of a kind phenomenon. *Completely isolated sentient beings, living out here among the ash. How do they manage?*

He mused on all the different life forms he had come across in his surf travels. From avians, to insects, to species that were harder to describe. *Like Mike and Claude.* He smiled to himself. *Ha— speaking of my furry friends... I better check on the boys.*

Max told Vern he'd be back up after doing the rounds and activated the portal door. He leapt off his feet and glided through the anti-gravity passageway to the main compartment. The door recognized him and opened automatically with a hiss.

"What's up, boys?" Max found Blob hovering over the twins by a large holoscreen.

"Hey, Max," they replied in turn, without taking their eyes off the imagery on display.

Blob had a frown across his whole face. "Cap, I'm having second thoughts. I was telling the twins, maybe that vision was just a vision, not the *actual* future. It's a long way back to the Abandoned, and we don't have kilos of supplies."

"Yeah, Cap," Mike threw in. "We need to get back to Oreldychyne."

"I wish we could call them to warn them…" Max mused out loud.

Claude had a quick reply. "I've already tried the Uweb code messaging system—there's too many pulsars blasting into deep space in between Centaurus and the Abandoned. There's only one way to get in touch with Angus's people…"

Max considered for a moment. "Hmm." On the one hand, they were pushing it pretty thin. They had prepared for a trip from the Last Ugov Outpost to Uehara and back. No asteroid belts or volcanoes were in the plan. There were emergency rations and water, but they had already begun to dip into those reserves.

Max was conflicted. *But what about Angus, Ariel… the* Terrastroid *and all those great people? They saved our lives, after all… no matter how special a pilot Vern is, we wouldn't have lasted long. It would have only been a matter of time until we were pulverized.*

"Blob," Max said, patting his auburn hair. "I think we're going to have to trust your instincts on this one… I mean, your visions seemed pretty specific.."

"Yep, Captain," Blob nodded, his monobrow straightening. "Those see-through space bubble things were there, and, immediately after, the *Terrastroid*. Our friends. There were explosions going on too. Big ones! Bigger than what you would expect from what passes for a normal Uday in that crazy place."

"That's enough for me," declared Max. "We met those Vapor Peoples for a reason. This must be why. We have to go there and change the future! We have to find the *Terrastroid* and get them out of danger! Maybe the far reaches of the Abandoned will be spared, and they can relocate their people out of harm's way."

"Yeah, I agree," Claude put in. "We owe it to them. This surf safari would be all over if it weren't for them, and we'd already be reborn in another manifestation on another planet in another galaxy."

"Whoa—dude." Mike gave his brother the stink eye. "Have you been taking your medication again, Claude? Reborn manifestations? Wow, rabbit. You're hallucinating—and you don't have that gem on top of your head like Blob, so you have no excuse!" His brother couldn't help but heckle his twin whenever the opportunity arose.

Claude took the bait as if it were a huge purple carrot, as he had a billion times before. "In case you forgot, Mike," Claude responded to the jibe, his furry chin held up high and his whiskers twitching to and fro, "all the greatest roboscientists experimented in Ri-Ri cacti dust—otherwise we could never have solved the algorithms to create AI in the first place."

"You mean we'd have no Vern?" Mike yelped into the holoscreen, expecting a sardonic reply from the half android up in the cockpit, who was always tuned in to what was going on inside the *Planet Hopper*.

When no simulated voice came back. Mike twitched his whiskers at Max. "I guess I'm up for heading back too, Cap. Especially for Ariel's amazing 'fresh made' vittles! Just kidding. *Terrastroid* food doesn't compare to Ueharan turnips, but hey, it beats what the *P Hop* is nuking up for us right now."

"I agree," Claude said. "We have to tell them about Blob's vision, restock our food and water, and then get out of there—quickly—before the giant freaks come and trash the place. Star maps don't do much good when there's debris in the way."

Mike clicked the holocom button to alert Vern of the change in plans, seeming annoyed that he hadn't responded yet. When Vern was occupied by dallying with the hyperspace settings, he didn't want to be bothered.

"Yo, Vern." Mike sent an audiocall.

"What's up, Mike?" Vern finally replied, sticking with audio.

"We're gonna step off the transition platform alongside the asteroid belt," Mike informed him. "But we're not going to continue on to Outer Cygnus. Yet."

Max took over. "Vern, we're going to have to find the *Terrastroid* and pay them a quick visit. Can you get the AI programmed?"

"Fine." Vern shook his head.

Vern knows this is risky, Max took a deep inhale.

***

As Max worked his way back to the cockpit, he performed a quick tour of the ship, to make sure everything was ready for the jump to hyperspace. The task consisted of checking portal doors, adjusting the climate control settings, and finding equipment needing to be stored away properly. The big, blue-skinned Algorean started on the front sector of the ship, this time doing forward somersaults to pass the distance in the anti-gravity passageway.

The *Planet Hopper* wasn't an ordinary spaceship, neither in design nor function. Consisting of four compact levels, its front sector was divided into chambers, each with their own purpose, while the rear sector housed the engine. Under the cockpit, which was located on the nose of the top floor of the ship, were the three chambers the crew used most often, stacked on top of each other with an express air tube connecting them. On the bottom floor was Blob's domain: neatly arranged mechanical equipment and tools stored in and around a wide vehicle maintenance bay.

He turned on the low emission lightning by voice command, and clicked off the anti-gravity so he could get his feet on the flooring and inspect the grappling hooks and struts for the post holders of the landing gear. They kept the central part of this chamber wide open and free of clutter, that way they (mostly Blob) could work on a sizable piece of equipment without space limitations. Robotic retractable arms extended from the top of the ceiling where his big Boorish friend had cleaned off the botcopters—both terrestrial flyers had been caked in hardened lava and stained with dark blotches from the spouts of gas that had bombarded their hulls back on the Orb. The botcopters were probably the most valuable vehicles they had on board, it was the best way to get from the landing zone to the surf spots when the terrain was to difficult to hike over.

Max continued on to the adjacent vehicle maintenance zone. It was divided from the equipment storage area by a sliding force field wall that he opened by depressing the proper holobutton, automatically popping up when he approached. This was the sector of the ship where everything entered and exited. The only other way out of the ship was through the emergency space pods lodged into place along the posterior hull of the ship.

Max peeked through a synthglass window into a sub-compartment serving as a transition between the main hatch and the loading zone. He squinted to make out the colors of the sensors on the ramp housing, and on the hulls of the landing gear prods. *Green is good,* Max thought, moving on.

The Captain whistled to himself as he floated past a low deck view port. A flicker in the darkness caught his eye—a stark white moon of the Orb was becoming visible as it emerged from behind the red shadow of its parent. *Gorgeous.*

He walked over to one of the bot copters and ran his hand over the synthmetal exterior. Smooth as a whistle. Blob had put a legitimate amount of elbow grease into it.

All of their modes of travel outside of the *Planet Hopper* were stored here. A multi-loader with enormous track wheels; two land rovers that converted to submarine functionality and could safely transport the crew under oceans, rivers, and lakes; two mini-hovercraft; a beaten down old air car—the urban-based, planet-bound traveling machine when living the terrestrial lifestyle—and, of course, rows and rows of surf boards. All sizes, all shapes, each resting in a custom-made, cushioned, vertical storage cocoon, ready to be grabbed and thrown into action in a flash. The vehicle storage area was separated from the engine room by an impenetrable wall, therefore in order to exit he was compelled to check out the surfboards again. A twang of surf froth brewed in his belly; he forced himself to move on.

Next on the inspection list was the resting quarters. *Usually a problem area,* noted Max. Especially near Mike's unkempt bed and changing area. To the Captain's surprise, the quarters were all tidy, and energy level outputs set to conservation settings, the preferred mode when going through a wormhole.

He jumped back on the small circular platform of the air tube and zipped up one more level to the leisure quarters. A chamber as wide as the vehicle storage area, it held all of their entertainment—hologames, mind-surfing balance boards, and other time-consuming activities meant to break up the monotony of waiting for the surf to clean up. Max smiled and lifted his chin up as he recalled being the champion of pretty much every single pastime residing there in front of him.

Up to the star deck, it is, thought Max. It was his favorite part of the ship, and when the air tube spit him out he immediately went over and ran his fingers across the synthglass window. A trillion twinkling stars shone back on him. He took it all in for a moment before resigning himself to his duties.

How are we going to find them? Max racked his brain as he headed to the air tube to check in on Vern. He was trying hard to keep from second-guessing himself. It was his call, ultimately, to return to the Abandoned asteroid belt, to warn them about... a dream. *This ship goes where* I *decide it goes.* The dynamic among his crew was immutable—they were all equals, up until when a final decision needed to be made. *Now we make the wave or we fall, and it's up to me to make sure we stay afloat.*

CHAPTER SEVENTEEN

Gemstone Visions

Another Uday on the Terrastroid, Ariel thought as she paused at the portal before passing through, like always, preparing herself for the assault on her nose, the smell of organic decay. *Another Uday to tend to the wonderfully stinky gardens!*

She stepped through with her olfactory organ pulsing, as she had done for many, many years at exactly the same time every Uday. Wrinkling her face instinctively, she stepped on the circular platform of the air tube and dropped in a slow spiral to the subfloor below the growing space.

She craned her neck searching the dimly lit area. *Ah ha, there she is!*

"Murriel!" Ariel called out to her daughter, stepping onto the ramp leading to the underbelly of the hydroponic gardens.

"Mother!" Murriel came over and embraced her.

Ariel hugged her back and then held her out at arm's length. "Well, my darling, what's on the list this rotation? Algae bloom eradications? Argon mixture fiddlings? Hydrologic hieroglyphs?

No, wait—let me guess—there must be a bit of harvesting prep we can get our hands on?"

"Oh, I've got a chore for us all right. This way please, madam." Murriel smiled and performed a mock curtsy, before leading her mother past a cluster of subfloor workers. Each of them spent a moment to smile and greet them before getting back to their tasks.

Ariel took note of the hanging roots dangling from the gourds growing above. They twisted into long entanglements of white flesh, with brown crackling skin on the edges, and sinewy, long golden hairs covering the open areas with patches of fuzz. Encasing these tentacle-like protuberances was a faint light, the green halo of a growth enhancement beam. Each set of roots had its own personal oval of light within which it basked. These protective auras were one of the myriad of indispensable methods her people had mastered—*had to master*—in order for them to be able to live so far out in the cold. Their artificial atmosphere, which made breathing and horticulture possible, was in a constant state of flux, and therefore oxygen levels were carefully monitored, with frequent adjustments made each Uday. Ratios of oxygen were paramount to their survival, and the exact numbers were displayed in every corner of every wall screen in the *Terrastroid*— a constant reminder of their perilous plight. Ariel glanced at the closest display and was pleased with the good balance between oxygen, nitrogen and argon.

Sweet breathable air, she filled her lungs with it. *But tomorrow... Maybe we'll have a bad moisture production Uday, changing the mixture ever so slightly, and everyone might have to be wearing space helmets in all the common areas. It's happened before.*

Just as Ariel had supposed, Murriel had led her to one of the sun strip operating rooms. A manufacturing droid was on sleep mode next to a two-meter square of opaque sun strip tile; it still held the tools it had been using prior to being shut off.

"Not a glitch in the pre-fab again?" Ariel wondered out loud.

"No," her daughter replied. "I think maybe the application software wasn't installed properly. Each time we get a tile into the final processors, it goes haywire, and shuts down automatically."

"Well, that's not good."

Murriel moaned. "We can fix most of them manually, but we don't have enough hands to do all that fine motor skill work. There are other more important jobs to do in the garden. So we have the lighting team—" Murriel pointed to a group of four men and two women gathered around holoscreens and conversing back and forth while gesturing—"trying to figure out a way to update the software again. But this time, factoring in the new mold specifications." Murriel snapped her fingers together rhythmically as she talked, meandering with her mother around the control room.

"Okay, sounds good." Ariel smiled with pride at her young prodigy. "Well, what shall we get into then?"

"How about you and I run the numbers and do some tests on this last unit." Murriel picked up the broken sun tile from the processor table. "Maybe we can give this group of geeks over here a head start." She motioned with her thumb to her fellow Abandoned men and women, huddled in concentration at their work.

Ariel did not veil her sarcasm. "Sun strip processor malfunctions, huh? Weird. Never would have guessed *that's* what we'd be working on today." Tending to the sun strips was a task that rejected completion. No energy—no life. It was up to them to make their synthetic sun shine.

"We're never finished with work, are we, Mother?"

"I'm afraid not, darling." Ariel sighed. "Dawning Day will be here before we know it, another year as independents. We must push through and prepare for the festivities…"

Ariel lost her train of thought as one of her visions crossed her subconscious.

Murriel frowned. "Mother, what's wrong?"

Ariel turned away. "I've... nothing, it's nothing."

"Oh, come on. It's obviously not nothing. What is it, tell me?"

Ariel sighed. In her pocket she fondled a rare gemstone, one passed on to her from her great grandfather and original explorer of the Centaurus Arm of the Milky Way. "I have been having strange visions lately..."

"What kind of visions?"

"Scary ones."

Ariel fielded her daughter's caress on her shoulder by placing her hand on top of hers. She could sense the concern in Murriel's voice. She didn't want to upset her daughter, but she couldn't lie to her.

"About what?" Murriel prodded. "The *Terrastroid* getting hit by a meteor? I'm sure the three brothers and their team can get our rock moving fast enough to dodge even the worst of meteor storms."

"No, I'm talking about the opposite of collision."

Murriel furrowed her brows and put up her palms.

"Magnetism," Ariel confessed the truth. "The Giant Beings have made a black hole. I've seen them activate it in my visions."

"Do you think the surfing aliens father brought here have endangered us?" Murriel asked.

"Well, dear, I think that goes without saying," she said, calmly at first, but her voice giving way to desperation. "But I'm talking about... well, I have this horrible feeling... if Perseans made it to Uehara, what's to stop them from coming to the Abandoned and clearing us all out with one fell swoop of their hands? They have already cast the first throw. Uehara is no more. One of our most important sources of exotic spices and a magnificent world of indigenous life—boom! Gone, just like that. It's disgusting."

"So, what, you think that was the first of *many* Planet Ball tournaments?"

When Ariel didn't reply, Murriel seemed to be considering what to say for a moment, before breaking the silence. "Mother, we can't let the terror consume us. The Persean game is awful, yes, but nothing can be worse than the threat of darkness we endure on a daily basis. We have to manufacture Uday and night, with these." She held up the tile again for emphasis. "Sun strips. Without them, our plants and Stroidtrees don't grow, we don't eat. Whether a toss of a planet ball, a random collision here among the Abandoned that we can't avoid, or a black hole… something will get us, eventually. We aren't Ucitizens. Virtual immortality is for the weak. We are the proud Abandoned! We live by the Uhour. And *this* Uhour if we don't fix these sun strips to allow variable tinting, we'll have crispy crops—that won't make a good stew, Mother."

Ariel gazed deeply into the eyes of her daughter. Without beating an eyelash, the young woman had transitioned her mother from a fearful dreamer to an applied farmer. The grace with which she spoke—it was uncanny for her age. *She's barely old enough for a suitor, and yet she sounds as if she could be leading the entire horticulture sector. How did Angus and I get so lucky? We have two of the finest children one could hope to rear.* She made sure to not fawn over Murriel alone, but to think of her son, Markus, as well. *The future pilot extraordinaire—if his father has anything to do with it.*

"I guess you're right, dear." Ariel said. "Maybe I'm just projecting… maybe these visions are just manifestations of my fears. There's so much work to do here, within our little rocky world, without worrying about a game played by giants. We can only control what we can control, here, on *Terrastroid*." But as the words came out the gemstone in her pocket seemed to radiate heat into her skin.

Murriel stomped her foot and made the declaration: "We're the Abandoned! Not even giants can stomp on what they cannot find! We are invisible among the cosmos!"

They smiled and hugged, side to side, with Ariel resting her head for a moment on her taller daughter's shoulder. Respite was brief for the Abandoned. *Time to get back to keeping our dark rock habitable,* Ariel thought. She hoped the sun tile solution would present itself soon. Then they could examine the root system of the Stroidtrees for leaks. Another never-ending task. *Ah, the glory of being Abandoned...*

***

Shaking out the cobwebs in his head, Max was standing in the mess quarters trying to make sense of Blob's blabbering. After coming out of hyperspace it was mandatory for the crew to take in electrolytes and sustenance, and Max's stomach ached as if he hadn't eaten in... well—thousands of light years. The Captain imagined that if *he* was hungry, then Blob must be *starving*. The crew gathered around the mess table had to suffer the big alien's absurdly loud mastication.

"Good Boorish cheese!" Blob exclaimed. "Yum!"

"I hate to break it to you, my friend," Mike told him matter-of-factly. "But that's *not* Boorish cheese."

"Well..." Blob closed his eyes, smiled, breathed in deeply, and opened them back up again. "It *tastes* like Boorish cheese to me, creamy, but not too grainy. Lots of moldy green crevasses on the outside!" He held out a chunk of... Max couldn't identify exactly what—but it definitely wasn't appetizing.

Mike turned his nose and whiskers away with chagrin. "Get that green stuff out of my face!"

"All right, all right, enough, you two," Max broke in. "Blob, stop embellishing. Mike, don't complain too much, it's all we've got left. Let's finish these vittles and go up to the mainframe compartment. Hopefully, Claude can find the *Terrastroid*."

They finished up every last crumb of synthfood and floated down one floor. Once they were surrounding Claude in his floating chair he reminded everyone Rymon had given them a movement signature code to help locate them.

"Okay, watch this," when Claude plugged in the code a graph popped up on one of the many holoscreens he had floating in the air.

Claude pointed. "Those jagged red spikes, they're the *Terrastroid*'s movements over the past few Udays. Oh, and there—yep—right there! That's their current location."

"Wow!" Mike cried. "How lucky are we? It's within minimal thrusters range!"

"Yep," Claude added. "Good thing they remained in this quadrant of the asteroid belt—otherwise the signature code would be useless."

Max nodded, his red eyebrows lifting up and going straight. He patted his friend on the head and back. "Nice work, Claude! Now send those numbers up to Vern. I'm heading up there now." He gave them his serious face before exiting. "Hey, keep an eye out for rogue rocks, will you guys?"

It took a few dozen Algorean heartbeats for Max to ride the air tube up and stomp into the cockpit, yet Vern already had the navigation cued up on Max's personal mini holoscreen, emanating from the armrests of his floating chair.

"Captain, I processed the data from Claude to plot our route."

Max lifted up his lower lip and marveled at Vern as he sidled into his floating chair. The synthmetal skin man was something to behold. *Impossible! How could he have finished the computations so fast?* He gave the order for Vern to hit the thrusters and the *Planet Hopper* lurched toward the cluster of asteroids taking up the entire front portal view.

"Hey, Claude?" Max hit the com.

After a pause his first officer responded. "What's up, Cap?"

"I'm just thinking... these guys weren't really expecting us, you catch my drift?"

"Uh-uh," Claude said. "I'm using all the hailing channels, every language in the Milky Way, and sending out any expendable probes, a few sonar blasts."

Good, Max thought. Claude was of the same mind. He was trying to make the *Planet Hopper* as easy to observe as possible. They didn't want to sneak up on their *Terrastroid* friends and be mistaken as a threat.

"But I don't know if it'll work." Claude admitted.

"Hmm. I pray to Algor they don't think we're a Ugov space ranger. They probably would want to run from them though, not vaporize them, right?"

"We better hope so," Vern threw in, "because I'm picking up a reading on a perfectly round asteroid moving unlike any of the others."

"Well," Claude said, his voice echoing through the cockpit "I'm pretty sure that Rymon, when he gave me this code, said to expect *them* to find us before *we* found them."

A Usecond after the words came out of the rabbit's mouth, there was a green flash and a locator signal popped up on the main cockpit holoscreen. Max could make out the oblate shape of the *Terrastroid.*

It was traveling with great speed—directly for them.

"Uh, Max," Vern said across the cockpit, stress simulated in his voice. "Do we need to warn the others to brace for impact, or what?"

"Steady, Vern. Do not veer off course." Max was certain they would recognize them... *Any Usecond, now.*

A moment of tension passed as the Captain and his pilot watched the *Terrastroid* approach relentlessly. The hailing frequency beeped on at long last.

"Is that you, Max?" It was the familiar voice of the leader of the Abandoned. "What a surprise! Good to know those hyperspace sheaths weren't faulty. Heh heh!"

"Yeah, Angus," Max cried happily. "Can you believe it? We made it back!"

"Why in the Milky Way would you guys come back here? You guys didn't find any volcanoes to ride in Centaurus, so what—you wanted to surf bareback on a comet, or what?"

Max laughed. "No, that's hilarious though! We've never tried that. Maybe we should! We got great waves at the volcano... and... uh, well, we wanted to visit and talk. Permission to land on your lovely little rock? We want to show you holovideos of our surf session and we, er—Blob—wants to tell you about an experience he had on a planet we named the Orb."

"Well," Angus drawled. "I'm sure Rymon and his brothers will be curious and excited. And Ariel hasn't been very happy cooking for the same old taste buds every night, she's fond of Blob, as you may remember."

"Well," Max warned, "since we've got hyperspace hangovers, we're all famished. Ariel might regret ever saying that after she sees how much he can put away!"

"Sounds good—she loves a challenge! Get into a stall pattern, I'll have our men open the landing tunnel. On my mark..."

***

Max led the crew up the causeway to warm greetings from Angus and his family, along with scores of other curious Abandoned people. After the buzz had died down and the small congregation had left them alone, they walked back to Angus's home to eat a meal befitting the only friends the people from the dark rocks had ever known.

When the laughter and conversation waned, and the food and purified comet water cleared from the feasting table, Max locked his gaze on Blob. He had already tried to get Blob's attention during the meal several times, prodding him to broach the topic none of them were eager to discuss: the big Boor's vision. But Blob had ignored his Captain, stuffing his face and staying silent. *Guess it's on me,* the Captain grunted to himself when Blob still avoided eye contact.

"So, um," began Max, "Angus, Ariel, listen, there is something—um—something we wanted to talk to you about, something that, Blob… *saw*. When we were on the Orb. Well, he didn't exactly *see* it…"

Despite his usual bravado, Max faltered. He was trying to come up with the right words to share the horrible news.

"Angus!" Blob blurted out, saving Max from stammering any longer. Everyone at the table turned their heads at the big Boor. His monobrow titled over his eyes. "I saw the Abandoned being destroyed. I had a vision, so clear and so true, that I could not have been dreaming it."

Angus stood up with an intense frown forming on his face. "What do you mean you had a vision? A vision of us, of the *Terrastroid*?"

Max and the rest of the crew were silent. It was up to Blob to convince Angus—*he* was the reason the surfers were in the middle of the largest asteroid belt in the Milky Way, instead of chilling out on Oreldychyne and surfing epic point breaks.

Blob's voice was deep and resonating as he revealed more shocking news, "We were so busy telling you about the volcanoes and our epic surf sessions that we haven't told you about the people we met on the Orb—"

"What?" Angus was turning red in the cheeks. "People? On this planet you speak of? Impossible!"

"It's true, Angus," Max was inclined to chip in, giving extra weight to Blob's words. "We were all there. We all met them. Vapor People."

"Yeah," the big Boor said, "and they were the most peculiar alien humanoids, like shaggy ghosts. They seemed to breathe and exhale vapor, not from mouths, I don't think they even had mouths, did they, guys? It came out from their skin; the gases seeped out from cracks in their skin. And they had three eyes, in a triangle formation, they wore long metal cloaks and they seemed expressionless, with just their red eyes visible from the dark hoods over their heads. They beckoned us to some sort of edifice, made from lava stone and dug into the ground. Inside were these orange hot springs, and that's when we noticed the stones."

Angus was wide-eyed. He went to stand by Ariel's side. His son had been listening intently, and now Markus replicated the same bewilderment.

"Wait," Angus asked, "you mean to tell me you had contact with another race of aliens? In the Centaurus Arm? There are no sentient beings anywhere near there. Even our old mining missions corroborate that. There's no way it's possible! It's too hot! That solar system, around the planet you call the Orb, there is no way it can sustain life."

"It *does*..." Blob said emphatically. "We hung out with them. Well..." He shrugged at his crew mates. "Really, I guess it was mostly me. I interacted with the Orb beings. Earlier in the Uday when we were surfing, I fell through a hole in the volcano crust, and I found an incredibly beautiful gemstone. And I pocketed it. Well, later on, when they saw I possessed this big, purple colored gemstone, they acted like they wanted it, so I gave it to them. In response they took a different gem and placed it over the top of my head, like this." He pantomimed for them, making his dominant hand into the shape of a small circle and holding it slightly above his head. "The thing literally hovered there, aren't I right, guys?"

The four others nodded, confirming his story.

A loud gasp from Ariel made the group around the dinner table snap their heads in her direction for a moment. When she looked away with pursed lips, Blob continued his story.

"And suddenly, I was... *transported*, as if I went through a hyperspace sheath without a spaceship or anything. And I saw the *Terrastroid*. Floating by itself. I felt as if I was right there!"

"What else?" Ariel asked, surprising everyone, including Angus.

Blob appeased his hostess. "Then I saw scores of Persean dome walkers, all in motion, all moving in the direction of the Abandoned. There were explosions, and white light, and I felt this... this terror coming from within the asteroids... Angus, Ariel... I believe they're going to hold a Planet Ball tournament here." He pointed to the floor with his massive, stubby finger.

"That's insane!" Angus yelled. "And you expect us to believe, what—a vision?"

Silence reigned. Max glanced at the boys while trying to get a read on what their mortal friend would say next. *Was this a bad idea?* Max fretted to himself, rocking his body weight back and forth from his left foot to his right. *Did we really expect to just show up here, drop this on them, and they would believe us?*

Ariel's voice was much quieter than Max was used to when she broke the silence. "It's true."

"What's true?" Angus asked.

"Mother!" Murriel gasped from the next floating chair. "Your visions!"

"Yes, child." Ariel reached over and patted her daughter's shoulder.

208

Max could sense the pressure building up in the family's dining room. Angus seemed perturbed now. "What visions? What is our daughter talking about, Ariel?"

Murriel spoke for her mom after Ariel refused to respond right away. "Mother has been having visions. Of Planet Ballers… and the use of a black hole to suck up our homeland."

It was everyone else in the room's turn to gasp when Ariel reached into her pocket and pulled out a glowing purple gemstone.

"What the…" Max said, "that's exactly like the one Blob found on Centaurus!"

Angus shook his head. "I've hardly ever seen that stone, you always keep it on your altar, tucked away in your meditation chambers! You're saying its—psychoactive? Why didn't you tell me you were having these visions, Ari?"

Ariel batted her eyelids. "I—I'm sorry, my love. I didn't want to worry you." She turned her attention to Max and the crew. "It was a gift from my great grandfather. He was part of the original mining trip to Centaurus…"

Any speck of Max that had been unsure of Blob's gem prophecy evaporated in a flash.

"I knew it!" Blob exclaimed, his monobrow lifting. "The vapor-breathing people were trying to help us—we needed to come here to convince Ariel what she has envisioned is true. It's a warning! No one in the galaxy likes those giants aliens—even as far out there as Centaurus!"

"Strange friends," Angus said, "you have come bearing extremely bad news. This might be permissible, *if* you have a solution to the problem. Have you one?" The grizzled Abandoned elder glared at Blob, then at Max. Neither could muster a reply. "Because… you've come all this way to… to what? Warn us? Well, now you've done that. My family is distressed. You've upset our sacred community. What is the next step you propose we take?

Run away? To where, I ask you? This is our home, we don't run from our home. We spent hundreds of Uyears running from the grasp of the Ugov. I don't care how big the Perseans are or what weapon they carry. This is our home and we will not flee from it. We'll fight if we have to! So tell us, crew of the *Planet Hopper*, how will you lead us to victory in battle against the enemy you've released in our midst?"

Mike laughed out loud, but sucked it in when Claude gave him a forepaw to the stomach.

"Um, Angus..." Max said, stifling a grin himself. "We're not really the warrior-types." He probably sounded like a fool to a man as fierce as Angus, but couldn't think of anything else to say. "Don't get me wrong, the rumors about Algoreans are true—we're trained in self-defense at birth, the boys and the girls, and Blob is no slouch when it comes to being a bodyguard, but... none of us has ever picked up a shock wand, much less a deadly weapon. I'm sure you probably guessed this, but we don't have ion cannons on the *Hopper*."

"We *have* to leave, Angus!" Ariel cried, tears pouring down her cheeks. "We can't let our people be annihilated by their stupid game!"

"Darling," Angus said, "what do you propose we do? Fly the *Terrastroid* across interstellar space on thruster turbines? We don't have a hyperspace worthy spaceship that can fit all our people in it. This is our home, and it is portable, to a degree. But we can't possibly get out of range of a Planet Ball tournament—much less run from a black hole!"

Ariel was getting hysterical, "Well, we have to do *something*... we can't just sit here, Ang. This alien Blob saw what I saw. The Giants are coming to do their dirty pastime in our backyard."

Max pointed out a glum fact: "We have several extra hyperspace chambers onboard the *Planet Hopper*, but obviously we can't fit the entire population of the *Terrastroid*."

"You want us to evacuate?" Markus yelped. "We don't even know how long we have! They could be on their way right now!"

"Actually…"

Above the center of the dining table a small holoscreen popped up from Vern's wrist implant. Persean Planet Ball tournament data scrolled, emphasizing his point. Everyone turned their gaze onto the half-man, half-machine who spoke his thoughts through the AI mind meld translator. "No, that is not the case. Perseans historically take a full Umonth to celebrate their previous tournament."

Angus tilted his head. "We don't go by galactic standard time here among the rocks?"

Max translated. "What Vern is saying is we do have a little time."

"Time is great, Max," Angus said. "But it doesn't solve the problem of evacuating our entire race of people without the means—or desire—to do so."

"So what—" Markus whined, "—we do nothing but sit here and *die*?"

Murriel admonished him. "We aren't going to die, Markus, be quiet! There has to be another solution besides us leaving the asteroid belt?"

"Murriel," Markus rallied, "we can't even scratch the skin of a single one of those Giant Beings with our puny arsenal. We would need a trillion *Terrastroids*—working all in concert—to even put up something resembling a resistance—"

"*We* aren't going to fight them," another voice said from across the table.

Max was as surprised as anyone. Claude had yet to enter the discussion, instead, during the entire post-dinner dialogue, he had been immersed with a mini-holoscreen, tapping and swiping periodically. Everyone waited for him to finish his point.

"Someone else will," Claude flicked his dread behind his back. "You're right, Markus. The Abandoned cannot win a fight against the Perseans," he continued, dragging his holoscreen to the center airspace of the room and tossing it up over the previous page still hanging there, superseding it, and revealing to all what he had been researching privately. The images displayed had nothing to do with the Giant Beings, as everyone would have guessed. Instead a Ugovernment Information Site glared with babel in many languages. "But these guys can. In fact, they've already defeated them once."

Angus stomped the grated floor. "What? The Ugov! No way, no chance. They forced us into exile here, they've tried to imprison us and destroy our way of life! They won't fight for us, they could care less about our dark realm of stone and ice."

"Angus..." Claude eased in. "This is our *only* chance. We have to alert the Ugov to the activity of the Perseans. When they annihilated Uehara they breached the treaty. It's a straight up cause for war, and if we tell them where they are going to hold their next tournament, the Sun People will *have* to act. They want more than anything to maintain order in the galaxy, and to keep their tight grip on the bitcoin making it all go around.

That's my rabbit! Max thought, glad to have him as his first officer and friend, for the ten millionth time.

Claude paused, his long ears twitching as if seeking dissent from the hosts. None came, so he pressed a few buttons and the holoscreen image shifted onto the face of a dark-haired, dark-eyed Earthish man. "I know someone in the Ugov who would listen to us. I met him a long time ago when I was involved in getting Mike and I's home planet to get better representation in the Ugov. His name is Adonis, and I was doing some research on him. He has gone on to become one of the fourteen, who has fought consistently to maintain the status quo in the Milky Way. From what I read, he devotes his time to keeping all the arms of the galaxy under the direct oversight of the Ugov. I'm guessing he has the clout to steer the military into action."

"Claude!" his twin, Mike, protested loudly as he swung his dreadlocks aside to reveal his twitching whiskers and beady, marbled eyes. "Come on now, are you *serious*? We can't go back to New Earth. We'll be arrested, tortured for information, and shipped off to Galaxy's End!"

"We have to go back, Mike." Claude responded. He stared in the Captain's direction, the one who's opinion *really* mattered. "Max, we have to go back. To help save our friends. They risked their lives to save us from the Perseans once, we have to repay them. Plus—we've got to save the entire asteroid belt—and the Outer Cygnan solar systems for that matter. Those Giant Beings could destroy them all—one by one. I mean... think about poor Uehara."

"I agree," Blob croaked, petting the brown patch of hair on top of his head.

Mike grumbled something but didn't protest any further.

Max studied the image of Adonis on the screen hovering above them. The face was handsome and wore a wry little smile, as if clued into something you weren't. Could Max allow their fate—and the fate of the Milky Way—to be in *his* hands? The answer, Max decided, was *yes*. He *had* to trust that face. For the sake of many others beside himself. But the Captain was smart enough to know they were going to need more than idle rumors of Persean advancements into Outer Cygnus to persuade the man depicted on the screen.

Good thing Claude was able to nab the data to make those star maps, he thought. *They ought to be enough to keep us off Galaxy's End. Praise Algor?*

CHAPTER EIGHTEEN

Boots on the Ground

Piper was pouring over biological composition scan results of Uehiron's surface, sent via satellite from the first probes Marjorie had sent a Uhour ago, when Carrysa walked into the *Lifebringer*'s lab. She had a smile on her face and the tan skin on her cheeks glowed.

"Piper, check this out!" Carrysa took both sets of thumbs and forefingers, pinched them together, then drew them out and away, opening up a small holoscreen page. She relayed to Piper how she couldn't believe the feedback regarding atmosphere, mean surface temperatures, and, more importantly, the number of estimated freshwater lakes and rivers. "This place is absolutely amazing! It's similar to the initial scans we had of Uehara, in many respects. Uehiron. Cool name." As Carrysa spoke she dragged the holoscreen by the top corner and made it slightly bigger, and therefore easier for Piper to read.

"Yes, Carrysa," Piper sighed. "A pretty twin of poor Uehara... I can't *believe* how lucky we are! How often are there two undiscovered habitable worlds this close to each other? Outer Cygnus is a boon to the field of astrobiology!" Piper took a moment to compose herself. She shared Carrysa's enthusiasm, but was still concerned about this pearl of a planet's fate. *We cannot let Zander get his fangs into her sister.* Piper liked to envision prospective terraform projects in the feminine sense; she was literally giving birth to life after all. *Uehiron has to be a different story. We can't let her suffer the same fate as her twin, which is yet another mystery to solve...*

"Yes, Carrysa," Piper finally said. "I have to admit, I'm in disbelief myself. I keep waiting for negative data, but every single test, every single model I run—it's one continuous confirmation. Like my father said: 'Data don't lie!' This place *has* to have sentient life. I mean, you already proved it, the air's practically breathable. Would the descent team even have to wear helmets down there?"

"No, I don't think so," Carrysa replied. "Obviously, if we are close enough to the poles, it could get pretty cold in places. Tundra frost biomes could be an issue. It appears there is an ice cap on the northern pole that does drop quite a ways, and the northern hemisphere seems to be nearly inundated by frozen oceans." She tapped the screen a few more times, calling up a drone flyby image of the northern pole of Uehiron, and zoomed in.

Regarding the image, Piper was prompted to click the com button: "Hey, Melia?"

"What's up?" came Melia's voice after a click.

"Carrysa's got a handle on the atmosphere, it's definitely breathable, there's ample water. My bio comp readings are off the chart. This is a mature, living, breathing sister of Uehara. Billions of years of living matter stomped on top of itself. I think we're getting pretty close to having to make a reconnaissance. We've got life readings, all we need is live holo confirmation... then we can sanction this place on the grounds of astrobiological law."

Melia guessed. "You want me to get the team together?"

"Yes."

"How soon?"

"I think the sooner the better, don't you agree?"

"Yes, definitely. We've got other systems with viable exoplanets still to monitor out here. Any favorable data on one of those uninhabited worlds—"

"We send it straight to the fourteen," Piper finished for her friend. "That will quench their thirst and give them reason to open up the Ugov's permanently black bitcoin. Mel, this place is special, maybe the equivalent of Uehara in every way. We need to be careful about our documentation, do you follow me?"

Melia's voice was stern, attentive. "Absolutely. I'll keep a holo feed for you, and you can control what goes to the memory banks of the mainframe."

"This has to be for our eyes only. I want to be able to edit the original version and encode it. Let's take the proper security measures—before the Ugov gets their hands on it."

"Understood, Piper."

"Good, good. This is awesome! All right, I'll get John to put the *Lifebringer* in an access orbit. Marjorie goes with you, as always. Please have her get the sampling robotics in order. I'll com you when we're thirty Uminutes from the drop zone and check on your progress. Got it?"

Melia's image on the holoscreen nodded and logged out, the screen flashing off.

"On my way!" Carrysa predicted her chief's orders, jumping up and exiting the lab. She had been waiting and listening patiently during the holocall to dismiss herself. One of her assignments aboard the *Lifebringer* was prepping the landing team. Piper smiled at her crew mate's eagerness to appease. It gave her such satisfaction when projects operated so smoothly.

The truth was, Piper had such a close bond, and had built such genuine friendships with her crew, assuming the role of strict boss every Uminute of every Uday was simply not tenable. But the girls had adapted. She had to be both: Piper and *Chief* Piper.

And the boys… Knox and her pilot—well, they were different.

She turned to the holoscreen displaying the live cockpit feed and informed John they were going to need a lower orbit. In order for the descent shuttle to execute a simple drop into the warmer central latitudes of Uehiron's wide continental expanse, the *Lifebringer* would have to scoot in pretty close.

Piper expressed her concerns to John. "Melia and Marjorie need enough time to make accurate surveillance, and it could be *very* cold. Weather could be an issue. Will you check the descent vehicle standard settings, and adjust them if necessary?" Piper asked/ordered, her continuous balancing trick between polite and demanding.

"I'm on it." More than willing to please, John smiled into the camera. He liked to be perfect. She never had to ask him to do anything twice. Her whole crew was the same: a dedicated and close-knit group, resembling a religious order, each of them beholden to their intrepid leader in their own unique way.

***

Bracing for the turbulence, Marjorie squinted her eyes and gripped tightly to the stationary bars attached to the side of her seat. It was an even bumpier ride than she had expected. The half-Algorean woman fought off the nausea. She hated this part, but if she wanted the glory of being the first to touch her boots on the ground, she had to suck it up.

Once their shuttle dropped through the clouds, a vision of the deep, dark cyan blues of the vast oceans overwhelmed Marjorie. She exchanged a bright-eyed look with Melia, sitting in the other seat. Descending ever faster the sepia landmass came into focus. John's voice blared over the intercom.

218

"Five, four, three—"

Marjorie gasped upon the sickening jolt of touchdown.

Melia was unstrapped from her seat before Marjorie had even opened her eyes, and her slim body brushed against her as she shimmied past, heading up to the bot copter launch pad. Marjorie took a deep breath of recycled air before unbuckling herself and gathering the robotics kit.

Once they were locked into the botcopter the top hatch of their descent shuttle retracted and they were airborne again, but not nearly so fast, and minus the intense jarring of the shuttle. *Much nicer,* thought Marjorie, her eyes adjusting to the pure sunlight filtering through her visor.

Her nausea faded and the excitement of what they were about to do became palpable. In the top left corner of her helmet holoscreen was an image showing the eager faces of the rest of the crew, gathered around the monitors up aboard *Lifebringer,* keeping a close eye on them. Hopefully. Extractions could be tricky if things were to go awry. But Marjorie was certain the safety of her crew mates was the most important thing to Piper, and it eased her nerves a touch.

Marjorie spotted a cluster of forest below, as the botcopter glided in a parallel pathway five hundred meters above the ground. A substantial river bisected the greenery, with numerous tributaries flaring outward, each of them flooding into a lake a kilometer or two from the forest's edge. She motioned to Melia, indicating where she wanted to set down.

"Yeah..." Marjorie's blue lips spread wide to reveal sharp white incisors. "Right there, that flat, grassy clump! Yep, bring us in, Melia."

"Who's first?" Marjorie stuck out her closed fist, ready to play the ancient three-option decision maker, *used by the Ugov to decide the fate of billions, if you believe Piper's rants!* "Let's do Asteroid-Laser-Pulsar."

"You can go, Marjorie, I have enough firsts—"

"Yeah," Marjorie chuckled at her. "This will be fourteen, I believe…"

"Thirteen," came the terse response over the com from the spaceship above, as always, Carrysa loved to take stock of Melia's exploits.

"Whatever, Carrysa," said Melia. "You're just jealous. Thirteen, fourteen, none of that matters if this place is even remotely close to what the models have indicated. Marj, are you going for it? If you don't I will. I've got to make sure Carrysa is keeping track up there."

Marjorie didn't need to be asked twice, and leapt off the edge of the copter platform. The ground was… spongy. It was so buoyant, so elastic! She marveled at the organic material beneath her boots—unlike any texture she had ever tread upon.

"It's springy!" She bounced up and down off the Uehiron surface, getting higher after each recoil, bursting upward with glee. "Yahoo!"

Melia followed her to the ground and activated the robotics control. A hatch opened alongside the rear of the botcopter in response. A few moments later, out popped a rounded drone with a thousand capabilities. *Yes!* Marjorie petted the smooth synthmetal. Sometimes the crew teased her for her special relationship with, in her words, "the ultimate tool for boots-on-the-ground biodata collection."

The camera affixed to the center of the drone, mimicking a pupil inside an eyeball, transmitted a live feed to Marjorie's handheld device. With a nanosecond delay, the holo bounced off their copter, made it to the shuttle, and ricocheted on up to *Lifebringer,* roughly two thousand kilometers above Uehiron.

"Insects!" Melia said excitedly, swatting a few buzzing gnats away, but her inflection quickly changed. "*Lots* of them, actually."

Let's see what's in that cluster of trees, thought Marjorie. *Seems the perfect place to find a shy critter.*

She steered the drone up and over Melia's head, and took a course to enter the forest at a height of about ten meters above the under story. The audio astonished first—as an avian song, vibrant and repetitive, rang out, preceding the image that would change the course of astrobiology.

A Uehiron bird flew from one limb to another, its speckled yellow and green plumage showing a shade of the color spectrum never before cataloged.

Marjorie struggled to control the adrenaline running through her, hands beginning to shake. She managed to click on the hover function for the drone, and it ceased moving, hanging in midair. She pressed a few more buttons to minimize any exhaust throttle sounds in an attempt to disguise their machine as a harmless organic life form. They didn't want to cause the bird to flee before they could get data on it.

Oh, good galaxy, we did it! Marjorie stifled a squeal and bounced over the springy tundra to hug Melia. Their celebratory hug, mixed with the joyous shouts of their teammates from the mini holoscreens inside their helmets, and all time stopped.

"Should I?" Marjorie asked, reaching for the release lever on her helmet to make the final validation of Uehiron. If she could breathe the air the special planet would meet the terraform humanocentric criterion of being inhabitable.

"Go for it!" Melia replied, waiting, per protocol, to follow suit.

The typical hissing sound accompanied Marjorie's helmet removal; immediately the cool breeze hit her cheeks. She inhaled a deep, deep breath of nitrogen, oxygen, and a minuscule amount of several other gases. When she exhaled, she smiled and closed her eyes for a moment. When she opened them, Melia had pulled off her helmet as well and was standing there breathing the chilly Uehiron air, with a grin covering the entire span of her face.

***

Groggy and lightheaded, Max sat in the cockpit rubbing his neck. It usually took him half a Uhour before he could truly regain a sense of reality. *Those virtual coffins suck! It's the sleep of death— except you actually do wake up.*

Max found himself with a spare moment, so he messed around with the sensory equipment. He figured he might as well check out the initial readings on the unexplored twin solar system of Uehara. In a manipulated view on the holo, the yellow star was shining brightly, all of its orbiting matter basking peacefully in the light. He was curious about the elemental make-up of the stars they passed by during their travels, and he liked to keep data about them on file. He pet his auburn hair absentmindedly. What kind of surf breaks might be lurking there? *Mind surfing again!* He had to laugh at himself. Then, something stood out to him on one of the visual displays. The movement of all fifteen planets and forty-three moons was constant.

But the holoscreen kept showing a slight deviation. A bit of movement in direct contrast of gravitational projections. Little orange lines on the holo showing… what, exactly?

Just as Max was going to mention it, Vern spoke from the pilot's chair a few meters away. "Captain, an unidentified object just popped up on the scanners.

Inspecting the trajectory statistics, Max discovered the object made drastic changes to its pathway resonance. There was only one thing capable of…

Uh oh.

An intergalactic spaceship was orbiting an attractive little world, the seventh planet out from the parent star.

"Vern? Can you confirm what I'm getting on the sensors?" Max prompted.

"Yes," Vern's artificial voice droned. "It is confirmed. The spaceship appears to be… exiting orbit. Altering its bearing and…"

"And?" Max prodded after too long a pause from his half-android pilot. He had a premonition he wasn't going to have a chance to defuse his hyperspace sickness with a dip in the laser sauna.

"Yeah, Max, it's heading our way," Vern said with unintentional nonchalance in his voice.

The *Planet Hopper*'s override switched on, swathing every room in the ship with red light, while the AI voice took over the intercom: "Alert! Alert! Weapons lock sensor readings. Alert! Alert!"

Max gulped. "What have we got, Vern? Details, please…"

"Where shall I begin?" Vern replied. "We have an IG spaceship, with extreme acceleration capabilities, possessing an elite level weapons arsenal, and its attempting to lock on to the *Planet Hopper*. The fact it was in orbit around a solid core planet more than likely indicates a pirate ship. Or worse a space ranger. Considering our location, far from the Ugov auspices, and the fact we have no defense, and can't jump into hyperspace right now, we are… *screwed*."

"Thanks for your honest assessment, Vern." His friend was dead on, they were easy pickings. But he held out hope Vern might have something up his sleeve. There was no point in trying to outmaneuver them now, and if they were going to blast them, they would have already fired. Max ordered the crew up to the cockpit.

By the time the crew had assembled next to Max and Vern the unidentified spaceship was within hailing frequency, and attempted to contact them. Max nodded to Vern who activated the holocall.

A pretty Sunish woman stood, arms crossed, with a cast of others huddled in the background. Including what appeared to be—*Is that an Algorean?* Max did a double take.

The brown-haired woman's stern voice indicated she meant business. "Identify yourself."

"Hey there!" Max said in his most charismatic theater voice. "We're the *Planet Hopper*... a... a *recreational* spaceship traveling in Cygnus." He turned and winked at his crew mates, who rolled their eyes back at him.

"You're a long way from legal territory, *Planet Hopper*. This is an official Ugov mission you are interfering with. I'm not a patient woman, and we have a lot of work to do. Now, the Intergalactic Dividing Line is a good twenty-five thousand light years from here, therefore you are breaking Ugovernment law. Explain why I shouldn't blast you into oblivion and move on with my assignment?"

"Uh, well, ma'am, I..." Max stuttered.

"Don't call me *ma'am*," she said sharply.

"Sorry, lady, I..."

"I'm *not* your lady, either."

"Sorry, so sorry. My name is Max. I'm the Captain of the *Planet Hopper*. My crew is a humble group of five. That's Vern, my pilot, we also have a couple of twins on board, named Claude and Mike, they're big rabbits, and then, last but *definitely* not least, my large best buddy over there, we call him Blob. We were forced to use the hyperspace platform here to avoid becoming causalities."

Max tried to kick start his brain and come up with a plausible scenario excusing their transgression. *I know—a distraction!* "We witnessed a Planet Ball attack on the solar system known, well, that *used* to be know as Uehara."

"What did you *just* say?" the Ugov official shouted.

"Yeah," Max lamented, "Perseans carried out a tournament there, and destroyed the entire solar system. It was awful."

Several voices came through the holo from the ship.

"But—how could that be?"

"That's a break of the treaty! That's an act of war!"

"Great galaxies! No!"

"Impossible!"

"That's why there was so much debris!"

"No way! No way!"

"This is ludicrous!"

"This can't be happening!"

The chorus of voices chimed on and on until the Ugov official finally put a stop to it with a vigorous wave of her arms.

"Everyone—*quiet!*" she yelled. Once her crew were quelled, she turned back to the holoscreen and said in a calm voice: "My name is Piper Crane, I'm the Chief Executive Officer of the Terraform Division of the Ugovernment. This is an official mission to the Outer Cygnus Arm. You have broken several Ugov laws. The punishment is severe for crossing the IDL—*regardless* of what you *may* have witnessed. You haven't told us why you're out here yet, either. We will be attaching a tracking beacon to your ship. Once your ship has been stamped, you will have to return straight to the Last Ugov Outpost and turn yourselves in. Ugov officials will be automatically alerted of your arrival, location, and offense. If you do not turn yourselves in immediately, they will send out the space rangers to destroy your ship upon location."

Max's jaw dropped. "Now wait just a Uminute! Hold on now, Miss Piper, there's no need for such drastic measures! Surely we can discuss this amicably! We are too far to send a warning all the way to Orion, and… you want to continue to your studies here, as I understand it."

Max watched her expression soften slightly. *There's my angle!*

He pounced on it. "We understand how important your work is and we want to support that. But isn't it also your duty as Ucitizens to alert New Earth of Persean activity immediately? That would force you to leave your work—a shame, no doubt. We were planning on returning to New Earth ourselves, in order to report the Persean crisis. Could we do the honor of getting this awful but important news straight to the right members of the council for you? I am sure they would send support right away, and this area would be safe for your labors."

The executive named Crane seemed to be considering. She muted and blacked her holo for half a Uminute. The image clicked back on. "Okay, Captain Max. We agree we could use your help… but that does *not* change the fact that you are going to get an arrest stamp on your ship."

Max and his crew groaned in dismay.

The executive smiled in response. "Don't worry, you can still do your duty as Ugov citizens. You can deliver our message for us—loud and clear—and then… go to Galaxy's End afterward."

"Whoa!" Max called out, all pleasantries dissipated, a trickle of that infamous Algorean adrenaline entering his blood stream. "Easy now, esteemed Executive—Crane is it? We're all friends here!"

"Piper," a soft voice cut the silence over the holo after Max's plea. A slim, dark-featured woman was speaking, but he could barely make out the words. "They look like nice aliens. I sense that they have good intentions. They were going to return on their own volition for the good of the galaxy. Perseans are a threat not only to our endeavors, but to the entire Milky Way."

"He's Algorean," another of the Ugov Terraformers said. "What'd I tell you, Marjorie? Nala's always right, they *are* good aliens. Didn't you say you've never met an Algorean who didn't have a good conscience?"

"True!" The woman named Marjorie pushed past the others in the image to post up in front, alongside the executive, who was also studying the screen. "Yep, look at the blue muscles! Those pretty tattoos! Well, well, Captain Max, eh? So what is another Algorean doing way out here?"

"All right, Marjorie," the executive said, frowning at the largest member of her crew, "that's enough—we're not at a social mixer here."

"What?" The Algorean woman put out her tattooed blue arms. "A girl can't flirt? I'm fifty thousand light years from the nearest elixir bar…"

The executive ignored her crew mate and addressed the one with the soft voice. "Nala, what did you mean when you said you *sense* that they are good people? They're obviously low-level pirates, out here profiting from the abundance in these hidden worlds—the ones we are trying to save. Nothing angers me more than aliens breaking protocol and making premature contact with other possible new species."

Max swallowed a lump as big as one of the gourds the twins devoured back at the Ucharan native's feast. *Probably better not to mention we pretty much do that all the time.*

He had to say something quick, though. "Executive, I promise you, if you let us go, without the stamp, but with our own integrity on the line, we will go straight to New Earth and report what we have seen and deliver any message you desire. I promise you that. We have family and friends, just like you guys do. They could be endangered if the Perseans advance. Blob here is a Boor, he's been through worse than any of us can imagine. My pilot here Vern, he was once Oreldychynean —but got shot down during the war and had to get all wired up. He gave half of himself for the galaxy. I don't want to go back to… er, I mean, *we* don't want to go to Galaxy's End." Max didn't need to fake the desperation in his voice. "*Please…* let us help each other."

"Piper," the soft-spoken one said, brown eyes fixed on the screen. "Let them go, *please*. I trust him. I can sense his goodness. Those of us aboard *Lifebringer* are committed, even with the danger of another attack, to finish our mission. None of us want to leave Uehiron. This could be the greatest discovery of the Ucentury. I know you're not going to turn back now, Piper, not when we're so close. When the councilmen find out we had knowledge of a tournament being held and didn't return right away to warn them... it could be bad for our division. And we undoubtedly won't finish our studies if we go back right now, they'll never let us near this place again."

The executive sighed and said, "Or worse, they'll let Executive Zander get his teeth into it first, by claiming it's located inside a zone that's too dangerous for our division to study."

Max's eyes widened. Angle number two! "We even know of an influential councilman who will definitely react to the news," he blurted out, quieting both groups in their respected spaceships. "He will listen to our report, and take action. Our friend Claude here has worked with him in the past in other altruistic up takings."

Claude stepped into view on the holoimage. "I do know a councilman, it's true. His name is Adonis. I believe he worked in the—"

The gasps stopped Mike cold.

"*Adonis?*" the chief executive threw up her arms and let them drop by her sides.

"Yes," Claude affirmed, his whiskers twitching. "He was instrumental in saving our people from tyranny. We set up a voting system to help Animal Worlds get better status with the Ugov, freeing mutants from their creators."

"I can't ever get away from him, can I?" Chief Crane seemed to ask nobody in particular. She breathed out as if she had been holding it for awhile. "Fine, Captain Max. Having a veteran onboard, who served the galaxy bravely, I'll admit, it earns a bit of trust from me. And Mr. Rabbit, or whatever your name is, you say you know Councilman Adonis, eh? And, what, I'm to assume you're close personal buddies with one of the fourteen? Really? Well, I order you to go straight to him and deliver a message for me. These *exact* words, do you understand? '*Now* do you believe me?' "

CHAPTER NINETEEN

A Conscious Leader

There were few councilors in the Milky Way more popular than Adonis, and he utilized his notoriety because… well, because the job required it of him.

Without me, the fourteen would be ruled by Blackons.

He cringed when the infamous group of corporate magnates came across his mind. They had one concern and one concern only: how much black was on their bitcoin. But, despite his revulsion to what Blackons represented, he *had* to placate them to some degree, otherwise the galaxy would descend into chaos and war.

Adonis couldn't resist gazing up at the immense edifices towering above him as he rode the chain string expressway across a massive divide between moonscrapers. A line of chairs, connected by unbreakable megacoil cable, strung out behind him limply. Most of the seats were occupied at the mid Uday hour, with scores of officials traveling from building to building to barter for their various causes. Albeit archaic, the ride on the chain string was a much more thrilling (not to mention faster) mode of travel than waiting in crowded lines for the air tubes and horizontal sky walkways, and it reminded him of playing as a kid in the old post-urban metropolis.

Zipping through the sky, he spied the chain string terminus point. A small landing bay came into focus with androids there to service the arrivals. The black synthmetal bay protruded out in a half-circle from the sheer vertical sides of the building, with a million synthglass windows reflecting the dull gray-blues of a partially overcast Uday in Sun City.

Stepping onto the synthmetal landing pad, he wished he was already done with this first meeting. The next one literally couldn't come any sooner, because it would be at one of those lounges where every kind of elixir was served, and the music played on and on.

After taking the air tube exit from the chain string expressway terminal, all he had was a short ride on a hover board to the location of his first meeting. Once he got there, he handed his hover board to a porter bot, and got a crook in his neck trying to see the top of the building. He would have to go *way* up into the Ugov moonscraper this Uday, into a high security zone allowing credentialed diplomats to meet in relative candor. *What is it, the one-thousand somethingth floor?*

After scanning his wrist pad to pass through security he entered the main hall. He smiled at those he recognized, their gazes lightening as he passed them by. Adonis was fitted with a tertiary brain implant. It worked like a mainframe, storing his constituents' personal data, so he could access the information instantly, and ask personal questions about their families. When he consistently recalled fellow Ugov employees by their relatives' first names, and recited facts about them, it created a rapport and built a trust.

The fact he was a long, lean and muscular man, with an impressive cluster of salt and pepper hair attached to a handsome face... well, that didn't hurt either.

And he made sure to show off his most natural asset. The standard Ugov neurolink cheek plate, worn by most high councilors, remained idle at home. He never used it. He preferred the subtlety of the implant. *It's more human to show one's whole face,* he thought. *Besides, who wants to talk to synthmetal, lights and sensor beams? We're becoming more like Gen-3ers everyday, I swear it...*

Once on the thousand-somethingth floor, he exited the air tube and paced his way to the council room. A shrill voice called out the Usecond he stepped through the doors. "Councilman Adonis, welcome, come, sit!" Councilwoman Martins greeted him warmly and bid him to an open and waiting floating chair. Councilman Shuler was with her, as always. They seemed like morbid twins attached at the hip—related, but always competing.

Their cheek plates might as well be linked. But Adonis knew better, the two of them were not exactly on the same page; in fact other councilors had gossiped the pair of them formed a binary system of checks and balances. *Yeah—when they interrupt each other, that's their form of checks and balances.*

After returning pleasant salutations, Adonis turned to the minimized holoscreen hovering in the center of the meeting room. He pressed the enlarge button, and the screen filled up the big space with an image of Uehara—a miracle of turquoise textures flanked by billows of bright white clouds. The planet was so alive it pulsated! He squinted at the screen and cleared his voice.

Adonis dived right in. "So, the updated agreement from the last Terraform Division meeting, tell me, I'm curious, how were we able to manage to get Zander to come on board with it? I thought the extraction guys wouldn't agree to be limited by astrobiological—"

"Yes, yes, of course," Shuler cut in, "the Extraction Division has to follow the recommendations of the high councils. But those are just initial guidelines that—"

"That *what?*" Adonis talked right back over him. "Can be circumvented? Is that what you were going to say?"

"Councilman Adonis, please—" Shuler started to speak again, but Martins broke in.

"Zander can't simply ignore the Terraform Division's findings in Outer Cygnus. If he wanted to bypass them, and start extracting rare elements, he would have to get yet another council approval overriding this last one. And Zander's not the patient type..."

"To say the least!" Shuler blurted out, fielding a disgruntled mumble for the remark from the councilwoman sitting next to him.

They *were* a funny pair, Adonis chuckled before responding. "Well, why don't you two tell me something I don't know... such as the crux of the agreement." Adonis's voice shifted up an octave as he prodded, "Was it authored by Chief Executive Officer Crane? Any movements on planetesimals by extractors would have to be clear of any sentient life and would fall below protocol standards of the Terraform Division, correct? Their mindset has precedent. If a world has a chance of being habitable, they *will* reserve it and protect it—no matter what. The last thing we want is more strife between those two divisions of governance, are we in agreement?"

"Yes," Shuler informed him, "Zander signed off on it already. Executive Crane made sure to entice him thoroughly with the readings of drone flybys. Initial readings showed a lot of rare element deposits in the other Outer Cygnus planetesimals. For example, the moons orbiting this one." Shuler pointed at the holoscreen image of the planet.

"It was curious, though," Martins said, shifting her cheek plate to the side. "Uehara readings came back, but then the transmission relay was cut. Irretrievably."

"That *is* odd." Adonis turned his head. "Did anyone investigate further?"

"Not much to find. Probably smashed by random debris," Martins surmised.

"Well," Adonis gazed up at the ceiling of the meeting chambers, smiling as he envisioned Piper and her team of fearless explorers orbiting some strange new exoplanet aboard the *Lifebringer*. "Hopefully she's flying safe up there."

Councilors Martins and Shuler raised their eyebrows in a mirror image of each other. The three finished up the rest of their debriefing and parted ways, with Martins and Shuler heading back to the floating city to be with their families for the evening. Adonis, coughing idly, cracking his neck with a practiced sharp twisting motion, one hand on his chin and the other on the back of his head, stepped on his hover board and headed to a sky cab platform.

Time for my second meeting. This time, though, the location was in a much more low profile location, and it was with one of his biggest political adversaries. Chief Executive Officer of the Extraction Division of the Ugovernment, Zander.

I wonder why he wanted to meet outside capital grounds? Another devious plot, I'm sure. Maybe I'll find out the real reason he signed off on the terraformers' plans.

Adonis could never guess what was on the man's mind—other than, of course, the constant desire to be cracking the proverbial egg of yet another planet, in order to take out its yoke of minerals and rare elements.

Once I have an elixir in me, I'll be able to sit within arms distance without wanting to reach over and strangle him. Adonis sincerely hoped so at least. It wasn't good media for councilmen to get into physical altercations at elixir bars. *"Diplomacy first,"—how does the saying go?* He licked his lips as he rode his hover board a little too close to a group of pedestrians who shot him a glance.

"First diplomacy, then combat!" he called over his shoulder.

***

Adonis found Zander waiting for him at a floating lounge table, overlooking a group of large breed Istabanian musicians warming up on a stage below. *What a cool, unique sound, I'll bet their songs are amazing!* Adonis, unprompted, sidled into a floating chair. And there was the pocked, gray-skinned face of the man he had imagined punching so many times.

"Executive Zander."

"Councilman Adonis."

Neither smiled, neither made a gesture, but instead stared at each other's eyes for a long moment. Adonis's pupils adjusted to the lounge lighting and were able to perceive the standard reddish glaze across the whites of his rival's eyes. One of the side effects of the herbal elixirs served there. Bloodshot eyes.

Speaking of which, I need to get on this guy's same level here. Adonis hailed the closest android waiter and ordered his favorite potion, sure to redden his eyes as well.

"Zander," Adonis said, gesturing about at the flunkies and riffraff congregated in the Low Town establishment Zander had chosen for their rendezvous. "Can you explain to me why we're meeting, and, more importantly, why *here?* I'm not afraid of a little face time with the general public, but this place isn't exactly mainstream."

Zander laughed and glanced around. He wasn't nervous, but there was something about his behavior... *He wants anonymity for a reason, why?*

236

"What, Adonis, you forgot where they serve the best seaman's salad in the Orion Arm?"

"It's all about the elixirs," said Adonis as he snatched and sipped the edge of the glass the drone waiter had arrived with. "You want to talk about the best? Ahh. This is the best solar soda in Sun City. Best in the *whole* Arm, though? That's a whole different story."

The energy mogul didn't dally long before beginning his pitch. "All pleasantries aside, I brought you here, Councilman, to discuss the Outer Cygnus situation. It holds our mutual interest, I imagine, does it not?"

Adonis puffed out his lower lip and lifted his eyebrows. "Yes, I suppose that's a fact. Ironic, though, isn't it? You and I sharing a mutual interest. But to make it clear, I am *not* interested in manufacturing hyperspace sheaths, as you are. I don't care what kind of rare elements are needed—"

"But you *do* care about the Terraforming Division, yes? And the ongoing exploration of the Outer Cygnan reaches..."

"Yes," grunted Adonis, annoyed with the parlay already. "Of course I do, as should every Ugov citizen who possesses a conscience. Astrobiology is part of the very fabric of our existence. It is essential for our galaxy to progress."

Zander clicked on his neurolink cheek plate extender, and the synthmetal strip came out to cover most of the bottom left portion of his face. He pressed on it gently and out came scrolling text projected in large font in the open space between the two rivals. Words scrolled upward slowly and disappeared, but held there long enough to be legible. "Have you read Universal Law lately? You might want to read this..."

Adonis didn't answer; it wasn't a question. He was meant to read it. Zander stopped the scroll, clicked a few more times and a portion of the ledger became boldfaced and zoomed in, to be distinguished easily.

"Maybe you haven't studied lately," Zander continued. "Let me read this part for you… 'No resource of the Ugovernment may be partitioned to any singular division, nor a singular high council ruling.' When it says: 'no resource,' Councilman, this part of the ledger—if you click further—includes a large body of things of the utmost importance to the integrity of our Sunish doctrine. None of which, I must dutifully point out, are more important than continuing to keep hyperspace travel an *expanding* industry— forgive the pun. It's really not complicated. To make the sheaths, we need rare elements. The limits on how far we can travel, how far we can extend our reach, how quickly we can get there and back—it's all dependent upon the building of sheaths. Without safe sheaths, we can't send the astrobiologists to the far reaches of the galaxy. Without safe sheaths, we can't secure our galactic hegemony, and we *cannot* progress as the leaders of the known universe."

"Oh, spare me the Suncentrism, Zander. Get to the point. What does all this have to do with me?"

Zander lost any sign of affability on the exposed right side of his face. His voice deepened. "You have the ability to reason with other council leaders, Adonis. You need to talk to the Terraforming Division and get them to okay our extraction plans. They have identified Uehara as a planetesimal with all the makings of a rare element producer. There may be other 'twin' systems in Outer Cygnus as well. But Crane and her people are going to want to keep them for their own purposes. To study them! Ha! Of all the absurd things! They probably don't even want to actually terraform them—just tinker with their astrobiological toys, and let them *sit* there. It's not their galaxy, however. We believe the exoplanet Uehara contains a scarce resource, critical for the stability of Sun Peoples. It cannot be partitioned. It will not be partitioned."

Will not? Adonis was discomforted by Zander's intimations about loopholes in Universal Law. He had just about hit the limit of his patience, so he sipped on his solar soda and took a breath to calm himself. "So, Zander, I guess I'll ask you again: what in the name of the Milky Way does this have to do with me? You don't really think I can actually talk them out of it?"

"Well..." Zander turned away, folding his arms across his chest. "We don't want to waste time arguing in council rooms for approval. The Terraformers' loyalist councilors are good at wasting Utime. Valuable Utime. Blackon investors have already staked claims. This project is happening, Councilman, and I am hoping you can speed up the process. Talk a little sense into Chief Executive Crane. Since you have a history with her..."

Adonis glared at him. The provocation of his rival now lacked all discretion. "And why, *exactly*, would I do that for a conniver like you?"

Zander chuckled before answering. "Because if you do *not*, Councilman, we may be forced to send out the extractor teams prematurely, which could potentially endanger the exploration team. Correct me if I'm wrong, wasn't Crane's father infamous for creating blockades and putting together resistance groups over prospected sites? We wouldn't want to have a repeat of *that* dark chapter in Ugov history, now would we? His daughter, your *close* friend Piper, seems to have a rebel streak in her, and believe me, this line of thinking won't be tolerated. Blackon investors who are counting on rare element extractions have more than enough bitcoin to hire non-military private security. Sagittar-built killing machines."

Adonis shook his head disgustedly while regarding the viper of a man float-sitting in front of him. The bastard smiled, stuck his chin forward, and moved his head and shoulders to the rhythm of the music filtering up from below.

He's mocking me. Mentioning my prior relationship with Piper? Talking about Blackon mercenary droids? Really? What a scumbag. He took another long sip of elixir, closed his eyes and repeated the mantra in his head: *First diplomacy, then combat.*

"All right, Executive Zander, you got me this time, I will do your bidding. Although, I can't guarantee you I can convince a woman so entrenched in her beliefs to risk compromising even one of her selected worlds, but I will attempt to do so. For the good of the galaxy."

"For the good of the galaxy—of course." Zander laughed.

"But I'll expect something in return—a favor for a favor."

Zander's mouth went straight. "I assumed as much. So... how can I be of service?" All the while he moved his upper body faster to the rhythm of the enthralling music.

Adonis shook his head. The despicable man had probably never gone to a dance hall in his entire life. "I'm not sure yet," the councilman said. "I'll holo you." And with that, he finished his elixir, roughly set the glass on the floating table, and exited without speaking.

***

He was being followed. After noting the same air car several times, while flying the short distance from Low Town back up to the floating city, it couldn't be a coincidence. Easy to identify by its sleek, modern design, the pursuing vehicle had the dark polished finish of a Ugov issue. A mere mirage at first, dangling at the edge of Adonis's paranoid subconscious, the black air car was about to force him into having a third meeting of the Uday.

He told his taxi android to bring him to the closest landing island, and the air cab banked and dived for the brightly lit platform hovering in mid air. Other air cars were landing and taking off, so they had to wait for their turn and do a loop around it.

"Stay here, please," Adonis ordered his cabbie. "This shouldn't take too long."

Councilman Adonis craned his neck to glance out the portal. *Yep, there it is again.* The dark shape initiating a slow approach to the island landing platform. *Who are you?*

He rarely called for security backup. The days of threats to Ugov councilors were long over. He could travel in relative peace, and Ucitizens often gave him gifts or invited them into their domiciles in an effort to show their appreciation for his work in keeping the galactic peace. Nevertheless, he considered calling for help. He reached for his wrist pad to bring up a quick hail emergency holocall… but he hesitated, relaxed, and waited for the inevitable to happen.

It's just another meeting.

Once standing on the platform, Adonis had to wait for the melodramatic appearance of one Royce Knox, head of security for the Terraform Division. As the boxy man strutted out from under the white emissions coming from the rear end of his expensive air car, Adonis chuckled to himself: *Wow, these terraformer guys ride in style! Us comely councilors don't get to fly around in those kind of machines.*

Knox, as wide as he was tall, came forward and saluted appropriately. "Good Uday, Councilman Adonis. Sorry for the scene…"

"Royce Knox, the terraformer bodyguard extraordinaire. How are you, man?" Adonis slapped him on the back in a semi-friendly/semi-aggressive manner, his hand stinging afterward. *Damn, the guy's made of synthmetal!*

Knox narrowed his eyes at him. "Adonis, I'll get right to it. We have reason to believe that Zander is going to endanger the terraform mission in Outer Cygnus. We need assurance you will hold him at bay."

The elder Sunish man's consternation was palpable. His blond eyebrows met in the center of his forehead, creating a uniform brow of hair all the way around a balding dome of pink skin.

"Well," Adonis said, acting oblivious, "that's random... I just now finished meeting with the aforementioned rogue." Adonis pretended to gape at him. "Oh, I see. That's not a surprise to you, is it? Wow—I thought my fame had bought me anonymity in Low Town. But I guess when everyone knows I'm fond of elixirs, and everyone knows where the best solar sodas are served, I'm probably not very hard to locate, am I?"

"Councilman Adonis," Knox leaned in to emphasize his words. His nicked up face got so close Adonis could smell his breath. "We need your help. Can you keep Executive Piper and the exploration team safe from him?"

Not the best hygiene, but he is one tough guy. Adonis wasn't an idiot, the man was not to be trifled with. *This is utter hilarity! I'm getting flack from all sides.* Shuler and Martins wanted him for information, Zander wanted him for corruption, and Knox wanted him for protection. As if Adonis the magician could get everyone to hold hands? He had to admit though, he *did* have a history of bringing people together, especially the castaway types, mostly Cygnan aliens displaced by wars, but also a time with Animal Worlds activism. *Who was that one rabbit I worked with? He had a twin who was a total wisecrack, both surfers too. They rode some pretty big scary waves on Hare Island. And those coiled up, stinky braids he had? There must have been sea crabs and lice living in there by the dozen. What a smart mutant he was...*

Adonis pulled his head away and stepped back. "My dear Knox, the closer you lean, the more I learn about your diet. Vegan to the extreme. How very permaculture of you. Now... I can assure you, my main consideration is what is in the best interest of the Ugov as a *whole*, and that *includes* terraforming projects. I always have—and will continue to—support your team's endeavors. Now, if there's anything else, sir? I've got to get some rest before I have to lobby at the high councils tomorrow…"

Adonis walked past a disgruntled Royce Knox, purposefully bumping his shoulder to further his angst. It didn't budge a millimeter. *Galaxies he's strong!*

Adonis hailed an air cab idling on the platform after dropping off its last fare, hopped in, and sped off into the twilight.

***

On his way home Adonis gazed out the window of his air cab and observed deep, dark tendrils of clouds, lit from behind by a recently set sun. A macabre scene of red and pink blotches dripped down the gray panels of the sky around him. There had never been war on the soil below him. When the Ugov chose the latest replica of Planet Earth, they made sure to place it in an untarnished solar system, the right age and distance from its host star, forever to be renamed: New Sun.

It might as well be called New Ugov. Ever since the capital of the galaxy had an official location, everything had changed… less representation and more corporatization. Blackons are blood-sucking leeches. Hard to shake off.

The air cab swooped around a curving skyway exit, marked by virtual laser dividers, letting all the other air cars pass safely above them. His tenement was easy to spot among the shorter buildings surrounding it: a large half shell design, quartered by spindly towers, with a million perfectly aligned lights coming from within the curve.

"I know what you're thinking, it's not much to look at from above," he winked to his cabbie, who was designed to resemble a famous actor of the past. *What was that guy's name... he starred in a comedy series I binge watched like a madman.*

"I'm sure it's befitting a man of *your* caliber, Councilman!" the android jibed.

"Ah ha, flattery. Is that how they're programming you guys these days?" Adonis shot back.

"Oh, absolutely not, sir. Try the word sarcasm. It's a word meaning—"

"So you do, or you don't placate high government councilors?" Adonis pretended to be serious.

"*High* Councilor? I had no idea. Oh, what precious cargo I carry this evening! Thank the Milky Way. But wait a Usecond... a high-ranking member of the Ugov? Who lives in the floating shell building? That seems contrary to my programming. I would assume one of the fourteen—*esteemed*—councilors, like yourself, live in the Shore View mansions, no?"

"Councilman Adonis lives among his constituents, haven't you heard the Uweb news holos? A cabbie of your caliber, I would think, should be able to instantly recognize my signature 'sans-cheek-plate-style', thus I assumed the reason for your excessive platitudes. No other Ugov high councilor refuses to wear one, and no other councilor lives in a floating shell—just little old me!"

"My oh my, since my data banks have you listed as 'unmarried' the ladies must love Adonis, the 'cheek-plate-free' councilman! Ah, but wait. Hold on... oh, dear. This *is* troubling. I just checked the media files going all the way back to before puberty. No marriages or long-term relationships with members of the opposite sex on record? Hmm. *Very* interesting. That's worth a story... multisexuality is accepted, Council-*person*, since before the Age of Orion, as a matter of fact, several thousand years ago. There's no need to be shy about anything."

"You, too, Cabbie? If I had a trillion black on my bitcoin for every media mogul that asked me why I'm not married, or made conjectures into my 'multisexuality' I would—"

The cabbie was processing faster than Adonis's tertiary brain implant, "Be extremely wealthy, indeed. I ran the holos and had them processed. You were asked the question by interviewers one thousand two hundred and thirty-two times in the past five Uyears alone."

"I have gone on a few Uweb virtual dates, okay? Since you're asking. It's not that. I work hard, long hours. Someone's gotta keep you AIs running and the Milky Way safe."

"My hero!" The cabbie's voice altered to a woman's high-pitched cry, probably sampled from an actress of the past. "Belittling the Sagittarians, eh? That doesn't sound like a heroic councilman to me."

"Well, heroes aren't always what they're made out to be... your tip will be transferred *some* Uday, I'm sure of it..." Adonis tried warding off the synthetic mocking from the ornery cabbie. But, as he stepped out onto the landing platform, he lost the next round as well.

"I'm sure it will..." his verbal abuser railed through a speaker attached to the top of the air cab, "what with all the extra bit coin you must have after the cheap rent you pay at this dump of a floating shell... ha ha ha!" And off into the night it scooted, leaving Adonis with his bitcoin in his hand. He shook his head as he inserted his bitcoin back into its slot on his wrist. *No wonder there was an AI War.*

Before going into the air tube from the roof of the landing pad, he took in the expanse of the floating city. Spread out across the wide blue waters and around the edges of Sky Lake were millions of people, stacked together on retractable moonscrapers, with portable Low Town buildings clustered in bunches beneath their shadows. Circling the metropolis were non stop whisks of light, air cabs' contrails and sensor beams, flashing on and off with each acceleration boost. *Like glowing flies buzzing in a forest,* he thought. Turning around, as he sank into the air tube, he caught a fleeting glimpse of Mount Sun, ten thousand kilometers above lake level, ringed and shrouded by clouds of every shape, moving to and fro.

Another Uday on New Earth, another dramatic sunset. It was hard for him to imagine life before the passing of "island civilization" laws. Consumption gave way to conservation, and all post-urban areas were required to build upward or downward into the earth—never to expand outward. Using this technique the majority of land between cities was able to revert to its wild state, ensuring the long-term health of the environment.

But it made for crowded conditions almost everywhere in the cities.

Which definitely included Adonis's residence. As he walked through the tenement, hundreds of neighbors smiled and talked in the air tubes and passageways. Music was playing through the common areas, with groups of friends dancing together.

Wait, what Uday is it? His heartbeat increased. *Did I forget it's a Uholiday?*

Brightening with the possibility of some much-needed time off, his stoke was shattered when a reminder holotab popped up off his wrist pad. Palm to forehead he scrolled through the damage. More meetings. More talking. Udays to him were nothing more than never ending conversations, where each word had the potential to change the fate of the galaxy. *Yeah, right.* He flashed his wrist at the security panel and the door to his apartment slid open, revealing...

Dear demons of the Milky Way—did I forget to program my AI maid service again? It was a sight to behold, a quintessential bachelor pad to say the least: old food containers and clothes strewn everywhere, buzzing gnats hovering in every room, elixir bottles standing like marionettes, robotics parts discarded into piles on (and below) floating chairs that hadn't been charged in so long they weren't floating anymore, instead they were plunked on the ground like shot-down space cruisers. A smell of decay made the scene even less welcoming. *Ugh.*

He turned around and headed back out the door. *Might as well go hit up the shell lounge and get a bite to eat and an elixir... at least it'll be a bit cleaner.*

CHAPTER TWENTY

The Persean Threat

Beep boo beep boo. Beep boo beep boo. Beep boo beep boo. Adonis's eyelids slowly unfurled as he reached over and clicked off the holocom signal.

What time is it?

He may have had an extra elixir after dinner. Or two? He found himself lying on the floor of his dirty apartment, still in his councilor's outfit. *Yep, shouldn't have had the last one.*

With hands holding each temple firmly, he crawled to his knees first, and then staggered to his feet. A holocall this early meant it was important. After downing an entire liter of water in one long gulp, he pressed a button to activate just the audio. It was his main assistant, calling from his office at the Ugov moonscraper.

"Councilman?"

"Yes, Audra?"

"Sorry to bother you at this Uhour, but we have an unsanctioned intergalactic spaceship that has been escorted to the

security wing of the landing port. There are Cygnan aliens, and…
others on board."

"So what? Audra, I'm kinda out of sorts. Too many elixirs last night… can this please wait for—"

"Councilman, they have asked *specifically* for you."

His consciousness lifted from dream to reality. "What? Asked for *me*, personally?"

"They arrived a half Uhour ago. I thought I would call you first, so Ugov security teams don't take over…"

Adonis closed his eyes, his head was ringing. "Yes, yes, good thinking, yes. Umm. Can you… uh, can you call Whitegull for me?"

Now he couldn't stop scratching his head and itching the back of his neck. He was glad it was an audio call, he hated for Audra to catch him in this disheveled state.

"I already did, Councilman. He's en route, so he should be at the site first."

"Thank you, Audra."

Adonis clicked off the com and raced out the door. He took the express cube directly to the landing port and was egging on his android pilot to speed up soon after, skipping the counseling session and the satirical ribbing this time.

When he finally made it there, bursting into the security detainment quarters, a large gathering of people were huddled together in the center of the chamber. He couldn't make out what they were staring at until he gazed up. A large, blue-skinned head was sticking up over the crowd.

"Move!" Adonis yelled, pushing through the gapers. "Get out of the way! Move! He stopped short at the front of the crowd, astonished at the unlikely sight of the aliens and mutants and…
What is that platinum guy, anyway? A Gen-3er?

"Councilman Adonis," A large, gray-furred rabbit hopped up to him, lifted his chin and wiggled his nose, evidently sniffing him out. "Do you remember me?"

Adonis silently regarded the rabbit. He scanned the whole lot of them a second time. The reintegration chamber where this strange bunch had been shuffled into had gone quiet.

"Adonis." Whitegull entered, the air lock on the door hissing open and closed. The councilman saluted his longtime friend and ally.

"What's the deal?" Adonis nodded to the group of... *what in Galaxies name* are *they?*

"Councilman," Whitegull pointed to an image on the main holoscreen, "these aliens have admitted to flying their spaceship to the Outer Cygnus Arm, deliberately crossing the Intergalactic Dividing Line."

"That's insane!" Adonis shouted. "Why would they do that? Moreover, *how* would they do that? No one possesses the star map data to travel beyond the Last Ugov Outpost!"

This was not the kind of news he needed to start his Uday. Especially after all the elixirs. He glared at the mutant rabbit who'd said his name a moment ago. "And who are *you?* How do you know me, again? What do you ragtag group of loafers want—other than a hefty prison colony sentence on Galaxy's End? Crossing the IDL is a major breach of Ugov regulations. Be quick about it, now, I've got a council or two to win over."

The mutant rabbit's reply was calm and measured. "Well, we may be able to help you do that."

Adonis's stomach growled. He had skipped his morning restorative beverage. "Is that right? And exactly how could your derelict posse help me sway a council?" He scanned the crew with a frown.

"Please watch this." The gray-furred rabbit hopped forward and clicked on a holoscreen message box from his wrist implant.

Adonis's jaw dropped. The box loaded a holoimage of Piper Crane. "*Councilman Adonis. These five Ucitizens have witnessed a Persean Planet Ball tournament in the Outer Cygnus Arm. Perseans have destroyed the Ueharan solar system. They have turned themselves in, voluntarily, in order to warn New Earth of this danger.*"

There was a long pause before she moved closer to the camera and said: "Now *do you believe me?*"

Adonis shied away from the holoimage, as if she were going to reach through the screen and grab his collar. Thankfully, it clicked off.

The Algorean took over diplomacy for the rabbit. "We came into contact with Piper and the *Lifebringer* while trying to return to the Last Ugov outpost from Uehara. We saw the dome walkers approach and... we had to jet out of the solar system in order to avoid the debris from Uehara."

"And you are?" Adonis cocked his head up at the big alien, who was patting his auburn hair nervously.

"Captain Max, Councilman. This is my crew of four—"

Adonis furrowed his brow. "Captain Max, eh? Well, what do you have to say in your defense, Captain Max? What were you doing flying past the IDL to Uehara in the first place? Only pirate ships travel there without Ugov permits—am I to assume that's what you are? Pirates?"

Whitegull added from the side, "Chief Executive Crane made no mention of such—"

"Um, Councilman, if I may?" The buffed out Captain put on a pleasant face. "We are the humble crew of the *Planet Hopper*. We are on a mission to surf. These are my best friends and crew mates. We travel from planet to planet scoring the best waves the galaxy has to offer. As I said, I'm Max, the Captain of our ship. This is Blob, our Boorish 'eating specialist' and gear head. That's Vern, he's half android, but as much of an alien as any other in the Milky

Way, and a fine Oreldychynean pilot, I might add. He's a veteran—and served in the war. And these furry little dudes are twins, Mike and I believe, you're acquainted with Claude already… they were both born and raised on Rabbit World."

Adonis had the flash of recognition. *Is that really Claude and Mike Rabbit? I just thought about them yesterday! Weird…*

"Hi, Councilman." The rabbit with all gray fur titled his head, his left ear pointed up. "Do you remember me now?"

"Of course!" Adonis smiled, pointing at him. "Now I recognize you—you're that crazy rabbit with the bug up his butt, always fighting for equal rights for all mutants!"

The rabbit laughed at first, then frowned when the insinuation sunk in.

"My brother was a hero—you should respect that…" His twin with the brown spots said with annoyance in his voice.

"Easy now, Mike," the Captain whispered, using two fingers to grab his friend by the nape and move him back a bit. "This is our only chance here…"

Adonis kept beaming his quadrillion-bit smile. "That's the biggest compliment I give—believe me. Nothing gets done without Claude's kind of persistence." Adonis turned and addressed the Algorean, recognizing his authority. "So… Captain of the *Planet Hopper,* let me get this straight: your crew flew past the IDL to the Ueharan system… *to surf?*"

"Well, um…" The Algorean hesitated, his baritone rising an octave. "Yes, but we also—on our own good will, mind you—came back with crucial reconnaissance needed by the Ugov. Doesn't that earn us a little leeway?" The blue-skinned alien tried his broad smile again.

Adonis wasn't buying it. *Crucial reconnaissance?* "And exactly how did you ascertain a star map to Uchara? Divulge all, please, or this will not be pretty." Adonis motioned to Whitegull to be ready to call for back up.

The Captain pressed at the corners of his auburn hair. "We won it. Fair and square, I might add. Gambling."

Adonis paced a bit on the floor, hands clasped behind his back. "So... let me get this straight. You traveled past the IDL—forbidden. Visited a Class C planet—*very* forbidden. A planet possibly harboring sentient alien life never before seen in this galaxy... *extremely* forbidden. All those transgressions... to *surf*? Must be a fun pastime. I watched Claude do his thing once, pretty impressive, I admit. But prior to your dalliance to Uehara, you were also breaking Universal Law by gambling in a non-sanctioned casino, and possessing an illegal star map. Any other offense you want to let me in on? You know, just so I'm ahead of it... you might as well tell me, Whitegull is probably downloading files on your history as we speak."

Whitegull, standing to the side of Adonis, flashed a wry smile at the crew.

The Captain shrugged. "We won the star map from a renowned pirate, you've probably heard of him, he goes by the name Carney."

"*Ha!*" Adonis shouted. "And the list goes on... I'm tapping into my brain link to add 'associating with pirates' to the list."

The crew of the *Planet Hopper* all stared at the carbon fiber flooring.

Adonis laughed out loud, but he wasn't amused. "What else? What other law, oath, code, or whatever you want to call it, did you violate? Come on now, don't hold back on me!"

"Well..." The Algorean avoided eye contact with Adonis. "There is something else. We also need your help..."

Now Adonis was officially miffed. "You need my help? This just keeps getting *better*... go on now, I'm envisioning a reality holovideo series—yes, that's it—one that follows you guys around from transgression to transgression!"

"Councilor," the Captain said. "We met these… people. Believe it or not they are living *inside* the Abandoned asteroid belt, and they're the ones that need help. And, well, it's kind of hard to explain, but they're also in danger from the Planet Ballers, and need protection. Can you send ships out there to, like, stop them from advancing?"

Adonis was out of incredulous looks to give. "Captain Max of the Ugov Space Fleet, ordering military action—now you've gone too far."

"Come on, Councilor! We've given you crucial info that can help save the galaxy! We've turned ourselves in. All we're asking is for you to help innocent, good people from being casualties of Planet Ball. Isn't there *anything* you can do?"

Adonis filled his lungs with a deep breath. He had to give the Algorean Captain credit, he was good at the art of the parlay. *This alien's better at it than most councilors I know.* "Okay, listen. I can tell you guys are sincere. And I *am* grateful for the intel. If Piper Crane vouches for you, okay, I'll see what I can do. But, Captain Max, a bit of advice to you and your surf buddies, let me handle the Ugov policy making, got it?"

When Max didn't answer, Adonis circled his hands in the air. The Captain nodded and motioned to his crew, who grunted their assents.

"Very well, follow Whitegull here, he'll take you to your— *temporary* confinement quarters." Adonis stomped off, his tertiary implant throbbing with data.

***

"The Perseans? Councilman Adonis, don't tell us you have brought together this council to speak of Perseans!"

Councilors stirred at the bellow coming from one of their own. The man worked his way through the crowd to the middle of the meeting chamber by maneuvering his floating chair around those in his way. "That's ancient history. Our time is limited, Councilman Adonis, we have many pressing matters. We don't have time to waste discussing the past."

"Councilman..."Adonis read the young man's name from a holodisplay floating next to him, squinting his eyes as if it was difficult for him to read—he was well acquainted with the man, but wanted to disparage him a bit for the interruption. "*Dorayne*— is it? The Terraform exploration team has witnessed the aftermath of a Persean Planet Ball tournament."

A loud murmur jolted through the proceedings. Incredulous councilors spun in their hovering chairs and made gestures of disbelief. Those accursed words had not been uttered in many, many Uyears: *Planet Ball.*

"It's true," Adonis calmly stated. "The Uehara solar system has been turned to dust. The Giant Beings have broken the treaty. That's a fact. It didn't happen in the past, it happened within the last Umonth. Chief Executive Officer Piper Crane of the Terraform Division passed on the warning through a group of alien messengers who are in custody now."

A councilwoman said, "Doesn't the Terraform Division have an active expedition right now in Outer Cygnus?"

Her question provoked a waterfall of inquiries from the group.

"How do they know it was Perseans?"

"What system has been destroyed?"

"Are you telling us the treaty is broken?"

"What kind of nonsense is this, Councilman Adonis?"

"This cannot be true. Has this been corroborated by Ugov drones?"

"There hasn't been evidence of Persean action for Udecades!"

The jumble of voices became one long undecipherable sound forcing Adonis to resort to pressing an alarm signal on the side of his chair. The short but powerful screeching sound put an end to the fulmination. He floated the chair higher than the others and stood on the seat instead of the step, for oratory effect.

"Fellow councilors," Adonis said, using his practiced candor. "This is an act of war. The Perseans must be dealt with swiftly if we are to avoid any protracted campaign and loss of life. We need to consider the responsibility we have as the leaders of the free galaxy, to value and protect all life forms here, *and* in Outer Cygnus. And our Terraform exploration team is out there, in danger, as we speak. I motion we gather military councils to decide on a course of action—*immediately!*"

The gravity of his request brought silence to the chamber. Voices emerged from the councilors' mouths, resembling amphibian croaks on a pond at full moon, one on top of another, until reaching a crescendo, with everyone trying to speak at the same time. A cacophony of opinions battling for supremacy.

***

During the tumult, Councilman Dorayne floated his chair to the floor and stood up. He motioned to the nearest councilor and mouthed the word "restroom," then back-peddled to the rear of the chamber, hoping not to garner attention. The councilors kept gesticulating and yelling, not one of them noticing as he slipped out of the portal. He nearly collided with a Ugov employee the moment he turned into the corridor, cursing under his breath as he scooted around the surprised woman. He rode the nearest air tube to the laser spa, two floors below. Once inside the facility he walked into the restroom and locked himself in a private stall, activating his wrist implant holoscreen.

The stern face of Myrtel frowned back at him, deepening as he was made aware of the situation.

Dorayne whispered, "I think Adonis is trying to muster military action to Outer Cygnus. He is basing this on a message from Piper Crane. It was delivered by strange aliens—who evidently met with the expedition team at the next system over from Uehara. They claim to have witnessed the destruction of the Ueharan solar system. By Planet Ball."

"Piper Crane?"

"Yes, I was just sitting in on the meeting."

"And strange aliens?"

"Along with mutants from Animal World and a Gen-3er."

"Dorayne," Myrtel's voice was hoarse and ragged. "Make sure you put your best agents on those alien freaks' location, and notify me if there is any change in status. Don't lose them. I'll take care of the Terraformer situation."

"Will do." Dorayne clicked off his holoscreen, and peeked around the rest room stall, ducking as a Ugov official walked past. When the man was gone he tiptoed out of the restroom and into the hallway, soon merging seamlessly with the rest of the foot traffic, as if on an ordinary Ugov assignment.

CHAPTER TWENTY-ONE

Speaking to a Giant

Finding a translator to allow Giant Beings to speak to the other races in the Milky Way was impossible at the end of the Persean Age. After the war between the ants and the elephants, all such communication devices—translator applications, computer simulators, AI language processors—were confiscated. The Ugovernment preferred to be the sole entity capable of the trick.

So, for Myrtel to talk to the grand master in high definition, he had his tech team concoct a way to project the image of his face as big as the size of a small planet, while at the same time shrinking an image of the face of Stergis. When initiated, massive processors took the data sent from Persar, decoded it into tiny wavelengths, reconstituted them, and then projected them from a string of spaceships extending out past the edge of the galactic core, across the Intergalactic Dividing Line, and through the bulk of the Perseus Arm.

An important key to the efficacy of the system was the use of an *extinct* hyperspace sheath used for sending Sunish armies into

Persean territories during wartime. Myrtel hired unsanctioned hyperspace scientists to operate the communication tubes—not to reopen them for spaceship travel, but in order to send pixels through the darkness of deep space. Any time Ugov space rangers or other random travelers came across the string ships they had no idea of their true function because they were disguised as shipping ports. All the regulatory codes were intact so everything checked out as legal and insured if Ugov auditors happened to fly past.

He was still in a bad mood several Udays after his meeting with Dmitri Stack. The man typified Blackon insolence, something Myrtel would have to deal with as he shifted power in the galaxy. Expecting Blackons like Stack to show allegiance to him was never going to happen. The question was, could Myrtel get *cooperation*. Not from Stack alone, but also from the Grand Master of Persar.

Myrtel's luxury spaceship jetted off Myrtel World to the far side of his solar system, settling into a slow orbit around one of the gas giants, poking through the blackness, a marbled, beige pebble. Myrtel gave the order to fire up the janky, makeshift communication system. Soon, the spotted and checkered image of Stergis, and the equally erratic audio of his voice, bounced off the surface of the gas planet.

"Myrtel."

"Grand Master Stergis."

"Always forward."

Myrtel did not return the greeting, but couldn't help reciting it in his head.

A moment of silence was followed by Stergis's voice—as each syllable ricocheted off the atmosphere of the projection planet. "Myrtel, you have news for me regarding our situation in Outer Cygnus? Hopefully all is in order?"

"No. All is not in order. A group of aliens arrived in Sun City. They claimed to have traveled to Outer Cygnus, witnessed the destruction of the planet Uehara and—"

"*What?*" exclaimed Stergis.

Myrtel continued, "There's more. They met with a terraformer team in the next system over, alerting them of our involvement."

Myrtel imagined the grand master in his robes, way over on his side of the galaxy, grasping a small planetoid in his hands the way a child would hold a bouncy ball.

"What is it?" Myrtel prompted when the grand master didn't respond right away.

"It's... about those aliens." Stergis paused, then said, "That spaceship, traveling in Outer Cygnus, weren't they traveling illegally?"

"Yes, absolutely," Myrtel's eyebrows went up. "No unauthorized spacecraft can fly beyond the IDL, they were definitely breaking Ugov mandates. Why does it matter?"

"Here's the thing, Myrtel. I believe we can identify who these aliens are. When we approached Uehara for our preliminary Planet Ball tournament, an unidentified alien spacecraft was detected by our military team. They were able to use a rare form of energy resonance detection, and they—well, they escaped. They slipped right past us as we were coming out of hyperspace from the platform off the edge of the Abandoned asteroid belt. Reverse sheath travel. We're aware the Ugov possesses this technology, but it has to be illegal for Ucitizens?"

"It most definitely is. Not even we Blackons are privileged enough to have it on our starships. Well, go on, what happened to the aliens?"

"We gave chase, but they committed suicide—so we thought. After all, they entered the asteroid belt! No spacecraft could possibly survive in such chaos for long. We kept a sensor drone nearby to keep an eye out, but we never received any readings to suggest a ship escaped from there."

"Let me get this straight…" Myrtel was in disbelief. *This is supposed to be my accomplice?* he thought. *And he can't take care of one tiny spaceship of aliens?* "You let spies through your grasp? You kept your drones there after returning to Persar, right?"

"No," Stergis replied. "I don't believe we did. In case of a random Ugov inspection by Space Rangers, we bring our technology back with us."

"So this is undoubtedly the same group of aliens… well, you may have jeopardized everything by letting them survive. Our element of surprise…"

"Myrtel, we don't have many Uweeks before this tournament is under way, and when that Uday comes, so does our new galactic era. Regardless of any… 'element of surprise.' "

"You may think differently when I tell you the ramifications of those aliens squealing to the Ugov. A major councilman has proposed to the high councils for immediate military action in Outer Cygnus."

"A preemptive move? Ha! I would love to see them try that!" Stergis's reaction boomed off the light brown planet's gaseous canvas. "We Perseans have been preparing for many Uyears. A new galactic age is near. A new age of legalized Planet Ball. I want to avoid a war if possible, that's why I'm counting on you and your Blackons, but if they move on Outer Cygnus I can't promise the *Amalgamator*'s canons won't annihilate them."

"Even if you defeat the Ugovernment's initial response, you realize it will interfere with the tournament?"

"Yes, I suppose it will."

"Grand Master, I will continue to inform you of the Ugov's plans, but you need to be more careful. We cannot further alarm the Sun capital. If we do, the councils will have that much more reason to support the military aims of this upstart councilman, Adonis. And we *cannot* have any more encounters with aliens."

"Speaking of… those aliens—they now possess the star map data to get from Outer Cygnus to the hyperspace platform near the Abandoned asteroid belt. It's a short sheath, but it ends close to the platform to our home. If the Ugov have their hands on that star map—that would take away our tactical advantage… the Abandoned platform is crucial to controlling Outer Cygnus."

"If there *is* such a star map, I'll get it from those pesky aliens," said Myrtel assuredly. "According to my sources, there was no mention of it yet, so if they *do* have it… well, let's just say I have my methods…"

"Excellent." The grand master's face brightened.

"And… the new weapon, are the buffers in place yet? Can your scientists truly mimic the collapse of a star?"

"We believe it will be ready for the tournament. We plan to test it afterward. If it works as planned, and a temporary black hole is manifested, it will perform janitorial duties after a match of Planet Ball. All the remnants and chunks of matter, sucked away clean, and ejected to an unknown location in another universe…"

Myrtel controlled the urge to raise his voice. "Stergis, you realize, if not contained by the buffers, creating a black hole that close to the IDL…"

"Oh, don't worry, my little alien friend," Stergis chuckled as he half-tossed the small planet in his hands, jumbling the image of his red-bearded face on the surface, stretching his features out. "The buffers will snuff out the black hole, and it will be as if the emptiness of space has always been there."

I'm not your friend. Myrtel furrowed his brow and swallowed. "Well," he said, "you need to be sure. Why not try a test in a remote part of Perseus? Wouldn't that be… *sensible?*"

Stergis laughed. "You tiny aliens… sensible! Ha!"

"Yes, sensible. I am the key to your victory, Grand Master Stergis. Without my help you have little chance of defeating the Ugov. This isn't going to be easy. So *I* will be counseling *you* on certain matters, such as those concerning Outer Cygnus. Right now the best thing to do is put the tournament on hold until we know for sure the Ugov won't be sending troops out there right as the games are supposed to begin. Think about it, Stergis, my *friend—*" the word enunciated with blatant sarcasm—"it would be an unmitigated disaster for Persean culture if the first official Planet Ball tournament were to be darkened by military action. It's supposed to be the dawning of a new era of competitions, yes? This era needs to be beckoned in with glory and honor."

"What do you know of honor and glory, little Sunish man?"

"I seek it, Grand Master, I reach for honor and glory, as you do. And I *will grasp it in the very near future.* I will rule this side of the galaxy, you will rule that side. As we agreed."

"All right, Myrtel. I will hold off—for one Umonth. We go on as planned if you have not resolved the issue. Get those star maps, and get rid of those terraformers."

"No. *You* are on hold. You will not throw planets until confirmation from me, personally. If you want my help with this war—you better let *me* do the strategizing. You can do the fighting."

They stared at each other's slightly delayed images. Clearly there was no need to say goodbye. Or use the moniker. But Myrtel recited it in his head, from rote. *Always Forward!*

***

Myrtel's poor mood had been worsened by the meeting. The grand master's flippancy about allowing spies to escape, and his refusal to accept Myrtel's advice regarding when to commence the tournament were making him second guess everything. He needed to gain leverage on Stergis. *I need that star map,* he lashed out in the air and swore he would supplant Stergis with a giant crony—one of his choice—that would honor the code of black and red bitcoin, and would allow trade across the Intergalactic Dividing Line. Out of the portal of his spaceship, he watched the gaseous planet fade into a pinprick, disappearing among the black fabric of space behind it. Stars speckled brightly, and a local nebulae explosion draped the scenery with a dull green hue, extending from the bright epicenter in every direction.

He contemplated the vastness of it all for another moment or two before reapplying his gaze on a holocall screen, pressing the necessary buttons to hail New Earth.

"Yes, sir?" Dorayne answered, his skin gone gray from lack of blood flow to his face. His eyes were rolling around slightly in their sockets.

"Dorayne. I have new errand for you. Of the utmost importance."

"Yes?"

"I need you to get access to the Ugov files on those aliens. Check their transgressions page... I'm quite confident you will find something—anything—to use as a pretense for collecting a bounty. I want you to detain one of them without any Ugov officials becoming aware. When you have one of the aliens in your possession, confine them and contact me immediately. Do you understand?"

"Yes."

Myrtel clicked off the holocall and leaned back in his hovering chair, interlocking his fingers with his hands cradling his head. *A hostage always helps motivate those who need a touch of...* prodding.

CHAPTER TWENTY-TWO

"Is that you, Vern?"

When the holoscreen buzzed next to the front door, it shook Vern from rest mode. He righted himself in his floating chair and gathered himself, waiting for the sensors in his legs to warm up before walking over to the display screen. His synthmetal limbs were creaking with each step he took.

Vern peeked at the holoimage from the camera outside the door. It was Adonis. He gave Vern "the look." The door retracted with a snap and hiss, even though Vern hadn't pressed the open button.

Adonis stepped in and waved his arms around. "Where are the rest of your... friends?"

Vern shrugged and reminded Adonis—through pantomime—he couldn't speak without connecting to an AI voice simulator. He motioned vaguely toward the back of the long, narrow confinement room, indicating to Adonis where the boys might be.

Vern typed a warning message as soon as the councilor had walked past him. *Hey Max! Adonis is here!*

The crew's quick response was impressive. As Vern followed Adonis into the main compartment he caught sight of Claude collapsing his microcomputer into a small cube. The rabbit slyly stuffed it into the dense, furry part of the center of his head, beneath a substantial chunk of greasy dreadlocks. It was doubtful anyone would go searching there for contraband unless they really, *really* wanted to. Meanwhile, Mike was trying to act casual, scratching his fur while staring at the synthmetal ceiling. Blob was humming to himself, wide-eyed, stepping from right to left. All while Max approached the councilman at the perfect angle to ward off a clear view, buying Claude a little more time to make sure his microcomputer wasn't emitting sound or light. It wasn't legal to gamble on the Uweb, which Vern assumed they were doing, much less even be on the Uweb in the first place, while under confinement of the Ugov. Communication with the outside world was supposed to be closely monitored, and it needed to be approved well beforehand.

"What's going on, back there?" Adonis leaned over to the side of Max, as if sniffing out the suspicious behavior they were displaying. "Hey, what are you guys doing?"

"Oh, uh…" Max stuttered.

"Storytelling!" Claude blurted out. "Yeah, storytelling—we were… we were talking surf. Remember that set, Blob, at Outside Overheads Reef? You got caught inside and rolled for a quarter mile? It took you *forever* to make it back out! Ha!"

Blob grimaced. "What are you talking about, Claude?"

You're not helping with the guise, Blob, Vern thought. Not a shocker. A Boor was as good at avoiding attention as a high-pitched alarm going off.

Adonis studied their faces. He puffed out one cheek, shook his head a few times, and then shrugged. Vern guessed Adonis knew they were lying, but figured they couldn't be up to anything *too* serious. "All right, so here's the deal, listen up. You two, come over here. Where's the Gen-3er?" Adonis beckoned Mike and Blob, who were lingering on the far side of the compartment, to come closer. Vern stiffly walked over to huddle near the councilman. "I managed to get you guys a furlough—"

Vern tried to hoot, but his AI wasn't connected to the voice modulator. By the way his friends were jumping up and down and screaming, he would have guessed they had just won a trillion bit lottery.

Adonis talked loudly over the hubbub, quelling it. "*Provided...* that you adhere to strict Ugov guidelines. I downloaded them onto your wrist implants a few Uminutes ago, so don't try to claim you 'weren't aware.'"

The Captain beamed. "Oh, of course, Adonis. Come on now, you can trust us!"

Typical Max, thought Vern, *already campaigning before the deal was done.*

Adonis shook his head again and motioned to the blue-skinned alien. "Settle down, Captain Max. Before you and your crew get all excited, let's get something clear: this furlough is an agreement I made with Ugov authorities, my reputation is on the line. You and your crew better stay within Sun City district limits, and keep a *very* low profile. Don't make a scene, or you'll be right back in here, but it'll be the last time you get to leave until you go in front of a Ucourt."

Max's grin was as wide as his whole face. "We'll take in the sights, have a bite to eat, taste the local fare... you know, like normal tourists do."

"Councilor," Blob asked, "any update on the Planet Ball dudes or getting help for our friends out there in the Abandoned?"

Adonis sighed. "Believe me—I'm working on it. As far as our Space Rangers can tell, there's no action in the Outer Cygnus area—nor the asteroid belt a few thousand light years away. We can't risk provoking any action at this time, I'll let you know when

I can send a transport ship their way. But I'll be honest—I can't say for sure when that will be."

Blob slumped in reaction.

"Nothing much we can do about it now, Blob." Max said.

Adonis patted Blob's furry shoulder. "Hey, listen, I'm going to do what I can, okay? Now, you guys go enjoy yourselves—not too much, though—come on, out you go!" Adonis activated a scanning beam on his wrist implant and motioned for Max to put out his wrist. With a beep Max was free, with the pulsator unlocking a code, giving him relatively unfettered access to the outside world. Adonis focused the beam on the others, one by one, and Vern had to shake his head and sigh, as the boys wrestled to get out of their confinement quarters. *Max won again, shocker.*

***

Earth Elixir was a bar serving the finest tasting beverages in the entire galaxy—at least that's what the gorgeous Sunish hostess proclaimed as Max led the boys through the rotating door into the establishment. *I guess dudes like us don't come in here too often,* Max concluded from her stares.

The place was relatively dead, a few regulars sapped their tall clear synthglasses from a row of hovering chairs, and a few couples were eating a meal in the rear of the establishment. Images of the natural world adorned the full wall holoscreens: forests of trees waving in the wind, gushing waterfalls, cloudy mountaintops, and a variety of animals charging around in their habitats, played on repeat, over and over. Sun City was the quintessential definition of an island civilization, which was the preferred mode of post-urban architecture among the hierarchy of the Ugov. The wild lands surrounding the capital of the Milky Way were renowned for their magnificence and their beauty, as well as their vast array of organic life forms.

Earth Elixir is definitely playing up that last angle, Max smiled, *big time!* The imagery on the walls made him flash back to Uehara. The glory of the coastline, forest, and the natives with beautiful skin and incredible food…

Max spotted a waiter and called him over. The man slowly, reluctantly, ambled over to their section. Was he a Sunish man or a well-disguised android? "Good evening! My friends and I would love to try one of your house elixirs, is there one you recommend?" Max asked politely.

"What kind of aliens are you, anyway?" The tender pointed to Mike and Claude. "I've never seen creatures as strange as you."

Clearly no need for pleasantries, I guess, Max thought.

"We're not aliens, brah," Mike hopped on his hind paws to emphasize the fact. "We're rabbits!" The gesture didn't seem to go over well. The tender grumbled something, but retreated to the filling station behind the bar to brew them a fresh batch of elixir—hopefully with no boogers in it.

Mike thrust his chin at the tender. "Galaxies, what's his problem?"

"Yeah, he's rude." Blob's monobrow tilted inward.

"No worries, bro," Claude laughed and swatted with his paws at the long white and gray frayed cords of fur, a meter long, which draped his brother's head on either side of his long ears. "The tender doesn't know fine dreadlocks when he sees them!"

***

Vern didn't drink elixirs. But he was well versed in *the effects* of drinking them from watching the guys over the Uyears. He had never taken any of the metabolic enhancing drinks on Oreldychync growing up, and by the time he was in the military—where imbibing euphorics was forbidden—he had missed the window when the properties in the beverage would have become

271

addictive. Most aliens who had imbibed elixirs during adolescence continued to drink them in one form or another for the rest of their lives. Lacking major side effects—other than the short, nasty hang over—elixirs gave the user a desired state of consciousness, such as serenity or resolution or "iration." Elixirs could allow one to become more talkative, or meditative, or, conversely, could increase libido or stimulate the brain cortex. There were many categories of elixirs to choose from, and it didn't take too many for the crew to get carried away. Which, if Vern was being honest, they had a habit of doing at elixir bars throughout a large portion of the inhabited Milky Way. The results of which were mixed, at best, and rarely favored the dude with synthmetal around most of his body.

I better get out of here and make sure to arrange a transport so they don't try to go to another elixir bar. Vern kicked at the ground. *This isn't a partying tour, it's a furlough. And whatever happened to the intergalactic surf safari, anyway? It's turning out to be something entirely different...*

Vern sent a pre-fabricated all-text to his crew's wrist pads: "Be right back," and slipped out of the entrance, drawing a long stare from the hostess.

Vern shuffled away until he was standing by himself on a sky deck—one of hundreds of rounded berths—connected to the long curving passageway, climbing its way up the moonscraper. Everywhere around him were moving aliens and machines. Moonscrapers lurched up in an absurd contest of who's the tallest.

Typical Sun People, Vern thought, *they're always competing to be the best, the grandest, the tallest. Oreldychyne is the direct opposite of this. Minimalism to the extreme.*

He walked along the rail of the sky deck for a bit longer. Every passerby, whether riding a hover board or on foot, paused and did a second take when catching sight of him.

Vern simulated a sigh. *I guess I am a freak. Definitely not pure organic—that's for sure, otherwise they wouldn't be gaping at me. But I'm not metallic either, I've got plenty of skin and most of my internal organs.* He peeked over the rail into a nook of business fronts. There were a few androids tending to menial chores. *Slave labor. Of course. They must all be property on New Earth—wait, there's a free android right there!* A Gen-3 was approaching him with a confident stride that belied newly retrofitted hydraulics. The face scanned him and made recognition.

"Vern? Is that really you?"

Vern stared at the synthmetal AI "person" who had hailed him. His own recognition scan was showing a spinning ball, meaning it wasn't able to process the sensory data.

The polished Gen-3er spoke in a haughty voice simulation setting. "It's me... Gene Genie. I can't believe this! We last saw each other what... a Ucentury ago?"

Vern stared in disbelief. *No way...*

"Vern, what in the name of the Milky Way are you doing here? What are the odds of our meeting here?"

Before Vern could get his voice activator revved up, the android seemed to be processing new information and constantly spat out more words. "Hold on a minute—why aren't you arrested? This is Sun City, the Ugov capital, you're... I'm accessing data bases right now... whoa! You are part of a group of—" An emotive pattern crossed the pretty face of the android. "You're an outlaw! I should call the security robots! The latest Uweb feed shows you're supposed to be under confinement! Stay back!" The Gen-3er retreated with two palms extended.

"Wait just a Usecond, Gene!" Vern turned up the volume on his voice simulator as it finally kicked on.

Gene stopped his diatribe and contemplated Vern for a moment.

"Stop talking! For a single Usecond, for galaxies sake! You never modified that personality setting did you, Gene?"

Gene tried to reply, before Vern put up a gloved hand. "No, it's my turn now—you listen. Let me talk. You will *not* call security robots. I'm with my crew, yes. We are... guests. Guests of Councilman Adonis. We came to Sun City on our own accord, well—despite my protests, but that's beside the point... anyway, I argued we shouldn't have come, but it's a long story..."

"Intriguing. It's not as if I don't have the time. Virtual immortality—ha! Let the organics have it, right Vern? All you and I need to do is transfer files from one metal husk to another, on and on it goes!"

"Uh... sure, whatever." That wasn't the case for Vern, he had plenty of organic tissue and vital organs.

"Let's catch up! I've been working on several amazing projects. Leisure and entertainment projects. One of them is for surfers, actually. Are you still into surfing, like last time I saw you?"

Now Vern was intrigued. "Yes. We still surf. In fact, we should be surfing right now, but instead we're in this landlocked Sun City fairyland."

"Once a surfer always a surfer, eh? Such an odd cult you belong to..."

Cult? Vern almost took offense. It was true, he obsessed over the sport, evidenced by the next thing his simulated voice droned out. "What do you mean projects, Gene? What kind of projects have you been doing? Projects for... did you say *surfers?*"

"Where are your friends?" Gene's head rotated on axis one hundred and eight degrees, giving away his synthetic identity.

"Right in there." Vern pointed to the Earth Elixir portal a few hundred meters down the long, white-walled pathways buzzing with people.

Once inside the bar, the loud voices of Max, Blob, and the twins were immediately perceptible.

The guys must have imbibed the firewater. Vern shook his head. *They're supposed to drink that stuff to get into the mood before a big wave session—not to get fired up to go back into confinement.*

The Usecond Max spotted them he called out. "Vern! You found a girlfriend! Or—" His Captain's face blushed a darker shade of blue. "Is it… *boyfriend?*"

Vern made a gesture. *Real funny, Max, real funny.*

"Hi!" Vern's old friend went ahead and introduced himself. "I'm Gene Genie, a Gen-3er, manufactured in the prefects of Sagittarius! Vern and I go way back! And, yes—I'm androgynous. But no, we're not an item." Regardless of the statement, Gene Genie slapped Vern on the backside causing him to jolt.

After everyone got in a hearty laugh at his expense, Vern introduced the boys, who in turn said hello and hugged the Gen-3er like he was *their* long lost friend. Gene scanned each of his crew mate's wrist as it met the receptor in his palm. He was probably discovering quite a bit about their biological compositions, including the confirmation that, yes, indeed they had all been drinking something the establishment called *firewater* elixir.

The group of six retreated to a floating lounge table and listened to Gene Genie tell stories about Vern, much to the half-android's dismay. They weren't particularly flattering, the tales from Sagittar. After the catch-up session, the topic of choice inevitably took over the conversation.

"So, Vern tells me you guys still surf?" Gene asked.

"Heck yeah!" Max pumped out his chest and flexed his arms with fists by his ears, his enormous pectorals, triceps, and biceps displaying his thoroughly tattooed blue skin. "Best collection of five surfers in the Milky Way!"

Gene Genie chuckled. "Is that right? Well, you'll be interested in what I recently installed—right here in the biggest park in Sun City. A synthetic *wave* pool."

It went quiet for several moments, which meant the locals sensed the sudden evaporation of background noise from the rowdiest table among the patrons, and craned their necks over at them.

"A what?" Mike broke the silence, hopping from his hovering chair and bouncing off the bar floor a full half meter in the air.

"Did you say, *wave* pool?" Claude copied his brother's antics, but one-upped him by hopping onto his floating chair, pretending it was a surfboard, squatting into a tube riding stance, and throwing out a shaka with his opposable thumb and pinkie.

"Holy Milky Way! A wave pool? Seriously?" Blob cried loudly, his voice deep, rattling the synthglasses on the table.

Gene turned his head side to side, the axial rotation getting jerked back and forth as he tried to face whomever was speaking. "My processors cannot confirm if your friends' loud response is aversion or glee?"

"Glee, Gene," Vern simulated. "We're all stoked. We could really use a surf, and we weren't exactly sure when, or *if* we were leaving here. Although, our boards and everything we own is sitting onboard the *Planet Hopper,* under a billion tons of soil, rock, and synthmetal."

"Well," Gene said, "you guys are going to enjoy this. I am extremely proud of the project. I brought in builders from the best manufacturers—all the way from Droid Land. This wave is the best ever created—professionals have tested it and said so themselves."

"Uh," Mike said. "*We'll* be judge of that."

"Where. Is. This. Place." Max enunciated each word. There was saliva dripping from the corner of his mouth.

Gene fixed his glowing eyes on the Captain, floating his chair back. A slobbering, flexing Algorean wasn't something to be taken lightly. "We can go there right now if you want, although it's open surf Uhours, so I can't give you an empty pool, like you probably desire."

"Tender!" Max yelled. "We'll pay our tab, right now!"

Vern had to smile as he watched his hearty leader suck up the rest of the dark red liquid in his synthglass, slam it down and yell: "Let's go boys! Drink up! Tubes await!"

CHAPTER TWENTY-THREE

Synthetic Surf-off

Ten Uminutes later the boys were standing on the pool deck near the jump-in spot, edging closer to the group of locals who were intentionally hogging the space. The Sunish surfers gave Max and the boys angry scowls. They weren't about to just step aside for them.

The Captain was first to handle the locals wherever they went on their surf travels—although it didn't hurt to have the massive form of Blob always looming over his shoulder—so he took his board, pointed the nose straight out, and marched right into the locals. They parted. It was better than getting impaled by the big Algorean's borrowed surfboard, but one of them expressed his vitriol.

"Synth Point is ours, you alien freaks. You can't surf here!" It was a larger Sunish dude who had the gumption to move in front of Max. Despite being outweighed by many kilos, the human seemed formidable, and Max stopped short of making contact with his surfboard.

The man jerked his thumb toward the exit as his friends encircled Max, emboldened by their leader. "Locals only. Get outta here."

"Hey, little human," Max said, dipping the point of his board at him, "we're close friends with Gene Genie. He built this wave—so step out of the way!"

Max charged on, bumping the local with the nose of his board to pry him out of the way. The rest of the Sunish surfers blocking the way grumbled uneasily to themselves, but reluctantly moved aside. Max motioned to the *Planet Hopper* crew to follow him, which they quickly did, trying not to make eye contact with any of the surfers—other than Blob, who's massive unibrow was folded over. The Big Boor peered at the human, who had boldly stepped in front of his Captain, as if he was an appetizer before dinner.

"Whatever, dudes!" exclaimed one of the other locals. "You probably can't surf anyway, you're a bunch of alien kooks!"

Max snapped his head around and stared at the Sunish man who had slung the insult, who immediately stepped back behind the bigger guy. "Watch and learn, little man, watch and learn."

Max leapt off the edge and splashed into the sienna water, submerging for a moment before popping up and landing sideways on his board. He wiggled onto his chest and straightened out his torso to align with the tail and nose. The borrowed board was clearly too small, lacking the volume necessary for the big humanoid. He struggled to paddle, but eventually managed to find the balance point, sprinting to the take-off zone. There were a few locals who were so shocked by the sight of an Algorean surfer, they sat on their boards and let him paddle straight past them to the top of the food chain. A wake splashed the Sunish dudes as if a small boat had buzzed them.

The next pulse from the underwater turbines bumped together, rebounding the energy off the walls, and he aimed his board at the forming peak. He spun, paddled, and kicked furiously to slide into the wave. Dropping in, Max took a diagonal line to maximize speed, the exact second his momentum waned he pressed hard on his fins, coming up the face to obliterate the breaking lip. Water sprayed ten meters up to the roof.

Max landed ahead of the whitewater, see sawed the board up and down by stomping on the tail again and again. Responding to the motion, his borrowed board snaked forward, gaining speed as he turned the corner of Synth Point.

A couple of glomming surfers tried to shoulder hop him at the middle section as he sped along. When he pointed straight at them, they spun their boards around, barely dodging out of the way.

Captain Max did several more full power cutbacks, etching the water with letter Ss, over and over. The big Algorean crouched as he approached the mega tube, which showed itself right as middle peak subsided. The tube was gathering into a hollow hole, intensely sucking in on itself, as it readied to unload its tremendous energy onto the synthetic reef below the surface. Stalling to slow himself underneath the lip, Max cruised within the brown round curtain, adjusting his weight to his inside rail, as he enjoyed the view.

***

"Whoa! That guy rips!"

Back on the deck, one of the local surfers couldn't help himself and blurted out what they were all realizing. Claude laughed as the dude had to duck a *thwack* from one of his friends for his disloyalty.

"Yeah, Max!" Blob cried. "Go!"

Claude gave Blob the "shaka" hand symbol as the Boor jumped off the edge and paddled to the top peak on his borrowed board. Claude elbowed Mike and they shared a giggle at the sight of their poor crew mate. Although he was on the absolute biggest shape Gene had in storage, even wider than Max's, nevertheless his hulking mass resembled a sinking ship attempting to make headway against a strong current.

A few of the locals pushed past Claude and his brother to the edge of the pool, and jumped off, following after Blob, catching up with ease. With Vern still hanging back with Gene Genie, Claude waited too, allowing things to manifest. Without Max and Blob standing on the deck in front of them, Claude felt a bit naked in his fur. *At least we get to surf without our suits on, although Mike and I are gonna need a shampoo treatment after.*

Claude and Mike snickered a bit more as the group of four local surfers who had entered the water, led by the guy who was bold enough to be willing to step in front of a perturbed Algorean, passed by the floundering Blob with ease. The locals were stroking with earnest sweeps of their arms and made a few derogatory comments loud enough for everyone on the deck of the wave pool to pick up.

"Whales don't surf!"

"Yeah, fat guy, get out of the water before you sink!"

"He probably can't even stand up!"

"Ever heard of a salad, dude?"

Claude flopped an ear at his brother and said, "This is turning into an old fashioned surf battle."

"Dude," Mike said, elbowing him, "it's a synthetic surf-off!"

***

Vern had a lot of questions for his old friend Gene Genie and memories flooded his data chip processors. *What happened to all that Utime?* Since his time serving in the Persean Wars, when it took the combined forces of the Orion, Cygnus, and Sagittarius Arms to defeat the Giant Beings, Vern avoided those memories.

He and his team of pilots from Oreldychyne were merely microscopic antibodies to the Giant Peoples attacking the Sagittarius Arm. The enemy was attempting to gain control of artificial intelligence—with the hopes of turning it against the Ugov forces. Vern and his crew of pilots attempted to thwart an advance on the next system over from Sagittar, and his best friends were all killed in the resulting firefight. Vern had somehow been spared by fate—trading death for a new *kind* of life. A life as both man *and* machine.

As it turned out, Gene Genie happened to be taking refuge on the small moon where Vern had crash-landed. A group of Sagittarians, led by Gene, revived him and nursed him back to health. But in order to do so—and without Vern's permission—they operated on him. The team of Gen-3ers equipped him with an AI overhaul, synced with any surviving neurons in his brain or spine. During the process, much of Vern's mutilated body tissue was replaced by specialized synthmetals, and several of his organs replaced by artiforgs. His eyes were gone, along with most of the skin on his face, and in their place was a visor and mask to cover the grotesque features of his mangled complexion.

One Uday, Vern had awoken to a new reality. He was now half android. Fuzzy details of his past life as an Oreldychynean hung in his consciousness; reoccurring dreams never fully forgotten. After a period of healing, Gene had paid for Vern's passage home to the Inner Cygnus. Vern wasn't the type to stay in touch, so they had not spoken since he left the Sagittar solar system, all those Uyears ago.

Vern stood on the wave pool deck facing Gene, conflicting emotions running through him. He owed the Gen-3er his life, and yet, he wanted to curse him out. *For being alive. And for becoming what I've become. A synthmetal half-breed.*

"Amazing coincidence!" Gene Genie's features were androgynous, seeming to fluctuate between masculine and feminine, depending on the situation and conversation. "I *cannot* believe we are standing here together right now!"

Vern inquired about his old savior's personal life. "Do you still reside on the moon when you're not on New Earth?"

"Oh, my goodness, no! That feels like a Ucentury ago... my expertise in mechanics allowed me to move to Sagittar and work for the head of infrastructure during the rebuilding era after the war. When I got bored with making moonscrapers for Sun Peoples, and making bitcoin for the Sagittarian leaders—who, I might add, oddly resemble Blackons in many ways—I went out on my own. Private contractor. That's how I came to New Earth—I was hired to work on the recreation parks of the capital. So I started a few Uyears ago, and my crew completed the wave pool a few Umonths ago. And, wow, you should have seen the locals that flocked here from the coastal cities of New Earth, Vern. Bringing that cultish behavior I was referring to earlier. Which, evidently, includes something you surfers dub as 'localism.'" Gene Genie extended his finger to the wave pool below them. There was a huddle of guys sitting on their boards, surrounding Blob at the take-off zone, preventing him from paddling in any direction. "I don't think they approve of me bringing outsiders to the wave pool."

***

Vern grabbed his borrowed board, jogged to the end of the wave pool deck and shuffled up to Mike and Claude, who were still hesitant to join the fray.

"What's up, dudes?" Vern said, trying to fire them up. "No barrels for the twins?"

"Look!" Mike growled, pointing his forearm paw to the top of the lineup. "Not even Blob can catch a wave. These guys are

284

blocking him and snaking him left and right, and talking a lot trash, too."

"Max seemed to do fine." Vern pointed at Max who was stomping back up the causeway after finishing his ride.

"C'mon boys!" Max cried when he made it to the three of them. "Whatcha waitin' for! Let's go schralp it up! Why are you still standing here?"

Claude motioned. "You don't see Blob?"

"Yeah, so what?" Max shook his broad blue shoulders and water droplets flew everywhere. "We've surfed crowded breaks before. C'mon, I'll clear things out for you guys a bit."

Following Max into the brackish water, Vern grabbed his borrowed surfboard by the rail and tossed it in ahead of him, hoping his water guard synthetic liner held up. *That disgusting water better not affect my system!*

Mike and Claude leapt in and paddled behind their two friends, forming a convoy of boards steaming to the line-up with authority.

A chorus of protests came from the group of locals sitting around Blob in a circle, their boards bobbing with the pulses of wave energy moving through the water. Every time the Boor attempted to paddle for a wave, two or three of the locals quickly took up the space, blocked for each other, and one of them would drop-in and holler back at him.

"Get out of here, large breed freak!"

"This is our wave—you kook!"

"You're not getting crap out here!"

"Don't paddle right to the top—fatso—go sit inside!"

"You need to respect the local scene. Come back next Uyear!"

When the Max-led convoy of four made it to the edge of the take-off zone, Vern could sense the animosity coming from the cluster of locals. They were waving their arms, splashing water, and coming up with such good epithets that he catalogued them in his tertiary brain layer for later reference.

"Listen, dudes," Max said, pointing his thick blue finger at the leader who had first stood in his way, "I don't really dig your alienism, we large breeds have just as much rights as a human or small breed, and we can either share this wave, or... listen, it's a wave pool. It's automatic until Gene Genie shuts it off for the night. We're not at some finicky reef break in the middle of the ocean, waiting forever for the rare sets. Let's share the goods!" Max paddled right through the flotilla, knocking a few of the locals off their boards as he made a B-line to Blob and the takeoff zone. Vern scooted into the wake left by his Captain and tried to keep up, with the twins lining up behind him.

"Go, Blob, go!" Max shouted as the next pulse from the wave machine drew near.

Blocking the other locals from getting in Blob's way, Max yanked on the nose of his board and jerked aside at the last Usecond, giving his crew mate a perfect wide open lane to the oncoming bulge of water.

Blob's eyes widened, then focused tight. The Boor paddled hard with his thick white arms and was swept up by the crest of the next wave. Unfortunately, the chippy borrowed board was nearly impossible for him to balance on. Of the entire crew, because of his odd morphology, Blob was the one who *had* to have the right surfboard design in order for him to shred.

Borrowed board or not the big alien found his equilibrium and re-corrected his foot positioning mid-drop. Forming a squat, he cranked a powerful bottom turn. The nose of his board went nearly vertical when he came up and smashed the lip with all of his momentum.

Vern was impressed by the consistent almond shape of the glassy wave as it continued to peel along the bottom contour of the wave pool. Gene Genie had done his homework when he built this incredible machine.

"Check him out, Vern!" Max pointed up at the holoscreen. The live feed image showed Blob as he pumped his way through the middle peak, about to enter the mega tube section. With impeccable timing, he wedged his bulky arm into the curling wave, stalling his momentum right under the most annular part, and he became totally shrouded. Vern could make out a brown silhouette tracing Blob's rotund shape, as it raced through the barrel.

The boys all hooted and hollered for their Boorish buddy until he was out of sight, watching the rest of his ride on the holoscreen above.

It was the last straw for the locals; they stirred into action. Outsider aliens encroaching on their territory was one thing—but to dominate the line-up and rip their waves better than them? Vern guessed they weren't going to be very stoked.

Oh, well, gotta go! Vern crept up behind Max and tried to get in position for the next wave, hoping Max would block for him too. A pair of locals trailed him, arm's distance away. Max peeled off again with impeccable timing, just as the next wave was ready to throw, allowing Vern to scramble over the edge and make the drop with ease. But when he peeked over his shoulder—one of the locals had dropped in behind him! The rider sped past Vern, reached out with both hands and shoved him hard off his surfboard. Without the normal retractable magnetic straps of his regular board to hold him on, Vern went flying to the bottom of the trough headfirst and penetrated the surface of the water with a hard thwack.

***

"Hey! What the heck, dude!" Mike yelled.

Max narrowed his eyes at the leader of the Sunish surfers, who was laughing with his buddies and pointing at Vern, who had just popped up from his fall, and was floundering in the impact zone, about to dive under another row of whitewater.

"Cheap move, dudes!" Claude growled at the group.

"I guess you locals don't know any better do you?" Max laid prone on his board and pointed at the Sunish surfer. "It's not a good idea to piss off any large breed, much less an Algorean man." He nodded to a bulging, refracting ball of brown coming their way. "But if *that's* how you want to play it—all right, we can do full contact as well! You want a piece of me?"

He stroked hard for the next wave, indicating he was going for it, but slowed at the last Usecond, purposefully allowing one of the Sun City surfers to drop-in directly in front of him. Before even making it to the bottom of the wave, the surfer found himself grasped from the waist, lifted clear off his board, and cradled in Max's arms. The Sunish man was flailing his arms and legs to free himself, but Max rode for the middle peak, carrying his living burden like a stork with a baby in a sling.

The guy screeched in a high-pitched voice to be let go.

Reaching the flat portion of the wave, Max lifted the Sunish surfer up above his head, with arms extended, and body-slammed him into the pit of breaking whitewater.

***

"Ooo!" Claude winced. "Ouch—that has *got* to hurt!"

With the locals distracted, his opportunity arose. He weaved past the pack of surfers at the edge of the take-off zone and clawed hard for the next wave. One of the rival surfers followed after him, making up the gap easily, despite Claude's head start.

It was too late to pull back from the oncoming rush of aqueous energy, Claude had to drop-in first. Right when he made a perfect carve off the bottom, successfully riding the foam ball to the shoulder, the rival caught him from behind, grabbed his tail, twisted it, and shook him, forcing Claude to fall off his board into the tan cauldron below.

This is going to suck, Claude gasped for a last breath while mid-air, bracing for impact. He closed his eyes and covered his temples with his paws, hoping his board wasn't about to guillotine him.

Boom! The crunch was a jolt to his system; all his fur stood up on end. *Lungs don't fail me now.* He kicked with all four paws trying to get to the surface before the next wave broke in front of him.

***

After completing his second ride Max jogged back up the pool deck. A blue mist rose from his trapezium muscles; his body core temperature was rising alongside his ire. The remaining locals, who had yet to enter the water, backed away at the sight of the stomping Algorean. Deciding on the spot they had better things to do, they grabbed their boards and gear bags in a panic, and ran for the exit of the facility.

Max did the simple math. There were equal crews of five surfers from the two rivaling groups. *Time to get it on.* He jumped off the deck into the lukewarm water and paddled back out.

When all ten surfers had bunched together at the top, the Sunish leader said to Max: "All right, dudes, you guys surf pretty good. But not as good as us. I challenge your crew. Let's find out who's better? Whichever group can get the most guys to stay on their feet all the way to the tunnel, wins. If we get more to the end—you guys have to bail. And if you do—you can have it all to yourselves."

"Deal!" Max smiled, thinking, *Got 'em right where I want 'em.*

The local dude's friends reacted angrily, not happy with the offer, and told him so in garbled surf slang not even Vern's AI simulator could have translated.

"Shut up, guys!" the leader quieted them with a roar. "Come on, stop being such weaklings, let's show these aliens how Sun People surf!" He sprint-paddled for the next wave, but then pulled his board out the back and chose not to go. Instead, he motioned to one of his buddies, who slipped into pole position.

Max searched his crew, contemplating whom he should send. He settled on Vern, figuring his friend would be seeking revenge, and called him into the wave. "Yo, Vern! Go get 'em! Your turn to do turns, brah!"

"Hey, dude?" the leader of the local surfers said to Max, as they floated side by side, waiting for an opportunity to catch a wave, "let's crank it up a notch, why don't we? To make things a little more interesting, what do you say?"

Max smirked at him. "Fine with me, dude, your funeral." The local guy was tough, Max had to give him that. Few Sunish men without a Ugov insignia on their breast would dare to talk so dismissively to an Algorean.

Max activated his wrist pad holoscreen and made the call. "Hey, Genie! Why don't you turn up the settings a few notches?"

Gene Genie's tiny image hovered there and spoke, his reply was measured, his voice and face reflecting his masculine side. "Maximillian, that's pushing it a bit. The one time Ugov inspectors let me to turn up the setting was when we were testing robot dummies. We haven't done any trial runs on the higher settings with actual humans or aliens or…" His head swiveled toward the twins.

Max puffed out his lips. "Okay, perfect! We can be your first test pilots! We'll do a verbal consent to waive our safety rights." He lifted his chin at the local who had been doing all the talking. "Hey dude, my crew is all good with being the lab robots for the higher settings, how about you guys? Are you guys good with being the first live trial runs on this thing? You must get bored with the *ramp,* how about we go with *ledge* setting?"

"Fine! You got it!" The rival surfer refused to be shaken.

Evidently Gene was fine with it too because all of a sudden the wave pool cranked to a halt. There was a moment of calm waters. A shudder. Then, a new sound emanated from the underwater turbines. The bulges moving across the surface of the pool became more and more refined. Everyone in the lineup watched in awe as sets morphed from the lurking masses of energy. The first waves that broke went unridden, as the surfers on the shoulder did nothing more than a few experimental paddle-bys, taking a gander at what they were about to drop-in to.

The lead Sunish dude motioned to one of his crew. "Chucky, your turn—*go!*"

The local named Chucky was focused and went for the next approaching wave with determination. Max nodded to Vern and his pilot paddled after the local, the predator pursuing the prey. After nailing their drop-ins, both surfers jockeyed along the face of the wave, carving arcs around each other, taking turns being in front. Each time they passed each other they reached out in an attempt to dislodge the other from their board. *Get 'em Vern!* Max watched them for a bit on the giant holoscreen, before turning his attention to the waves at hand.

Next in line at the take-off zone were Mike and Claude, their fur soaking wet and their rope-hard dreadlocks plastered to the sides of their heads. They looked much skinnier when soaked to the bone and two Sunish surfers shadowed them, with bad intent.

With all four competitors hovered near the peak, egging each other on, trying to get their opponent to bite, it was a game of who would go first. The advantage was clearly to whoever went second, as they would be able to watch their opponent ahead of them and push them off from behind. But if you got sucked over the falls, well, that was it, game over.

Finally, with Max's prodding, Mike broke from the small pack and sprint paddled for the oncoming peak. Claude made the conservative move and waited for both of the locals to go, dropping in right behind them to protect his blindside.

After the first three riders from each group of five had commenced their surf duels, it was time for the Hopper's jumbo crew mate to compete. Blob leveled a ferocious stare at his assigned adversary, which propelled the Sunish surfer over the ledge first. Blob pounced on the mistake, dropping like an ion bomb into the trough. The bulge of energy passed underneath the hapless human, knocking him from his board. The local dude skimmed across the surface, unable to penetrate, making his punishment worse. He was laid out helplessly as the aqueous guillotine came down.

"Ha! Ha! What a kook!" Max laughed as the holoscreen showed the thin, concentrated blade of the lip land right in the mid-section of the prone rider.

One-zero, us. Max and the best rider of the locals now sat alone at the top. Max assumed the guy must be pro, judging from how skillful his turns had been on the previous wave. The Sunish surfer rode with precision and confidence. The dude and his buddies had the upper hand in this synthetic surf-off, being familiar with the pool's trajectory.

Max cheered as the image of Vern flashed across the holoscreen. The half-android pumped his board through one particular section with a vertical ledge that was... *inimitable* by nature. *Not too shabby for a fake wave,* Max thought, as the screen switched to a live holo of the twins zipping along.

No contact had yet occurred between the twins or their rivals, but the mega tube section loomed ahead. As Max feared, the locals used their knowledge of the wave to their advantage. When the twins instinctively stuck their front paws into the wave to slow their momentum inside the hollow part of the tube, the local didn't stall. Instead they high-lined it onto the steepest part of the aqueous bulwark—forcing the wave to close out. Both rabbits were in the drink in a heartbeat, while the two locals landed top to bottom floaters and rode off, triumphantly shouting and pumping their fists. *Two to one, them, just like that.* Max slapped his hand on the water. *Damn.*

With the score settled in the twins' match up, the holo switched back to trusty old Vern. He was trying to even the score at middle peak. He jostled with his opponent until they were locked together in an angry ball. Both boards were riding parallel to each other, merely a Boor's hair away. Max thought they might both fall, but, at the last Usecond, Vern freed his arm and smacked it across the surfer's head. The local crumpled and was eaten up by the churning whitewater, limbs flailing like a rag doll.

Right on, Vern! Max thought. Now his pilot could enjoy the rest of the ride without a pesky human on his back. *Two-to-two. All tied up, with one matchup left.*

"I guess it's up to *us* to decide this!" Max smiled confidently. In all the surf contests he had entered in his life, not once had there ever been physical contact allowed. *Advantage two hundred kilogram Algorean.* He laughed out loud.

The talented local surfer remained unflustered, showing zero signs of intimidation, "Yep, it's you versus me. Why don't you go first, alien, if you're so confident in your skills, go in front of me, bro..."

"Be glad to. Catch me if you can—*kook!*" Max was amped with adrenaline. He only needed two long strokes with his arms and a few kicks with his legs and he was in.

Synth Point's *ledge* setting made the drop pretty sketchy, but he handled it with grace, and sped from high peak to middle peak, trying to get as big a lead as possible on the Sunish surfer, who had entered the wave a good ten meters behind him, but was coming on fast. Max expertly lined his rail with the contour of the oncoming lip, bashing roundhouse cutback after roundhouse cutback, in a powerful display, reminiscent of a wild animal trying to deter another animal from entering its territory. However, every time Max pointed his board back toward his opponent, the surfer did a cutback to stay out of range of Max's long blue arms. This human—despite his size disadvantage—was *not* giving up.

The middle peak crested in front of them and a perfect cylindrical barrel formed. The Captain's opponent respected the art of surfing as much as him, exemplified by an unspoken truce, allowing them a brief respite from their battle so they could enjoy the view from inside the tube.

But then the Sunish surfer tried to use speed as his weapon. He raised out of his stalling, drop-knee stance and pressed on his inside rail, projecting out of the tube with the spit, passing Max shrewdly on his blind side.

They were both through the mega tube, and the surf battle was still undecided. It became a sheer race as the speed track section peeled monotonously ahead of them. They gyrated and pumped, with Max bridging the gap moment by moment.

Algoreans had a habit of making physical competitions anti-climactic. The most athletic race in the galaxy owned every record in the Galactic Olympic Record Book. And Captain Max was no exception. He caught the surfer from behind, snatched him by his long flowing hair, and lifted him off his board—extending the human out as if he were a trophy—before dumping him in the whitewater. Game. Set. Match.

Time for me to show off. Max gave out a bellow and whipped his board rail to rail, gaining tremendous speed in a short distance. He aimed straight for the water outflow tunnel at the end of the wave, and let the whitewater propel him forward, crouching for one final tube *not* included in the designers' plan.

CHAPTER TWENTY-FOUR

Ethereal Discovery

Melia was speaking so fast Piper could barely understand her.

"Wow, this is truly amazing... can you believe it, Piper? How long have we been waiting for this Uday? I mean, this is unbelievable! A new species of sentient life? Out here in the farthest part of the Cygnus Arm? I can't believe it... I mean, if we didn't have the video..."

Melia was giddy—even for her. Ever since she and Marjorie had returned from their boots-on-the-ground mission to Uehiron, the entire crew was out of their minds with excitement. The initial chemical composition scans from the organic samples had confirmed what the astrobiology community liked to call "universal norms." The right mixture of nitrogen in the air and minerals in the soil. A thing of beauty. *I wish he could be here, be part of this...* Piper bit her lip.

"Piper?" Melia asked. "Everything okay?"

"Sure! Of course... this is *so* awesome!"

While they waited for fresh data to upload, Piper couldn't dodge Melia's concern.

"Piper, what is it?" That woman had her pegged better than anyone in the galaxy.

Piper sighed, and turned to Melia with tears welling and said: "It pains my heart... every planet we transform, every species we catalog, *he* would have had so many new perspectives on them. Ways of looking at things, ways of disseminating the information, breaking things down in a way I can't."

Melia reached out and held Piper's hand for a moment. "Hey, listen—it's sad he's not here, but he's always inside of you, and his work carries on *through* you. Your father would be very proud, Piper."

"I just miss him, I guess."

At least I've got Melia, Piper thought. *She'll always be here for me.* When the dam holding her tears came close to breaching, the holoscreen saved her. The green data symbol blinked. Marjorie's upload was ready to open. The chief executive's burst of emotion had evaporated, and now it was back to business as usual.

Piper focused her blurry eyes on the holoscreen. A still image of an animal was displayed there, and it was quite extraordinary. It was nothing but a puff of gas with eyes and a beak poking out. *Where is it's actual body?* She squinted harder, trying to make the resolution of the holo improve.

"Melia," she asked, "can you have Marj upload the cursory compositional readings on them?"

Melia tapped on a holopad for a few Useconds.

"I'm working on it," Marjorie replied over the com, obviously receiving Melia's text. "I'll send it up in a Usec..."

"What is *that?*" Melia asked, pointing at the still image.

Piper pressed and swiped until the short holoclip was playing on repeat.

Melia giggled. "What are those cute little things doing? They're there one Usec, gone the next."

To get the footage Marjorie had used one of her patented "silent-glide" drones. It was designed for reconnaissance flights into hard to access areas, and the rocky precipices in the part of Uehiron they were calling "the Highlands"—a forested area with large crevasses and extensive labyrinths of caverns—were perfect for the task. Tucked into one of these nooks, high among the vine covered trees, Marjorie and Melia made their revolutionary findings. A unique sentient alien species!

Piper edged off of her floating chair and stood closer to the holoscreen as if she was about to jump through it and pay the strange little critters a personal visit.

A cluster of ten or more of them flittered and fluttered around each other. At times the group emulated one big amoeba of grayish white gas, but at other times the mass split apart into multiple life forms, bounding alongside each other.

Are they ghosts? Piper stared in disbelief. She had never believed in the supernatural, but she did believe in astrobiology, which also necessitated a suspension of biases. But it was a suspension based on scientific facts—not on faith alone. *They're like—miniature clouds... but if they're made up of gas, how are they displaying characteristics of flocking behaviors? They don't have any noticeable wings...*

"There," Melia said. "That one to the far left of the screen—freeze it!"

The holovideo seemed to catch one of the creatures in a kind of transformational stage. Piper activated a frame-by-frame, slow motion rendering on the holoscreen. They both stood in amazement, Melia off her chair now as well, moving closer to the screen as if they were both trying to coax the fascinating image right into their spaceship. Nothing more than an ethereal, delicate wisp of gas, the singled-out special being seemed to break apart—

evaporating in the thin air. Immediately, a minuscule cloud formed about five meters away from the dissipation of the first.

"Now look!" Piper made a twirling motion with her finger. "It acts as if it's a microscopic tornado. Look at the cyclical vortex of gas moving about. Emissions?"

"An exhaling mechanism, maybe?" Melia posited.

"Maybe a new kind of internal organ? It has to breathe, though, that much is for sure, they are definitely breathing in the atmosphere. Yeah, here are the chemical readings right here. Marj just sent these." Piper pointed to a secondary, smaller holoscreen off to the side of the main display beginning to roll numbers and text.

"Or..." Melia put her hand on her chin. "What about heat exhaust? Maybe it's how they cool themselves? Similar to how species with fur can't sweat, they pant, to regulate their body temperature..."

"Doubt it. First of all they don't have fur, usually the panting method is used because the animal doesn't have the same skin cells as us. Second, it's far from toasty. Yeah, Mel, the mean temperature of the Highlands might be an issue. It's pretty cold up there. About five degrees Celsius."

"Cold for us," was Melia's astute reply. "Maybe hot for them."

"Mmm—could be true. My brain is fixed on carbon-based. You're right, Melia, we can't assume these little guys have anything resembling normal molecular structure."

Piper and Melia silently meditated on the special findings. The small compartment was filled with the noise of indicator beeps on various holoscreens large and small.

"Carrysa?" Piper hit the com button and waited for her to respond from the bowels of the ship where the lab was located.

"What's up, Piper?" Carrysa's voice came through the com within a few Useconds. The crew needed to have their com volume knobs set at high, and they had better be ready to answer, should the chief beckon.

"Can you come up here?" Piper politely requested. "I need another set of eyes and your astrobio expertise."

"*Expertise?*" Marjorie guffawed over the com, unprompted. "Come on, Piper, the girl hasn't even learned the new platform we're using!"

"All right, Marj." Piper tried to temper the half-Algorean's heckling. "Let's go easy on Carrysa, now."

"Why?" Marjorie continued. "Just cause her wrist implant goes on the fritz doesn't mean she gets a free pass, does she?"

Carrysa defended herself over the com. "I do *not* have anything wrong with my wrist implant. And even if I did, I somehow manage to produce the best astrobio charts in all of Orion, shocker, I know."

"Well," said Piper, "that's true, Carrysa, you do amazing work. But since Marjorie mentioned it... Marj, this evening you are now going to spend time helping our *challenged* friend with the platform transition calculations, sound good?"

Marj wouldn't want the extra responsibility. There was enough to do stuck in her compartment with synthmetals, exotic tools, and the multitude of projects paused in the middle of completion. Piper hated how it was usually a mess in Marjorie's compartment—there was so much clutter in there it was hard for anyone else to enter without stepping over and around the various gadgets she had displayed and arrayed in various stages of disrepair—but she always got the job done.

"I totally and completely rescind that last comment!" Marjorie whined. "Carrysa is perfectly capable on her own! Her wrist implant is working totally fine!"

Piper laughed at her half-Algorean crew mate through the intercom. "Marj, I swear, sometimes I think you should try to be a holovideo comedian. But sorry, that's an order. I want you two working together, not competing. Out."

A few Uminutes later Carrysa entered the chambers. Piper hadn't even noticed because her and Melia's faces were nearly touching the holoscreen they were so close to it.

Her singsong voice made Piper and Melia unglue their eyes. "Getting friendly with the technology, it appears? You guys give 'up-close-and-personal' assessment new meaning."

"My astro lab master." Piper beckoned her over with a sweeping motion of her hand. "Exactly who I needed to see. Check this out."

Carrysa came over and stood next to her crew mates and watched with anticipation as the magnified slow motion holo of the singled out special being came to life. After her first viewing she cried out: "Oh—great Milky Way! That's incredible! What kind of gas—does the composition reading show?"

"Methane mixture..." Melia answered for Piper even though the question wasn't directed at her. "Small percentages of other stuff... water vapor and nitrogen..."

"Hmm..." Carrysa ran her fingers through her golden curls, tucking the ends behind her ears. "*Wait!* Stop it—stop it right there!" She swished both hands in the air, gesticulating excitedly. "Now go back two frames—see that, see that? There's a solid core in there—a sort of physical structure. Skeletal or muscular. How else could they be interacting and even communicating with each other? They have to have a brain and central nervous system."

Scratching her head, perplexed, Piper had a tip of the tongue sense they were on the brink of *extremely* important findings. She meditated on Carrysa's observations for a moment.

"Yes, Carrysa," Melia agreed, "this is good. Now we know exactly what to search for: a gaseous-emitting life form—but from a solid interior. I'll send this concept back to the lab, I can run a few models from here, then Nala and I can try to identify any other distinguishing features. I get what you mean about the flocking behavior, Carrysa."

Melia had brought the screen back to a panned out image so the entire cluster of animals were doing their little dance together, smoky puffs appearing and disappearing as they jostled to and fro. The first officer of the *Lifebringer* gasped for the fiftieth time. "Good Galaxies, they are... amazing. And kind of cute too, huh?"

Wordlessly, the three women communicated their joy to each other with broad smiles and a group hug, unable to stop watching the holovideos over and over.

***

The signal of an approaching drone beeped loudly on the *Lifebringer*'s cockpit monitor, upsetting John from his thoughts. He groaned his disdain, and pressed a few buttons to shut off the noise. When he read the accompanying text, he grimaced. It was a Ugov special transport. *Piper is going to be so pissed...*

He reeled in the drone with an energy beam, resetting its orbit to make a narrow ellipse around their spaceship. He knew better than to watch the holomessage. His Queen of Terraforming—as he liked to refer to Chief Executive Crane—would want to be the first to see it.

"My queen?" he enunciated in his most sarcastic (yet embellishing) tone when her face showed on the holo.

Piper groaned, clearly perturbed by the interruption. "Yes, John, what is it?"

John shifted to serious mode. You had to be ready to toggle between "best friend ever" and "demanding boss" at a moment's notice with her. "Sorry, Piper, I'm sure you're busy down there, but... it's important. We've got a messenger drone just arrived. I stabilized it to a local orbit around our ship. It's from Sun City. From Councilman Adonis." He refrained from adding any vituperative comments about the infamous politician, but he sure wanted to.

"Are you *serious?*" she spat. "What does *he* want?"

John asked, "Do you want me to send the message to your holoscreen in your chambers?" He waited so long for a response he swiped a holobutton to make sure the com was still turned on.

"Yes, John," the chief's voice finally came through the cockpit audio. "That would be fine, thank you."

***

Piper examined herself in the mirror setting on the three-meter holoscreen bathing the center of her private quarters with light. She ran her fingers through her dark brown hair and puffed it out a little bit, but a Usecond later, deciding better, she tamped it back down. She did a half turn, gazing at herself as if she were a display holo. *Ugh,* she frowned, *what is my problem, right now?*

The truth was, she had been procrastinating. She was putting off watching Adonis's personal holomessage, as if it were a sign of weakness that she would run to her quarters and click play the Usecond she got inside.

After a few Uminutes of doing simple chores and tidying up, wasting time she could have been analyzing data in the lab with Nala, she halted to give herself a lecturing. *What are you doing, Piper, watch it already, will you!* She adjusted her jacket collar and activated the transmission John had downloaded to her private holoscreen.

"Greetings, Chief Executive Crane!" The holo revealed a most earnest smile from Adonis, but it dissolved quickly. "We have possession of the Cygnan aliens you sent to Sun City... but you're in grave danger! We have reason to believe there will be further advances by the Perseans in Outer Cygnus. Everything your father stood for could be gone in an instant! Piper—" his image moved closer to the camera—"*Lifebringer* and your team are the highest caliber terraformers the Ugov has ever had! You cannot jeopardize them, yourself, *or* that spaceship. Therefore, I'm sorry to inform you, a council has decided: you are under direct Ugov orders… to return to Sun City immediately. Decease all scientific duties. Record and store all data pursuant to your investigations. And get your crew out of there! Piper, this is not a choice… it's an order from the fourteen." After a long pause, his voice went from firm and authoritative to soft and sincere. "Please. Come back to Sun City. Before it's too late. Yes, I believe you now."

The image of Adonis faded away, leaving Piper staring at herself again, as the mirror setting was still activated on her holoscreen. It reflected back a trillion pixels instead of her flesh. She studied herself for a few moments as she massaged her temples. *Why do I always feel this way after? I'm all flustered now—galaxies!* She smacked her palm on the nearest console.

Adonis was not merely a high-ranking Ugov councilman with whom Piper was forced to deliberate with as part of the job, it was a bit more complicated. Quite a bit more complicated. *Best friends, that's really what we were. We were inseparable back in those days.*

Piper had met Adonis in their youth, as they had both been raised in the same floating city neighborhood on Sun Lake. Their families had close ties to the high-ranking councils of the Ugov, therefore both had been primed for duty with elite level academics. They studied together, eat together, and went to dances together. All of their professors adored them, and they were a couple in everyone's eyes—even though they had confided in those closest to them they had never once kissed. Nevertheless, both sets of parents had assumed the two inevitably would marry, have children, and go on to serve in the high councils together. *But it didn't go quite that way, did it?*

She answered her own question out loud to her image. "Nope."

He was so gregarious. So beloved by the faculty and the students. People wanted to be next to him, to listen to his voice. To watch him dance.

She traced the Uyears back in her mind to the fateful Uday when she had found out from her girlfriends he had been dating another woman at the university. The betrayal brought out a fury within her she had never experienced before. It scared her.

She remembered the Uday so clearly. She had arrived early to their usual meeting place, where the two went over morning study guides, and he had been there with... her. *Cozied right on up, talking into her ear, as if it was... me.* She pursed her lips tight, shaking her head.

After witnessing him in that way, smiling and laughing with another girl, she regretted having any kind of relationship with him—friendship or otherwise. She retroactively nullified their relationship. She barely said a word to him for Umonths. Once university graduation proceedings were over, she made sure to take a terraforming assignment in a faraway solar system, leaving Adonis back on New Earth learning how to rule the masses. She wanted to wield science. He wanted to wield *people*.

So, in a short matter of time, they went from being inseparable—laughing and carrying on with a flirtatious, jovial chemistry belying romantic love—to being one hundred percent out of contact with each other.

Many Uyears passed. Piper followed in the footsteps of her father by taking the mantle of Chief Executive Officer of the Terraform Division. And this meant she was forced to interact with Adonis again. Part of her job became attending councils to garner bitcoin, and since Councils and Adonis seemed to be synonymous...

The first time she saw him in person, after all those Uyears, was in a moonscraper hallway between council rooms. Without a sternum, her heart would have exploded out of her chest as he recognized her, smiled, and... for a flash, it was as if not one moment had passed since the time they were inseparable. For a split Usecond, it was if she was still in love.

***

Once Piper had the girls gathered in the main hall of the ship she paraphrased Adonis's message from Sun City. Bleakly, almost morbidly, she watched as their faces went through a metamorphosis from excitement and glee to disbelief and resignation.

"Guys, guys, come on..." Piper said. "Let's act professional. None of us want to leave—especially not now, after what we've found. A burden has been placed upon us. We must preserve this place, these creatures."

"Piper!" Marjorie's arms waved. She also had the typical muscular build of her kind, the blue skin had pink swirls, and the blood vessels seemed to pop out on her neck when she got flustered. Better not to rankle an Algorean, even a half-breed. "Why are you listening to the Ugov *now?* Damn the Milky Way if we came all the way out here, discovered a new life form, and have to just leave it and skedaddle on back home. As if we'll *ever* be back here again anytime soon. This is it! This is our *one* chance, Piper!"

Carrysa weighed in next: "Yeah, Piper, I mean we already made the commitment to stay after we met those weird surfer aliens. They told us what they saw. Uehara was blasted, and Uehiron is probably next. We understood the risks. I thought we agreed to stay, didn't we?" Carrysa asked, speaking shyly, not in the aggressive manner her crew mate had spoken.

"I understand." Piper said, folding her arms across her chest. "You are all frustrated. I am as well, believe me. More than you would ever know. But, ladies—oh, and gents (sorry John)—this is not a *choice* anymore. The Ugov had no knowledge of what was happening out here, so we took the liberties. We made the single most important discovery in astrobiology since my father found the Helganian species. That's more than we could have hoped. Yes, we all want to find out more about this new species, but we have to take what we were able to find and use it to our advantage. Of course the Ugov will have to fund another mission out here, are you kidding me? If we reveal our findings, they'll have to! We'll have support from every scientific council in the galaxy."

Her downcast crew were searching the synthmetal floors, unable to return Piper's gaze, no matter how hard she tried to garner it back.

"In the meantime," she figured she might as well continue since no one was saying anything, "we have to save this place. We must make sure it doesn't suffer the same fate as its twin sister Uehara. But I have a mandate for the crew, listen: none of us trust these Ugov councils, so I am ordering us to keep these findings in ship. No one peeps a word about the special beings—until I say so. Uehiron, as far as we know, is a Class C planet—with carbon based life forms, but no technology-based peoples. That may be good enough on its own to merit the necessary black bitcoin to cover our next trip, and if not—well, we still have the startling discoveries we've made here. I don't want this info going to the wrong hands. Does everyone understand?" Piper stepped forward, forcing each of her team to make eye contact, one by one, save Melia, who never failed to support her no matter what decision she made.

"I have a question," Nala asked softly from the back of the group who had assembled in the meeting chambers to discuss their next move.

"Yes, Nala, of course." Piper waved her hand for her to speak.

Nala stepped forward and everyone hushed. "How are you going to eliminate the data from the mainframe?"

Piper reached into her waist pocket and pulled out a memory cube for the answer. It was an expensive piece of technology, so expensive to manufacture in fact, there were merely a handful produced each Uyear. It shined silver and black, with a clean, glossy finish, and a freshly-polished arm runner. The mathematics behind its storage capacity was mind-boggling.

"What is *that?*" Marjorie asked excitedly. "Is that a Sagittarian memory cube?"

"Yes," Piper said triumphantly, holding it out on her palm at arm's length for all to behold. "This is state of the art. There aren't many in existence. It functions as a data receptor *and* a data eraser. Melia downloaded all of our data, holo, audio, and projection sheets from Uehiron, and I put them all onto this cube. I also had her clean *Lifebringer's* mainframe, which means there is one copy of this—our *only* proof of what we have achieved on this mission."

"Wow," Melia blinked and tossed her head side to side, a smidgen in each direction. "That thing's... incredible! You've been holding out on us, eh, Piper? It looks like a gaming cube, but more... sturdy?"

"Oh, *it's* sturdy, believe me. I'm pretty sure it can't be destroyed by anything short of tossing it into a solar storm."

Piper projected her smile on her crew, trying to get them to return it. But, in the moment, there could be no joy. They were being ordered to leave a life-changing astrobiological discovery, something they had worked for their entire professional careers.

Piper gulped and stiffened her spine. "Do I have your understanding? Please orally acknowledge. Sound off."

"Yes," Carrysa said immediately.

"Yes, *ma'am*," Marjorie said stiffly.

"Yes, Piper," Nala said.

"I've always got your back, Terraform Queen," John confirmed last.

Melia didn't answer out loud. There was no need.

"All right—girls—and John—please head back to your respected duty chains, and prepare the ship for hyperspace travel. Make sure you have no private communications regarding the findings on any devices. Melia, you stay with me."

They filed out one by one, with John asking before exiting: "What should we do with the video residue on the planet rover and other equipment we used?"

"Thanks for reminding me, John. You can go ahead and check all the vehicles and drones employed down there, and make sure the AI data cleaning device gives it a good wipe afterwards, will you?"

"Got it." John paused to raise an eyebrow at the two women before are walking out.

Once Piper was alone with Melia in the main hall she touched her arm and stopped her. "Melia, once we get back we need to meet with Royce immediately. We need to find out what he's hearing back on New Earth. Do you think there's really going to be another war?"

"Piper, please, promise me you aren't going to tell Adonis?"

"What? About our *real* findings? Of course not. I'll share them with Kennedy, and our most trusted team members back at Terraform headquarters, but that's it."

Melia nodded, but gave Piper the once-over.

CHAPTER TWENTY-FIVE

Return to Sun City

Familiar spires of moonscrapers became visible upon their descent. The biggest ones, poking through the clouds into the upper stratosphere, were the most recognizable—each with an obnoxious Blackon-produced corporate holoboard adorning it. John had *Lifebringer* on approach, and Piper paced on the bridge, the anxious tug of terrestrial gravity on her legs. Touching her feet to *real* ground, even synthmetal flooring, always felt *so* good. Interstellar travel could be tough on the equilibrium.

Once John had landed, and the crew were about to exit the ship, Piper took a moment to gather the troops at the portal door. She wanted to express her appreciation for their hard work and dedication on the (regrettably) abbreviated mission to Outer Cygnus.

"Now for the good news…"

"Drum roll please, Carrysa," Marjorie blurted out. "The chief's got good news—*for once!* Thank the Milky Way!"

Carrysa obliged Marjorie and verbalized a synthetic beat machine.

Piper blinked and shook her head in mock dismay. When she informed them they were being given the next few Udays off, a joyous hurrah burst out. Quieting them with a push of her palms to the floor, Piper reminded them how much work there was still to complete.

"Listen, girls—no, John, don't say it, I didn't forget you—this has been an amazing adventure... one of the craziest of my life! I feel privileged and honored to have led this mission. But it was stressful, and emotionally draining. We all deserve a break, but—then it's back to the base. Kennedy will have a billion tasks for us, and probably a trillion questions. So... enjoy the time off, we're back at headquarters in three Udays... thanks again, guys, I love you all! Rest and recuperate with your family and friends. That's an order!"

Piper put out her arms, and everyone joined into a big huddle for a final embrace. They had traveled a long, long way from New Earth, and returned together, safe and sound, harboring a secret that would undoubtedly cause upheaval in the galaxy. Whenever she assumed her crew couldn't get any tighter...

The doors hissed opened, and to her surprise, they had a welcoming committee at the bottom of the gangplank.

"Hey, look!" Marjorie pointed and there they were—the five crew members of the *Planet Hopper*, standing with big grins. "It's those surfer dudes!"

Melia groaned. "Oh, dear Milky Way, what now? Not these guys again."

"Hey, now!" The big blue guy, the one who had called himself Captain Max, was beckoning them to debark. The two giant rabbits were hopping and waving. The big fat furry one with the monobrow stood with arms crossed and a kind of... apathy on his face. While the androidish guy—or *whatever* he was—did not move a muscle... or a wire..

"So," Marjorie drawled, as she was the first to walk over and greet Max face to face. Piper watched in dismay as she walked all the way around him, fixated the whole time on his posterior. "You *are* a pure Algorean aren't you?"

"Ease off, Marj," said Carrysa, second to step off the ramp. She nodded "hello" to the rest of the weird creatures gathered to greet them. She had to physically nudge Marjorie to keep her from touching Max's humongous deltoid muscles. "You haven't been off assignment *that* long!"

"What a... *pleasant* surprise," Piper chimed in with unmasked sarcasm. She went and stood in front of Marjorie, partly because she was the leader of the whole darn mess, and partly because she wanted to block Marjorie from continuing her assessment of the Algorean Captain's fine athletic physique.

"Piper Crane, Chief Executive Officer of the Terraforming Division of the Ugovernment. Good to—" she reached out to shake hands with Max, but her eyes exploded from their sockets when she saw how humongous it was, and withdrew hers promptly—"meet you in person."

The alien's sincerity was no illusion. "Maximillian, Captain of the *Planet Hopper*. Likewise, it's a pleasure to meet you, ma'am— I mean, um, Chief Crane."

The rest of the crew members of the *Planet Hopper* and *Lifebringer* exchanged a few reserved greetings.

"I gather you were able to inform the authorities of the Perscan activity in Outer Cygnus," Piper said without disguising her disdain. "*And* managed to get Councilman Adonis to put out an order for our return. Thanks a lot!"

"Well, I, uh..." The Captain stammered. "We didn't tell him to do that, he kind of did it on his own. He was worried about you guys, I could tell, he wanted to make sure you were safe. You have to admit—for good reason."

"Oh, please," Piper spat out. "His one desire is placating those who monger the resources that come from our terraform explorations. He uses *our* expertise and talents for the benefit of the Ugov. He isn't concerned with our safety."

"Hey," Mike pointed out, "we *tried* to warn you too. We wanted you to get back to New Earth safely, don't forget that."

Melia glared at him. "Well, you got your wish, Mister Rabbit— we were forced to leave an amazing new world with others still to be explored. We had to abort our mission and return here without even skimming the surface of what's out there. Happy?"

The rabbit tried to reason with Piper's second. "Hey, come on now, dudette, what if the Perseans had come back and played round two on your amazing new world?"

"Yes, what *if?*"

A new voice spoke from the upper landing bay platform, clear and tempered, one Piper had heard a thousand times.

Adonis approached, stepping slowly and purposefully, breaking into his galaxy-famous smile. "Then we would not be able hear all about your adventures in Outer Cygnus. And then we wouldn't be able to send you back there as *soon* as it became safe to do so."

"Councilman," Piper addressed him while motioning to the crew of the *Planet Hopper*, "I should have guessed you'd be behind these proceedings. As… *endearing* as they are in person, can you explain why are these aliens not incarcerated for breaking Ugov laws? Don't tell me the councils are going soft on us."

Adonis lost his smile. "Mmm. Quite the contrary, Executive Crane. These aliens have done a great service to the galaxy by coming to us and reporting about the Perseans' dalliances in Outer Cygnus. We should laud these 'surfer dudes.' But, I assure you, none of us take it lightly they breached Ugov code. Until a council has determined how they will serve their punishment, they are on confinement."

Melia snickered. "They don't seem too confined right now." She punctuated her assessment with a nod in their direction and a wave of her hand.

"Well…" Adonis stroked his beard. "No need for you to worry, Melia. They're being watched after."

"Yeah, I'll bet they are…" Melia grunted before stomping off.

Adonis ignored her, addressing the rest of the bunch. "And I want to say thank you for sending the crew of the *Planet Hopper* to us, and also to say welcome home. I—we—we're all glad you're back safe. I promise I will do everything in my power to protect the Outer Cygnus Arm and get you back out there to complete your mission. I'm sure it was hard to leave. But it's really no different than if there was a supernovae explosion, or any other celestial event which could have put your mission in jeopardy. Ugov law is clear, in cases where there could be risk of harm—"

"Spare us, Councilman," John snapped. "You have us back on New Earth—right where you and your black bitcoin cronies want us. Saving black for the Ugov to spend on the destruction of the galaxy." John brushed past Adonis, making shoulder contact, the second to leave prematurely from the *Lifebringer*.

"Well," one of the rabbits said to the other, too loudly, "*that was awkward.*"

"I know, huh!" the other one replied, also loud enough for all to make out .

"Hey girls," the Algorean exclaimed, "I've got a great idea! How about meeting up with us later this Uweek, and we share a meal together?"

Piper had to admit, the alien had major charm. He posed with arms spread wide. "If, that is, the charitable councilman allows us another furlough?"

"Absolutely," Marjorie answered for Adonis, a good idea to her, evidently. "You big hunk!"

"Too busy," Piper said. "*All* of us... are too busy." She glared at Marjorie.

"What?" countered Marjorie. "You just gave us the rest of the Uweek off!"

Piper blushed, as her reasoning had been instantly stripped of its validity.

"If it pleases you," Nala asked the twins softly. "I would be curious to find out more about your genetics, Mike and... Claude, is it?"

The rabbits high-pawed each other, smiled, and nodded eagerly—eyes wide.

"Cool, then *I'll* go share a meal with you guys..." Nala arched her eyebrows at Carrysa.

Carrysa groaned. "All right, all right! I'll go with you weird aliens. Send me a holomessage when you know where and when. I've got to go visit my mother." And Carrysa was the next to stomp away.

"Awesome!" the more uppity rabbit cajoled after her. "It's a date! See you soon, *Carrie*..."

"It's Carrysa!" the twin brother elbowed him in the side, and they shoved each other playfully.

Piper laughed at the befuddlement on Adonis's face. Before the councilor had actually confirmed "the date," Max had already herded the twins back to the loitering duo of fatso and mute boy, returning Marjorie's adoring hand wave all the while.

"Well, I guess that'll be fine—" Adonis said, too late to stop anything anyway.

The last two crew members of the *Lifebringer* were next to vacate.

"Bye, Piper!" Melia hugged her.

"Thanks, Piper, for the Udays off..." Marjorie said with genuine affection.

"No problem, Marj. You deserve it. Later you guys! Thanks for everything!" Piper called after Marjorie and Melia as they headed off to find an air cab to take them to their homes.

That left Piper and Adonis standing there, both realizing they were the last ones on the causeway. It was quiet for a moment. Neither made eye contact at first.

She tried a casual joke. "So much for detention and punishment, eh?"

"Seriously!" Adonis laughed, sounding relieved. "Good thing I'm not such a push-over in the council rooms."

Double-meaning, Piper shook her head.

"Hey," he said before she could find another smart comment, "walk with me to the air tube, I wanted to talk to you about something..."

***

She had no idea how he did it, but somehow Adonis had convinced Piper to meet her the next Uday at his office on the four hundred and twentieth floor of the signature Ugov moonscraper, right in the center of Sun City.

"For a quick debriefing," he had said, so he could, "be more prepared to take his argument for the defense of Outer Cygnus to the high council." She had agreed, reluctantly, then, as each Uhour passed since making the appointment, she regretted it more and more. She nearly messaged him to cancel fifty times.

It was so damn frustrating. She should be able to say "no," and go about her business. But she couldn't. His intense gaze—the hazel eyes encompassed by the signature dark eyebrows. She privately longed to stare into those eyes again. It nearly brought her to tears, even after all this time. The betrayal seemed so...

palpable. When their relationship had ended abruptly, Uweeks before graduating from the university, it had been a blow not only to herself, but to everyone in her family. *I think my father was more disappointed than me...*

And yet, instead of canceling, the next Uday she resignedly hailed an air cab from the roof of her apartment in the southern suburbs. She rarely stayed there, in fact, she had a portable floating bed at Terraform Headquarters which served as her main resting place. Even when she did retire home, after a long Uday of work, she could barely get to sleep before her AI woke her. Back at it again.

Flying in the air cab gave her a beautiful perspective. The sun was rising above Mount Sun, and a sharp ray of fuzzy light penetrated through the mist. Contrasting the natural vista were Sun City's cluster of moonscrapers, with muddled purples reflecting off the synthglass in the morning glow.

Piper swallowed, despite a dry throat, and squeezed her hands into fists a few times. *Oh, well. Might as well go pretend. Again.* Her ability to conceal her infatuation with him was an issue of pride. They were both adults now—not students of the university. Both had gone through immense changes. Both had had other relationships. But still... she was unable to let go, and continually found herself getting agitated whenever she tried talking with him. *Maybe it's all the council debates.* The pair had quite the reputation for mixing it up in the chamber of floating chairs. Therefore, it was assumed this animosity was merely the result of a difference in political viewpoints—even though the dirty details of their private history were common knowledge. *That's what it is—history. Let it go. He's offering to help my division. I've got to give him the benefit of the doubt on this one. We need him on our side. Uehiron needs him on our side. Not me?*

She parlayed her emotions with rationality on the flight over, peering at the cradle of life on New Earth. An oval shaped

316

perimeter of massive urban structures formed a jagged mole growing from the skin of the unblemished natural ecosystem. The greenery of forests, the crystalline blues of freshwater lakes, the rugged iron hills bulging in every direction, they all served as reminders of how effective island civilization was. Outside the oval, nature ruled. Inside the oval, Sun Peoples twittered away the Uyears, pushing black and red numbers across glinting bitcoins, as the newly built moonscrapers reached higher and higher into the troposphere.

Piper shook her head in disgust. *And inside those monstrosities, councilors and Blackon lobbyists arguing over the fate of all the other sentient beings of the galaxy—it's all so phony.*

Even though she complained, deep down she was glad her job forced her into the council rooms to bicker and banter and barter. What better way to show your intentions were sincere than proving it with actions? Find new life. Protect new life. Create habitable worlds. The Terraform edicts. "The argument for life," as her father coined. It was something to live by. *Something for me to live for...*

***

"Chief Executive Crane!" Adonis practically jumped off his floating chair when she entered through the slide door to his office. "Thank you so much for coming!"

She tried to hold her tongue, but instinctively made a sardonic remark. It was her regular mode of talking to him, since their estrangement. "Councilman, I didn't really have a choice, did I? You claimed you wanted to help my division."

"Of course," he said, offering her a floating chair. "Listen... I get it, Piper, you're frustrated by the lack of Ugov financial support, and pissed off we had to bring you back early from your project. I understand why you're upset... believe me."

"No, you *don't* understand, Adonis." Piper sat, but kept the floating chair low to the ground and pivoted away from him. Easy getaway.

"Yes, actually, I do," Adonis said. Piper guessed he was used to her vitriol by now. But credit to him, he continued calmly, "And it's why I want to help. The Terraform Division of the Ugovernment is crucial to the integrity of the galaxy. I am one of the few councilors who understands—astrobiology is of the utmost importance. I can influence Zander and his cronies—*if* I have the information I need."

She rolled her eyes, shook her head, and pressed her lips together, as the density of the cube in her vest pocket became more palpable. Possibly the most important information in the galaxy was contained within the few grams of the object.

He moved across the room with a certain grace, sat in his floating chair, and ushered her to move hers opposite his. He pressed a holobutton and the virtual curtains drew back from his office window, unveiling a breathtaking view of Sun City.

Adonis smiled his trillion bit smile. "So tell me… what did your team find there? There's not much on the data banks uploaded to Ugov access channels. Almost nothing at all about this new system you discovered and named—Uehiron. But your team logs show boots on the ground. Is this a worthwhile venture? Can you terraform there? Or is there anything that would get Zander all in a huff and ready to support a military defense? Knowing the man, I doubt he will go for it unless there are signs of rare elements to dig for."

Piper described their journey, detailing their flyby of Uehara and the shock of its relegation to rocks and dust. She talked about Uehiron in broad, vague terms, and of their unlikely meeting with the crew of the *Planet Hopper*. Adonis smiled at her telling of the encounter, and laughed out loud when she described how the weird surfers thought they were going to be blasted to oblivion.

Piper did not take kindly to interference with her missions, nor did she particularly care for those who traveled past the IDL without permission, but she wasn't about to shoot them with ion cannons!

They finished their laugh and Adonis floated to the window. "Hmm. So definitely some form of carbon-based life on Uehiron... And what *else?* The thing is, although finding carbon-based life forms is wonderful, a scientific marvel, no doubt about it, it's not going to be enough to perk up the bitcoin automatons."

"Ahh, Councilman, believe me, I'm *well* aware of the way the Ugov sucks up to the Blackons. Like two hands slapping your face from either side." She mimicked the concept with her own hands and face, provoking Adonis's eyebrows to arch. "I told Zander before we left there was a distinct possibility one of Uehiron's moons contained the minerals he sought. We were yanked out of there—*by you*—before we could get the numbers to appease him. So there you go. I can't help Zander, so you can't help me, is that it, then? Shall I excuse myself?"

Her eyes turned to small beads as they scrutinized the man she used to love. But he did not return the venom. It was contrition on his face. After a pause, she sighed and let her shoulders drop. They had been pinned against her ears. She eased back into her chair; she had been on the edge of it, about to drop off the front.

Adonis seemed to relax too. He pressed with his fingertips and slid his thumb across an initiator, and a large holoscreen popped up in between them. "Listen, Piper, I know how passionate you are about all this. This is your life's work—to discover and create life. I get it."

He pointed to the holoscreen he had opened. She was taken aback. He had obviously been working on his computer for a while before she had arrived. All of her most recent projects became three-dimensional holoreplicas floating in the middle of the room. Which included several planets that had once been rocky wastelands devoid of even basic archaea. Now they were populated worlds, with working representative high councils, fully sanctioned by the Ugovernment. Many, many trillions of peoples—from Sunish to Algoreans to Boorish to Oreldychynean to Istabanian—were now prospering on these terraformed worlds.

"I, uh, I..." Piper was thrown off. Why was he studying her terraform projects? "This is a nice little holo show, but I don't understand..."

He engaged her with a smile. "Piper, we are the same in a lot of ways."

Her reflexes forced her to interject, but he cut her off. "Just let me talk for one Usecond, please, Piper."

She made the sardonic zipping motion across her lips with thumb and forefinger pinched together.

His smile widened. He was unceasingly able to fend off her abuse. "You and your amazing team are doing incredible work! Everyday you create life where there was none before, and discover life where it was believed not to exist. You are in the business of life. Saving life. Making life. So am I, Piper. My job as a high councilor is to *protect* the life of all Ucitizens—even its most marginalized aliens, even its non-indoctrinated constituents. You create and find life, and I want to protect it. I wish we could both be free to make these decisions on our own, but that's not representative Ugovernment. If we did not have mechanisms in place, the corporate Blackons would have even more sway in galactic politics than we do, as a voting entity."

"Okay—why are you telling me all this?"

"Well," Adonis rubbed his hands together. "It's just that... I want you to know... I study your projects. I study your techniques. I have followed all of them, Piper. Bismarch, Gladdenfield, Myrtel World, all of the—on a side note, I thought it was a fascinating technique to try..."

Piper lit up at the mention of the terraform method she and Melia had pioneered on Euclidae, located in the mid-Orion arm, many Udecades ago. "Yeah—and it would have worked, too—if I could have had more time to allocate to the fabrication of the wrapping material. It was the first time ever applying it. We couldn't trap enough heat and gas from the solar parent with that first batch of material. The initiator satellites were arranged perfectly, though, thanks to some risky orbital insertions. It was *supposed* to make a pseudo-atmosphere, and hopefully, over a few Uyears, bring the mean temperature above two hundred and seventy-three Kelvin."

"Such a remarkable idea! So much more innovative than the halocarbon factories spewing out nasty gas cocktails, non-stop, for eons..."

She blinked at him. He was shockingly versed in terraforming. Neither spoke for a moment.

Finally, he put out his hands with palms out. "I mean, who wants to study the geomorphology of a planet with all that going on?"

"I know, right? Hard to get work done amidst chaos. But the old fashioned way—hastening a given planet's ability to create its own atmosphere—it worked like a charm for my father and his predecessors."

Piper searched his face for whether mention of her father jarred any emotions. Cris Crane and Adonis had been close friends. Udecades ago. He bit his lip gently and sighed. *Yes, thought Piper. He misses him, too.*

Piper quickly got off the topic of her father: "Synthwrapping is being perfected right now by one of Kennedy's teams at Terraform Headquarters. Depending on what your councils decide, we might have the funds to try it on one of the Outer Cygnus target planets. But... I guess that's not going to happen anymore, is it?"

Out the synthglass windows the sunrise had given way to a glorious Uday. Little tastes of yellow light hibernated behind billowy precipitation clouds hovering above Sun Lake.

"Piper," the earnestness in Adonis's voice drew her to turn his way. "It's not over for Outer Cygnus. It's not decided yet. *Unless* the Perseans come in and start throwing things around. That's why it's so important we can get our minds together and figure out a way to prod the councils into action. Exogenesis is your ultimate goal, as it is mine. But without the Perseans confined to their corner of the Milky Way, all terraform projects will be tabled. The question is *how* can we convince them there aren't just military reasons to be out there..."

She rolled her eyes, floating her chair away.

"Yes, Piper," he pleaded, "I am referring to black bitcoin. We need to find value in what lies out there. Military generals are obstinate, whereas, extraction moguls are quick to action."

She mulled it over. She couldn't believe she was actually considering handing him over the cube. As she juggled with the decision, the imaginary voices of her team rang out in her head, inconsolable voices: *Why, Piper? Why? Why would you give him the data?* But the voices of Martins and Shuler, brushing off Outer Cygnus as if it were an insignificant portion of the galaxy, also replayed in her mind. There was one other idea she had...

"Piper?"

Her head twitched as she emerged from a fog of indecision to peer at the man she had known so well, so many Uyears ago. The man she had loved.

"Hey..." He scooted closer in his chair. "Can I take you somewhere? I really want to show you something special. Would you be willing to spend half the Uday with me? We can put off this talk of saving the arms of the galaxy for a little while. What do you say? I *promise* you'll love it! We can get out of the city for a bit." He was positively glowing as he stood, pushed his floating chair

322

out of the way, practically kneeled, as if a suitor, and reached for her hand. She paused before taking it timidly, and he lifted her out of her floating chair. She had forgotten how strong his compact physique was. And his hand—smooth and warm.

"All right," she replied softly. "*I guess.* I was planning on checking in with Kennedy at headquarters, but I did give the girls a few Udays off…"

"Piper, we're both workaholics. Let's get out of Sun City for the Uday."

"Where are we going—out of the city, where?"

"Trust me. You'll be amazed."

Great—trust him. I guess you don't remember the last time you trusted him, do you Piper? she asked herself privately.

Despite her normal instinct to reject his offer, she acquiesced and he followed her out the slide door of his office as he called for an air cab through his wrist pad to meet them on a lower sky deck.

***

As they hiked the wet and muddied trail, splashing through occasional puddles of brown mire, the scent of the forest became more and more noxious and intense. Piper took in deep breaths, her pulse racing faster with each meter of elevation they gained. No one else was hiking on the trail, although a few hover board chargers passed by, sliding and gliding through the puddles, but careful not to splash them.

Adonis led the way, his boots bore the Ugov insignia, although it was indecipherable from wear and tear, and his pace forced Piper to walk faster. Steeper and windier, the trail climbed along the edge of the westernmost ridge of Sun Mountains. Blues and greens dominated the landscape, the colors of the various leaves and needles jutting out into the trail. Although the foliage was dense, there were small avenues within the branches, animal pathways into the depths of the forest. And, of course, there were the Corwin trees! They were *unbelievably* tall in certain areas, upwards of one hundred and fifty meters, blocking out the clouds. It was almost as if they were trying in vain to outdo the moonscrapers reaching from the urban megalopolis into the lower atmosphere. And yet, they would be merely the size of a blade of grass on Persar.

Each Corwin tree was part of a family, a cluster of roots so deep and wide their interaction with the soil was a marvel of the biosphere; a symbiotic relationship between fungus and bacteria giving fertile ground for them to flourish, while it simultaneously fed the arboreal animals with seeds and nuts, and in turn, the predators that eat them. Even the under story was dependent on the sunlight filtering through the clouds. Below the curled and twisted limbs of the Corwin trees, several species of brush netted together to form a cushion of flora unlike anywhere else in the galaxy.

It was the middle of the Uday by the time they finished their ascent, and judging by the white-roofed sky, rain was coming soon. *You can smell it,* Piper thought. The foliage seemed to swell, as if forewarned, to catch the life-nourishing liquid on its way. *No wonder the trails are always filled with mud up here in the high forest.* During the warmer portions of the Uday the ground was transformed into a beige cake of hardened sludge. When the downpours came it could be like trying to walk through quick sand.

The trail leveled out, finally, and curved inward, away from the views of Sun City. Deeper and deeper the worn path plunged into the forest. Light filtered down through the canopy. Piper's eyes adjusted to the dimness of the inner forest, revealing the majesty of old growth arboreal species. Corwin trees grew taller up here, directly correlated with elevation.

Adonis checked behind him to make sure Piper was keeping pace. Everything was oddly *familiar* to her. Neither had spoken for a few kilometers, so Piper focused on her breath, and the calming sounds of insects creaking, birds jabbering, and the monotonous sound made by the squish of their boots. It was peaceful and delightful. Even as the clouds shed sprinkles, it could not deter their progress up the mountainside. Occasionally a flower or two emerged from beneath the blue and green hues of the local foliage, white orchids, adorned with fractal patterns resembling red dwarf stars materializing from the dark of space. Stamen tongues reached out to lick the drops of water from above.

For an astrobiologist, the smells emanating from the forest were *the* definition of organic life. Connecting to the natural world was something her father had instilled in her at an early age. He would often lead her on hikes with the purpose of getting away from island civilization, away from the shining silver towers of a billion Sun People living on top of each other. He had preached to her about the importance of respecting a given biosphere. Her father had believed each biome was its own unique entity, and therefore had the inalienable right to exist *as is*—without prodding by technologically-advanced people. Without restrictions on the natural growth of aliens in the galaxy, there would be nothing but synthmetals sprawling into every corner of every inhabitable planet. Cris Crane honed his daughter's natural aptitude for terraforming; he needed successors to be wardens of the vast, unchartered biomes existing out there. The art of creating new worlds and saving others was integral to the health of the Milky Way. Piper lived her father's legacy each and every Uday.

Now she hiked with a different man. A man who also knew her inner truths. *Perhaps more than anyone but my father,* she thought. *And Melia, of course.* She watched Adonis's sure-footed dexterity as he hopped over puddles and navigated around eroded rock piles spilling onto the trail.

I can't believe I let myself go hike alone with him. Whatever she told herself, she was still enamored, despite her bitterness toward him. Galaxies he was handsome—genetic advances did tend to maintain a person's appearance. And his black mane with graying streaks grew as if he were still in the peak of adulthood.

Soon it was raining hard. She could tell by the thunderous sound cascading downward from the tree tops. But, because of the umbrella-like constitution of the branches and leaves above, only singular drops penetrated to the ground, leaving them relatively dry.

Adonis had not spoken since before they sought shelter among the trees, and now he made mention of how much he loved coming to this place. He told her he had hiked there many times— *by himself, yes*—right after she had left for assignment all those Uyears ago.

"Piper, I need to tell you something." Adonis stopped and turned to her. "It's something I've always wanted to say to you, face-to-face, but you've avoided me so well all these Uyears, there wasn't a good opportunity for me to do it. So here goes…

Piper, I *never* meant to hurt you. I still can't forgive myself for seeing that other girl. But I was so young—I had no idea… what… *love* was. I was immature and trying to make you jealous, or something idiotic like that…" He searched the trees as if to deliver him the right words to say. "When you left, my heart longed for you. My soul was an empty vessel. I realized then, that I could *never* replace you with someone else. So I would hike these mountains and think of you. This became my refuge. I could come here to cry when I needed to."

"*You?* Cry?" Piper regretted her sarcasm when she saw the anguish cross his face. It was as if she was stuck in auto-speak mode, and was struggling to eliminate the contempt from her voice. A defensive mechanism she had deferred to for Uyears when having to deal with him at the Ugov moonscraper.

He sounded genuinely hurt this time, unable to placate her any longer. "Yes, Piper. I do. I'm human, just like you are. A Sunish man with real emotions. But you don't get the real version during council debates, or by watching news holovideos that spread stupid rumors and innuendos about me and my private life."

"*Ha!* You mean all the girls? What, those are made-up stories?" She regretted saying it immediately.

Adonis shrugged. "I mean, I've been with a few women. But if you watch those holovideos, you would think I was a pleasure droid. It's ludicrous!" Regardless of how many women he had dated, he had never committed, never had a binding love ceremony. "There was no love between any of those women and I. And anyways, that was Uyears ago."

"Yeah, right." She rolled her eyes, unable to stop herself from making a knee-jerk responses to every sentence coming off his lips. *Oh, but those lips...*

Adonis caught her eyes. "You have been with a few yourself. Charles, Theo..."

Now Piper went on the defensive, blushing. "What business of yours are my prior relationships?"

The serenity of their natural world setting faded into painful memories harbored from the past.

Adonis tried again. "Piper, I've paid close attention to your career. I studied your terraform projects as if they were my own... Piper, I've never stopped caring. I've never stopped... loving you."

His hazel eyes burned at her with passion. Clearly, her obsession with him was reciprocal. No witty response came to her after his revelation.

He continued to stare. "So many Uyears I waited for you to return to Sun City. And when you finally came, I hoped, I *prayed* that... that you would forget the past, and we could try a fresh start. That you would forgive me—some Uday."

His hands were grasping for hers. She accepted them. The warmth of his palms sent jolts down her spine, but she didn't pull away, they were pleasant somehow.

Piper gazed into the canopy. Individual drops of rain followed random vectors, ultimately hitting the soil below. One as large as a sip of water plinked as it hit her moist skin and she giggled. Piper started to catch them on her forehead. Adonis followed suit, and right away had a drop splash off his forehead. He opened his mouth and caught a few drops on his tongue, and she copied his approach. They laughed. When their eyes met again, their fingers still interlocked, there was a slight moment of hesitation before their faces moved toward each other. She pressed her lips against his.

And, in the span of a single kiss, Piper's vexation, building for Udecades, dissipated into the steam rising from the trunks of the Corwin trees.

CHAPTER TWENTY-SIX

The Crews' Date

"Hey ladies!" Max exclaimed as the three members of *Lifebringer*'s crew ambled into the restaurant. "We're over here!"

Max tried to gauge their mood as they filed in one by one: little Nala smiled, quick-witted Carrysa smirked, and bodacious Marjorie stormed right over to their floating table, extending one of her arms and offering the back of her hand, as if expecting Max to give it a kiss. Max obliged after a shrug. Time to let his natural charm take over. He beckoned their three supper companions to their own empty floating chairs. *Well,* Max thought, *I think I can guess which one is most excited to be here.*

Outside, through the massive synthglass windows surrounding the establishment on all four sides, the sun was setting over the mountains, painting the sky with pink and orange, while the Corwin tree forests lost their hue, merging into dark shadowy clusters, clinging to the edges of rocky precipices.

"Ladies," Max said, taking on the guise of a server. "We are *so* glad you could join us! Adonis suggested this place... well, actually, it was the only place he would give us a bit voucher for, but hey—the menu is fabulous! Of course, we're starved for something fresh. I'm sure you guys can relate—hyperspace food doesn't cut it." He motioned his thumb at Blob. "Our friend Blob here, he gets *very* hungry. I remember the first time we met... Vern, do you remember that? When Blob ate all the vittles supposed to last us for two Uweeks, where were we surfing again?"

Vern's speechless, emotionless, synthmetal face wasn't going to answer, so Max did it for him: "That fun point break in Oreldychyne! That's right, Vern! Not far from where you were living at the time." Max nodded enthusiastically. "It's all coming back to me now—we had to sell a few space instruments to the local guys in order to buy some fish so we had something to eat. We would have starved out there!"

"Oh, please!" Blob cried. "You exaggerate so much! But I promise you, tonight, when you're not looking, I'm gonna grab something off your plate!"

Everyone laughed except Carrysa and Vern. Vern was at the far end of the table, his floating chair significantly further away from the table than everyone else's. Carrysa still had a frown plastered on her face. It was going to take Max's sense of humor to break her out of her shell.

I love a challenge, he thought, giving her his full attention. "What's up with you, Ms. Pouty? Aren't you excited to eat with us, your fellow Outer Cygnus travelers? C'mon, now, Carrysa... you're too pretty to hold back that smile of yours!"

As Max cajoled her, Carrysa wiped her brow with her hand a few times, her consternation fading away a little bit. *Still no smile, though. But it's something...*

Conversations at the floating table naturally moved to those sitting closest together, so Nala talked to Claude, with Mike, as always, sitting right next to his brother and listening in, ready to interject (also a regular occurrence), if his twin was not saying the "right" things. Claude and Nala found they shared a love for science that superseded the rest of the group. Nala's hushed manner of speaking forced Max to lean in closer.

"Induced acromegaly?" Nala was asking Claude about their mutations. "Wasn't that the forte of Kane?"

Claude nodded. "Absolutely—wow—that's so cool you've heard of his work! His ideas *literally* made the two of us." He pointed a paw at Mike.

"Dr. Kane," she said. "I'm aware of his work. He was a geneticist from the early Orion days, when the rest of the Milky Way had not been fully colonized. From the holos I watched, he was quite the character."

"Yes," Claude replied, "he certainly had his quirks. But, bottom line: he brought mutation science to another level. He proved if you solved the genome code, you could replicate it perfectly—or, enhance it, customize it. Increase its brain size."

Mike was locked and loaded for a quip. "Yeah, and as you can tell, Nala, Dr. Kane favored me judging by how big mine is compared to my twin."

Claude ignored him, trying to concentrate on Nala. "Dr. Kane was an Originalist in every sense of the name, and a big proponent of gigantism. And those Originalists feared these Old Earth animals would never be seen again in their original form. I think, in his weird way, he thought he could preserve them by giving them full intellectual capacity."

"*Full* intellectual capacity?" joked his brother, motioning with his paws to his enlarged head. "Speak for yourself on that one, dude!"

Max cracked up, which would egg on Mike to become even more of a jokester, but Claude was undeterred.

"Ignore them, Nala," Claude said, "it's easy, I do it all the time. As I was saying... I read more than my share of Kane's holopages, and his theory was that, once empowered, animals would be able to save themselves. Seems a bit insane, but it's kind of true when you think about it... I mean just take our home in the Animal Worlds system, for example. We're all Ucitizens now!"

"Hyperplasia has its dangers, doesn't it?" Nala asked.

"It does," continued Claude, "but Kane perfected a way of shutting down the multiplication of cells once they had reached a target range. Organic tissue proliferates in its subject, then, with a secondary injection, it subsides to a rate constant with the common parameters of adulthood."

Max found himself intrigued by this petite, dark-featured woman who was a bit taller than the twins. Rare for a Sunish person to be so small. Especially considering, in the galactic age, physical features were chosen ahead of time by the parents of a newborn. Tall had been favored for time immemorial.

Max peered around the table. Blob had finally broken Carrysa out of her shell, and was busy talking to her while the twins continued to mull over genetics with Nala. The Captain leaned his head to listen in.

Carrysa, it turned out, was keenly interested in Boor, Blob's home world, and had even done a bit of research on Boorish people and their habits. When the Persean War came, many Boors were displaced, as the large species aliens were all but ignored by the humans, and Carrysa had worked on a terraform project to build an asylum world for the refuges. Max could tell she had won Blob's heart immediately.

Meanwhile, across the table, and without the distraction of the others talking, Max was in Marjorie's crosshairs. The weight of her stare was more intense than a scanning beam. She casually floated around the perimeter of the table, until she was practically on top of him. She traced her fingers on the numerous dark lines marring his deep blue skin. "How did you get this tattoo? And that one? What about that one?"

Max loved storytelling, so he was citing the traditional Algorean familial meaning of his skin demarcations.

"This one looks weird!" Marjorie touched an area on his upper back, above the shoulder blade.

When he told her it wasn't a tattoo but a scar, she wanted to know where he got it from. Incognizant of the implications, he blabbered something about the jungle of Uehara, and the sharp edges of the unique foliage there.

Marjorie's eyes went wide, and she floated back a touch. After staring at him for a moment, making Max uncomfortable, she whispered, "Um, Max. You should *not* have told me that! If Piper finds out, you guys are totally in for it... I mean, don't tell me you interacted with sentient beings. *Please* don't tell me that."

"Uh... um, I..." Max stammered. *Galaxies—what did my big mouth get us into now? This is usually Blob's territory. The guys are really going to heckle me for this one, especially the big fella.*

"No!" Marjorie hissed.

Max spread his palms wide. "Yeah, we did. There were natives that... we, uh, might have seen them."

"*Might* have seen them?"

"Well, yeah, we saw them. Incredibly beautiful people." He tried his diffusing grin to no avail.

Marjorie gasped. "Max! It is strictly, *strictly* forbidden to engage with unstudied aliens. It could upset the whole balance of evolution in the galactic biosphere—don't you get it?"

Max tried to figure out how to explain surf stoke? "Well, yeah, Marjorie, that's all true, but... there's this amazing tidal bore wave. Quite infamous, actually. Although, never surfed. We read about the Ueharan oceans and their massive bays on geography holovideos. We wanted to surf an epic wave—y'know? Knock it off the list..."

Max scanned his half-Algorean counterpart, hoping for less disappointment than was showing on her face. Unless you were a diehard surfer, it would be impossible to reconcile breaking Universal Law in order to surf a couple of waves.

Marjorie shook her head slowly, and for once wasn't beaming at him as if he could do wrong. She sighed and swallowed deeply. "Max, make sure you don't say anything about this to anyone else on our crew—or anyone on New Earth for that matter. I hope your crew knows better than to tell about your *highly* illegal foray there."

"Yes," he lied, "of course."

"Well, you better make sure." A drone waiter came by to take their orders, stopping their back and forth for a moment. Once it was gone, she gasped and put her hand over her mouth. "Uehara is destroyed! That means—"

Max recognized the look. It had been plastered on his friends' faces when they had been processing the fate of the blue-green pearl back at Outer Cygnus. "Yep," he said, dropping his chin and closing his eyes. "Those beautiful people—all the species on Uehara—gone forever."

***

Just as the food was finished, and mild elixirs were drained from their glasses, the eight of them were ready to leave, when, surprising everyone, Adonis and Piper showed up. Together. According to Max's estimation, for two people who were supposedly at odds, they were standing far too close.

With greetings complete, the two sat (next to each other) and joined in the conversation with the rest of the group for a few Uminutes. At one point Piper doubled over with laughter at a joke. She was speaking less rigidly to her crew.

As their voices came to a lull, Marjorie suggested they go listen to music and maybe... *Did she say dance?* "I know of *just* the place... they might even have actual *live* musicians!"

After everyone else had said "yes," and were staring at Piper and Adonis, awaiting their responses, Max sensed the awkwardness. Her crew weren't happy with how cozy the two were getting. Not one bit.

Piper waved. "Uh—I'll try to catch up with you guys in a bit."

Marjorie and Carrysa were giving Adonis the stink eye as they filed out.

***

Carrysa tried to get into the groove, but found herself moseying around the place, not so much dancing, as swaying back and forth. The establishment Marjorie suggested they go to had at least one hundred Sun People, along with a mixture of probably a few dozen Cygnan aliens, all of them bobbing and waving their arms, like a flock of seabirds on the waves, a rolling mixture of movement. On stage, the rhythmic beat entered the dancers' bodies, spurring them into choreographed movements. A kaleidoscope of lighting came from laser portals spread throughout the venue, each providing its own unique color and pattern. Depending on how many elixirs—and what type one imbued—the intensity of the scene was either enthralling or uncomfortably pervasive. Carrysa was in the later category.

Carrysa waded through the revelers until she got a glimpse of Adonis and Piper, who had naturally succumbed to the music and joined the fray. Their bodies moved in unison, as if no time had passed since their final dance. Piper was smiling, and allowed Adonis to grasp her hand and twirl her around as the music heightened pace. He barely took his eyes off of hers. Deftly and confidently he created a space among the patrons by sheer fluid movement. Other dancing couples and individuals on the dance floor couldn't help but join her in watching them.

Carrysa walked back to a floating table and sat. She twiddled her thumbs, wishing some strapping Sunish man would come ask her to dance and sweep her off her feet with class and charm. *I'll settle for an alien, at this point.* But her insecurities festered in the moment—what with her hair a tangled mess, her cloak not woven of fine synthetics and robust colors? And there was pretty Piper, being moved around the dance floor with adroitness by one of galaxy's most infamous bachelors. It was hard to shake herself from a touch of envy. Piper *always* had men courting her, and she waved them away without so much as a glance in their direction. *Good galaxy, I just want* one. So she idled again in her floating chair. Out of the corner of her eye, she glimpsed one of the rabbits—maybe Mike, but it was hard for her to tell him apart from his twin—hopping toward the sky deck.

Then something else.

At the edge of the crowd, a couple of darkly dressed men were loitering near the open-air exit doors, wearing shadowy complexions, most of their faces covered by extra long cheek plates and hoods hanging over their eyes. They did not seem to fit into the scene, it was euphoric in the dance hall, and they were... brooding. Dangerous.

Carrysa spied them heading for the same sky deck exit Mike had been hopping toward. *Hmm. That's weird.*

She stood from her floating chair and weaved her way through the stragglers at the edge of the dance floor. She attempted to blend in—keeping her head low—so they wouldn't notice she was following them. The shadowy men seemed intent on getting to the exit quickly, which meant a few patrons got a rude bump, displacing them slightly, and causing them to gawk at the three dark characters pushing through. But the patrons did nothing more than stare.

No one wants to mess with these guys.

Following them out the exit, Carrysa took the conveyor from the dance hall to the sky deck. Her lungs filled with the fresh, cool night air of a typical Sun City evening. She cocked her head to survey the patrons hanging around outside. A few were walking back into the fervor of the dance hall after cooling off. It didn't take long for her to pick out the shapes of the dark men. They walked with purpose and were gaining on Mike's relatively slow-hopping pace. She assumed he could probably get those paws bouncing him much faster if he needed to, but he had no clue he was being pursued.

He never had a chance. They fanned out in a half circle and closed in, snatching the giant rabbit by his two largest dreadlocks.

Carrysa gasped and was momentarily frozen, not sure what to do. Should she yell out? Get help? Sensing the insidious nature of the perpetrators, she grasped it would be better to maintain a low profile and not alert the kidnappers she had witnessed the crime.

A quick buzz of light flashed from within the trio of kidnappers.

Oh my Milky Way! Nausea overcame her. *They hit him with a shocking wand!* Those weapons were supposed to be exclusive to Ugovernment peacekeepers, yet these men brandished no official insignia on their lapels, nor any uniform indicating a status of authority.

What is going on here? That poor rabbit!

The assailants stepped onto a hovercraft, seeming to manifest out of thin air, and before she could even process what had happened, they jetted up and over the railing of the sky deck. Several people who were lounging outside recoiled, their long glasses of elixir tumbling from their floating table and shattering on the ground.

Carrysa followed the flight of the craft with her eyes, her head turning and tracking the flat, black platform of the hovercraft. *It's a short distance passenger machine. They can't be going far.*

337

A bundle of brown and gray fur wedged in between the huddle of the men; two paws hung limply over the edge.

CHAPTER TWENTY-SEVEN

The Outer Cygnus Dilemma

General Lorne paced back and forth nervously in front of wide synthglass windows, surveying the great city extending out below him. His view revealed low-lying networks of fly ways, filled with air cars, forming a matrix through rows and rows of beige complexes. Surrounding the hexagonal shaped buildings were layers upon layers of Persean fruit trees and berry bushes, each manicured seamlessly into the architecture.

One of the general's many responsibilities was his role as Weapons Director of the Planet Ball Development Center, a prestigious locale placed neatly on top of the highest hill in the capital city of Persar. Thus the first class view.

Designed to mimic the shape of a rounded planet, ripe for the throwing, a great white dome was perched upon the tower wall where his lab was constructed. There, he could consult holocharts and watch holofeeds while also keeping an eye on things in the production hangars. After all, Perk and his team of scientists were working feverishly to meet the deadline proposed by the Grand Master of Perseus, and Stergis would not accept excuses.

Yes, but with no buffer... The general folded his arms across his chest, staring out the synth window for an answer. If Perk could not perfect the weapon's safety measures, they risked creating an uncontrollable force that could endanger the entire galaxy— *including* the Perseus Arm. The first in line for reprimands and punishment would be him.

"General Lorne," the holoscreen above the entrance chirped with the voice of the grand master, who's call General Lorne had been expecting. He twitched slightly before responding, pressing the holobutton to open the tower doors. All of the assistants in the tower retreated to the air tubes. Stergis barely glanced at them as he walked directly in the general's direction.

"Grand Master!" said General Lorne, trying to sound enthusiastic. "Always Forward! Great of you to come visit the tower. I am sure you are here to check on the status of the new technology—you'll be happy to hear we have made significant progress..."

"Yes, yes," the grand master said, impatiently waving his hands. "Always Forward. I have been checking for myself on the digital logs. Impressive range coordinates. Unfortunately, we have a delay. The tournament is on hold—but praise Perseus—only for a short while."

"May I ask..." Lorne carefully prodded. "Why?"

Finally, the grand master spoke. "We have a problem with Outer Cygnus, General. The Sun People have been alerted of our activities—when you and your underling allowed those aliens to escape into the Abandoned asteroid belt they were *not* destroyed. In fact, it's a worst case scenario, for they now possess our star map data. Any Ugov aliens could potentially travel from the Outer

Cygnus solar systems to *our* home Arm. You failed me, General Lorne. You failed all of us. Perseans, our culture, our sport. By letting those specks of dust retreat to the galaxy arm whence they came—now *everything* could be in jeopardy." Stergis turned, his pale eyes belying his grave intentions.

"Sir—Grand Master—I am ashamed!" Lorne stepped forward, forcing his chin not to droop. "Buele believed the risk of damaging the *Amalgamator* was not worth chasing the bacterium scum. Truthfully, I didn't think they could have survived either—"

"*Silence!*" Stergis bellowed.

The tower quieted, other than the usual clicks and beeps from status signals emanating from the holoscreens hovering throughout the air space of the domed chamber.

In that moment General Lorne had the sickening realization his life was in the balance, so he took a chance and stammered, "Commander, I—I can make atonements for this failure! I have the most extensive knowledge of the new technology we are going to impose. Please, let me finish my work here... then you won't have to re-train a successor or promote an unworthy Perscan to my position. If my team creates the weapon and it helps the cause and you are still not satisfied with my performance... then I will gladly give my life, comforted by the fact the delay in my execution would allow me to serve Persar faithfully, one last time."

The grand master's face softened. Stergis needed the general to oversee Perk with the black hole technology. He prayed it would be enough.

A holocall signal buzzed. It was the high lady calling. Stergis nodded in the direction of the general as he stormed to the exit. The tall Grand Master stopped himself at the portal, turned around, put out his pointer finger straight up in the air, making it clear how many more chances he had to serve. *One.*

Lorne sighed deeply as he watched the grand master get sucked into the air tube.

When Stergis returned home he found Wella waiting for him on the veranda and they embraced. How she did it, he would never know, but with one peek at his face, she intuited his Uday's journey. His conversations, his planning, even his strategizing. Her turquoise necklace pulsed at her sternum as she wordlessly examined him.

After basking him in a benevolent smile for a few moments, she said in her singsong voice, "My love, you did not follow through with your conviction? I sense General Lorne is still serving you. Always Forward."

"Always Forward." Stergis lifted his chin. "Yes, your senses are true. When you called, I felt it a sign. I have decided he will follow through with his current assignment. I was close to executing him. After all, it is he I hold responsible for this tedious delay in the inaugural tournament."

"Stergis, I adamantly disagree with the delay. It gives a bad impression as Grand Master. An impression of hesitance."

He turned away from her sharp gaze. "You are wise, High Lady, you are able to peer directly into my soul. We must be cautious. The Sunish have great numbers. Remember, we are just one world, one sun, one planet, my dear. And we don't live forever. We have merely a billion of us—and although we are giant in comparison— there are quadrillions of them. Exactly how many of the tiny beings exist is difficult to comprehend, perhaps as many as there are stars in the sky, or rocks in the Abandoned…"

"Ahh—do not fret, Grand One," Wella purred, "we *can* and *will* defeat them. Every useful Persean soldier must remain in our service. We will need many allies. I am in the process of making new ones. As we speak, the words of your forefathers are spreading through newly fed mouths."

Stergis tried to remove the sour taste from his mouth. He pictured her buzzing around "making new allies" at the Arrangings. She was so attractive. *To my rivals, I'm sure even more so.* He studied her figure: tall and thin, with slightly textured but vibrant yellow skin, her arms coated with fine white hairs, and her long braided tail draped her back. He couldn't help but feel… somewhat emasculated. Most of the major decisions were made by his wife, the powerful woman whom many considered to be the *actual* leader of the new era of Planet Ball.

"And," she said, "I've been informed you have been making new allies of your own—among the tiny beings, is this true? Don't you think this also reflects poorly on your position."

He stared at her for a moment, parting his orange hair with his hands. *How does she know about my dealings with Myrtel?*

"I have, High Lady," Stergis finally responded. "It seemed prudent to have valuable spies at their level. And he has military power as well."

"Remember, Stergis," she said, kissing him on the cheek, and drawing him into her arms, melting his annoyance with her, "allies prove their worth when they serve a function."

Stergis considered her words, releasing himself from Wella's embrace, unwrapping one arm at a time, slowly.

"Wella," he said, the lines on his forehead forming perpendicular rows. "I worry about the younger generations. Whether or not they truly have a passion for the traditions of our forefathers."

"Many of them are soft," Wella's voice snapped, uncharacteristically. "They have no understanding of the war that destroyed our arm of the galaxy, no longing for the culture that perished in the war. But I have planted a seed among them, one that is strong and passionate for our cause."

"Bijr…"

"Yes." She raised an eyebrow at him.

Your turn to be surprised, my dear. "He's quite the handsome choice for a protégé in the Arrangings Dome, no?" he said.

"What is this now—do I detect jealousy, from the grand master, no less? A sign of weakness, according to the Rites of Persar."

She was teasing, but Stergis's cheeks flushed anyway.

"Now," she took his arm and turned him to face out on the capital city of Persar's jagged skyline, "look out there and tell me what you see."

He sighed, forcing himself to gaze out on his constituency. "The most beautiful city in the galaxy."

"That's right. And your leadership as grand master is crucial to making it the rightful capital of the *entire* galaxy. We remove New Earth's galactic status—their planet is nothing more than a ball for you to throw. Stergis, I am strongly advising you… you cannot delay the tournament any longer."

When she said nothing more he spoke again. "We need to be careful, High Lady. We cannot rush this. Our inaugural tournament is of the utmost importance. We cannot afford to have it tainted by interfering little bacterium."

She unlinked her arm brusquely. "As you wish, Grand Master. I have another meeting to attend this evening. Always Forward!"

Her sleek, nubile form glided past him. She went inside and gathered her things, opened a holoscreen to call for an air car, and was out the portal, gone into the night, leaving him on the veranda to brood.

***

To say Chyrone was surprised when he received a message from the high lady to meet in a discreet park on the outskirts of Persar would have been a gross understatement. He was still in shock when she emerged from the air car and strode toward him with tantalizingly long strides.

Her voice was pure as a songbird's. "Chyrone the Brave, Always Forward."

"High Lady—Always Forward—I—"

"Thank you for meeting me under these circumstances, Chyrone. This isn't the way I prefer to communicate, hiding out in a park after Persar has set."

"Yes, High Lady, I was—"

"Wondering why we're not speaking in the Arrangings Dome, as we normally do? Yes, well, I'm sure a man such as yourself has been conjecturing…"

Chyrone raised his eyebrows, feigning he misunderstood her.

"Grand Master Stergis."

He gulped. "Yes, High Lady, what about him?"

"Oh come now, don't play coy with me Chyrone, you are his biggest rival, his best challenger, you've seen the holovideos, there are more than a few who are partial to your playing style and, more importantly, how you envision Persean culture."

"Envision? I'm sorry, I don't follow you, High Lady."

"When we are alone, Chyrone, please call me Wella." Her smile nearly melted him. His heart surged through his chest as she squeezed his shoulder.

"Now," she purred, "why don't we talk together for a bit, take in the stars. Our sixth moon should be rising soon, although, I'm afraid the apogee makes it a bit dim. Much like the grand master's vision of the future. Far too dim."

Chyrone no longer doubted the intimations coming from the high lady as silly dreams of glory. They walked for a Uminute or two breathing in the cool night air, searching for celestial bodies. *This is my chance, what I've been waiting for my entire life, my path to grand master.*

He wanted her to spell it out. "Are you saying—"

The high lady shushed him. She put her hands on her hips.

"Let me ask you something, Chyrone, the one Planet Ball star capable of rivaling the grand master—but think carefully before you answer. I will not ask you again. Which do you hold more sacred: solar boards and dome walkers, or the promulgation of Persean culture?"

"I—I—"

"Which do you prefer: defeating a Planet Ball opponent, or ridding the galaxy of the tiny beings?"

They stopped at a small incline overlooking a pond with waterfowl floating in silent curled balls. Persar's mild yellow light infused the overcast skies. Chyrone was about to respond, but she continued to pelt him with questions.

"Can you guess how my husband, the *current* grand master, answers these essential inquiries?"

"Well, I—"

"How about his little clone, Ezran?"

"High Lady, it's—"

"Let me give you a little hint, Chyrone, I'm hoping your answers are different than theirs."

Enough time passed without her asking another question, so he prepared to tell her exactly the words she was asking for; he loved Planet Ball, but he wasn't an idiot. The position of Grand Master of Persar ran through the high lady.

***

One more meeting and this dreadful evening can be over, Wella thought as her air car dipped into a final approach to Planet Ball Headquarters. There was another figure she needed to bring into the fold, the final piece to the puzzle she had begun to put together, ever since trouble brewed in Outer Cygnus.

It was late, Persar had set hours ago and most were home gorging with their families, and there were few handlers in the docking bay when her air car landed. So she walked in anonymity, with a single security guard from her retinue pacing her long strides. When she reached the main entrance Wella dismissed him as another man emerged from the slide doors to greet her.

"High Lady!" General Lorne's voice called out to her. "Always Forward! To what do I owe this pleasure?"

"Yes, yes, Always Forward, General Lorne." She brushed past him, making sure to let her shoulder make firm contact. He had to spin around and follow her as she marched through the slide doors to his private meeting room.

Wella shrugged off several formalities, refused a glass of Persean juice, and would not even peek at him until comfortably seated in the privacy of his office. Only then did she cast her final spell.

"General Lorne, do you know why I'm here?"

Before he could babble she began peppering him with questions.

"In the middle of the night?"

Not quick enough to cut in, the general sunk in his floating chair.

"Without making any appointment?"

She didn't speak for such a long period he figured he ought to respond. "High Lady, let me assure you I—"

"You're not curious why I come, right at this most historic moment, under the cover of night... *without* the grand master?"

She loved watching their eyes bulge. *Ah, yes, Persean men. So fickle.*

"High Lady, I'm not sure exactly what—"

"Even the grand master is fallible, General Lorne. *That* is why I am here."

"Fallible?"

"Yes. Even the greatest Planet Baller of them all can lose a match. The problem is we—as Perseans—cannot afford to lose. And it's not this single tournament, in a faraway corner of Outer Cygnus, that I'm *really* concerned about. I'm here because I fear for the future of our kind."

The general was squirming. His floating chair reacted to his nervous twitching and he rocked side to side. "High Lady, I'm afraid I don't follow."

Her grunt of displeasure made him place his feet on the ground to stabilize his chair. "Your duty, as general and commander of the *Amalgamator* is not to be a caddy to the grand master during his Planet Ball forays, it's to protect the Persean people. Would you agree?"

He couldn't get an answer out.

"Because if you don't agree, that would mean you are privately admitting to me where your loyalty lies. Is that where your loyalty lies?"

Lorne stared at her, face gaunt, as if he might vomit. "No."

"No—your loyalty does not lie with the Persean people?"

"That's not what I said..."

"Confirm it for me, General Lorne, for once and for all—are you a Persean first or a Planet Baller first?"

"A Persean, of course, High Lady."

"Ahh—now we're getting somewhere." Her voice changed from the grating sound she used during Quarreling to a much softer tone. "I was certain I could trust you. Now you are beginning to find your answers. Why I came here, under cover, while Persar sleeps, while the grand master wallows in fear... I'm here because I knew I could trust you to protect the Persean race."

"Of course, High Lady, but how?"

"I'm glad you asked, General. Float in your chair, get comfortable. There are many things to discuss, and plans to put in place."

CHAPTER TWENTY-EIGHT

Tough Decisions

When Adonis walked onto the scene Claude was curled into a furry ball on the sky deck, moaning, his crew mates surrounding him. The poor mutant rabbit was inconsolable. And the councilman saw his buddies weren't in much better shape, but they were putting on their best faces, telling Claude not to worry, they were going to find his brother.

But there was no changing the reality—Mike was *gone*.

As soon as he heard the news, Adonis sprung to action and made a holocall to his most trusted assistant, Whitegull, to set in motion a team of investigators. If word got out about the kidnapping it would set off a backlash when it was discovered he had allowed the arrested Cygnans free rein of the city. After getting off with Whitegull, Adonis had promised Max he would do everything in his power to discover the whereabouts of their crew mate and instructed the terraform team to keep things hushed until he contacted them with further information.

Finally, Max lifted Claude to his hind paws and walked him to a waiting air cab. His crew mates followed.

"Come on, Piper, let's go!" Carrysa stood with Marjorie near the air cab landing strip conveyor, her hands on hips disapprovingly.

"Hold it a Usecond, will you!" Piper shot back over her shoulder.

After a whirlwind Uday, Adonis and Piper stood face to face on the sky deck. Staring into her brown eyes Adonis felt as if he were inside a bubble of serenity, insulating them from the bustle of air cabs flying to and fro.

Ignoring the frowns of Carrysa and Marjorie, Adonis drew her in closer by gently taking her arms.

"Adonis, I—"

"Shhh." He put his finger over his lips. "This has been an incredible Uday. Truthfully, I've been waiting my whole life for this Uday. I am so sorry we can't... well, I have to go... I've got to find out what's happening with our alien friends here. This could be a *very* serious matter. A security incident of this kind has the potential to affect the entire Ugovernment. But I want to... to see you again?" He grasped her hands in his. Her palms were warm as she squeezed back.

Piper had a tear forming in her right eye. "Adonis, I... I want you to look at something. But you must promise me to keep this to yourself." She reached into her vest pocket.

Something entered his palm discreetly from hers. A small, metallic cube cooled his hand.

A single tear rolled down her cheekbone, petering out below her jaw. "What wonders there are in this galaxy... I think this might be the key to saving Uehiron. Let's talk about it tomorrow."

She kissed him on the cheek and left him standing there, his palm closed around the object. When the terraformers had lifted off and flew into the night, he opened his hand and regarded the data cube. His head snapped to the dark sky, hoping for one last glimpse of her face, but their air cab was gone from sight.

***

After Uhours on holocalls trying to get any kind of lead on Mike's abduction, Adonis's crusty old apartment was somehow even crustier when he stumbled through the slide door late in the evening. It was so… empty. So much more so than it normal was. After the hike with Piper, kissing her lips for the first time, Adonis had been so ecstatic. Now, all by himself at the shell, the loneliness crept back in.

He tossed his blue suit coat on the cluttered floating couch, activated the auto settings on his kitchen droid, and per usual, the bar fixed him a nightcap elixir. *Galaxies, I wish she was here right now.*

Adonis yawned. He shook his head from side to side trying to resist the urge to collapse on the couch and sleep. *My brain hurts.*

He finally sat, sipping his elixir, but sprung back to his feet after barely getting comfortable. *Wait a Uminute, I know what to do!*

He shuffled through retractable storage drawers in the wall of his study, each opening and closing when he hit the holo button prompts. *Where is it? Where is it…? Hmm?*

"Oww!" He knocked his head against the edge of one of the drawers he thought he had closed. *Aha. Here it is.* He rubbed his head as he picked up an old, heavy, storage cube—nothing like the one she had given him. Piper's data cube was heavy in his pocket— by its sheer *presence* not its mass.

He found the closest holoscreen button, clicked it, and used his thumbs and pointer fingers to widen the screen as big as it would go, taking most of the air space in the room. Placing the cube in front of the scanner, he sat back.

"Play," he commanded.

The video was antiquated, a format hard to translate to modern holoscreens, and therefore poor quality. But the footage was rendered enough to clearly make out Piper's face, smiling, right into the camera, so young, and so alive.

The few times he had played the cube over the Uyears—usually after many elixirs and another excruciatingly lonely night—he hadn't the slightest inkling he'd be able to walk with her, hold her, kiss her, dance with her...

He watched the holoimage pan out and show the park they had been visiting that Uday. Adonis had been filming, and his voice was in the backdrop, squeaky and high-pitched, flirting with her incessantly. *A diatribe of comedic nonsense,* he thought. *I was so naive and insecure.* His mature self had an inordinate amount of disdain for his immature self. With one gulp, he downed the rest of the elixir in his glass.

After a few more Uminutes, he got up and left the room with the holovideo still playing. The four-dimensional imagery rotated, following his line of sight as he exited, as if her beautiful apparition were watching him.

Time to find out what this *is all about.*

He found the jacket he had been wearing earlier in the night strewn over a chair inside the front door. He reached in a small inner pocket and pulled out the dense metallic cube Piper had put in his palm. Regarding the complexity of the outer etchings, Adonis squinted and held it closer. A beep acknowledged a scan of his retina and the cube activated. A green hologram, a few millimeters wide, opened in the air alongside it.

Hmm. How did she get my retina scan and program it without me noticing? He smiled to himself. *Tricky, Piper, very tricky.*

He initiated the cube, unsure of what to expect. Judging from the passion in her voice, Piper must have given him something monumental. *But why would she trust me? After everything we've been through together? After one kiss? It was a great one, but...*

His expectations were soon met and exceeded, as the data cube proved to hold the incredible findings of the *Lifebringer* on their mission to Outer Cygnus. The wonderment of the ground footage on Uehiron and the accompanying data charts on the planet were astounding! There was such an eclectic mix of species, and the atmosphere was astonishingly similar to those found on most of the naturally inhabited worlds in the Orion Arm. He laughed as he listened to the girls of the *Lifebringer* discussing their amazing discovery—so much joy in their voices; with Nala always getting the last word, after all the louder voices died. He fast forwarded to the avian sighting and then other quick clips of insects flying about near running water, all shown from the perspective of the flyby drone.

Eventually he came across the holofiles on the ethereal beings. He watched the slow motion footage and nearly coughed out a lung. Their odd movements... and those puffy white emission clouds left in their wake... it was unlike any behavior ever recorded by astrobiologists.

She did it! Milky Way be blessed! Piper has made history—like father like daughter. Cristopher Crane—whom Adonis had adored—was the last astrobiologist to discover a unique species of sentient life form. Archaea and bacteria were far easier to find. This was a special discovery. One for the ages. *And she trusts me with this? No way. There's got to be something else...*

He dug deeper into the files, and opened the geological findings data charts. *Uh oh.* He scrolled and scanned, scrolled and scanned, reading some portions intently, while skipping others. He zoomed in on certain graphics while sweeping past others. No matter how he tried to analyze the data, it was clear the planet was rich in rare elements. It was as if Zander himself had authored the planet into existence so it could provide him with the most profitable mining opportunity. The whole continental ridge line of the northern hemisphere of Uehiron was stuffed with deposits needed to manufacture hyperspace sheaths.

Great Galaxies, it's everywhere. Adonis rubbed his temples, the elixir wasn't helping. *Really? Seriously? How could there be this much on one planet? Why did Piper show me this! She knows I could show this to Zander and get immediate military action going in Outer Cygnus—then Uehiron would be inundated with space machinery within a Umonth!*

It dawned on him. She was testing his loyalty. But the more he continued his research, the more stressed out he became. Section by section, hologram after hologram, the remarkable planet came to form on the screen in front of him. What a quandary! On the one hand, here was a planet with a healthy biosphere, a robust web of life containing unique alien species that could hold the answers to astrobiological puzzles that had been confounding terraformers for Ucenturies. On the other hand, it was a planet so rich in rare elements and minerals it could practically fund its own hyperspace sheath manufacturing company.

Adonis groaned, turning away from the holoscreen. *Maybe that's Zander's plan. Get a source of materials to build the means for hyperspace travel from Outer Cygnus inward, instead of shipping everything out there, he could build it from the Uehiron system backwards from planet to planet all the way to the IDL.*

Boiling it down, Adonis figured the Outer Cygnus dilemma was the essence of the conflict between two divisions of the Ugov: Terraformers, promoting responsible astrobiology as paramount to the success of the galaxy, and Extractors, claiming technological progress as more essential.

He closed his eyes, concentrating on his heart pulsing blood throughout his body. *And then there's the damned Blackons... with profit guiding their greed.*

He shut off the holoscreen angrily with a wild fling of his palm. He groaned falling into a floating chair at a bad angle, missing the seat, going all the way to the floor. He remained there, crumpled on the stinky floor; it matched his mood perfectly. *Dang, forgot to set the auto cleaner. Oh well, since I feel like garbage, I might as well lay in it.*

Was he really going to have to take this data cube to Martins and Shuler? It would ultimately mean Zander and his extraction team would have their way. How could he betray Piper? *But I can't endanger my fellow Ugov citizens.*

He pressed on his brow and squeezed his temples. Could he prod the Fourteen into action without substantial proof of Persean treaty violations? To many of the councilors, the words of a few delinquent aliens—and of the returned crew of the *Lifebringer* (who did not witness a single Planet Ball being hurled)—didn't amount to irrefutable evidence.

But this cube. He held it aloft and gazed at it sleepily. *This storage cube tells the real story of the multitude of wealth, both astrobiological and geological, to be found in the magical realm of Outer Cygnus. The true potential of Uehiron, as Piper's team has named it.* He recalled the holoimage of the shining green planet. It was a beacon of light sitting peacefully among the darkness of deep space, unaware its fate was being decided thousands of light years away.

Thoughts faded into gray and Adonis fell into an unconscious stupor, still grasping the metallic lump in his palm.

✳ ✳ ✳

When Mike awoke, he was lightheaded, nauseous, and his body ached. He swept away the dreadlocks from his face and tried to scoot onto his hind paws, but was so devoid of energy it took him nearly an entire Uminute to do so.

What the…? Where in the Milky Way am I? What happened to me?

He was pretty out of it, but he could tell right away he wasn't in Sun City anymore. He wiggled his nose and whiskers. In fact, the smells were so foreign...

A chill ran through him and he dropped his head. He wasn't on New Earth, either. He had been taken to another planet. *Claude!* Mike couldn't stand to be without his twin brother. They were rarely apart for long; Claude gave him comfort and confidence. So did his fellow crew mates—Vern, Blob and Max. With a rising dread in his chest, it truly dawned on him: they were not going to be able to help him this time.

The leftover effects of being hit with a shocking wand kept the victim comatose for sometimes as long as a Uday. Eventually the hangover lifted, as normal physiological functions returned. Mike hopped around his dark environs trying to make sense of it all. *Where was I? Yes, the dance hall. I hopped outside...*

His memory was less than full capacity, and he had no idea who had kidnapped him. But, having been hit with a wand before in some past adventure, at some faraway surf spot, on some faraway world, he was fairly certain he had been struck by one.

His surroundings were dim and not improving his state of affliction. It wasn't exactly a prison cell, but it might as well have been. There was one tiny portal window filtering in light from the top corner of a gray synthcrete ceiling. It was at least ten meters off the floor. *I ain't jumpin' that high.* There were a few cushions and a decrepit mattress where he had awoken in a daze. A bathroom. But otherwise it was a barren quarter, fit for a captive. He couldn't even make out a portal door until he noticed a pale blue flickering from one of the walls. *Must be the status indicator light. Well, my status is looking pretty lame right now.*

Mike didn't bother yelling or slapping his paws on the wall, he would have to wait for his captors to present themselves.

Settling into a ball on a cushion, he tried to figure out his predicament. Smells wafted through a filter in the high window.

The stink of ratite dung. His button nose involuntarily rolled in circles.

His eyes glowed in the dimness. The amazing tidal bore surf sessions on Uehara played in his mind, the smell of the air, the roar of the jungle. *Will I ever surf again?*

A holocall emanating from the portal sensor shook him.

"Well, well, Michael Rabbit."

The voice over the com was low and hoarse, a grating sound, and it shook Mike to his core, spreading fear throughout his recently restarted nervous system.

"Welcome to Planet Myrtel. I trust you slept... deeply. I hope you find your quarters appeasing. We may even find a carrot or two for you..."

Mike perceived from the blatant sarcasm that he was dealing with someone who had supreme confidence, someone with bad intentions. Nevertheless, his brazenness took control. "Where are you? Why don't you come face me!"

Shocking the large rabbit, the response to Mike's challenge was immediate, as an older man slid through the portal door, the hiss upsetting layers of dust which caught the light, as they rose and drifted. "Here I am, Mr. Rabbit. As you requested. Face to face."

Mike usually would attack with nails scraping if he was given an opportunity to strike back at an assailant or captor, but he was frozen; transfixed by the Sunish man standing before him. Of medium height and build, his embroidered skullcap covered most of his head, with silver and black strands of hair splaying out the back. A thick, gray beard covered his face with a large, mole-covered nose protruding from it. His deeply inset blue eyes were sunken within canyons of weathered skin on his face. On his black suit was the signature embossed golden circle of the Blackons.

"I am Myrtel Hemperley, and you, Originalist mutant, are privileged enough to be breathing on my planet."

"Privileged? Ha!" Mike shot back, his short term memory overcome by vitriol.

"Ease your tongue, Rabbit. You are here for one purpose, and one purpose only. And if you cannot provide me with what I want, you will be disposed of. Then, one by one, starting with your twin brother, I will dispose of the rest of your derelict crew of Cygnan scum."

"You wouldn't dare! We have friends—councilors and high-up people in the Ugov, so—"

"*Pfft!* I've got a hundredfold more."

The man wasn't bluffing. Mike deflated back into a ball and dropped his chin.

After a moment of silence, Myrtel resumed talking. "Surfing the Milky Way, eh? Hmm. Yes, I have seen you and your crew's exploits in holohistory news feeds. Your crew has broken so many Ugov laws in your eagerness to ride waves it really is comical. I was surprised you weren't already locked away at Galaxy's End. Although, that made it much easier to abduct you. Thank the Milky Way for typical Ugov inefficiency." He smiled and gazed upward as if sending a prayer to the stars above.

Mike stirred, rising to his hind paws. It took everything in his power to keep from crumpling, his thigh muscles were so weak. Lactic acid had hardened in his veins from the shocking wand.

"And so what do you want with me and my crew, *sir?*" Mike emphasized the sir with scorn. "What could we have possibly done to make you willing to… take me *here* and threaten our lives? Especially when we're already under Ugov supervision."

The older Sunish man smiled again, a creeping malice spreading across his jowls. "I just alluded to it… surfing and traveling to places you should not be. Congratulations, your crew finally went one place too far, and rode one wave too many. Now your life depends on how forthcoming you are. Remember, it's not just yours, it's yours *and* your friends' lives at stake here. Brother

358

Claude goes first. Sorry, Mister Rabbit, when you traveled to Outer Cygnus and landed on that bacteria-laden planet of Uehara, you made the choice to pass the IDL, and that was a very, *very* bad decision. But you made an even worse decision when you escaped. You have stolen something I need. A star map."

A light clicked on in Mike's head. He guessed what was coming next.

"When you used energy resonance—(by the way, where in the Milky Way did you get that technology from, I wonder?)—and traveled to the Abandoned hyperspace platform, I know you stored away that data somewhere. I want it. My understanding is this star map has not been shared with the Ugov, luckily for you and your crew—or you would be dead already. That might have been the single wise choice you made, not giving it to Councilman Adonis.

"Put your eyes back in your sockets, Michael, I'm privy to your little 'relationship.' If your crew can do these two simple things: one, get me that star map, and two, assure me your crew alone has seen this data, then I will bring you back to New Earth. Once you have met those conditions, I will let your crew go back to the Inner Cygnus Arm. And I'll assume that I will never have to hear about you surfing alien freaks again—because you will *not* be making any more forays to Outer Cygnus."

Ah ha! Mike thought. *This psychopath must be a Persean sympathizer. How else could he have any idea we were jumping hyperspace sheaths way out there on the edge of the Abandoned?*

"Fine." What choice did he have?

Mike's reply appeased his captor. "Good. I hoped you would be a sensible mutant, Mr. Rabbit. I will make the preparations. I will contact your twin brother and tell him the terms we have made. If he cannot deliver what we ask of him, I'll order the executions. Let me remind you—he'll be first."

The vicious Blackon named Myrtel wheeled around abruptly, his boots clacking on the synthstone floor. The door hissed open and clanged shut, leaving Mike in a depressed state, lying on the floor, with tears wetting the fur around his eyes.

CHAPTER TWENTY-NINE

Betrayals and Oaths

Adonis was torn when he entered the loud council meeting chambers, his stomach grumbling in protest. Thirteen councilors were engaged in pre-official conversations, which ranged broadly from personal life, all the way to dark secrets of intergalactic politics. One and all of the thirteen's voices paused—shaking their heads and grumbling to each other at his tardiness, then went straight back to their banter.

With a five hundred kilo weight on his soul, Adonis walked to his floating chair. He was harboring the most important secret in the Milky in his hip pocket. His duty was to the Ugovernment's citizenry, he shouldn't be giving preference to any one division, but Piper...

"Council, to order!" called Councilwoman Martins, with Shuler shuffling along right behind her. "We've much to discuss, and low and behold, the man who organized this meeting of the fourteen has finally arrived."

Adonis shook off the glares as he hopped on his floating chair, the hologram of his name bent across his body as he passed through the projection. *I must look even worse than I feel. Damn elixirs.* Zander's pink face examining him—as the older man eased into his chair—substantially increased Adonis's nausea.

"Yes, Councilman Adonis?" Zander croaked. "You said you had something I would be interested in? I'm assuming this has something to do with Outer Cygnus? Like every order of business brought to my table, lately…"

Adonis cleared his throat. "Umm… yes. I do. Here…" he motioned to a Gen-3 assistant android who retrieved the memory cube from his palm and went to plug it in. "Let's all take a look at this before we discuss anything further."

A few moments later the holoscreen image lit the space above the long floating table where the councilors now were settled. And there it was… the little green planet. Uehiron. An emerald ball glowing among the blackness. A single yellow star basked half the planet in light, while the other half was shadowed, but visible. Nearby, the brightest of a handful of moons reflected a different kind of radiance.

Adonis glanced at Zander for his reaction. *Ha! You can practically hear his slobber dropping onto the table.*

"As the image zooms in, these highlighted areas…" Adonis floated his chair over and pointed out where he was referring to. "I think you'll be pleasantly surprised by the amount of rare earths stored in the core deposits."

"How interesting you're showing the council this," Zander squinted at him despite being less than two meters away. "What *incredible* timing."

"What are you implying, Councilman?" Adonis floated away from the image to get a better read on his semi-adversary.

"Please, gentlemen, temper yourselves," Shuler interrupted. "We are the fourteen, and there is a situation developing here. We *must* come to a consensus. Please, let's be cordial with each other."

Adonis landed his chair on the synthfloor with a thunk. "You think *you* can do that, Executive Zander?"

"If *you* can."

Adonis rolled his eyes. "What do you mean by 'incredible timing?' "

The chief of extraction continued, "First, the Persean threat to Outer Cygnus—once again, brought to the fourteen's attention by your sources—and now you're showing us data that will provoke me to support military intervention… which is part of your agenda. I just think the timing is a little coincidental. Do we have any other evidence?"

Adonis stared at him for a Usecond before answering. "Do you *actually* believe Executive Crane's team would make up these findings? That's preposterous—you know as well as everyone here sitting in their floating chairs—her division is not fond of extracting from an unexplored exoplanet."

Zander seemed unperturbed. "Well, if the findings are real, I support an extraction team along with a military convoy, immediately."

"The numbers do seem promising." Martins had been scrolling through a separate holo from her cheek plate. "This could definitely help expand hyperspace sheath building capabilities."

Shuler said to the group, "We can't afford to ignore this, Councilors."

Adonis laughed and shook his head. *How quickly they fall in line…*

Zander chimed in, "So we should bring this to a vote? And what about Executive Crane?"

There was a loud commotion outside the chambers, the doors slid open, and in stormed a surly Piper Crane.

Dear Galaxies, Adonis gulped, *what have I done?*

"What *about* Executive Crane?" Piper shouted as she made a beeline straight for the Gen-3er assistant. She bumped it out of the way, and removed the data cube from the holoprojector input slot. Uehiron's majestic green hue left the room as the image vanished. She turned and stared at them for a moment. "The Council of Fourteen—ha! Look at you all! So pathetic. So eager to cut my budget, and cut *into* my planets."

Adonis floated over and reached out. "Piper, I—"

Piper stomped right past Adonis, shrugging off his arm on her shoulder and leaping onto the table. "Before you all bring to vote, maybe you'd care to view the *real* data!" She reached into her pocket and pulled out a gleaming memory cube, an exact replica of the one Adonis had brought to the meeting. "You'll find a different argument for action in Outer Cygnus—the argument for *life*." The Gen-3er wasn't about to wait for her to give the order, they had built in emotional sensors after all, so it walked over and took the other cube from Piper and plugged it in.

"What is this?" Zander cried out when the new image projected. "These numbers are completely different! There's barely any rare earths on that chunk of rock!"

"Exactly," Piper said, her eyes narrowing on Adonis.

She set me up. Adonis tried to speak, but she squealed over him.

"No, no, no! Don't try to placate me, Councilman Adonis. When I gave you the cube last night I said *specifically* not to share it with anyone… because it wasn't finalized."

She's covering her butt, now. Adonis bit his lower lip.

"Those weren't official numbers," Piper continued. "Now you've embarrassed my team, you've embarrassed me, and you've embarrassed this council."

Adonis slipped in a pathetic attempt to quell her ire. "I'm—I'm so sorry, Executive Crane, I was trying to—"

"Pardon me," Executive Zander called out loudly, "but this is a meeting of the fourteen, and with all due respect, Executive Crane, you weren't invited. Now you've come bursting in, claiming you've given the council false data... What kind of stunt are you pulling here?"

Adonis almost defended her when he was reminded it was never necessary with Piper Crane. Her father had trained her to be able to stand up for herself just fine.

She locked eyes with Zander and said, "There is no *stunt*. What there is is accurate data and Ugovernment law. In this galactic era, astrobiological imperatives override the desire of the greedy. Your kind, Executive, who can never realize when enough is enough."

"What are you blabbering about, Crane?" the elder Sunish man hissed back.

"Ugov law makes it quite clear: a newly discovered life form nullifies any extraction claims. I'm paraphrasing, of course, but I'll have the assistant pull up the exact code, if you'd like..." she backed her threat by waving at the Gen-3er, who obligingly filled the holoscreen with digital tomes of written laws.

Zander groaned. "Not necessary, thank you."

With a break in the main conversation, the fourteen leaned to each other and whispered to the side.

Piper wasn't done. "Council of Fourteen, hear me! I have unequivocal, boots on the ground proof of new life forms on Uehiron! The law is the law. I demand you vote to support military action to protect our astrobiologist teams in the field, not to chaperone mining operations. We must not allow the Perscans to destroy what could be the greatest discovery the galaxy has ever known!"

"Ha!" Zander laughed. "You're a clone of your father—a dreamer who partakes in Ri-Ri cactus dust..."

Don't, Piper, Adonis thought.

She walked across the table, becoming a predator, ready to pounce on Zander and tear him apart.

"Okay, that's enough!" shouted Adonis, getting out of his floating chair and stepping between Piper and Zander. "Zander, be respectful. Piper, can you please come down off the table and take a floating chair? We are all very much in appreciation of your findings. Let's discuss this amicably. I'm sure the council will allow you to sit in, considering the stakes…"

Her bloodthirsty gaze snapped from Zander to Adonis. Now he was the prey, and a lump formed in his throat. *Come on, Adonis, you can fix this. Think!*

"Amicably?" Piper yelled, pointing her finger in his face. "Are you out of your mind, Adonis? You lied to me, and to the council." She made a gesture to Zander. "This snake is insulting my father and you want me to speak amicably?"

"Piper, please—"

She jumped off the table and addressed the quieted fourteen one final time. "You have a duty to uphold the law! You are the highest council of the Ugovernment… I expect you to approve the data prepared by my team. It details how much bitcoin it's going to cost to get a military convoy out there. Believe it or not, my team also calculated the cost for bringing Zander's extraction team— solely for reconnaissance purposes, of course."

The pockmarked councilman protested, "But there aren't rare earths on Uehiron. We're not spending any resources there."

Piper gave him a knowing smile. "Exactly what I knew you would say. And you perfectly demonstrate *why* the Ulaws were written. For snakes of your ilk. When the data showed rare earths, you're slithering to get into a hyperspace sheath, but when the data shows rare *lives*, you want to shut it all down. You disgust me, Executive Zander."

There was a gasp, followed by mumbling amongst the councilors.

Before Adonis could try again to quell her tirade, Piper had shifted her wrath back squarely on him.

"And *you*... no words describe what you are, Councilman Adonis. The most famous councilor in the Ugov, they say. Ha! More like the most flip-flopping, untrustworthy, lying, cheating, backstabbing son of a..."

She charged out of the council meeting, leaving Adonis right where he began, with everyone staring at him.

***

The council approved the vote twelve to two. Of the abstainers, one was a given, the other was a mild surprise. Zander sure, but why Dorayne? He had argued against opening Outer Cygnus during a prior meeting, hadn't he? Adonis couldn't figure it out. What was his angle? He had connections with Blackons—but who *didn't* in the Ugov? Adonis himself had "associates" on that side of the ledger.

When the pasty man got up and excused himself, there was sweat condensing on his temples. As Ugov employees got the best genetic implants, Adonis found it curious. *How could he possibly have a fever?*

Adonis waited half a Uminute, then bailed out the door and searched for Dorayne's long blue and white cloak with the Ugov insignia on the back. He was rather tall, and therefore easy to spot among the busy sky deck. Adonis followed step, careful to keep his distance, squatting behind a passerby as Dorayne whipped around. *What is going on with this guy? He's definitely going to spot me. Time for emergency measures.*

Adonis got as close as he could, then darted behind a pillar and pressed his wrist implant. *I've got just the thing for this.*

A few clicks later, a small round object, the size of a small bee, protruded out from the synthmetal where skin used to be when he

367

was born. He activated it through voice command and the "bug cam"—as he liked to call it—fluttered off into the air. He linked up with a satellite and recorded the live feed directly to the data storage on his holopad. Every sight and sound would be Adonis's property. *Illegally, though. What in the name of the Milky Way am I doing right now?* He was conflicted, but he was going to have to trust his intuition on this one.

Adonis went to an unoccupied corner of the sky deck and followed the video in privacy. The bug had managed to wiggle through a closing air door, while following its appointed subject, and now landed on the edge of the bathroom stall the councilor had sequestered himself to. The feed showed Dorayne pacing back and forth and wiping the sweat from his brow. He was agitated to say the least, and Adonis fretted about pulling the bug cam. The guy was in the privy, after all.

A holocall signal from Dorayne's cheek plate glowed, and Adonis's eyes widened. Now it was official, his bug cam was making Adonis complicit in an illegal monitoring of a fellow Ugov councilor. If Dorayne detects his device and he was caught...

"Councilman Dorayne," droned the image of a man Adonis had never met but everyone in the galaxy new—Myrtel Hemperley. "I trust you have crucial information or you would not risk contacting me... a bathroom stall? Honestly, do you have any respect?"

"Myrtel," Dorayne's whimpering made Adonis ready to punch the rail of the sky deck. "I couldn't risk our communication being intercepted. It's too... sensitive."

"Well," Hemperley prodded, "go on, spit it out! And turn off the video will you, I don't want to see the inside of your moon scraper toilet!"

Adonis's video feed went blank, but the conversation continued to be recorded. He placed his wrist by his ear for privacy.

Dorayne's voice squeaked. "They've approved action to the exoplanet Uehiron. It's official. It was Crane and those surfer aliens—they ruined everything!"

Myrtel drawled, "Not to mention that pesky Adonis. That push-over worships the ground Crane walks..."

What the... Adonis did hit the rail, cursing from the self-inflicted pain in his knuckles. *Who does this Blackon flunky think he is?*

"You have the rabbit in custody. What should I do next?" Councilman Dorayne whined.

Unbelievable! Adonis shook his head. One of the fourteen was taking direct orders from the most unconscionable man in the history of the galaxy—who was also in on Mike's abduction! *This is getting way too crazy!*

A loud voice called out his name, forcing the audio to shut off. Adonis turned, who—

Wham! A punch nailed him straight in the jaw. At first he was numb with adrenaline. But the pain soon came, along with the salty taste of blood in his mouth. He wobbled, with stars dancing in his head, but managed not to crumple, getting into a defensive stance. No further punches came, and when his vision cleared there was the hulking figure of Royce Knox. His arms were by his sides, so Adonis dropped his guard, one hand rubbing his mouth instead.

"What the—"

"Shut it, Adonis, or I'll hit you on the other side of your face." Knox meant business.

Assaulting a Ugov councilor? Even for Knox that was pretty over-the-top. The balding man could be prosecuted and disciplined. But Adonis figured reciting Ugov law was probably not the best tact at the moment, so he refrained. Plus his jaw ached badly. Provoking a second punch could be catastrophic to his facial configuration... *Galaxies, that guy has synthmetal in his fists!*

"*That* was for Piper. You are a traitor, Adonis! I told her not to trust you!"

"What?" Adonis spat back. "A traitor who manages to get your division's most important exploration mission approved, protected by military convoy, and in record time, no less. If that's a traitor… And by the way, Piper is the one who gave me the fake data cube. She set me up!"

Knox shook his head. "You don't know when to stop do you? Don't you see what you have done? You've caused further discord amongst the fourteen. Now, Zander thinks that Piper *purposefully* made a fool of him in there." He pointed back to the council chambers entryway. "Shuler and Martins have their doubts now, too."

"Newsflash holo, Knox— they've *always* had their doubts about Piper. *I'm* the one that advocates for your division the most in there—*oww!*" Adonis grabbed his mouth, the bleeding had stopped, but the throbbing made it hard to speak.

Knox glared at him, nostrils flaring. "How do you live with yourself, Councilman?"

"Knox…" Adonis muttered, wishing he had an elixir. He had to push the words from the corner of his mouth to get them out. "I advocate for the citizenry, not any single division. I made the hard decision—from the findings Piper had on there originally, mind you—to turn over the data cube because… it was the right thing to do. We must stop the Persean threat. Period. We needed more motivation. I thought Zander and his extractors would be able to get that."

"Well they approved it after all…"

"Um…" Adonis would have smiled wryly if he could have. "Yeah. *Because* of the unique species clause. Piper was quite aware of what she was doing when she gave me that fake cube, Knox. She played me like a drum machine."

"Yeah, I feel *so* bad for you. She was testing you! She was genuinely heartbroken!"

"Heartbroken? What are you—her dating android? You've taken over security and matchmaking for her too, or what?"

Knox shook a fist at him.

Adonis took it down a notch. "I can build back her trust. And yours."

Knox winced. "What kind of new lie is this?"

"I'm serious, Knox." Adonis motioned him to the privacy of the sky deck rail. "I'm actually glad you're here—not that you punched me, of course, I could have done without that, but I probably would have come to you right after—"

"Right after what?" Knox shuffled his feet. "You're not making sense."

"Watch and listen."

Adonis played the holorecording of Dorayne's traitorous conversation with Myrtel Hemperley, getting a kick out of Royce Knox's widening eyes as the message droned on.

"But this means..." Knox was in disbelief.

"They're in with the Perseans, yes."

"It's illegal footage?"

"Yeah... that's why I was going to come to you first. Ha!" Adonis slapped him on the back, making Knox's frown bend.

"We can't use it as evidence."

"Duh!" Adonis winced, every facial expression sent a jolt through him.

"Okay," said Knox, "download that message to my holopad. I've got an idea."

"Uh oh," Adonis held his wrist over Knox's to complete the transfer. "I have a feeling this might have something to do with *those* things." He pointed to the man's enormous hands. "Don't go doing anything illegal now, mister head of security, wouldn't reflect well on your beautiful, fearless leader."

"Thanks for the advice," Knox said. With the download complete, he shoved Adonis hard to the ground, making him land on his bottom and back awkwardly. "Now I'll give *you* some friendly advice: Stay away from Piper."

"Yeah," Adonis yelled after him, sitting up and checking for more bruises. "Real friendly, Knox, real friendly!"

***

"What happened to you, dude?" Max smirked at Adonis as he buzzed himself into their confinement quarters, a healing pack pressed against his face. "You run into a wall, or what?"

The growl Max received warned him to leave well enough alone, so he offered Adonis a floating chair and called the boys over.

"All right," Adonis said, after fending off more questions about his puffed-out jaw and the scratches on his knuckles, "here's the deal: I found out where your crew mate Mike is being held."

Max turned to his buddies and grunted, "We already know where."

"*What?*"

"Yep, check this out," Claude said in a somber voice pressing his holopad.

A few Uhours ago, they had received a random, anonymous text with the instructions on how to retrieve him, which included "returning the information you stole." Vern hacked into the metadata and discovered the source of the message was Myrtel World.

"What is it you guys took from him?" Adonis asked point blank.

Max bulged his eyes at his crew mates so they wouldn't blab. "Nothing—what're you talking about?"

"Max," Adonis groaned, rubbing the healing pack on his bruised cheekbone, "I should tell you I had the *Planet Hopper* scanned thoroughly. It appears your ship has a rare technology built into it, and also has quite a bit of protected data in your mainframe's data banks. Anything you want to disclose at this point, Captain?"

Max shrugged. *He knows, might as well level with him.* "Here's the deal, dude. We do have something. But we can't give it to you—yet. You read the text. Penalty of death if we botch this. The message told us not to divulge anything to anyone."

"Max..." Adonis said in a patented Ugov form. "Do you realize I could have all of you confined in separate quarters and your ship hacked apart piece by piece, until I found what's on there?"

Threats. The classic Ugov stance. Not the right tact with Max. "Is that how you want to play it, Councilor?" His Algorean temper rose one notch. "After everything we've done? Even though you promised you would help us get our crew mate back? And what about our friends in the Abandoned, the threat to their home, you haven't mentioned a thing about them!"

Max watched Adonis wilt a bit. *Good, the guy may have a heart. Galaxies—it's hard to tell with this dude sometimes.*

"Okay," Adonis said, "I will not press this issue, but that's with the understanding that once we get Mike safely returned, you forfeit whatever it is that's so important Hemperley would go to such drastic measures to get it back."

"Agreed."

"All right," Max said, "now that that's settled, how are you gonna help us get Mike back? Can you send a nice armed ion cannon transport and we can go get Mike out and lock the Blackon scumbag up, or what?"

The way Adonis fidgeted wasn't promising.

"Um," the councilor finally said, "I hate to tell you this, but I can't help right now. All my resources are going to Outer Cygnus and the Persean problem. The best I can do is give you a furlough to talk to the Terraform team. I'll bet they can help you, Piper has contacts in the Myrtel World system you can use. As soon as Outer Cygnus is resolved, I can turn my attention to helping you guys get Mike safely returned. I'm sure we can help with your friends in the Abandoned afterward."

"Seriously, dude?" Claude growled, hopping away and shaking his dreadlocks. "You're nothing like the councilor I used to know."

Blob shook his fist at Adonis and turned and walked to another part of the quarters. "You're lucky I don't give you another shot!"

Max shook his head, his Algorean anger rose another level. But what could he do? He accepted Adonis's furlough scan and the boys got ready to go find out if they still had any friends on New Earth. Hopefully the crew of the *Lifebringer* were more keen on helping than the rest of the Ugov seemed to be.

***

Max rallied the troops with a fiery speech, and they took an air cab to Terraform Headquarters to meet with Piper and her crew. A Uhour later, both crews sat together in a meeting chamber, with the entirety of the two groups meeting for the first time face to face. Once the introductions and minor gossip were through, Max addressed Piper for the real reason for the visit.

"So," the Captain drawled, avoiding Marjorie's panting stares. "Executive Crane…"

"You can call me Piper here," the Terraformer extraordinaire said.

"Okay," Max said, smiling his trillion bit smile, "Piper it is. Pretty name… We've come a long way since we first chatted over holo in Outer Cygnus, eh?"

The crews both giggled a bit at his comment.

"So," Max said, "we're honestly pretty pissed off at Adonis."

Piper let out a groan. "You aren't the only ones, believe me."

"He's a conniving snake!" shouted Marjorie.

Out of the corner of his eye Max noticed Royce Knox, who stood by the exit door with arms crossed, flinch.

"Well," Max said, "he explicitly promised us he would help us rescue Mike. He's gone back on his word."

"Not surprising," Piper replied, "considering he just did the same thing to me... but I better not get into it now, go ahead, Max..."

"He said you would be able to help us." The Captain arched his eyebrows at her, pushing the auburn bangs out of his face.

"How could *I* help you?" Piper asked.

"We received an anonymous text message from his captor."

The *Lifebringer* crew gasped at the news.

"That's awful" Nala said during the silence ensuing Max's bombshell. "He's a notoriously corrupt Blackon—and one of the richest men in the galaxy."

"Ahhh..." Piper hummed. "Now I see why Adonis furloughed you guys over here."

Max confirmed her guess. "He told us you helped terraform Myrtel World, that you might have some good ideas for us on how to free Mike. The message makes it quite clear—if we don't give Myrtel what he wants, Mike dies. Then assassins come for us."

Piper's crew gasped again.

Piper cut straight to the chase. "What is it Myrtel wants from you?"

Max expected nothing less but had his answer prepared. "We can't tell you."

Piper wasn't having it. "You want our help, Captain, and you can't tell us that crucial bit of information? That's your only leverage at this point!"

"I'm not bluffing, I can't show you the message," Max countered. "If we reveal it to *anyone*—Mike is a dead rabbit."

Time for the fallout. Their new friends were far from pleased to have essential info withheld from them. The *Lifebringer* crew talked amongst themselves for a moment in sharp tones. Max got more than one stink eye.

Finally, Piper broke in. "Hmm. This is very, *very* bad. Myrtel is practically above Ugov law. He's got security systems in place I had no part installing. I'm not sure what you want me to do…"

"Help us," Vern said, out of the blue.

"How?" Melia asked for Piper.

Vern's droning AI voice answered. "Come with us to Myrtel World, work with whatever contacts you still have there, and help us get our crew mate back safe."

"I'm sorry," Piper said. "But in case you hadn't noticed, we are busy getting a terraform mission approved to Uehiron. Yes, I do still have contacts on Myrtel World—but I have no idea how reliable they are. It was two Udecades ago when I designed that place."

"Piper, I want to help them," Nala said, her eyes wide as saucers. "They are good aliens, and they've helped us. Uehiron might be gone without their warning of the Persean action in Outer Cygnus."

Piper seemed to consider her words. But her reply was disappointing to Max. "I'm sorry… I cannot help at this time. The discovery of a new species is too important to delay, especially with the risks."

Vern's visor went blank as he prodded further. "How about we strike a bargain?"

Max gave a "what's up?" look to Vern.

Piper regarded the emotionless faceplate. "What, Vern?"

"We need your help and we have something you want. I hate being the one to divulge this…" Vern droned. "Max usually is the one who does it—by accident, but we have discovered *another* undocumented alien species."

"Vern!" Claude shouted, giving him a wiggle with his whiskers. "Shut your voice modulator off, dude!"

"Yeah," Blob joined in, "seriously, Vern. What're you doing, you synthmetal head!"

Too late, Max thought as Piper jumped out of her floating chair and walked right up to Vern and put her face in front of his. Millimeters away.

"Say that again, Vern," she commanded.

"Uhhh… we found a new species?"

"Where?" shouted Melia, jumping out of her chair as well. Pretty soon, the entire crew of the *Lifebringer* was up and at 'em, peppering Vern with questions.

He remained silent and stoic until they were done.

"Sounds to me like your team is interested in making a deal," Vern said with matter-of-fact inflection.

Piper growled at him. "I could have your crew sent to Galaxy's End, Vern. None of you reported this?" She whirled on Max. *"You're* the Captain—what, you didn't think it was important enough to tell the foremost team of astrobiologists in the galaxy that little tidbit of information?"

Max tried to defend their actions. "It was a whirlwind experience, we were just surfing, no big deal…"

"Just surfing?" Melia chimed in. "Ha! Surfing and breaking intergalactic law.

"Let me start from the beginning…" Max said, giving a brief rundown of the crew's experience on the Orb. When he finished silence reigned. The *Lifebringer* crew settled back into their floating chairs, locked in their own thoughts.

"I know this is crazy news," Max began, "but I think this benefits both the *Planet Hopper* and the *Lifebringer.* Y'all help us get our beloved crew mate back, and we help you get to Centaurus and find the Vapor People."

"This all has to happen off the record?" the chief executive asked.

"Yes," Max replied. "Because if any of Myrtel's spies or contacts get wind of this, Mike is done for. Oh, and one other small detail..."

"Great! And what is that?" Piper breathed out deeply, unable to stop shaking her head.

Max flashed a sheepish grin before making the request. "You have to get the *Planet Hopper* out of lockdown. Not only do we need our suits and surfboards—cause don't think we're going to the Orb without surfing again—but it also happens to have the star map data that only Vern can process to get us all to Centaurus. And, um, the hyperspace sheath is a little... sketchy, too."

Max closed his eyes and praised to Algor Piper would be amenable. *Maybe I shouldn't have thrown in the last part?*

Piper stared at him for awhile. She searched the faces of her crew mates, seeing all wide eyes and smiles. "I might be able to swing that."

"What?" yelled Max. "You actually *want* to do this?"

Piper answered by ordering her team to prepare the *Lifebringer* and pull up her old files on the Myrtel World terraform project. "Well, I guess our mutual story isn't over yet, you strange surfer aliens..."

"Praise Algor!" Max shouted so loud Royce Knox was stirred to action. He walked over and whispered something in Piper's ear.

"Let's go boys!" Max cried to the three of them. "We've got a brother to save, and a surf session for our reward!"

Blob, Claude, and Vern followed Max out and they called an air cab to return to their "confinement" quarters.

CHAPTER THIRTY

Myrtel World

What would my father say to me right now? Piper couldn't help but picture his broad grin. Aiding and abetting alien fugitives against the Blackons? Breaking Ugov terraform privacy laws? And to top it off, taking a non-sanctioned trip to the Centaurus Arm to seek out a new alien species. She had to smile. *Yeah, pretty sure he would be proud.*

Piper stood in her chambers on the *Lifebringer*, en route to the hyperspace sheath to Myrtel World, staring at a holoimage of the great Cristopher Crane. Oh how she missed him.

"It's a whole different Milky Way now, Pops," she said to his holo. "The councils are rigged and the Blackons grow more influential by the Uyear... the discipline you founded—astrobiology—is now becoming an afterthought."

She pressed a button and her father's recorded voice said, "Piper! Happy birthday, sweet child of mine! May you have many more wonderful Uyears of exploration and discovery ahead of you! I'll see you soon, okay? Love you!"

Piper replayed the message again.

"Well," she said softly, "I've got the exploration and discovery part down pat, thanks to your great wisdom and guidance. Oh, Pops, if you could have seen Uehiron!"

A buzz came at her door and an image of a smiling Melia projected, her signature virtual knock emanating from her wrist implant every time she visited Piper.

"Come in!" Piper called.

The door shushed open and in came Melia, a smile on her face. Observing the wet mark on Piper's cheek she inquired, "You okay?"

Piper turned away. "Oh, being weird and talking to my father on the holo again."

Melia sighed. "Do you need some space? Do you want me to come back later?"

"No, no!" Piper motioned to a floating couch. "Sit. Tell me what's going on."

Once settled, Piper had her android pour two waters and they each took a sip.

"Well," Melia said, "here's the deal… We're taking a massive risk here. It needs to be stated up front. From your first officer."

Piper gave her a raised eyebrow. "Did the girls put you up to this? And John?"

Melia shook her head. "Not at all. This is all coming from me. If we are implicated in this ruse we are possibly damaging the name of our division."

"Oh, come on, Melia." Piper laughed off the suggestion. "My father was a rebel too. Especially when regarding a potential new alien species."

"Yes, and in order to do so, we are gambling everything on random alien surfers. Fake documents about the *Planet Hopper* being removed to a non-existent space mechanic? Abusing our power on a former private terraform project? Messing with Myrtel Hemperley? This is insane, Piper!"

"And what about Mike?" Piper shot back. "He deserves no help from Adonis or the Ugov? He should rot in a cell, with that wicked man controlling his fate?"

"Well…" Melia had no reply for that. It was a fact—no one else was going to help the crew of the *Planet Hopper* get the other twin back.

Piper persisted. "Once we're successful on Myrtel World, what is the end goal?"

Melia frowned. "Centaurus."

"Exactly."

Melia wasn't persuaded yet. "Still, we have to break Ugov law even to do that! We have no approvals, no justifications for being out there… some of the more conservative of the fourteen are liable to call us outlaws! Not to mention using a janky hyperspace sheath, constructed by mortals, living in an asteroid belt."

"Well…" Piper gave her a wink. "They called Cristopher Crane an outlaw too. He did some pretty crazy missions. And he's the one who is most responsible for building our division to where it is… I think we're living up to his legacy."

"If anything goes wrong and we get implicated in this, it could affect funding, Piper."

"Funding! Ha!" Piper stood up abruptly. "You know me better than that, Mel."

"I do, that's why I'm here talking to you right now. Reconsider, Piper, please. It's not too late to turn around. We can give a few contacts to the guys and head back and get legitimate Ugov certification for a trip to Centaurus."

"Wow. Okay, at least it's clear where *you* stand." Piper's cheeks turned red. Melia rarely disagreed with her decisions. *No wonder she came to see me in my chambers.* She would never openly challenge her boss and best friend in front of the rest of the crew. *Speaking of the rest of the crew…* "And I'm sure my first officer has a pulse on the others? Where do they stand?"

"Marjorie would follow that handsome captain to the edge of the galaxy!"

They both laughed at Melia's icebreaker.

"Okay," Piper said, "Marjorie—check… and Nala was the first to want to do this, so she's in, but what about Carrysa, John and—"

"I can't believe you brought Knox!" Melia said. "He can be as volatile as an ion cannon in the hands of a Gen-2er!"

"Royce will be on his best behavior. Adonis isn't around. Besides, don't you feel more comfortable having him to add to the those two giant alien ruffians? I do. They might be good in an elixir bar fight, but I'll take Royce Knox when it comes to tactical combat of any kind."

"Combat?" Melia's eyes bugged out. "Are you expecting violence?"

"No…" Piper groaned. "I am not expecting anything other than two successful missions. We get Mike and we get to Centaurus. That's why I hired this crew, and that's why I have you as my first officer. Come on, Melia, can you fire me up just a *little* bit?"

A buzz on the holocom stopped their conversation. A call from the cockpit.

"Chief!" John's voice came across the com. "It's time to get down into the hyperspace chambers and take a long nap. Shall I send out the all call?"

Piper tapped the com. "Okay, John, check that. Give me two Uminutes."

"Ten-four, Chief," John replied. "Timer's set. Meet you down there."

Piper gave Melia the "I'm boss, you're not, even though I love you" look.

Melia seemed resigned. "Okay, well, in case I couldn't change your mind... I did get those codes from the Myrtel project files you wanted. Also had Carrysa reach out to your ground contacts there. Most of the people who worked on the project are in different parts of the galaxy. That prissy moonscraper architect is still living there though, believe it or not."

"Valicius Creme." Piper pronounced the woman's full name. "Hmm... Val and I didn't exactly see eye to eye on everything, did we?"

Melia snorted. "A couple of preening peacocks, trying to outdo each other with your ideas."

"Well," Piper said, "she *did* hate that scumbag Myrtel as much as us. But why would she stay though?"

"Ever heard of the color black? That man's bitcoin must be the size of a Persean star ship."

Now Piper snorted. "Let's hope she hasn't been corrupted. We've got the codes, we've got Miss Creme... and we've got backup. We should be fine."

"Off to sleep we go!" Melia offered her arm.

Piper linked up and they exited her quarters. They took the air tube to the hyperspace chambers to gather with the whole crew for one last pep talk. Next stop: Myrtel World.

***

"You *can't* be serious?" Valicius Creme, Head of Terraform Maintenance, and the last holdout of Piper's original design team, placed her head against the wall of the elixir bar and closed her eyes.

Not the reaction Piper was hoping for, after fessing up to the real reason she was back on Myrtel World, and for the arranged meeting—but it could have been worse. She hadn't call for security, at least.

Had Piper badly misjudged their first move of the escape operation? *Val's got a good heart,* Piper thought, *but she wouldn't still be here without a tad of loyalty to Hemperley. And why did I pick* this *place to meet with her?* There were at least twenty-five Sunish Blackon types sitting in clusters at floating tables under the yellow glow of dimmed hololamps.

Piper replied, "I *am* being serious, Val, and let's keep our voices low... there are a lot of eyes and ears around." Piper's head swiveled to survey the nearest patrons of the elixir bar. They weren't paying them any attention.

Valicius was drop-dead gorgeous, bright orange hair made into perfect curling rolls, and a body that made Piper feel like a teenager. *How does she maintain that thing?* Piper frowned. There weren't many times when she wasn't the center of attention in a room full of men, but when Val was around, it had always been the case.

"Well," Val said after a long stare, her emerald green eyes shining at her former superior. "You better have a damn good reason to want to break a prisoner out of the one detention center on all of Myrtel World."

"I do."

"Because," Val continued, "crime is practically non-existent here. There are no courts. The rumors aren't rumors, Piper. This world's owner has no qualms making people who cause trouble 'magically' disappear. And I don't plan on being one of those. My bitcoin levels are a lot higher than when I worked for you and the Ugov, believe me..."

"This is about more than bitcoin," Piper said, "I can assure you that. Much more. For one thing, the prisoner is being held illegally, and he has committed no crime. In addition, it's what's at stake here… suffice to say it goes far beyond what you might imagine."

"Try me."

Piper made an effort not to spill *all* the beans while she updated Valicius on what the potential ally needed to know. Without a sense of trust between them, Piper would never be able to convince Val to help her.

Once she got a sense of the seriousness of the situation, Val groaned. "I *knew* I shouldn't have answered your holocall… damn the Milky Way!" She slapped the table.

"So," Piper said, trying to calm Val, "as you can see, this is about new life forms. Protecting them. From the Giant Beings—and any who would align themselves with those murderers. It appears your current employer is on the wrong side of things…"

"My current employer, like you said, is a murderer. If I cross him, my virtual immortality becomes instantaneously defunct."

"That can't be your reason for not helping me."

"Oh? I should not care about a threat to my own life?"

"That's the whole point, Val! This is a threat to *all* life. Not just yours. Not just mine."

"Why don't you get your Ugov councilors to prosecute him and free your friend that way?"

"It's time sensitive."

Val laughed. "That's all you needed to say… Galaxies, when I think about how many times we had to pause our projects because we were waiting for Ugov approval… Speaking of Ugov approval, what makes you think *I* can get you into the detention facility? That would have to come from above me. I'm nothing but an employee of Myrtel World now.

"That's just it, you're an employee who works on the terraforming systems."

Val took a long sip from her elixir. She had already finished off two of them, and Piper had barely taken a sip from her first one. "Keep going…"

So that's what she's been doing, all this time, Piper thought, *drinking elixirs and kicking back without a care in the universe.*

"You can lead us in, we'll be a team of researchers from Terraform headquarters on Sun City, doing our every Udecade check on our former projects."

Valicius spat out a sip of elixir. "What?"

Piper came prepared. It wasn't going to be an easy sell. She hadn't been in contact with Miss Creme for many, many Uyears, and from what Piper could recall, it wasn't the "best" conversation to go out on, either. Come to think of it, there might have been some blaming and finger pointing over glitches in the system. Piper recalled the moment when the pretty woman stomped away from her on the last Uday she had set foot on Myrtel World. Her red hair had been flapping in the wind, as her hourglass figure tip-toed away.

"Yeah!" Piper tried to sound enthusiastic. "It will be a perfect pretense for visiting the detention facility. When we terraform, there is a high precedent set on the natural systems being kept in tact. We can bring monitoring gear and pretend you're taking us for an official check-in, you know, to make sure it's up to standard and working properly and everything."

"Wow." Valicius wasn't pleased, but the surprise was gone from her face, replaced by what Piper would have labeled as resignation. "This is a serious bomb you are dropping on me, Executive Crane. I worked so hard on this project… yeah, it's true, it was you who gave me this big break and assigned me here, and it's given me a luxurious lifestyle and certain—let's just say, *liberties*, but…"

"But what?"

386

"You seriously don't remember? The end of things? How it went down?"

Piper did, but played clueless.

Valicius grimaced. "Too preoccupied with the next project. That's your whole MO, Piper. I was expendable, no matter how hard I worked for you, it was never enough. The Usecond you were finished, I was part of the old project."

"That's not true. I valued your work highly."

Valicius snorted. "Yeah, sure, is that why you blamed me for the lava flows in the southern continent? Among other things…"

"Val," Piper gave her a wry smile. "Come on, now. Listen, I'm sorry. I'm apologizing to you, right now, right here. You're right. I get very focused on the job at hand. Sometimes, I don't treat my crew or my other associates with the care they deserve. But right now, I'm trying to do something more important than any other project or job I've ever been faced with. And you're the only person I can turn to for help."

Valicius coughed on a sip of elixir.

"Ironic, isn't it?" Piper laughed despite herself and the situation.

After a moment of awkward silence, long enough to make her emotions run the gamut from: *Yes! she's going to help* to, *uh oh, she's going to call security.*

"Okay," Piper's former employee finally said. "Apology accepted. And I am grateful for the opportunity you gave me, without your trusting me to work on this world, I would never have been hired to stay here."

"Awesome!" Piper blurted out, sinking into her seat a little, as several sets of eyes gave them the once over. *Galaxies, can you ever tone it down?* Piper lectured herself in her head. "Then… you'll lead us?"

Valicius's face paled. "Uh, *no.*"

"What do you mean, *no?*"

"That's not going to happen, Chief Executive Crane."

"Call me Piper."

"You used to dock me points on my evaluation if I called you anything but that!"

"Times have changed, my dear." Piper smirked. "Next project—remember?"

"Ah, yes." Val sniggered. "Regardless, I am not putting my life on the line. I am going to help you, but there's no way I'm leading a fake mission *into* the detention center to remove a detainee. *That's* crazy. To tell you the truth, helping in *any* way is crazy..."

"But you're going to..."

Valicius Creme's emerald eyes beamed at Piper. "I still can't help you unless you get an official Ugov holo approving a terraform systems review. And I mean for *any* location on Myrtel World, not just the detention facility. Oh, and by the way, good luck making a fake one unless you happen to know a Gen-3 android that isn't programmed to follow Ugov law."

Vern! Piper pictured the half-alien, with his visor and masked face showing no emotions whatsoever. "If you've got an old copy of a past review, I have a friend who can help."

"Oh?" Valicius's thin and perfectly manicured eyebrows lifted. Two parallel red lines. "You brought your team with you, did you?"

For a moment Piper worried if she was being played. *Is she going to report me right after we leave this bar? I have absolutely zero leverage on this woman...*

"I did bring the crew, but you would only remember Melia. The rest are new—well, not new, but you know what I mean..."

"Okay, so let's say you've got a copy from me and it can be converted. You've got your old codes on your wrist implant, don't you?"

"Yes, but will they still work?"

"They don't now, but they *will* work."

"What do you mean? How?"

"If you tell me the exact Utime when you go in for your 'inspection,' I can revert back to old code systems and yours and Melia's will work. But just for a short time, there will be alarm settings activated, and I'll have to update the system. I can only stall for so long. Once I do a reboot, and it comes back online, at that point, the old codes will no longer work."

Piper tapped her chin. "Hmm. Well, that's going to have to do. How long?"

"Ten Uminutes. Tops."

"Seriously?" Piper put out her palms.

"Yeah, and you're going to have to deal with the Gen-3er in charge there. He's not an easy one to fool, and with one holobutton, Myrtel's head of security, a freakish Algorean named Drummond, will be all over the scene in a jiffy."

Piper took a deep breath, and chugged half of her elixir in one gulp.

"Whoa, girl!" Valicius laughed as Piper nearly fainted when the psychoactive component of the beverage hit her. "You've got to sip it... or you won't be waking up early tomorrow."

"I've got hyperspace hangover anyway," Piper sighed, "this can't be any worse." She finished the rest of her glass.

"Piper?" Valicius reached out a hand to grab Piper's forearm as she stood to go.

"Yeah?"

"Listen, I've got to be honest with you. I'm not taking the fall for this. If you get caught, I am going to plead I was completely in the dark. I'll say the document was fabricated by you. Once you get in there, and I revert the codes for ten Uminutes, you're on your own. I will disavow all knowledge of this. You understand that, right?"

The Sunish woman's smile was so pretty it seemed unnatural. What could Piper say? She had to trust Creme and take whatever help she could give her team.

CHAPTER THIRTY-ONE

Escape From Myrtel World

Max wasn't used to taking directions from anyone—especially a puny Sunish man with a paranoid complex. He frowned as Royce Knox droned on about the details of the plan, gauging his buddies for their reactions.

"Hey, dude!" Claude was *definitely* paying attention. Max always loved that about his little furry friend—his mind was a veritable memory cube. "You've briefed us like fifty times! We know what the deal is, okay?"

Royce Knox stared at the moody rabbit. The head of security shrugged and grumbled. "Fine. Have it your way. We'll skip the final briefing. But it's your brother's life on the line, isn't it?"

Claude squinted at him. "Yeah."

The Sunish man nodded. "Well, I'm doing my best to make sure we get him out safely. This is my area of expertise. So cut me some slack—isn't that your surf slang saying?"

"All right, Claude," Max ordered, "easy now. Chill for a moment, dude. Go get a breath. We're leaving in five Uminutes. You're staying here and keeping an eye on the *Hopper* and ready to make an emergency evac."

"Captain," Claude said, whiskers taut. "This isn't fair. I should be going with you guys into the detention center…"

"Claude," Max said, "we went over this, dude. Knox agreed with me. It's better to keep a mutant rabbit out of sight, considering we're trying to *break free* a mutant rabbit, you know what I mean? Vern is going in with team one, his skills are needed on the ground, so we're counting on you to fly, dude… *Mike* is counting on you."

Claude's eyes were down, one paw tapping the synthmetal flooring.

Max patted his furry shoulder. "Hey, dude, come on, now, we've all got to be sharp, play our parts here. You think I'm looking forward to being put in restraints and pretending to go back into lockup?"

"We needed a pretense to get our muscle in there without causing too much commotion," Knox threw in. "At least initially. Knowing Myrtel, there may be some resistance there to meet us, a few droid guards, or worse…"

Max turned to face Knox. "What's worse than droids?"

Knox grunted. "Myrtel's head of security is no slouch. We trained at the same university on New Earth."

"Nothing Blob or I can't handle!" Max's confident laugh following his words. "Believe me—we've had our fair share of scraps, me and Blob."

"Drummond is an Algorean, FYI." Knox said. "About the size of you, actually," he surveyed Blob from the ground up. "Although, I'd say Myrtel's guy has got better abs…"

Blob stomped one of his gargantuan feet on the synthmetal floor. "Like Max said, nothing we can't deal with."

***

Beep. Beep. Beep. Three beeps, repeated. Myrtel groaned. *What now?* He was happily imbibing an elixir and waiting for the next ratite race, floating in his most comfortable chair with the best of view of the Dome's racetrack.

But an alarm code on his wrist implant meant it was serious, so he placed down his glass and shuffled to the door of his private viewing box.

He was about to activate a mini holoscreen when a holocall popped up, superseding the other image in magnitude and brilliance. Drummond. *This can't be good news.*

"Sir," Myrtel's head of security roared. "We've got a problem!"

"What is it, Drummond?"

"Security breach."

"On my world— impossible?"

"It's confirmed, sir."

"Where?"

"It's at the detention facility, sir."

"What? No!"

"I'm afraid so, sir. I'm en route—but I thought you should hear it from me."

"Yes, thank you, Drummond."

"It must be those renegade pirates trying to break out one of their friends we incarcerated last Uweek."

Myrtel groaned and smacked his own head with his hand. "It's not renegade gambling addicts, Drummond. I have a feeling this is much worse—"

"Ah, I'm seeing it now, sir. An alert code sent from the warden?" Drummond's holoimage flickered.

"Make sure—"

"The asset is secure."

"Drummond, that freak rabbit better still be rotting in his cell. Send me video proof the Usecond you arrive, got it?"

"Got it, sir."

Myrtel watched the image of Drummond disappear and yelled for an air cab. *Who would dare come to my world and make trouble at the detention center?* He doubted it could be the derelict crew coming for their mate—how could they possibly get out of the Ugov's hands and enough resources to fly out to this part of the Orion Arm? But who else could it be?

When he loaded into the back of his luxury air cab he roared at the android pilot. "Go! The detention center! What in the name of the galaxy are you waiting for? I'll chop you up for parts if you don't get me there on time!"

Myrtel had to hold on to his seat as the air cab zipped off the landing deck and into the sky.

***

"Okay, Royce and Max," Piper whispered into her wrist com. "We're approaching the warden now, get ready to get in here quick if things go south." She had just sent the text message to Val to deactivate the codes.

"We're in position," Knox's voice replied. "I repeat, we're in position."

Now that they were about to do this, for real, she was so glad she brought her security chief. And those two aliens seemed to be

394

quite the scrappy types. But she sincerely hoped they could pull this off in a more discreet manner—minus the fisticuffs. Myrtel was a merciless Blackon and the rumors of what he did to his enemies… *Well, safe to say I'm his enemy now.*

She squeezed Melia's hand and started forward. Trailing right behind them were Carrysa and Nala, and lastly, Vern—stiff-legged walk and all—trudged along at the tail of their group. Marjorie and John were back on the *Lifebringer*, holding down the ship and ready to fly in and scoop them up if necessary.

Right away, the warden was on alert. The Gen-3er was a modern, state of the art android, with a smoothly polished, Ugov-quality, synthmetal exterior, making Vern's janky suit look like it was left out in a hailstorm. Several whistles, beeps, and noises emitted from the thing as it emerged from behind a floating desk. Its red eyes scanned them with multiple beams.

"Halt right there!" the voice was effeminate, its body—definitely masculine. "State your business. I have nothing on record for any face to face meetings this Uhour."

Piper did as they were asked and put her hands out. "Okay, we're stopped. Official Ugov business—there should be a record of our—"

"There is no record."

The warden's voice was too much. *Seriously, with* that *build?* The voice and body did *not* go together. Piper tried ignoring the intonation, but found herself suppressing laughter each time the android spoke, despite the precariousness of the encounter.

"Vern?" Piper turned and beckoned the half-alien to approach.

A trio of droid guards floated into the waiting area, forming a synthmetal barrier between team number one and the entrance to a hallway leading to the detention cells.

Vern stepped over and activated a holoscreen. On it was the counterfeit Ugov work document he had created from Valicius Creme's file deck.

"This is extremely odd..." The warden downloaded the information on the document, but didn't seem to be buying any of it. "Your document seems to check out. It's certified, but... Terraform Division sends a team with a half-android clear across the Orion Arm to 'quality inspect' a detention center?"

Piper hoped Royce was listening to a live feed. This could go off the rails any moment. Time to leverage...

"Excuse me, Warden!" Piper tried her authoritative Ugov voice she used during contentious council meetings. "You already certified our business. Now my team has scanners and holocubes to download. I expect your full cooperation. We're going to need to check inside the detainment cell area. Please lead the way." She wagged her hand at the android, impatiently waving it on.

"Executive Crane, is it?" the Gen-3er had no doubt done a retina scan while Piper had been standing close to it. "There is no mention on your Ugov feed regarding..."

"Warden," Piper was ready to pull the rip cord, but tried another tact. "You understand *I* designed this world? I'm sure you're pulling up the data now. Part of our terraform manifest is making sure our work is properly maintained. Up to specs. That includes major infrastructure: the detention center, gambling halls, the Ratite Arena..."

"And..." The warden wasn't budging.

"And..." Piper stalled. *Think. Think.* "Well, I could easily interpret the data as coming up short of minimum parameters... Would you care for a team of inspectors to arrive from Sun City to check your database every Uhour, on the Uhour? You're a busy android. It would be a big disturbance, and set your schedule back."

The android seemed to twitch. *Processors with a kick.* Piper shook her head. *The worst invention ever made by humans.*

"Fine. But I'll be guiding you. Several portions of the center are strictly off limits—even to the highest level security clearance on Myrtel World."

Team number one exchanged nervous looks and followed behind the warden as it used a retina scan of one of its synthetic red eyeballs to open the entrance to the interior of the detention center. One droid guard shepherded the group's rear, while the other two posted at the entrance near the waiting area.

Piper nodded to Melia, who quickly typed a message to Royce Knox's wrist implant to acknowledge they were in, and for the others to proceed with the plan. The hope was that when team two brought the fake prisoners to the front, the droid guards would call for the warden, leaving team one on their own to find Mike's cell.

Nine Uminutes, Piper calculated, *this is going to be tight.*

***

"Go time!" Knox said, perturbing Max.

That's my line! The Algorean Captain was psyched to get Mike to safety, but the Sunish security chief was bugging him, keeping his blood from boiling.

Max marched along with Blob, the big aliens flanking Knox on either side, their wrists shackled and their heads down, as if resigned to their fates. Knox held out a shock wand in one hand, while in the other he held a synthcable attached to both of his "prisoners."

"Halt!" the duo of guards hummed as they neared the front of the detention center entryway.

"Where is your warden?" cried Knox. "I've got two newbies to add to your collection. Got 'em fresh from the gambling halls, trying to cheat a Blackon!"

The droids' heads swiveled as they leveled scanning rays on team number two.

"Remain there," one of the droids ordered, zipping over to the floating desk several meters away. A holocall screen popped up.

Max couldn't get the gist of what they were saying from where he was standing, so he surveyed the detention center live stream cam mounted on the wall adjacent to the floating desk. There's team one! The stream showed the warden in front of Vern, Piper, and the others. He was gesturing at them. Were they arguing?

Max shrugged at Knox. *Should we go?*

Knox gave him the palms down fingers spread gesture: *Hold on.*

Max could feel his Algorean temperament creeping into his nervous system. Part of what made him such an amazing surfer was simply the alien blood coursing through his veins. He *had* to get Mike to safety. His reputation as a Captain and a leader were at stake. And yet he was letting Royce give the orders. *We'll see for how long...*

The first drone came back with the orders to wait for the warden, so Max spent the next two Uminutes listening to Knox try to distract the drone guards with idle chat, as if they were two Istabanian nitwit mercenaries, the most gullible aliens in the galaxy.

When the warden entered the room it nearly imploded. Scanning rays and alert codes flashed from the top of its head. "Two unscheduled visits within a half Uhour? Probability less than point seven three percent. State your business, Sunish man."

"Warden, Security Officer Royce Knox here, good to meet you. I caught these cheaters at the gambling hall making fake win claims for their bitcoin. I brought them straight to you."

"Officer Knox, you did not follow protocol." The sultry voice of the warden made Max give Blob a wink. "You must report all arrests and enter them in the database before..."

After a long spiel falling deaf on Max's ears, a stalemate manifested. The warden was requiring data entry before admitting the offenders. They weren't going to get past this stingy gatekeeper with their lame alibi.

Max spied movement on the holoscreen monitors. There was Vern and team one, still in a cluster, with another of those droid guards floating alongside them.

The warden caught Max staring. "Prisoner? What's so interesting there? Ahh. The surprise visitors? Hmm. My scanners are picking up recognition on your prisoner's facial features. Officer Knox, step closer, I need to scan your retina and identify your security credentials. When did Myrtel hire you? Because I vet all the—"

Bam! In one foul stroke with the bottoms of his shackled hands, Blob had smashed the warden so hard on the head it's legs had snapped off. It crumpled into a pile of jagged synthmetal.

"Blob! What the—" Max protested—before he had to dive out of the way of a laser blast from the droid guard. The Captain crawled behind a floating couch in the waiting room and peeked over the edge. A loud zap, accompanied by a pulse of energy that reverberated inside Max's chest, hit the room with incredible force. There was Royce Knox, shock wand still in hand, the droid guard relegated to a frozen mass. *I guess the Ugov model works on the non-living too*, Max remarked to himself.

"Blob!" Max popped to his feet and stomped over to his crew mate, the pile that was once the warden stuffed under his armpit. "That wasn't the plan! What're you doing, you big, fat—"

Knox surprised Max. "Actually, he might have the right idea. The retina scanner on the warden, we need it to get inside and help team one, and if that thing had scanned me, we were shot. Cover blown. Hopefully this thing doesn't have an automatic alarm activation system. Most of them do. We don't have much time—let's go!"

Max and Blob followed Knox to the entry to the hallway and Blob held the sizzling but still slightly functioning android, aligned its eye with the holoscanner, and they all sighed with relief when the doors slid open.

"I saw Vern and Piper on one of the monitors—it's that way!" Max pointed to the left and they charged down the narrow hallway. "To get to the main detention cell block, we need to take that air tube—Blob, the eyeball!"

Blob held up the warden again and they were able to squeeze into the air tube. During the short ride, there were fewer lights and less audible beeps emitting from the warden. Max prayed to Algor the thing could hold together a little longer.

As soon as they popped out of the air tube, familiar voices hit Max's ears, reminding him to be wary. The hallway exiting from the air tube platform curved to the left, providing them a moment of cover.

"Knox—the droid!" Max tapped the Sunish man on his shoulder. "We can't sneak up on it, and from this range one of those laser blasts…"

Knox pointed to a belt fastened to his waist. "Don't worry, I've got plenty of little toys in here. Hmm… Yes, I've got the right thing for this!"

When they peeked around the corner of the hall into the main cellblock, there was team one, with a droid clearly preventing them from going anywhere. The warden had probably ordered them to stay put until he came back. *He ain't coming back looking like he used to, that's for sure.* Max chuckled. The crumpled figure of the once immaculate warden was still jammed under the gray fur between Blob's massive arm and back.

The Captain peeked around the corner again. Where was Nala? The little quiet one didn't seem to be with the group and Max was sure she was supposed to be part of team one.

Knox grumbled something to himself as he fidgeted with his belt, producing a small, black, oblong ball made of synthmetal. "Here it is!"

"What's that?" Blob asked. "One of those flybot cams?"

Royce Knox smiled at him, the bald dome of his head glinting in the hallway lights. "Better. When I say charge, we rush in there, whoever gets to that droid first—disable it. The other two, get team one to safety and out of range of any stray lasers. Got it?"

Here we go again, taking orders from a Sunish man as if he's a general ordering us into battle for the Ugov. But Max sucked up his pride and muttered, along with Blob, "Got it."

They watched a miniholo from Knox's wrist implant. They could tell the group around the corner hadn't yet been alerted to their arrival. The image feed came from the little black ball rolling along the synthmetal floor, quietly, sticking to the bottom corner of the seam of the hallway to be indistinguishable. Once it got within a short distance of the droid guard, it paused. Knox looked at Max, then at Blob. They nodded back.

"Charge!"

Knox's little black ball had zipped underneath the droid and a dark gaseous cloud shot out from it. In less than a Usecond the droid was completely veiled by the cloud. Blinded, the machine rang out confused alarm patterns. Max was fastest, and had plenty of Algorean boiling blood now. With a few giant strides and a massive leap, the Captain went into a two-footed flying leg kick aimed into the middle of the cloud. A loud sound came from within the temporary storm, and the droid guard was violently shoved into the closest wall. Max didn't hesitate to pounce on the machine again, grabbing it by its rigid arms and twirling it around and around until he let it go with all his might. *Crunch.* The droid collapsed against the wall, sizzling. Hand to hand combat was not the strong suit of this type of guard, and the experienced Knox was well aware that, once you disabled their lasers, they were susceptible to ruffians like Blob and Max.

Piper smiled at Max. "Well, well, it appears team one has a new consign, eh?" She pointed to the warden's body still safely tucked under Blob's arm.

"I don't know about that..." Max beamed back. "Now, we've got to get our furry buddy out of here—how many Uminutes do we have left until those codes deactivate and this entire charade is up?"

"Four," Knox responded, checking a miniholo timer.

Piper gasped. "Where's Nala?"

"Good galaxies!" Carrysa cried. "She's so sly she must have snuck away without the droid even noticing!"

"I bet she's found Mike!" Melia yelled. "Let's go—we find Nala, we find your crew mate!"

An incoming holocall signal on Piper's wrist implant beeped. Sure enough, it was Nala, and she had already plugged in coordinates for Mike's cell.

Team one and two meshed into one entity, racing down the hallways of the cellblock, with Knox reminding them of their elapsing time in annoyingly short intervals.

"Okay, okay!" Max yelled at him. "We get it!"

"Fine," Knox replied, "but let's keep following the holobeam. I set it to Nala's coordinates."

"Max!" Blob cried from behind him. "Check this out!"

Max slowed and let the rest of the group pass by so he could address his big crew mate. "What's up buddy?" But Max recognized the problem. The warden had gone totally dark. Its red eyes had lost their glow. "No more retina scan..."

"Piper!" Max yelled, rushing back to the group. "We've got no access to get the cell open!" He jerked a thumb back to Blob who tossed aside the sizzling Gen-3er.

Knox must have overheard. "Max—don't forget about this!" He tapped his belt.

What else does the guy have in there? Max got his answer when they made it to Nala's location. She was standing in front of one of the cells, talking with the occupant.

The Captain shouted out with glee—there were two paws sticking out through the bars touching Nala's hands. "Mike!" Max bellowed.

The yell awoke several of the other prisoners, who started yapping in several languages and sticking their various shaped (and colored) limbs out of their cells.

"Dudes!" Mike yelled back, tears pouring from his eyes. Max and Blob were reaching in and hugging him through the cage.

"Thank you, Nala!" Max said to the shadowy shape of the *Lifebringer*'s most dainty crew member, who had stepped back to allow the boys to have their tearful reunion.

"Out of the way, Captain!" Knox ordered him. "We've got less than a Uminute before the codes expire—then a supernovae of security are going to descend on this place!"

Max did as he was asked and watched as Knox pulled out a miniature laser saw from his belt. Only Ugov quality could possibly cut though synthmetal bars, and of course, Royce had nothing but the best at his disposal. *Ucitizen taxes paid for that saw,* Max noted with a frown.

It took awhile to warm up the laser saw, and by the time Knox had cut a hole big enough for Mike to slip out, deafening alarm codes had begun to drown out the agitated prisoner's voices.

"Follow me!" Piper cried to the group. "I've got the tracking beam on."

Max scooped Mike in his arms and transferred him onto his back. "Hold on, my furry friend! We're gonna get you out of here!"

They stormed back the same way they had come through, passing what was left of the warden, and stuffing themselves (beyond capacity) into the waiting air tube. Inside the confined space, the panting from the mouths of the combined crew members made the stress more palpable. No one spoke. Mike was a limp sack over his shoulder. *What in the name of the Milky Way is going to be up there waiting for us?* Max wondered.

He received his cryptic answer when the air tube doors slid open and they filed out into the last hallway before the exit of the detention center. Barring the way was a mean-looking Algorean man staring straight at Max. He was flanked by a dozen Sunish troopers in body armor with handheld ion lasers drawn.

Hmm. I'm changing my mind about needing Knox. "What do we do?" Max asked Piper's chief of security, whose eyes had steeled as the bald-headed man assessed the situation they faced.

After a pause, Knox took control. "Okay, Max, Blob, Vern, we've got to get these goons away from the exit so Piper and the rest can make it through the slide doors. Let's try to stall them, and then we try to get out behind Piper's team once they're safely through the exit."

"Try?" Blob said more than asked. "There *is* no try. We freed Mike, and I plan on getting him to his brother on that ship."

"I like your enthusiasm, Blob!" Piper smiled at him despite Drummond's force of troops approaching them with a purposeful gait.

"You got any more of those smoke bombs?" Max asked.

"No." Knox turned his head to Max, who frowned. "But I've got something better."

"A portable ion cannon?" Max asked. "Because we're a bit outgunned with seven handheld lasers versus one shock wand and our bare hands."

"Better than an ion cannon. Less messy, too. Piper, keep your team way back out of range. Max you and your crew mates will know when it's time to mix it up." Knox gave him a wily smile, then turned and walked away from their group with his hands up, intercepting the security team at the midpoint of the entry hall.

"What is he doing, Piper?" Carrysa whispered.

"I have absolutely no idea," Piper replied, "but let's get our group ready to run for that exit!"

Max, Blob, and Vern could simply watch and follow Knox's cue. The impressively buffed out Algorean leading Myrtel's security forces shouted for Knox to stop or he would have his men open fire.

Max whispered to Blob, "Let me have that dude, okay, big guy? Don't let Vern take any heat either—he's gotta fly us out of here."

"Got it, Cap." Blob's monobrow sunk over his eyes, his bodyguard persona was ready to rumble. *Praise Algor!* Max closed his eyes in prayer. *I'm so glad I've got my big Boor backing me up!*

Max gently set Mike down and motioned to Carrysa and Melia, who came over to make sure he was supported on his wobbly paws. Myrtel had obviously been malnourishing his crew mate. Max's blood boiled. His hands curled into two large blue fists.

Amazingly, Knox hadn't been bluffing about having another trick gadget on his belt. When two of Drummond's officers went to put shackles on him, there was a flash from Knox's midsection. A bright light initiated at Knox's waist, formed into a circular beam, and then, one by one, the beam extended out, finding its way onto the handheld lasers of Myrtel's security team. An anti-ion charge spread through each of their weapons, forcing them to drop them as they heated to a melting point. The handhelds made a sizzling crackle as they hit the floor, one after the other. The Terraform heavyweight had instantaneously disarmed the security team!

Vern stayed back a bit as Max and Blob charged forward and engaged the first two guards who were grappling with Knox. With synthmetal body armor, punching them would be useless, so Max relied on pure strength, wrestling one of the guards into submission. Blob merely reached out and grabbed the back of the other man's tunic and lifted him off the ground. Having done it before, the best friends didn't need to confirm their next move. They held each of the guards aloft and, on the count of three, smashed their bodies into each other, knocking them unconscious to the floor.

Five to four odds, no weapons? I'll take it. As Max stalked Drummond, a well of adrenaline surged in his veins, as if he was dropping in on a monster wave. His Algorean counterpart showed zero signs of hesitation, however, and even leveled a smile at Max.

"A tough guy, eh?" Max called out. "Let's find out how tough you are against one of your own!"

Drummond shoved aside two of his guards who were dutifully standing between he and Max, and stepped forward with brash confidence. Without warning the head security officer accelerated and leapt. His blue shape became nothing more than a large blur as he clocked Max in the side of the head with an open hand strike, landing his maneuver with perfect balance, safely out of the Captain's reach.

But Max was in no position to strike back. His knees buckled, and his head was spinning from the blow. The dude was fast and strong. But how hot was his blood?

The Captain's main method for subduing an opponent in martial combat, especially after suffering a heavy blow, was to grapple, so he tried to grasp Drummond in a body lock. He used all his strength to wrap his arms around the alien's waist and neck, but his foe was well trained in the discipline. The Algorean security chief simply shifted his weight to the side, yanked his neck out from Max's hold, and took his free hand and pummeled the Captain in his solar plexus.

This time Max did collapse. All oxygen was removed from his lungs, and a bit of blue blood trickled from his smarting ear. He instinctively went to fetal position, covering his head, expecting a kick or another blow. Nothing came.

Max struggled to his feet and tried to make sense of a wobbly scene, his equilibrium affected by Drummond's strike. Once the room stopped spinning around him, there was the figure of Royce Knox, shock wand out, whipping it and jabbing it toward a dodging and ducking Drummond. Even an Algorean tough guy wasn't keen on taking a zap from one of those things. Piper's bodyguard had saved Max from further damage. Time to repay the favor.

Max patted his red hair, wiped the blood from his cheek, and sprinted back into the fray—just in time—as one of Drummond's guards observed Knox was too focused on his quarry and had left his back exposed. The guard pounced to deliver a blow to the rear of Knox's head, but Max was there in time. He caught the Sunish man's hand inside his own big blue fist and wrenched the man's arm to the side. The guard screamed as his shoulder joint popped out of the socket. Max followed it with a solid punch to the jaw. The man fell motionless. Four-to-three.

Drummond had a chair and was using it as a buffer between a still charging and attacking Royce Knox. *This Knox guy's nuts!* Max was being won over. *I'll take orders from this guy anytime...*

Max barged over, jumped off a floating table, and landed with all his weight on the chair Drummond was wielding as defense. The weight of Max and the chair was too much, and Drummond was forced to drop them. Max stuck his tongue out while he crashed to the ground because he was sure Knox would take advantage of the opportunity he just created.

When the wand struck the big Algorean brute in the chest, his teeth lit up, a miniature lightning storm exploded inside his mouth. Drummond dropped face first to the floor with a huge crash.

Advantage, us. Max turned his head to witness Blob finishing off two guards at once with massive wild hammer punches. Vern was getting into the act: he used his synthmetal shin to kick one of the guards, clearing the way for Piper and the rest of the team to run for the exit. The last guard standing had recovered from Vern's initial kick and reached for a weapon in his pocket—maybe a shock wand of his own.

"Hey, dude!" Max yelled, turning into a red and blue fireball of fury. "You ought to think twice about that…"

The sight of Blob and Max plodding toward the guard provoked him to cry out and flee.

Max snorted. *Smart choice, dude.*

"Let's go!" Max roared, and Blob and Vern followed him for the exit.

CHAPTER THIRTY-TWO

Just Another Epic Sesh

"I can't believe you talked me into this…" Mike was hovering on his board, peering over a familiar ledge. But for some reason, the mega volcano's slope seemed ten times longer and much, much steeper than last time.

"Yeah, sure," Max said, "as if it took *that* much convincing." The Captain stepped on his board and activated the magnetic deck to lock in his boots. He tested the grip by pumping back and forth from tail to nose a few times.

Claude floated over next to Mike. "Are you kidding me, bro? We were all fighting over who was going to be first to tell you the good news—that the first thing we're doing after we get you off Myrtel World is shred the mega!"

Blob was strapped in already, his enormous shoulders and chest stretching out his synthsuit. "Mike, don't lie—you know you froth more than all of us combined."

"Hey," Max said, "not to worry, my furry friend! We'll ride close together, like last time, and you can ride in the middle of the pack, okay?"

Although weary from his ordeal, Mike couldn't help let his machismo shine. "Oh yeah?" he cried, stomping on his turbo booster. "Middle of the pack, huh, Cap? Try and catch me!"

With a jolt Mike launched over the edge. No turning back now. He shut off the levitation feature and his board touched the black and gray talus slope. He waited for the pressure of his fins digging into the sloughy material before putting any weight on his boots, then carved a gouging S-turn, sending a fan of black debris in the opposite direction.

Max called over the helmet holo, "Easy now, Mike. Your energy levels are coming in low, and your nutrient and hydration numbers aren't too good, either!"

"What—you can't catch me?" Mike cried, blasting an aerial off a cornice of segmented volcanic rock. For extra flair and style points, at the apex of his jump, he bent his lower paws and jerked his board out to the side, grabbing the rail with his gloved paw for maximum, stalling extension. Completely and totally weightless for a few satisfying Useconds, Mike could sneak in a gloat. *Ahh, the closest thing to flying!*

After he landed, Mike crouched into a tuck, speeding off. This time his brother's voice came through the holo. "Bro! You gotta slow down. The lava flow hasn't triggered yet, we've got to time this right—hold on!"

Mike still refused to scrub his speed with turns. He peeked over his shoulder and smiled. He was still well out in front of the guys.

"Dude!" Claude yelled. "That's not the way! Stop! Stop!"

When he turned his focus back on the terrain it was too late—all Mike could do was cry out as he reached a false edge to the talus slope. There was a moment of complete vertigo. He found himself gliding along a razor thin black edge. To the left, a twenty meter drop into a bubbling molten lava pit. To the right, a slope curving back to the main bowl of the volcano. His momentum was taking him the wrong way! He stomped on his tail pad—to no avail—and went over. *Uh oh.* He spiraled as he fell, losing complete control of his body.

"No!" Claude cried over the holo. "Mike!"

Helplessly wiggling his forepaws, Mike watched his brother drop over the edge, trying in vain to catch him. From the scorching heat below, Mike didn't have to conjecture long to figure out where his descent terminated—an orange pool of hot death.

Levitating and free-falling were merely gravitational cousins, and the gap between the twins widened.

He had no choice but to save himself. He managed to grab the nose of his board with his forepaws, interlocking his human-like fingers. He concentrated all his lower body energy on swinging his dangling rear paw back onto the deck of the board. Even if he could tap the aerial booster pedal, it could change the direction of his fall. He recognized the dark flat area of dried lava, forming a rim around the orange lake below. If he could aim for that...

He reached and reached until one toe gripped the synthresin deck of his board. A second toe made contact, then a third. The orange light below was growing in size as he plummeted. He was about to experience the *virtual* part of his virtual immortality.

Mike shut his eyes and braced for intense heat.

Wham!

"Uhhh!" Mike was broadsided by a large alien body. A ball of gray fur and blue skin tumbled onto the rim of the lava lake.

Max! He must have dived off his board and "wing suited" it to me!

"Dude, thanks!" Mike cried out, checking his suit for tears.

Max smiled back. "That's what a Captain's for... but, my little furry friend, you've gotta be a little more careful." The Algorean inspected his board for damage.

Claude hovered down and jumped off his board and raced over to his brother. "Bro—I thought you were a burnt hare!" He embraced Mike in a big hug.

Vern retrieved Max's board from hover mode and he and Blob got off their boards to join the *Planet Hopper* team huddle.

Max did a three sixty. "Where are we now, Claude?"

Claude checked his helmet holo. "Uh oh."

Mike struggled to his forepaws and went to get his board. *Trouble's coming.*

Claude confirmed a moment later. "Captain, dudes, that earthquake is hitting in... thirty Useconds. When it does, the pyroclastic flow starts, and it begins coming down this slope with earnest. I have no idea where the side shoots go—I've only mapped out the safest pathway to the lava bars at the bottom. We were supposed to stick to that line..."

"Judging from this orange lake," Vern said, pointing over the rim's edge, "safe to say the flow makes it down here." His visor faced the long drop-off they had descended to retrieve Mike.

"Strap in, boys!" Max ordered. "Mike—I ain't kiddin' this time. Stay in the middle of the pack. Claude's in front, I'm right behind him. Big dude, I want you to go after me. Vern, you take rear and tell us when the flow is coming!"

"Uh, Max?" Vern asked, his visor now pointed at the crater of the volcano.

"Yeah, Vern?"

"It's coming."

A red line was easing through a tight shaft and funneling toward the lava lake.

"Well, this sucks," Vern said. "A new fissure must have formed!"

"Go! Go! Go!" Max's voice belied true fear.

Claude zipped around the edge of the lava lake and when Max was off, Mike kicked his tail thruster and followed after them.

"Where are we going, dude?" Mike asked through the helmet com.

Claude shot back. "I'm trying to find a way over this embankment… if we can find a way over we should be able to ride the talus slope to the lower levels of the mega volcano. From there we can cut over and, hopefully, make it before the lavafall morphs into a wave."

"That would suck to miss out on the wave!" Mike cried.

"Well," Blob groaned, "we wouldn't have had to if you hadn't fallen, dude!"

"Quit it!" Max roared. "Keep the com clear for Claude's and my directions. No chatter. Wave or no wave, we're getting off this mega volcano safely, okay?"

With his helmet silent, Mike focused on pumping his surfboard's thruster pads to keep the correct pace. He wasn't about to cross Max again, not tonight.

Claude directed everyone into a wide shoot he claimed would funnel them to where they wanted to be. He dropped in first, taking his board back off lev mode, letting his fins, rails, and rocker get him grooving on the talus.

Now this is what I'm talking about! Mike let himself relax a bit, carving behind his brother with mellow turns. *Phew—that was pretty close, though… almost smells like… my fur is singed. Wait, what's—*

A crackle underneath his board made him twitch. The funnel was made of thin sections, so brittle the weight of the surfers and their boards was enough to break through.

"Guys!" Mike yelled as an opening big enough to swallow him ripped apart in front of him.

And for the second time during the same sesh, unheard of for a surfer of his skill level, Mike was falling. Both his magnetic boot soles held to the deck this time, and he was able to land ten meters below the crack. He found himself inside a black tunnel of perfectly smooth, dried lava rock. The swales, lit by Mike's helmet cam, rolled ever downward, dropping off into a catacomb of tunnels, similar in circumference and made from the same igneous rock.

"Are you serious, Mike?" Claude said, floating on his board and pausing alongside him. "You fell again?"

The rest of the crew dropped through the crevice and they hovered on their boards staring at Mike.

"Claude," Mike pointed to the dark hole. "Where's *that* go?"

"No way, dude, don't even think about it..." Claude replied.

"What?" Mike put out his paws. "This is epic, let's ride down this hole!"

"Oh yeah?" Blob asked. "Where to, Mike, the molten core of the Orb?"

"What's that sound?" Claude's ears extended as far as they could inside his helmet.

Thirty Useconds had passed. At first the earthquake manifested with two separate, sharp and powerful jolts, enough to make their boards jump. But soon after it came on in earnest, forcing the surfers to squat and grab their rails with both arms to keep from losing control and falling off. The whole thing didn't last too long, but was violent enough to freak them all out.

A new sensation crept into Mike's consciousness. His helmet became stuffy—too stuffy for a climate controlled airspace. If he could have sweated, he would have, as an immense wave of heat came blasting through the tunnel from higher elevation, blowing straight *through* them into the darkness.

Mike yelled out. "Lava tube! We're in a lava tube!"

"This is not my idea of a fun tube..." Blob busted out.

"We've got no choice, Max!" Vern's voice modulator simulated his panic.

"Mike, get in the middle!" Max cried. "Claude—go! *Go!*"

Mike waited for his brother and the Captain to pass, stomped the tail thrusters, and followed them into the volcanic catacombs.

"I've—got—a—sensor—looking—for—routes—out!" Claude's voice enunciated one word at a time as his board chattered from the friction. He led the crew through the first few sloping turns using a bright headlamp to illuminate their progress.

As he rode along the smooth terrain, Mike was mesmerized by the colorful patterns on the walls. The charred black rock, common closer to the surface, seemed to have been cleansed away. Now reds and oranges, in striated, whirled patterns, flashed past his wide eyes.

Another heat wave pulsed from behind them, and Mike swore his tail had caught on fire his synthsuit was getting so hot.

Alarm codes flashed inside his helmet. He ignored them and tried to focus on Max's line, maintaining a safe distance to keep from bashing into him from behind.

The heat intensified. The lava flow had entered the tube at a higher elevation and was now flushing downward with gravity's pull.

"Claude?" Max's voice came through the holo. "Get us out of here, quick!"

Claude responded immediately. "There's a fork ahead—everyone go left!"

Even though Mike saw it coming he barely made the turn, having to ride along the concave side of the tunnel wall in order to pull it off.

"Thrusters on! Straight ahead—there, go!" his brother yelled.

The fresh air was palpable even through the recirculating air of his helmet. Mike charged for the fissure in the roof of the cave and glimpsed starlight peeking through. *Go! Go! Go!*

Once they had popped out, one by one, with Blob unintentionally excavating a sizable chunk of lava rock with the top of his helmet, the crew charged after Claude. He was making a beeline for the lava bars. *Yeah, bro!* Mike loved it, even in the face of all this danger, his crew's love for surfing trumped everything. They had made it in time to catch the wave! The orange pinnacle rose, jacking in height, preparing to unload its viscous energy.

Just another epic sesh! Mike had to laugh, pumping his board toward the drop-in.

***

Piper's heartbeat was in her throat as she instructed John where to land the *Lifebringer*. The coordinates matched with Vern's, but the exoplanet the surfers had dubbed the Orb was so desolate, so empty. Nothing but dried lava rock fields and active volcanoes. Cellular, sentient life? How?

At one point during the *Lifebringer's* initial flyby she gave consideration to the possibility the alien surfers were using her to get in another surf session. No carbon-based life readings of any kind had come back yet. How did these specialized alien species survive out here? What did they eat? Drink?

A sensor alarm beeped. "Got something." Melia said.

The entire crew was congregated on the bridge, and everyone huddled around the first officer's holoscreen.

"What is it?" Piper gently moved to the front of the group. "A life form reading finally?"

"No," Melia replied, "still no reading of any kind, at least nothing with carbon based signatures. There's weird plants—more like rocks—with metallic roots growing out of them. Some hearty-shelled insects, fire-resistant ants and beetles and such, *but...*"

416

"What?"

"This x-ray scan reveals a kind of... structure?" Melia pointed out the chart readings, zooming into a miniature map of their local surroundings.

Piper agreed. It was definitely built by something relatively large, and with decent intelligence. "Okay, that's got to be it. Vern mentioned they went to a sunken hovel. John, let's keep our distance and we can use the rover to get us through the last part. We don't want to scare anybody off."

When Piper turned to regard her crew she had one of those flashes of pride. They came to her when she was leading the girls on an important terraform mission. She basked them in a benevolent smile and cleared her voice. "Ladies—and Royce and John—we are on the brink of something incredibly special. Remember that feeling of disappointment we had with Uehiron? Well, life in the Milky Way can be strange. The possibilities unlimited. Opportunities? They come and they go. The most important thing is we take advantage of them when they *do* come. I, for one, could not be prouder standing here in front of you right now as we are on the precipice of making Uhistory."

"Woo—yeah, Piper!" Marjorie bellowed.

"Making Uhistory..." Carrysa mused. "I'm starting to get used to this!"

Piper gave Carrysa a playful poke in the ribs. "Well, I have exciting news for everyone, and you'll be especially pleased, Carrysa."

"Double rations!" Marjorie said in jest.

"Much better than that." Piper waved her hand to the vista through the synthglass window of the bridge, ribbed black plains with a slight dull red glow. "I'm going against protocol on this special occasion. We're *all* getting a first contact today!"

There was a moment of shock among the crew. Piper giggled as Carrysa's jaw dropped. Even Nala's eyebrows raised, with a smile brightening her face like a blush-colored sunrise on the west facing mountains.

"Are you serious?" Melia questioned.

"Totally serious—even John's coming!" Piper cried out, making eye contact with her pilot.

"Piper—really—I?" John seemed as surprised as Melia, but Piper wasn't expecting them to take this in stride.

"Executive Crane," the only person to ever call her that said, "with all due respect, the security and safety of the team can be at risk without following—"

"Protocols," Piper finished for Royce. "But one of the reasons I'm okay doing it this way is because you're here. Vern assured us these Centaurians are innocuous, and I am fully confident you will keep us safe—after all, look what you did for us on Myrtel World? Everyone? Can I get a 'whoop-whoop' for Mr. Royce Knox, best *ever* head of security for the Terraform Division of the Ugovernment? Wow, you *really* stepped it up. We all thank you!"

The bridge resounded with cheers for a few Useconds. And then it happened ... Royce Knox smiled. Nala and Royce both? Within that short a period of time? Impossible. The feel good session was working. Piper had a knack for figuring out the apt time to boost morale.

Piper put on her serious face. "Okay, team, we've got quite a bit more prep to get to, with all of us going. Carrysa, test all of those extra spacesuits, get the gear ready. Knox you're on emergency supplies. John, program the AI to fly over to the marked location of the Vapor People's supposed home in case we need a quick pickup. Marjorie—you're on the rover. Nala, get all astrobio test kits prepped, I'll send Melia in a Uminute to help you. Everyone got it?"

Piper pumped her fist in satisfaction as she watched her crew zip off to tend their assignments. Melia shook her head, and laughed at her.

"What?" Piper asked.

"Nothing," Melia said, "but you're a born leader, you know that?"

"You think so, eh? Well, even so, you're my next-in-command. You're the one who's got to keep this crew in line for me. You're the behind-the-scenes leader."

"I'm just saying…" Melia closed the holoscreen from the mainframe in the bridge and then approached her friend and gave her a big hug, still beaming. "Your father would be proud is all."

Piper exhaled deeply while in the embrace, so grateful to have Melia to confide in, and to explore the galaxy with.

***

The Terraform team's rover bounced and bumped along the jagged terrain, John behind the controls, the rest of the crew strapped in tight. The one time Piper tried to talk she nipped the tip of her tongue, as her chin was forced shut when one of the struts of the rover fell victim to the uneven lava plains. After the route finally leveled, she could get her orders out through clenched teeth. She tasted a bit of salty blood.

"John," she said loudly over the grinding tires. "Let's park it a good three hundred meters away, at least."

"Check that, Chief Crane." John was all business when flying, and even more so when driving the rover. He once told her it was more "visceral" than piloting the *Lifebringer*. He brought them to a rumbling stop and Piper gave the thumbs up to the crew.

By the time they were all standing on the great flat stretch of the plains, the reality had sunk in for Piper. *Whoa! We're standing on an exoplanet in the Centaurus Arm!*

Nala walked forward with her ghostly gait, even more exaggerated in space boots, leaned over, and took a soil sample with a synthmetal receptacle.

"And we have our first firsts!" Marjorie joked.

"Let's head for the coordinates," Knox said, leading the group with a sensor beam linked to his wrist implant.

The crew hiked on for a few peaceful, beautiful Uminutes. Their boot falls created an arrhythmia over the monotonous black and gray rock. The looming mega volcano dominated the skyline, with a single orange stripe running through its midst. Piper shook her head in disbelief. *Are those crazy surf derelicts really going to try to surf that?*

"Straight ahead," Knox said, "there it is—whoa! We've got movement." He put out his arm and waved it to signal for the crew to stop.

"What do we do, now?" asked Marjorie. "Do we just stand here?"

"Well," Carrysa said, "I'm going to take a wild guess and say they aren't used to having a lot of drop-in visitors."

"Knox?" Piper deferred.

"We want to minimize any sign of aggression," he replied. "Let's allow them to come to us. The crew of the *Planet Hopper* mentioned being "chaperoned" by the strange aliens. That's the word Captain Max used."

Sure enough, a group of eight of them approached, the reddish glow of their trio of eyes cutting through the dark night sky. One of them gesticulated. It extended a hand out, with the palm facing down.

Piper gasped and jumped back when a burst of blue flame hit the ground a few meters away from where her crew was standing.

"Don't worry—" Knox reassured them. "It's a physical manifestation of communication. I'm guessing reactionary more than anything menacing. They don't have the ability to enunciate. Literally no mouths. I am adjusting the translator program in my helmet now, I should be able to at least get the gist of what they're trying to tell us by analyzing their movements."

Piper motioned for the team to form up alongside Knox.

"Yes," Knox said, his helmet bobbing. "The flame burst was just a greeting, according to the translator, at least."

"That's a pretty scary way to say 'hello!'" Marjorie said. "I'd hate to see how they show affection!"

The leader continued to approach while the other black-cloaked figures stayed back in a huddle, gray gaseous clouds drifting upward from—

They're respirating through their skin! Piper now had to acknowledge that, so far, everything Vern and Max and the surf crew had told her had been accurate. It gave her a touch of satisfaction her decision to help them free Mike was paying dividends.

"What're you getting, Knox?" Piper asked.

"Well, the translator could be wrong," Knox said, tapping the side of his helmet as if trying to clear a fuzzy channel in his holocom, "but it's showing... recognition."

"Recognition?" Piper asked. "On who's part?"

"Mmm," Knox stalled. "Unless there's a glitch, they seem to have been expecting us."

"How's that possible?" gasped Carrysa.

"Dear Milky Way..." John mumbled.

"What a first contact!" Marjorie slapped Piper on the back, too hard, knocking Piper forward a step.

The chief gave her crew mate the evil eye. *You don't know your own strength, Marj!*

Turning her attention back to the dark-cloaked alien in front of her, Piper couldn't help but translate the next movement made by the leader. He beckoned them with earnest arm swings, motioned to the hovel.

"Unbelievable!" Melia cried.

"We're being invited to dinner with a new alien species?" Marjorie joked.

"Something else…" Knox said with seriousness. "An important ritual."

Quintessential Nala: While everyone stood dumbfounded—even Knox—she had slipped past everyone and was walking lockstep with the alien. Its long cloak shrouded its lower body so Piper couldn't tell if was bipedal, or how it locomoted.

"Nala!" Knox cautioned. "Wait! I prefer to go first…" Always the loyal shepherd, he leap-stepped in the light gravity of the Orb and caught her in an instant.

Piper waved the crew on, and they followed from a cautious distance, until they reached the sloping entrance into the Centaurian hovel.

"Should we all go in?" Melia asked her commander.

"Knox?" Piper deferred.

"Scanner shows it's a pretty tight chamber in there." Knox grunted. "Let me go in first…"

The other seven Centaurians had already descended inside, leaving the leader alone at the opening. The alien pointed at Piper and motioned to a kind of slot near the top of its head.

"Knox?" Piper tried to sound calm, but her heart rate increased, and an odd cloud of nostalgia overcame her senses.

"It's refusing to let me pass," Knox said. "It wants just *you* to come inside."

The *Lifebringer* crew's eyes were drawn to their leader like chips of metal to a dense magnet.

"Okay…" Piper considered what to do. She pictured Max's broad smile and auburn hair; Blob's monobrow, a great, curving parabola; the twins' spindly dreadlocks and goofy big-toothed grins; and their half-synthetic, low-key pilot, Vern, who had briefed Piper on what to expect on the Orb.

"Knox, guys," Piper said, "everything those surfers have said has been black on the bitcoin. What are these Centaurians going to do, burn me alive? Why? They have no mouths—they're certainly not going to eat me, ha!"

"That's not funny, Piper." Knox wasn't amused.

If it weren't for the automatic volume adjustor in the helmet com, Nala's voice would be imperceptible. "Piper, I'll slip in and watch over you. I'll signal Knox in the unlikely case it becomes necessary."

Knox liked that better. "Excellent, Nala! Okay, Chief Crane, I'm right here at the door. Anything comes up, I'll be in faster than zipping through a hyperspace sheath!"

Piper followed the still-beckoning leader into the chiseled lava rock chamber. Once inside, she spied a shadowy wisp. Nala had already entered the hovel and was perched in a dark corner watching over her. *That's my team!* Piper beamed, trying to draw courage from them.

A Usecond later she found herself kneeling in front of a shelf, chipped into the side of the hovel wall with a rudimentary digging tool. Resting on the shelf were fragrant bundles of dried vegetation, singed on the edges, alongside several saucers. One of the saucers, more ornate in design and larger, held a purple gemstone bigger than the eyeball of a Ratite Arena mount. *Dear Milky Way—it's beautiful!* The impeccably flawless luster on the stone drew her eyes to it.

How long she stared at it for, she wasn't sure, but her consciousness seemed to have a cloud pass over it. She felt relieved, as if given a respite from too much direct sunlight. A calmness overcame Piper. Happily immobilized, her arms limp by her sides, she watched as the leader took the gemstone and brought it to her. He placed it delicately near the crown of her head and, somehow, it didn't fall off but seemed to hover there, connected through an undetectable energy force.

A dream state took over and she lifted out of her body, an enormous pull drawing her into the night sky. Soon she was zipping through and out of the thin atmosphere of the Orb, taking heed of the signature chemical compositions... and then *noticing* her noticing. *I'm—neither awake nor asleep—what is happening to me?*

Her father's face appeared. Clear as Uday. His voice speaking a million words all at once, and yet... Piper could decipher the meaning of every sentence he spoke. As if she was transported, instantly, to every conversation she had ever had with her father in her entire life, from childhood until... their last conversation. The hair on her arms lifted and she pet them with her fingers— what? There was no spacesuit, she could feel her goose-bumped flesh. *How...*

Next, she "passed through" her career in Terraforming. Her wins and losses in the council rooms became more than mere memories—she *lived* them again. It didn't take long for Melia's face to occupy front and center of whatever trip she was on. Piper was overcome with a glowing in her heart. Love and support buoyed her in a soft cloud. Her entire crew stepped into the vision, and they were now all laughing together on the bridge of the *Lifebringer.*

Next came Adonis. He stood in front of her, smiling that galactic smile of his. She tried to shake off the feelings: visceral attraction and rejection, clawing at each other for supremacy in the middle of her chest.

A bright flash, an explosion, and his face was gone, in its place the leftover rubble of Uehara. A clear, crystal sphere with a gigantic Persean inside. Its hand emerged from the protective bubble and grasped a moon. She knew what was coming without needing to envision it. They were rolling their dome walkers toward Uehiron. The next tournament location.

When the terror in the pit of her stomach ceased, a new fear grew there, turning into tiny butterflies spreading to every corner of her body, culminating in her brain. Her last vision was of the

Abandoned Asteroid Belt. One asteroid in particular became prominent. It moved and gyrated and... was inhabited! Faces flashed in front of her, and Sunish words were spoken aloud, overlaid as before with her father's visions. The *Planet Hopper* flew through the spinning forest of rocks, and the crew's voices were shouting loud warnings. A wave of anguish flooded her as she witnessed the darkness of space warping, close outside the edge of the Abandoned. A tiny black hole was sucking in the first of the outermost scrabble. *Oh... no...*

With a shocking jolt, Piper was returned to her present moment and all clarity of the visions subsided into fuzzy, dreamlike memories. They seemed to fade by the Usecond, and Piper was desperate not to lose them. She reached for her head and touched the synthglass of her helmet visor instead of hair, and when she squeezed her wrists, the synthetic material of her spacesuit was back. She waved to the Centaurians and rushed for the exit ramp. The fleeting memories were driving her to make haste.

It's a warning—I've got to talk to Max and the crew immediately!

CHAPTER THIRTY-THREE

To Parlay and To Connive

The *Amalgamator* was locked into a smooth orbit within Uehiron's parental solar system, and Stergis found time to confer with Ezran about the upcoming match.

His nephew wore the traditional apprentice tournament robes and the lengthy bottom whipped up air as he paced the bridge of the most powerful spaceship in the Persean arsenal. He seemed nervous. "Grand Master, I applaud your bravery in wanting to face a difficult opponent in your first official match… but Chyrone has been hoping to upend the rankings since he was my age."

Stergis whipped around and glared at Ezran. "Have you not the utmost confidence in my abilities?"

"I do, Grand Master." Ezran paused. "But the climate in the Arrangings Dome has been stormy to say the least. I fear Chyrone is going to—"

"What? " Stergis laughed off his nephew's warnings as paranoia. He had enough of that himself, he didn't need another dose. "The Uday our great blue star finally explodes into a supernova, is the Uday my rival can finally have his victory Uday!"

"He has won several miniature Planet Ball tournaments, as you're well aware…"

"Ezran! What has come over you? I brought you to Outer Cygnus to learn and to advise me on throw probabilities—not to inflate my opponent's resume!"

Ezran continued his pacing. Stergis could tell he was bothered by something. "And then there's the threat of the tiny beings…"

"Threat?"

Ezran stopped. "Uncle, can I be forward with you?"

"Always Forward, my little prodigy…"

"I know you well, Uncle. You value the tradition of Planet Ball as much as any Persean ever has… but you aren't going to risk our entire world for this one tournament, are you?"

Ah, Stergis thought, *the very question I struggle with each and every waking moment.*

A holocall beep came through the bridge: General Lorne with information.

"Grand Master!" His voice sounded winded, as if he had run to the holocam as fast as he could to deliver the news.

"General Lorne, I'm discussing strategy with my neph—"

"Always Forward!" the general cried. "We've got tiny being convoys coming out of hyperspace on the edge of our tournament's solar system!"

"Unbelievable!" The grand master slammed his fist against the console.

"There is a call coming through a special channel. The video will be fuzzy, but you should be able to communicate without too much delay. Should I patch him through, Grand Master?"

Stergis fielded an I-told-you-so look from his nephew. "Yes, patch him through."

A staticky voice came through the bridge holocom. "Grand Master Stergis of Persar, this is Universal Government High Councilor Adonis. Can you hear me?"

"Yes."

"Great! I wasn't sure if this was going to work, I—"

"Silence!" growled the grand master. "This is not one of your council meetings. You've breached our truce by crossing the Intergalactic Dividing Line! How dare you arrive here and cast your tiny shadows on our great Uday. This is our first official tournament of the new age!"

"Well..." the voice replied, "that's why I'm here. That's why I'm reaching out to you right now. You must be aware you are in breach of our contract."

"You have no jurisdiction on this side of the invisible line you have drawn."

"Respectfully, Grand Master, that is not accurate."

"Unless you've been sending spies illegally to Outer Cygnus, you should have no knowledge of our movements." Stergis peeked at Ezran for his reaction to the parlay.

"Well...we have not been sending spies, however—"

"Ah ha! As I thought, breaking the pact!"

"Hold on, please—let me finish. In the agreement it clearly states two provisions you are forgetting. One, no actual Planet Ball. And two, the Ugovernment specifically holds the rights to explore for new life forms and to protect them, even if they lie across the IDL."

"Oh, I'm quite aware of the pathological provisions my forefathers were forced to agree to. To paraphrase: there can't even be a speck of bacteria near a Solar Board. And yet, you tiny beings have the right to hollow out any planet you please, no matter where it is, or what's on it, you have the right to extract every last drop of its minerals and rare earths."

"Again, Grand Master, I did not draft these provisions, as you yourself did not agree to them, personally. But as you said, your forefathers *did* agree to them… for a good reason: to avoid more warfare and destruction."

Something inside him snapped. Stergis sighed. "I'm afraid it might be too late for that."

"I apologize, Grand Master, but too late for what?"

"Your viral desire to profligate has angered those who preside in the Arrangings Dome. There are certain things even I, as Grand Master, cannot control. The will of the Persean people."

"I highly doubt it is the will of your people to engage in conflict that will cost lives."

"Councilman Adonis, you seem like a decent piece of bacterium. Not as bloodthirsty as I imagined you Ugovernment-types. However, you have exactly ten Uminutes before I allow my generals to demonstrate how powerful the *Amalgamator*'s laser canons are… I expect all of your ships to be out of range of the tournament debris path, or face the consequences."

Stergis waited for the delay, but it took longer for the Sunish man to compose his thoughts so he watched the com blankly.

"Grand Master, I want you to know we are aware of your dealings with the Blackon Myrtel and your attempts at bringing back your traditional pastime on a permanent basis."

Stergis ignored the Myrtel comment. *He better not have lost that star map data. That's most of my leverage.* "You know nothing of traditions, puny Sun man!"

"That's just not true, we have long-established traditions, the same as your great culture of Persar."

He's placating me! "Great culture? How dare you talk of Perseans in this way? You murdered millions of my people in the war!"

"We took heavy losses ourselves. Billions—maybe trillions—of good people. War is awful. I'm not a big fan. But, as beautiful an art form as your game is, the facts are clear: it destroys worlds. Innocent life."

"Many policies your Ugovernment support destroy life. Especially the smaller life forms you consider insignificant. The loss of animals, plants, and insects from your destructive mining techniques."

"There is truth in what you say..." The councilor sounded conciliatory. It was throwing Stergis off in his dealings with the little man.

"Yes," Stergis said, "there is. And you value the larger life forms, the sentient ones, the ones who insert an implant into their wrists at birth...whereas, the smaller, wild life forms are an afterthought to you. Well, holonews flash for you, Councilman— we see things *exactly* the same way. You are nothing but a virus threatening to ruin our culture and our traditions. A galactic pandemic to be exorcised."

"Listen, Grand Master, I understand your point of view. Believe me I do. I'm one of the few on the council who want to make changes to the truce. To help your people and your tradition. I'm being honest. I want to help, but... that being said, I am first and foremost indebted to save as many Ucitizen lives as I can. And to protect them. Therefore... we simply cannot accept tournament play anywhere in the Milky Way."

"You can't accept it? Oh, and tell me one reason why I shouldn't vaporize your pathetic little convoys right now? I have strategies to go over and warm-up exercises to complete."

"Well, two reasons. First, the entire galaxy is on alert. Second, you're cognizant of what happened the last time we faced off in battle."

"That's when your little viruses were able to get through a sheath to the Perseus Arm of the galaxy. Did you already forget you erected space blocks and removed the sheath platforms? Our hyperspace scientists have the exclusive ability to get in and out of our part of the galaxy now. You can't strike what you can't reach, Councilor."

"Grand Master... please listen to reason. I am against preemptive strikes. But this will start a war. Many of both of our people will suffer and lose loved ones in a conflict. What if I can negotiate with my leaders and we can agree to allow you to play on your side of the IDL? Real, full tournament games?"

Stergis motioned to Ezran. His nephew nodded, this was an opportunity.

Stergis chose his next words carefully. "You would allow us to throw real planet balls, play on real solar boards? Not the simulated nonsense we've been forced to use over the past generation?"

"Yes! Of course, in order to get the councils to agree, there would have to be *some* form of Ugovernment oversight, vetting solar systems for rare or intelligent life forms..."

Stergis put his hands on his hips and shook his head in unison with Ezran. "You tiny beings.... Solar Board quality is not determined by the Ugovernment. Can you still not comprehend we are the superior species?"

"Grand Master, please, give me a Uhour to contact my people in Orion. Let me explore a few options and find out what I can come up with."

"I'm not going to give you anything, tiny Sunish man. We are scheduled for first throw in two Uhours. Talk with whomever you please, but I would suggest you tell your little convoy to get back on your side of the IDL."

***

"Chyrone, what news have you of the tournament preparation?"

Wella hated being disturbed while in meditation. She liked to prepare for a tournament with a relaxation breathing exercise and a sip of Persean fruit juice. Instead, as she was entering a state of bliss, she was forced to go inside, which meant leaving the veranda, and the view of the rolling hills of yellow and green, with the pointed buildings of the capital stretching to the sky in the distance. A holocall from the grand master's rival this close to the first throw was not part of their plan.

Unless there was a problem.

"Always Forward! High Lady, I have unfortunate tidings."

"That *is* very unfortunate, as I haven't even had my fruit juice yet." She squinted. The holoimage of Chyrone on the *Amalgamator* was shaky at best. She could barely make out his handsome features or read his facial expressions. *But that's why there's voice tone,* she smiled.

"Convoys of tiny aliens have arrived in Outer Cygnus."

She couldn't say she was totally surprised. They were an indefatigable bacterium, she had to admit. "Quite unfortunate indeed. And the grand master, how has he reacted?"

"I cannot say for sure, High Lady. But he has parlayed with one of the tiny being leaders."

"Parlayed, eh?"

"There is a general evacuation warning right now onboard the ship. However, it *is* normal protocol when our enemy is within striking range."

"I see…" Wella breathed in deeply.

"How shall I proceed, High Lady?"

"As before. Stergis will make his choice. He is with Persar or against. The question is, has your loyalty wavered, Chyrone?"

"Of course not, High Lady!"

She liked the quick reply. "Excellent. Because General Lorne can easily do my bidding without your help—but I'm trying to do more for you. Raise you to the highest position in the galaxy—to hold the mantel of Grand Master. Does that not still interest you? The right to throw first, the right to be intimate with the High Lady of Persar?"

"Yes, High Lady."

"*That* is the answer I wanted to hear. Now, go check on the status of the tournament and keep me informed. If there is no planet tossed, if the grand master dares to retreat back to the hyperspace platform near the Abandoned… you know what to do. Go to Lorne. Get the special weapon activated and throw in that traitorous fake—along with his whiny nephew! And make sure the platform is disabled before you return to Persar, or don't bother coming back!"

* * *

He wasn't sure if it was the elixirs Jonah had "made" him drink after they knocked off crushing boulders for the Uday, but Angus's head was aching. He told Jonah he was heading home, ostensibly before Ariel bugged him about starting dinner on time, which was as good an excuse as any, because… well, it was probably true. It was Dawning Day after all. A Uday to celebrate their independence.

"Whoa!" Jonah was looking worse for the wear, his spacesuit's exterior covered in a layer of white dust. "Hold on, friend, one more before you go!"

"Can't, gotta go. Till tomorrow, Jonah."

Jonah growled and turned away, scanning for someone else to talk to in the nearly empty elixir bar. *I guess he's not hungry,* Angus thought, *otherwise he would say so.*

"Hey, Angus!" said a fellow Abandoned passerby in the hall.

"Greetings." Angus smiled and tipped his head.

Morale had been strong on the *Terrastroid.* The strange visitors had brought an opportunity for his people to converse about things other than solar panels or ice water melt storage. Angus had that familiar sense of pride in being a leader of this marginalized group of hearty survivors.

All his positivity evaporated the instant he walked in the door. His wife's face was ashen white.

Uh oh, I'm not late am I? "Hello, Ariel, my love, everything okay? You look like you've just seen a rogue asteroid on course for us."

"Angus—I received a distress text message from the hyperspace platform near the edge of the Abandoned."

"A distress call—from who?"

"The surfer aliens! Captain Max—here... read it. Dear one, I fear the visions I was having are coming true!"

Angus clicked the holoscreen and read the grim news. Planet Ballers. Mini black holes. Evacuation. The rest of the words were a blur.

"Oh my..." He placed his hands on his gray, bushy hair, the dark goggles matting it against his head.

"Evacuation? Angus, please tell me this is false... a bad joke?" Ariel had tears pouring over her cheeks now.

He went to hug her, held her tight for a moment, extending her by the arms away from him. "My love, our world may be coming to end, but the most important thing is we save our people. Where are the children?"

"I sent them to fetch Rymon and his brothers. I wanted to make sure this message checks out."

"I'm afraid your visions are true, Ari. Somehow, those gemstones from Centaurus allow the future to be seen."

"It's true... I *have* to accept it now. Yet another vision confirmed it. Max's holomessage said they have brought another spaceship to help us get our people to safety... but where will we go, Angus? Where?"

"I don't know, my love. But we *will* persevere. That much I know. Our people have been through too much to have our way of life exterminated. We will rebuild and find safe haven somewhere out there in the galaxy. I promise."

They embraced again. Ariel now weeping, and Angus soothed her with pets to her back.

"But, Ang," she moaned, "it's Dawning Day, this is supposed to be our biggest celebration! I prepared a feast!"

"We must be brave now," Angus said, not feeling at all that way. "We will have a Second Dawning Day. Somewhere, somehow. I will call the elders and start the evacuation protocol. Have Rymon talk to the tower and send a locator signal to the *Planet Hopper*."

He rushed out the door with a kiss on her cheek and a squeeze to her hand.

***

The *Terrastroid* docking bay was a frantic scene of moving parts, both organic and synthetic. Abandoned people and their droids and equipment were packing vitals into storage compartments on the aft of the *Lifebringer* and the *Planet Hopper*. Voices were mingled with crying babies and children. Occasionally, an order barked out over an intercom, Sunish words repeating basic evacuation protocols.

Max tried his best to keep a smile on his face as he greeted Abandoned women and children who had been assigned to his spaceship's limited hyperspace chambers. There were two dozen aboard the *Planet Hopper*.

Thank the Milky Way the terraform ship has an emergency hyperspace bay, he thought, helping a boy into his mother's arms as she made her way into an uncomfortably tight chamber. The estimate for maximum occupancy was going to fall well short. And judging from Angus's face, the Abandoned leader had internalized the glum truth as well.

Max watched Piper Crane and her crew busily tend to the traumatized Abandoned people who were moping across the causeway in a long, single file line. *The* Lifebringer *crew are good people,* Max thought, *I guess the saying is true—you can't judge a Sunish person by their morphology, you have to judge by their policy. And this one is extra special.* He focused on Piper as she wiped the tears off a child's face and whispered in the little girl's ear. It warmed Max's heart for a moment.

I better check on how close we are to getting off this rock. Max made his way through the congregation to talk to Royce Knox, who was standing guard, probably assuming he would have to do crowd control when things got ugly. And, judging from how clustered it was near the entrance to the *Lifebringer*, they were about to.

"Knox!" Max said, having to push a bit to get through the wild-haired Abandoned men who, so far, were following directions. But they were getting antsy. Evacuations were bad enough, but the prospect of having your wife and children board a ship without enough room for you… it was brutal to watch the men's faces. "How's it going over here?"

Knox snapped his head at Max. "I may need Blob soon." There was plenty of jostling among the younger Abandoned men over who was in line first. "Hmm. Maybe Marjorie, too."

Max watched the two men nearly come to blows before he figured he better intervene. He caught one of the man's flying fists before it could make contact, and held it at bay, stepping in between them.

"Come on now, honorable men of the Abandoned!" Max said loudly. "We must allow women and children onboard first. After, we can get all of you on…"

"*All* of us?" The man—who's punch Max had caught in mid-air with his palm—cried. "We're not stupid! There's only two hyperspace-capable ships in this docking bay. You're not going to be able to fit us all—and Gabriel here cut me! He's not even married! My wife is aboard that ship, and I plan on getting on it!"

There was a loud chorus of cheers and yells after the man's short, impassioned speech.

Max shook his head at Knox, who was drawing his shock wand. Was it really going to come to this? Max lost his smile as the desperation became tangible in the docking bay. *Where is Angus? He's got to help us out here!* Max hit the holo on his implant and made sure Blob was coming over to provide extra muscular deterrent.

"On my way!" Blob reported over the com. "We had to shut the exterior doors to the *Hopper*. We're maxed out on stowaways."

"Okay, make sure our crew stays put, and come give us support with that big old body of yours!" Max clicked off the holo, still searching for Angus's big gray afro among the crowd. *There he is!*

"Knox," Max cried to the beleaguered security chief. "Blob's on his way—I'm going to get their leader over here to talk some sense into them!"

Max shoved his way through the men until he reached Angus, grabbing him forcibly by the arm. "Come on! Your men are getting aggro!"

It took only a Uminute before they made it back to Knox's position, but things had already deteriorated. Knox had to shock wand the one man who had been violent earlier, and his Abandoned friends were encircling the Ugov tough guy.

Blob burst on the scene with clenched fists.

Angus ripped his arm free of Max and pinballed his way through the crowd to get in front of Knox and Blob. He was screaming for order. "Abandoned men! Do not dishonor our name! Stand back— move back away from the platform!"

Most of the angered men reluctantly backed away, reminding Max that Angus had a lot of rep with his people.

"People of the Abandoned!" Angus yelled. "This is a Uday we hoped would never come. The chaos of our home is something all of us cherish. But this proud life we chose… it came with a certain element of danger. Impermanence. That is why we sought to separate from the immortal ones. That is why we came here. And that is why *I* am staying here."

Max's eyes popped out. *What the…*

"Dude!" Max scrunched low so he could talk in Angus's ear. "What are you *doing*?"

The aging Abandoned man wore a steely-eyed, composed face. "I know perfectly well what I'm doing."

"Angus!" yelled one of the tallest of the Abandoned, who was standing right in front. "If you stay—I stay."

"I, too, will stay and sacrifice myself with honor!" Another Abandoned man took the initiative of the first.

"And I!" cried another.

One man standing near the front said, "I have no children, no wife—I'll stay. I give my position in line to you, Angus!"

"No!" Angus roared. "My fellow Abandoned… this is a sacrifice I must make as a leader. We are reaching capacity soon. I call to all Abandoned men of age, first those with no family, then, if need be, others, to join me. Stay here on the *Terrastroid*. Face the fate we are destined to receive. At the same time, those who stand with me do the honor of making sure our great people continue on. We will call this Uday ever forward as the Second Dawning. The Uday our people were saved. Remember, this rescue is happening thanks to the help of our friend here! Do not endanger our saviors! They have come, despite great peril, to help us retain our culture. Stay orderly. Wait your turn. Peacefully. And if you stand with me, and humbly volunteer to give your space away, your memory will live on in the songs our future generations sing!"

Angus had done it, the panic was quelled, and resignation was setting in for those who sat on the bubble of either being left as a sitting duck for the Perseans, or leaving every single bit of their lives behind. Max stymied a tear. This was going to be a difficult process, coming to the *Terrastroid* and asking them to leave everything behind—including a few of their loved ones—but every Usecond, as more and more unoccupied hyperspace chambers were filled, the dread increased exponentially in his gut.

CHAPTER THIRTY-FOUR

Outer Cygnus Showdown

As soon as the hyperspace chamber door slid open, Max had every intention of bolting straight to the cockpit. Before going in for the instantaneous long sleep, his last thoughts had been about the dangers facing them the Usecond they emerged on the other side of the wormhole. The Captain could envision scenarios where the AI would do nothing to avoid a cataclysm—an abrupt ending to their journey to Outer Cygnus. Old debris from Uehara, creating a new asteroid belt around the parent star, was foremost on his mind. As he lay there on his back, paralyzed by lack of significant blood flow due to his abnormally low heart rate after hyperspace travel, he had a nightmare about the *Planet Hopper* getting dashed by rocks.

Finally his legs thawed enough he was able to struggle to his feet and exit the hyperspace chamber. Curled next to him still, asleep, was Markus, Angus's son. The crew had gotten so desperate at the end, they started putting more than one person in each chamber. Max pushed back a pang of remorse—the young man might never be with his father again. *Why did you stay, Angus?*

Heart rate normalizing, Max zipped through the ship listening for sounds of material hitting the shell of the *Hopper*. Nothing. *That's good.* No one was out of their chambers yet, with the exception of Vern—who had an extra hearty constitution when it came to withstanding hyperspace hangovers. Max made sure to program the auto wake settings to let his pilot and him be alone on the ship when they first arrived, otherwise Claude would be pestering him with questions.

"Vern!" Max greeted his friend. Did he ever smile behind that synthmetal mask of his? "What's the low down? I was having nightmares, dude, bad ones..."

"All clear so far, Captain," Vern responded without a trace of concern in his voice. "No debris. But the Planet Baller alarm code is about to wake up the ship, it's already on the long range scanner. One massive ship. The same one we ran into last time."

"Mmm. Not the best news. But we knew they were probably gonna beat us here. Please tell me Adonis kept his word and is somewhere in the vicinity?"

"Indeed he has. That cluster of pixels right there." Vern pointed on the cockpit's main holoscreen. "A modest convoy. Got to be what—at least twenty starships."

"That ain't much against that thing," Max said, putting his finger through the light woven image of the Persean ship. Twenty Ugov starships were merely specks of dust in comparison.

"True."

"Well, let's get the councilman his star map data!" Max nodded, and Vern did the rest, jetting their ship for the Ugov convoy—and not a moment too soon. The Planet Ball warning sensor triggered, and loud alarms blasted automatically throughout the ship.

Max swallowed a dry lump in his throat. "Not the best way for those poor Abandoned people to come out of their first deep sleep, huh Vern?"

"Seriously. Such a bummer. I still hope we can change the course of the future and save the *Terrastroid*, maybe get all these people back home to their loved ones we couldn't fit onboard."

"I guess what else can we do but get Adonis this star map data, huh? You've got it all cued up, right?"

Vern nodded.

"I'll go make sure everyone stays locked into the anti-gravity of their chambers until after we get across to the convoy."

Max turned and sprinted out of the cockpit to roust the rest of the crew. Blob was going to be especially cranky. *And hangry.*

Adonis took a deep breath before clicking the holocom. *Well, this is it. My last chance to avoid war.* Once he activated the audio device and hailed the Persean leader there was no going back. He didn't reflect on his virtual immortality often, but at that moment he found his mind straying to the morbid realization one of the possible outcomes of this holocall would be his convoy getting obliterated in a ball of fire. He breathed out and activated the com.

It took a full half Uminute for the rendering to load, by then Adonis had a trickle of sweat rolling down his back. The grand master's fuzzy outline became visible, with his voice booming the standard greeting of his people.

"Always Forward," Adonis replied in turn, he figured he ought to say it, although some Ugov councilors would try to have him removed from office for uttering the Persean motto. But he had to somehow quell the alien's fury, and deescalate things in Outer Cygnus. "Grand Master, I have good news!"

"Is that right?" Stergis had clear sarcasm in his voice. Not a good sign. "Your convoy will be leaving soon and Planet Ball has returned to the Milky Way for good? Excellent!"

"Uh," Adonis had to snort at the man's insolence. "No. Well, yes. Well, not exactly."

"Then *what* 'exactly,' puny human? We are about to launch the dome walkers—I don't have time for this constant parlaying you bacterium love so much."

"I've gotten the council to approve Planet Ball play!"

During the ensuing silence, Adonis figured the grand master was waiting for him to elaborate, but he wanted to push the Persean's buttons a little bit.

"And? Go on, tiny being!" the Persean leader roared. "There's obviously a catch."

"Well, yes, Grand Master, you are quite perceptive."

"Enough with the platitudes. I'm warning you, don't test my temper on a tournament Uday."

"There is a catch, but it's exactly as I said before. You must allow us to vet your solar boards. There must be criteria. If we discover no crucial life forms, and the tournament is played far away on the other side of the IDL, we've agreed to let you play."

"*Let* us play? Here we go again—the presumptive nature of you viral specks of dust. It's pure lunacy. I'll say the same thing I said last time: you have no leverage. Now, remove your convoy before it gets pulverized. And if you take one shot, even one single ion canon blast, I'll throw my first satellite right at your ships!"

"Hold on, Grand Master. You might want to think twice about making anymore threats."

"Oh—and what could you possibly do to my *Amalgamator* with those little chips of synthmetal you call starships?"

"I've been very cordial with you, Grand Master. But the insults and the threats stop now. When I reveal what has recently come into my possession, you might not be talking in this manner. A cooler head will prevail—I'm sure of it."

There was a long, awkward silence. Way too long for Adonis's liking, especially after tossing out a threat to a beleaguered enemy.

"Go on..." The calmness in the grand master's voice made Adonis perk up.

"With all due respect," Adonis said, unable to calm his ire, "I want to remind you—I *detest* war. I do not believe it is the best solution to our galactic strife. But you need to be aware of a certain fact... I have possession of the star map data to get Ugovernment forces to the Perseus Arm."

"Liar."

"I thought we agreed no more name calling?"

"I agreed to no such thing, you bacterial scum! You're threatening my home world!"

"You are threatening mine!"

Quiet again.

Adonis tread lightly. "Now listen, I am not—I repeat—I am *not* advocating for this. I've told you my belief on what is the best solution for both parties. You keep your tradition going, you play your wonderful game—but you do it safely, you do it on your side of the galaxy, and you let us vet the solar boards first. We can create an intergalactic ambassador for each of our worlds and make sure you are involved in the process. How does all that sound? Isn't that a better alternative to destruction and death?"

It had been so long since the grand master spoke, Adonis feared for a moment he had disconnected the call. When he spoke again, Adonis jolted out of his floating chair.

"Fine. You have won the parlay this time..."

"Adonis—my name's Councilman Adonis. Oh, thank the Milky Way, Grand Master! You will not regret this decision, I promise you!" Adonis was so ecstatic he danced around his quarters.

"Councilman Adonis, I warn you, do *not* use that star map. Do *not* follow us back to Persar. Always Forward!"

The holocall went dead with a final crackle. *I've done it!* Adonis shook his head. *I've brokered peace for the Milky Way. This has got to be the best Uday of my—*

Boom! Boom! Boom!

Massive blasts hit the side of his starship.

***

"Max!" Claude yelled over the holo.

"What's up, furry friend?" Max clicked the holocall button from the cockpit, winking at Vern as he did—the twins didn't necessarily love the Captain's propensity to use the nickname. "All good down there on the mainframe?"

"No!" Claude shouted. "Far from good! The Perseans are firing on the convoy!"

"I guess that star map wasn't as important as everyone thought," Max posited.

"It was—look!" Vern said, pointing at the long range display. "Now they're bailing out of here!"

On the monitor the giant ship swiveled around, pointing away from Uehiron and the convoy orbiting between the two large gravitational bodies. A lustrous glow came from the Persean starship's rear thrusters and it zipped off for the hyperspace platform.

"Holocall from the *Lifebringer*, Max!" Vern said.

"Patch it through!"

Piper and most of the crew of the *Lifebringer* came to life in miniature holoform.

"Captain!" Piper cried.

"We saw! They took a shot at the convoy then took off for the platform! What should we do?" Max had no recourse but to defer to the chief executive.

Piper moaned. "*Nooo!* Adonis! He's on one of those ships—many good people are on those ships... Damn the Milky Way!" Piper's image punched at the air. "We've got such an important payload in our hyperspace bowels we can't afford to make a run at the Perseans."

"A run at them?" Max was mortified by the implication, but also curious.

"We could easily catch them," Piper answered him. "You could distract them with the *Planet Hopper,* and we could drop one of our terraform tools on them. We've got worldbuilding detonators we use to induce planet core heating. They would probably do the trick, even on a huge ship like that."

Max channeled his past. "Well, my mother back on Algor taught me many things, Miss Piper. One of them was you never go after someone retreating from you. You've already won. If you chase them, and catch them—then what? You might lose a battle you've already won, or worse, use anger instead of reason for achieving your valor."

Piper blinked. "She said all that, eh?"

"Well," Max countered, "not verbatim."

Vern pasted a laughing face emoji on the holoscreen to tease Max.

Piper sighed before speaking. "I'm certain Knox would agree with you, Maximillian of Algor—we'll have to let the Giant Beings go with zero reparation. Let's go check on the convoy and maybe we can help save some lives. We don't have to jump into hyperspace anymore, so we can load escape pods into our bays and wait for reinforcements to come to Outer Cygnus."

"Great idea! Let's go!" Max cried.

"Catch you out there, surfer dudes!" Marjorie yelled before the holoscreen clicked off.

Max and Vern gave each other a grin.

"Hit it, Vern!"

The *Planet Hopper* jerked as it changed course and headed for the smoking mass of the convoy.

***

When Chyrone burst into General Lorne's quarters, not long after the *Amalgamator* popped out of the hyperspace sheath near the edge of the Abandoned asteroid belt, he feared he had given the career military man a cardiac arrest.

"Always Forward, General Lorne, you look awful!"

"Always Forward, Chyrone—to what do I owe this visit?"

"Do not play innocent. You have a duty to uphold."

"Excuse me?"

"I spoke to the high lady, General. I'm fully aware of what you agreed to. There is no turning back now. You are looking at the new Grand Master, and if you want a place in my armada of the greatest starships in the galaxy, well, you better start pretending you remember how to bow."

Chyrone took note of how the general stared at him, pale yellow eyes reflecting neutrality. He would have to be dealt with, if not now, eventually. "Lorne, we are committed. Stergis has proven to be weak. He is fearful of the tiny beings and he disgraces our tradition of moving Always Forward. The time has come. You know what to do."

General Lorne's pink lips pressed together, his eyes never leaving Chyrone's.

Chyrone persisted. "I need you to acknowledge you understand your duty. Or shall I call the High Lady of Persar and declare your intentions to bow to a tiny leader, rather than your new grand master?"

That did it. Blush colored the general's cheeks and he broke the stare. "I understand. There is no need to alarm the high lady."

"Good. Much better." Chyrone slapped the general on his back. "Perhaps when we've rid ourselves of this traitorous fake leader, we can work together to restore Perseus to glory. Yes?"

Lorne nodded.

"Excellent. When I walk out of this room, I'll expect you to make the call to Perk. He is to give you all the access codes, and if he shows the slightest sign of protest, he's going in too."

Chyrone flipped his styled hair to the side and exited through the slide door, grinning as the thrill of what was about to happen grew closer moment by moment.

***

"You made the right decision, Uncle," Ezran said, jerking Stergis from his thoughts. He was staring at the holoscreen indicating their distance from the hyperspace platform. Fifteen Perscan minutes, no more.

"Oh?" Stergis was in no mood. "Is that right, nephew? Are you my lead counsel now?"

"No, sorry, it's not my place." Ezran went quiet.

Stergis had a flash of guilt for snapping at him. "Go on, it's fine. I'm going to get it from Wella, I might as well get your honest opinion, too."

"Why did you fire on them before we left?" Ezran asked the question Stergis hoped he would be brave enough to ask.

Stergis smiled at him. "If you are going to take the mantle of grand master someday, you must practice making these difficult decisions. So, tell me, Ezran the Great, I would like you to tell me your best estimation: why did this old—some say washed-up—grand master fire upon the tiny beings?"

Ezran squinted. "A message. You were sending a bold, clear message."

"Go on..."

"If you take away our tournament, you will pay a price."

"That's right. And why not destroy the entire fleet?"

"A ploy."

"Ezran, I'm impressed. And the ploy?"

"Draw them in, to follow us here, where the trap is set."

"Your acumen is ahead of its time! Yes, and speaking of the trap, Perk should be calling any—".

A buzz on the holo.

"There he is!" The grand master was a bit deflated for not having thrown a planet ball, but the satisfaction of destroying the tiny beings while unleashing the weapon he had been waiting so long to unveil, well—that would be his tonic. Until he had to face Wella back on Persar. There was no tincture to deal with her wrath.

"Grand Master, we are prepared to activate the weapon. We are picking up the remaining Ugovernment starships coming out of the wormhole now. General Lorne requested you both come to witness from the forward berth."

"Fabulous, Perk, we'll be right down."

***

"Adonis!" Max yelled over the holocom. The Captain was panicking. Where were the unscathed Ugov ships going?

"Captain Max!" Adonis's image came across—the bridge on his Ugov starship was pristine and fully staffed, which meant it was undamaged and revving up to follow the others. "What's going on? Hey, thanks so much for saving so many of our soldiers! You guys have been amazing!"

"No problem, Councilor Dude, but listen—in all the hubbub I forgot to tell you about the black hole weapon!"

"The *what*? Max, listen, I can't talk about that right now… we're about to enter the sheath to chase after those damn Perseans. We think we can still catch them before they leapfrog to the Persean Arm."

Max got apoplectic. "*Stop!* That's it! Don't go! Tell your captain full halt!. Get all your ships back here!"

"What? I don't understand."

"It's a trap—the Perseans are going to set off a black hole weapon right next to the Abandoned hyperspace platform! Stop the troops!"

Adonis's image flickered off.

"Adonis? No! Did they go to hyperspace, Vern?"

"Their engines are prepping…"

***

"What is this?" Stergis stopped halfway across the weapons deployment chamber at the bottom of the belly of the *Amalgamator*. "Why is *he* here?"

Chyrone's presence froze Stergis in his tracks.

"Grab him!" Chyrone pointed, and several armed guards wrestled the grand master and his nephew to the ground.

"This is lunacy!" Stergis yelled, struggling to shake free. "I'll have you all executed!"

"Silence, traitor." Chyrone leveled a cold stare at him. "Your time as grand master has come to an end."

"What? No! Stop!" Stergis flailed his arms. "Let me go! Guards—I'll have every nerve in your body severed!"

"Perk?"

Chyrone had called out his assistant's name! Perk was in on it too? Impossible!

"Activate the weapon!"

Upon Chyrone's command Perk stepped forward, along with a twitchy General Lorne. It finally dawned on Stergis. *Curse Persar—they're all in on it...* Everything was making sense now. *Even Wella? No, never.*

"I have loyals!" Stergis tried a last vestige threat, hollow even to him. "They'll have you all killed the moment you return to Persar. The high lady will—"

"Oh," Chyrone said loudly, "she sends her regards. And her farewells. And she said to make sure you don't meet your maker alone."

No! Not Ezran, please. A snap in his back drove all the breath from his lungs. One of the guards had hit him with a laser whip! Ezran cried out in pain from somewhere behind him.

The doors to the weapons bay slid open as the guards dragged Stergis and Ezran into the adjacent air lock compartment. Using the laser whips to keep them from pushing their way out, the guards pressed the interior doors closed.

A flash of bright light came through the weapons bay. A single loud boom resounded through the *Amalgamator*, shaking the ship to its core.

Stergis slammed on the door with his hands screaming for them to let them out. When the hatch doors slid open the immense gravitational pull and frigid air of space greeted him with malice. The sharpness of being frozen alive hit his skin next. His last vision was Ezran's white body spinning off into space.

EPILOGUE

Smack! Max hit the lip of the unfurling wave with every bit of force he could muster. After stalling at the point of impact, the rails and fins of his board reconnected with the concave part of the wave, and he free-fell to the trough. With the whitewater ball about to catch him, he straightened out. Dropping prone, he let the force of crashing water behind him propel him for shore. It wasn't the best wave in the galaxy—no Ueharan tidal bore, that was for sure—but hey, he and the boys were surfing again. Amazingly.

Max rode the whitewater on his belly like a bodyboarder, hands cupped over the nose of his board, taking the mellow way back in to the dark beach. The Uehiron sand on this part of the coastline was the deepest of black, with shining flakes of mica stuffed within, making for a picturesque coastline glistening under every drop of sun. As he cruised along the last fifty Umeters to shore, a whirlwind of memories overwhelmed him. It had been by far the craziest Umonth the crew had ever experienced in their lives.

What started out as a mission to save Mike and score waves turned into something much, much more.

Max waved to Marjorie and a few of the *Lifebringer* crew who were milling about on the water's edge. The Terraformers were camped out on Uehiron as well, doing their astrobiological thing, while Max and the boys surfed. Piper had managed to finagle a special Ugov certification for the crew of the *Planet Hopper* to "study oceanic processes"—i.e. surfing hall pass. *Good to have friends in high places.* He smiled. *Speaking of friends in high places,,*

He pictured the handsome face of Adonis. The enigmatic councilman had managed to heed Max's warning in time and get the convoy to turn around—avoiding the awful fate of being sucked into the Persean black hole weapon. He was back on New Earth, no doubt drinking elixirs at night and arguing passionately in the Sun City moonscrapers by Uday, trying to maintain order in the galaxy.

Even the refugees from the *Terrastroid* were coming along, despite many of them losing family members. *Oh, that wild Angus—he was a cool dude.* Max swore to the big, gray-haired Abandoned man, on the docking platform before they left, that he would look after his son Markus and make sure his family had safe haven. While the Ugov was trying to figure out what to do with the refugees, Adonis established a temporary shelter, with all the amenities—not far from where the two crews were camped.

As the whitewater finally petered out, losing the strength to carry his big blue frame into shore, Max stepped his feet into the water and waded the rest of the way to the beach. It was great to surf naturally, no suit, no boots—Max had even turned off all the extra mechanical functions of his board so he could rely purely on his surfing skill.

He turned and there was Claude, off in the distance, dropping in on a wave. His brother hooting him on from the shoulder, so loud Max could hear it from the beach. It brought him great joy to see the twins together, surfing, out of harm's way.

The point break at Uehiron refracted the gentle swells, shepherding the curls into a wide cove. The waves were nicely formed and easy to catch, and it gave Max a great idea. *I'll bring Markus out here tomorrow and give him his very first surf lesson!*

Once he was a few steps up the sloping black sand beach, Max stuck his surfboard in tail first, nose pointing to the clear dusk sky, then turned back around to face out to sea. Saltwater dripped down his forehead as he gazed out to the horizon. He saw Blob and Vern sitting outside waiting for a set. Above them alien bird species called out happily as they cycled in the air, diving again and again into the water, occasionally plucking a tiny writhing fish in their beaks. Uehiron's parent star was setting, and dusk approached. A few bright dots poked through the darker parts of the sky, above the long blue plane of ocean spread out before him. The various moons and brightest stars were ready to shine and reflect for the evening, basking their Outer Cygnan paradise in a pleasant glow.